Praise for Irene Hannon's Books

"This latest page-turning thriller from Hannon will keep readers guessing until the end."
Library Journal starred review of *Over the Edge*

"The sweet romance and suspenseful mystery elements combine seamlessly."
Booklist on *Over the Edge*

"An impressively original, carefully crafted and fascinating read from first page to last."
Midwest Book Reviews on *Over the Edge*

"The narrative crackles with suspense all the way through its surprising conclusion."
Publishers Weekly on *Into the Fire*

"A compelling mystery with a palpable love story."
Booklist on *Into the Fire*

"This author never disappoints."
Interviews & Reviews on *Into the Fire*

"A suspenseful whodunit to the end."
Evangelical Church Library Association on *Body of Evidence*

"One of the best offerings by master of romantic suspense Hannon."
Library Journal starred review of *Labyrinth of Lies*

"Hannon's winning inspirational thriller will please fans and newcomers alike."
Publishers Weekly on *Labyrinth of Lies*

"Riveting suspense."
Relz Reviewz on *Point of Danger*

OUT OF TIME

BOOKS BY IRENE HANNON

HEROES OF QUANTICO
Against All Odds
An Eye for an Eye
In Harm's Way

GUARDIANS OF JUSTICE
Fatal Judgment
Deadly Pursuit
Lethal Legacy

PRIVATE JUSTICE
Vanished
Trapped
Deceived

MEN OF VALOR
Buried Secrets
Thin Ice
Tangled Webs

CODE OF HONOR
Dangerous Illusions
Hidden Peril
Dark Ambitions

TRIPLE THREAT
Point of Danger
Labyrinth of Lies
Body of Evidence

UNDAUNTED COURAGE
Into the Fire
Over the Edge
Out of Time

HOPE HARBOR
Hope Harbor
Sea Rose Lane
Sandpiper Cove
Pelican Point
Driftwood Bay
Starfish Pier
Blackberry Beach
Sea Glass Cottage
Windswept Way
Sandcastle Inn
Sunrise Reef

STANDALONE NOVELS
That Certain Summer
One Perfect Spring

UNDAUNTED COURAGE · 3

OUT OF TIME

IRENE HANNON

Revell

a division of Baker Publishing Group
Grand Rapids, Michigan

© 2025 by Irene Hannon

Published by Revell
a division of Baker Publishing Group
Grand Rapids, Michigan
RevellBooks.com

Printed in the United States of America

All rights reserved. No part of this publication may be reproduced, stored in a retrieval system, used for generative AI training, or transmitted in any form or by any means—for example, electronic, photocopy, recording—without the prior written permission of the publisher. The only exception is brief quotations in printed reviews.

Library of Congress Cataloging-in-Publication Data
Names: Hannon, Irene, author.
Title: Out of time / Irene Hannon.
Description: Grand Rapids, Michigan : Revell, a division of Baker Publishing Group, 2025. | Series: Undaunted courage ; #3
Identifiers: LCCN 2025000907 | ISBN 9780800741907 (paper) | ISBN 9780800747480 (cloth) | ISBN 9781493451487 (ebook)
Subjects: LCGFT: Christian fiction. | Thrillers (Fiction) | Novels.
Classification: LCC PS3558.A4793 O93 2025 | DDC 813/.54—dc23/eng/20240214
LC record available at https://lccn.loc.gov/2025000907

Cover design: James Iacobelli

This book is a work of fiction. Names, characters, places, and incidents are the product of the author's imagination or are used fictitiously. Any resemblance to actual events, locales, or persons, living or dead, is coincidental.

Baker Publishing Group publications use paper produced from sustainable forestry practices and postconsumer waste whenever possible.

25 26 27 28 29 30 31   7 6 5 4 3 2 1

To Jennifer Leep,
my editor for thirty-four books.

Thank you for taking a chance on my first suspense novel—
and for believing in Hope Harbor as much as I did.
It has been a joy to work with you.

I'm grateful beyond words for
the phenomenal run we had together,
and I will always cherish our friendship and partnership.

May your star continue to rise!

ONE

HER DREAM SABBATICAL was *not* off to an auspicious start.

Easing back on the gas pedal, Cara Tucker frowned at the flashing lights in the distance as she rounded a bend in the two-lane, rural Missouri road.

Why was a police cruiser blocking the entrance to Natalie Boyer's secluded estate—her destination on this early September Tuesday?

Cara coasted forward on the deserted road and squeezed onto the narrow shoulder a dozen yards back from the squad car emblazoned with the county sheriff logo. When a deputy emerged from behind the wheel and walked back to join her, she lowered her window, cringing as a wave of late-summer heat surged in.

"Morning, ma'am." He stopped beside her car. "Can I help you?"

"I hope so. The owner of this property is expecting me. What's going on?"

Instead of answering her question, he posed one of his own. "What's your name, ma'am?"

She passed it on. "Is Natalie all right?"

"Give me a minute." He pulled out his radio, walked several yards away, and angled sideways.

Cara peered at him through the haze of heat. He appeared to be talking, but his words were indecipherable.

Not a surprise, but frustrating nonetheless.

She shut her window, cranked up the AC to compensate for the humidity-laden air that had infiltrated the car, and tapped her fingers on the steering wheel while she waited for the deputy to return.

A minute ticked by. Two. Three.

What was going on?

Had something happened to Natalie?

And if it had, how would she manage to pull off the project that had won her a prestigious fellowship for the fall semester? Natalie and her journals were key to the research.

At a sudden prod from her conscience, she winced. Banished those selfish thoughts. The safety of the older woman should be more important than career considerations. Rather than worrying about the feather this project would add to her academic cap, she ought to be saying a prayer for—

The deputy ended his conversation and strode back to her.

Gripping the wheel with one hand, Cara opened her window again and gave him her full attention.

"I just spoke with the sheriff, ma'am. He'll meet you in front of the house. Give me a minute to move my car."

They were letting her in.

Yes!

One hurdle cleared.

While the deputy returned to his cruiser, Cara rolled up her window and put her car in gear.

Once access to the driveway was restored, she rolled forward and swung in, tires crunching on the gravel as she traversed the long lane that wound among the pin oaks, sweetgums, maples, cedars, and white pines that had been left to grow in their natural state on the rolling terrain, with scant room for one car to get through.

Rounding the last curve, she gave the clearing ahead of her a sweep.

The house was just as she remembered it from her one visit back in April. Similar in design to the style favored by the Missouri French settlers who'd arrived in the area in the 1700s, it was slightly elevated off the ground, with a steeply pitched hipped roof, wraparound galérie, and a multitude of French doors and windows.

New in the picture were the squad car like the one at the entrance—and an ambulance.

Her stomach clenched.

Natalie had sounded hale and hearty during their phone conversation to finalize all the arrangements, but she *was* in her early eighties. And she did have long-standing physical challenges. While people developed workarounds for those sorts of things, health-related conditions could create problems on occasion.

Grimacing, Cara pulled to the side of the drive and set the brake. Been there, done that. Experience was an excellent teacher.

Hopefully whatever had happened in this house wasn't as bad as it appeared.

A fit-looking man in uniform exited through the front door, and Cara slid from behind the wheel to meet him by the hood.

"Cara Tucker, I presume." He extended his hand. "Brad Mitchell."

She returned his firm clasp. "I'd say it was nice to meet you, but I'm not certain that's the most appropriate sentiment under the circumstances. Is Natalie okay?"

"She claims to be. The EMTs aren't convinced yet."

"What happened?"

"According to her, she felt lightheaded, lost her balance,

and fell when she got up after her nap. The housekeeper heard the fall, found Ms. Boyer in a disoriented state, and called 911."

"Did she hit her head?"

"She says she didn't. I told her you were here, and she confirmed you were expected. Maybe you can convince her to go to the ER and get checked out. She hasn't been receptive to that suggestion so far."

Cara shook her head. "I doubt I can change her mind. Our one face-to-face meeting won't buy me much influence."

His eyebrows rose. "I got the impression you were friends."

Flattering, but a bit of a stretch.

"More like acquaintances. My association with her is professional. I'll be spending weekdays here during the fall semester to work on an academic paper."

She left it at that. The sheriff likely wouldn't be interested in hundred-year-old journals written in a vanishing language. Even her siblings' eyes glazed over if she went on too long about her research project.

"Are you a student?"

Her lips twitched in anticipation of his reaction. "No. Associate professor at SEMO. Historical anthropology."

He did a double take.

Not surprising.

At thirty-four she still looked more like a typical undergrad than a professor.

But the sheriff recovered quickly. "Impressive. What sort of paper are you writing?"

She studied him.

Did he have a genuine interest in her project? Or was he simply being a thorough law enforcement officer and digging for more information about the woman who'd appeared out of the blue in the midst of a crisis?

Didn't matter. A top-line answer would suffice in either case.

"French culture around Old Mines. Natalie has material that will be helpful to me and offered to assist. Since commuting two hours each way every day wasn't practical, she also offered me a place to stay."

"Interesting." A beat passed as he considered her, but rather than follow up on that comment, he motioned toward the house. "Why don't we go in? It's too hot to stand out here in the sun. If you were able to convince Ms. Boyer to let you invade her turf, I'm still hopeful you may be able to persuade her to pay a quick visit to the ER."

"Don't count on it."

"You can't do any worse than we have. Shall we?"

He let her precede him up the walkway and the steps that led to the galérie but reached around to twist the knob when she arrived at the door, giving her a subtle whiff of an enticing aftershave.

As she entered the house, it was clear the activity was centered in the living room to her right.

"Ah. Cara." Mouth contorting into a rueful twist, Natalie lifted a hand in greeting from her seat on an upholstered chair. "This wasn't the welcome I had planned for you. I'm sorry for all the turmoil."

"No worries." Cara crossed to her, and the hovering EMTs moved aside. She perched on a chair beside the older woman, whose leg was propped on an ottoman. "Are you okay?"

"I feel fine now. I know Lydia meant well, but she overreacted. The lightheadedness has passed, and my leg will heal."

Cara inspected the woman's exposed black and blue knee. "Do you think it would be wise to have a doctor weigh in on that?"

"No." Her tone was decisive. "I've seen too many doctors in my day. And I know my body far better than they do. I can't explain my earlier fuzzy-headedness, but that happened before I fell. I did *not* hit my head. My brain is working fine, and no harm was done to my knee other than a bruise. This is much ado about nothing."

Cara gave the sheriff a slight shrug and telegraphed a silent apology. She was in no position to push the woman, who seemed in total control of her faculties and fully capable of making decisions about her health care.

He acknowledged the message with a slight nod and joined them. "Ms. Boyer, the EMTs will have you sign a form indicating you declined transport and further treatment. Once you do that, we'll leave you in peace."

"Thank you, Sheriff. I do appreciate your prompt response. I'm sorry to have wasted everyone's time."

"To tell you the truth, we prefer calls that end this way." He smiled at her, displaying a killer dimple.

Cara's pulse picked up as she gave him a closer inspection. Broad shoulders that seemed capable of carrying a heavy load. At least half a foot taller than her five-six frame. Toned physique, suggesting workouts were part of his regular schedule. Light brown hair, neatly trimmed. Green eyes the color of imperial jade. Strong jawline. Firm lips, softened now into an appealing flex, that looked like they knew how to kiss.

She blinked.

Where on earth had *that* fanciful notion come from?

As if sensing her scrutiny, the sheriff transferred his attention to her.

Warmth suffusing her cheeks, Cara shifted away on the pretense of watching Natalie converse with the EMT who'd handed her a clipboard while the other medical technician spoke into his radio. Ogling wasn't her style, even if a man was ogle-worthy. Nor was it her practice to dwell on a stranger's physical attributes.

Besides, getting carried away by a handsome stranger was foolish. Her focus this fall needed to be on her research, not on the opposite sex. Just because her sister and brother had both found The One over the past eighteen months didn't mean the same kind of happy ending was in the cards for her. That was a reality she'd accepted long before Cupid came to call on Bri and Jack.

So getting all hot and bothered about a man she'd met mere minutes ago and would have little or no contact with in the future was crazy. She ought to—

At a touch on her shoulder, she swiveled back to find the sheriff watching her with a quizzical expression.

Whoops.

She must have missed something he'd said.

"Sorry. Did you ask me a question?"

"Yes. Would you mind walking out with me while Ms. Boyer finishes up with the EMTs?"

Hard as she tried, she couldn't come up with an excuse to refuse his request short of telling him he discombobulated her. And that wasn't an option.

"Of course."

She rose and followed him to the door, keeping her distance from the captivating aftershave that was obviously messing with her brain.

After letting her precede him onto the galérie, he took up a position near the railing. "Are you familiar with Ms. Boyer's situation here?"

A faint scent of spice and sandalwood tickled her nostrils, and she eased farther away. "Not in any detail."

"Let me fill you in on what I know, which isn't much. She's a very private person. More so since she retired eight years ago. As I understand it, her housekeeper is only here two days a week. A groundskeeper who doubles as a handyman lives on the premises, but I doubt he interacts with her on a daily basis. He has a few . . . issues . . . and tends to keep to himself. You'll be seeing more of her than anyone. Falls at her age can be dangerous, and injuries don't always manifest themselves immediately. I'd appreciate it if you'd keep an eye on her for the next several days."

The sheriff had a caring heart under his badge.

Nice.

"I'll be happy to do that."

"Good enough." He held out his hand. "A pleasure to meet you. Don't hesitate to call us again if you need any assistance while you're here."

"Thanks, but I'm hoping today's incident was the most excitement I'll experience."

"Hold that thought. Enjoy your stay out here. It's a beautiful spot."

With that, he descended the steps and returned to his patrol car, the EMTs on his heels.

Cara waited until the two vehicles drove off, then retrieved her purse from her car and locked the doors. No doubt an unnecessary precaution out here in the countryside, but it was hard to shake long-ingrained concerns about safety.

At the doorway, she paused to glance back toward the drive. A cloud of dissipating dust was the only evidence that Natalie's property had been visited by emergency vehicles today. And hopefully, they wouldn't return.

Even if she wouldn't mind seeing that hot sheriff again.

EXCELLENT NEWS.

Fingertips tingling, I lowered the cell from my ear, pressed the end button, and smiled.

Everything was falling into place with minimal effort on my part.

Slipping the phone back in my pocket, I walked over to the counter. Opened the cabinet that held the liquor. Hesitated.

It would be nice to celebrate with a scotch, but I had to keep a clear head going forward.

I poured a glass of iced tea instead, crossed to the back door, and slipped out. Heat shimmered in the air, suffocating and oppressive, and I took a sip of the cold liquid.

One episode of dizziness wouldn't help me accomplish my goal, of course—but if Natalie continued to have difficulties, it would be harder to write them off as anomalies. It wasn't uncommon for people in their eighties to begin to have health problems, after all.

A notion well worth exploiting.

A bead of sweat trickled down my forehead, and I took another sip of tea.

The key on my end was patience. Everything had to evolve naturally so no one got suspicious.

But patience was going to be a challenge now that the stakes had been raised and the clock was ticking.

The visiting professor was also a complication I hadn't expected and didn't need. If she became a hindrance, I might have to persuade her that hanging around Natalie wasn't in her best interest.

I tightened my grip on the glass.

Persuasion could get messy—and I didn't relish hurting anyone. This plan was supposed to be bloodless.

Sometimes, however, circumstances required a person to venture outside their comfort zone. Do things they wouldn't normally do.

So if it became necessary, I'd take whatever action I needed to. Carefully, of course, even if no one would ever suspect me. I'd played my role well for a long time.

A bead of moisture trickled down my forehead, and I retreated to the coolness inside.

Despite the air-conditioning, however, I continued to sweat—

thanks to the second thoughts that were hiking up my blood pressure and stress.

Backing out wasn't an option, though. I'd already considered the situation from every angle, and this was the optimal solution.

I finished my tea, set the glass in the sink, sat at the table, and booted up my laptop. Seconds after opening the Tor browser, I was on the dark web and diving back into my research.

It was amazing how much information you could find these days with the click of a mouse. The internet was a virtual smorgasbord for criminals.

Not that I was one of those. Not at heart. My ambitions were modest.

But it never hurt to be prepared in case the situation ratcheted up and I was forced to take a detour down a road that was dangerous . . . and deadly.

TWO

"**LET ME GUESS.** You want the Tuesday meatloaf special."

Brad arched an eyebrow at the fortysomething waitress standing beside his table. "Am I that predictable?"

"Not always. But I know you're partial to Chuck's meatloaf. You and half the town." Angie waved a hand over the crowded diner, wrote down the order, and stuck her pencil behind her ear. "I keep telling him it should be a regular menu item, but does he listen to me? Ha." She snorted. "That man can drive a body crazy. Talk about a temperamental chef."

Chef?

That was a generous term for the taciturn hash slinger who owned Chuck's Place.

On the other hand, the hearty fare the man whipped up was close to homemade—a godsend over the past three years. Plus, stopping in here for dinner was better than eating alone in a house that always felt too empty.

Brad shrugged. "I suppose you can be temperamental if you have a loyal customer base."

"Tell me about it." Angie rolled her eyes. "Say, I heard Natalie Boyer took a fall. She okay?"

No point asking how she'd heard the news. In small communities, gossip had wings—and ambulance calls were big news.

"As far as we could tell."

"She's awfully old to be living alone out there."

"Micah lives on the property too, and Lydia's there on a regular basis."

Angie affected a shiver. "Micah gives me the creeps. I wouldn't want him lurking around *my* house, let me tell you. And I doubt he'd be of much use in an emergency. Lucky for Ms. Boyer that Lydia was out there today. With the spotty cell service around here, I don't know what she'd do if she ever needed help and no one was close by. 'Course, she'll have the professor on hand this fall. You get to meet her while you were there?"

"How did you hear about *that*?" Even Lydia hadn't known about Natalie's guest until late last week, from what the housekeeper had said earlier today. And a houseguest wasn't in the same gossip league as an ambulance visit.

"Lydia mentioned it to her brother, who told his girlfriend, who passed on the news to my sister at the hair salon. Lydia had to make a special trip out yesterday to clean the guest cottage because Ms. Boyer's cousin came down from St. Louis for the weekend."

As usual, Angie was a font of information.

"We could use you as a detective if you ever want to switch careers."

"Very funny." She smirked at him. "It's all a matter of keeping your ear to the ground. No special skill involved. I also picked up a few unrelated tidbits at the church picnic this weekend. You should have come."

Brad averted his gaze, straightened his cutlery, and took a deep breath. The mere thought of facing the inflatable bounce house and slide, or the face painter and balloon artist, had unleashed an avalanche of memories best kept buried.

"I wasn't in a picnic mood."

Angie sized him up with the practiced once-over she used

on customers. "Well, you missed a good time. Father Johnson was in fine form in the dunking booth."

The corners of Brad's mouth twitched. "I would have enjoyed seeing that."

"He drew quite a crowd—and raised a fair amount of money for the mobile rural clinic. So what's she like?"

At the abrupt change of topic, Brad squinted at her. "Who?"

"The visiting history professor."

An image of Cara Tucker materialized in his mind—early thirties, lithe and graceful, with wavy dark brown hair, a focused demeanor, and perceptive hazel eyes that radiated warmth.

"It wasn't a hard question." Angie inspected him.

He smoothed out the edge of his paper napkin. "She was pleasant and professional."

"What sort of research is she doing?"

"Something to do with French culture around Old Mines."

"Hmm." Angie pursed her lips and tapped her order pad against her palm. "I wonder if it has anything to do with those old journals Ms. Boyer has. Paul Coleman's been after her to donate them to the historical society."

"What kind of journals?"

Angie hiked up her eyebrows. "You don't know about those?"

"Should I?"

"No, I suppose not. I doubt many people do. But Paul mentioned them once while he was having lunch here. Let me get your order placed and I'll fill you in on what little I know. Hang tight."

She zipped off, detouring to top off coffee mugs at another table after a patron summoned her.

Brad leaned back and scanned the street outside the window of the corner booth that let him keep tabs on the action inside and out. Tonight was quiet, though. Not many people had ventured out into the steamy weather. Despite the waning day, heat still shimmered from the sidewalks, more intense now than it had been while he'd stood outside Natalie Boyer's house this morning talking to the professor he'd mistaken for a student.

He flinched.

That had been a major faux pas.

But her tank top and slim capris hadn't been stereotypical professor attire.

Fortunately, she'd seemed to take his gaffe in stride. Found a touch of humor in it even, if his reading on the tiny flex in her lips had been correct.

Her very generous, soft-looking lips.

He took a sip of his cold water and erased that image.

Strange that he was still thinking about her hours later. And blaming his musings on the prompt from Angie would be disingenuous. The truth was, she'd been on his mind since they met. Not just because she was beautiful, though she was, but also because of her intensity and singular focus. While they'd conversed, she'd given him her rapt attention. As if every word he said mattered.

There'd also been a unique quality to her speech. An accent, perhaps. Almost as if English wasn't her first language. What was the story there?

Whatever it was, there wasn't much chance he'd hear it. She'd be sequestered at Natalie's for the duration of her stay in the area, and he had no excuse to venture out there again.

Too bad.

Cara Tucker was an intriguing woman, and it was rare for intriguing women to cross his path these days. Not that he had any interest in her personally, of course, but she did pique his curiosity.

"Sorry. I had to straighten out an order with Chuck." Angie paused beside his booth and propped her hands on her hips. "Where were we?"

"You were going to tell me about the journals."

"Right. According to Paul, Ms. Boyer has some journals written in Paw Paw French by one of her relatives. Paul said they're one of a kind, because as you know, Paw Paw was a spoken, not written, dialect, and unique to this area. Maybe the professor got wind of the journals and convinced Ms. Boyer to let her use them for research." Angie lifted one shoulder. "I can't imagine what else at that house would merit an extended stay."

Brad didn't try to hide his skepticism. "Unless the professor speaks the dialect, they won't help her much."

"But Ms. Boyer speaks it. Or she used to. I'm thinking the professor may have sweet-talked her into translating them for her. Why else would she be staying out there for the semester?"

It was hard to fault Angie's logic.

"You may be right. But how on earth did she convince Ms. Boyer to let a virtual stranger invade her privacy?"

"You've got me. Either they clicked, or the professor charmed her into agreeing. Did she strike you as—" A loud *brrriiinnng* sounded from the call bell, and Angie cast an annoyed glance toward the pickup window. "Oh, for pity's sake. After all these years, does Chuck really think I'm going to let an order sit on the counter and get cold? Sheesh." She smoothed out the apron she wore over her jeans. "I'll have your food out in a jiffy, hon."

"No rush on my end."

"We don't like to keep our customers waiting." She winked and bustled off.

That was a fact. The service at Chuck's Place was quick and efficient. If this visit ran true to form, his food would be out in less than ten minutes. And no matter how long he stretched out his meal, he'd be done far too fast.

He drummed his fingers on the table.

If he relieved one of the deputies on duty for an hour or

two after he finished, he could delay going home. Larry would grab the chance to run back to his house and play with the grandkids until bedtime. They didn't get down from St. Louis often enough to suit his senior deputy.

Of course, going on a patrol circuit would extend his already long day—but it beat wandering around his empty, silent house where the love and laughter that had once filled the rooms were only a distant echo in the recesses of his heart.

Outside the window, a couple strolled past hand-in-hand on the other side of the street, and Brad's stomach hollowed out.

Strange how the loneliness and sorrow and despair he'd learned to keep at bay felt more acute tonight.

Stranger yet?

He had the oddest feeling his melancholy state was somehow related to his encounter with Cara Tucker.

"THAT WAS A WONDERFUL WELCOME MEAL, Natalie." Cara set her napkin on the table. "But I wish you hadn't gone to so much trouble after all the excitement earlier today. A sandwich would have been fine."

"Nonsense." The older woman waved her concern aside. "I did most of the prep yesterday. Besides, I've dealt with far worse than a bruised knee in my day."

Hard to dispute that. For someone who'd suffered through polio in her youth and continued to live with the aftereffects decades later, a bruise or two would be nothing more than a minor inconvenience.

"At least let me handle cleanup."

"Now that I won't argue with. Much as I enjoyed cooking while my father was alive, I must admit I never liked the pot-scrubbing part."

"Why don't you give me fifteen minutes to take care of the

dishes, and then we can discuss our schedule for tomorrow. Shall I meet you in the living room?"

"That will be fine. And don't rush on my account." Natalie pushed herself to her feet and grasped her cane. "I'll crochet a few more rows on my latest project while I wait for you."

As her hostess limped toward the doorway, Cara assessed her. While her gait did seem a tad stiffer tonight than it had during their visit back in April, the other woman would never move with agility or grace. How could she, with one leg shorter than the other? Even with a brace and heel lift to help compensate for the discrepancy, she had to use a cane for stability. In all likelihood, her awkward carriage had more to do with the lingering effects of polio than her fall today.

Cara sighed.

So many people had challenges the able-bodied never stopped to think about.

She began clearing the table as the woman disappeared through the door.

Was that why Natalie had contacted her after the interview in the Cape Girardeau newspaper? Any story about twentieth-century French culture around Old Mines would no doubt catch the woman's eye, but perhaps Natalie had also sensed a kindred spirit when the interview briefly took a personal turn. Had that compelled her to extend a helping hand?

Hard to know for certain. All her benefactor had offered was that the project would give her the incentive to follow through on the promise she'd made to her father to translate the journals.

Whatever the motive, it was foolish to look a gift horse in the mouth. There were amazing resources under this roof, and she didn't intend to waste a second of this once-in-a-lifetime opportunity.

After restoring order to the kitchen, she joined Natalie in the living room.

"That was fast." The woman paused in her crocheting.

"I try not to linger over disagreeable chores." Cara smiled and motioned toward the pile of pink yarn on Natalie's lap as she took a seat at a right angle to her. "Pretty."

"Baby afghan. I crochet them for a pregnancy resource center. It's a worthwhile use of my spare hours." She finished a stitch and put down the hook and yarn. "Before we talk schedules and routines, are you certain the guest cottage is adequate? I don't get out there often, and while my cousin never complains when he comes to visit, men tend to view accommodations through a different lens than women."

"It's perfect. Spacious and clean and welcoming. I also caught a glimpse through the trees outside the back window of a lake in the distance. Is that on your property?"

"Yes. I should have mentioned that when I gave you a tour of the house earlier. Feel free to wander about on the grounds. Micah keeps a walking path cut that Steven, my cousin, likes to use."

"Who's Micah?"

"My groundskeeper. He lives in a tiny cabin not far from the lake. You won't see much of him if you ramble around. He keeps to himself. And you met Lydia earlier today."

"Yes." Not that the housekeeper had been very amiable. While Natalie napped after the emergency crew departed, the housekeeper had gone about her work with quiet efficiency. Her responses had been polite, but she hadn't initiated any exchanges.

A taciturn groundskeeper whom the sheriff said had issues, a reticent housekeeper, and a woman who spoke an arcane language that would be extinct once the handful of remaining older people who could converse in it were gone.

It was quite a cast of characters.

Natalie picked up the conversation. "In terms of our schedule—what we discussed last week is most acceptable. We'll work on my aunt's journals from nine until eleven each morning, which is all these old eyes can handle of faded, antique handwriting. You can record as I translate. The rest of the day will be yours for further research and writing, and I hope a bit of relaxation. Is the desk in the cottage adequate? It's the one I used until my father died and I took over his study."

"Yes. Much nicer than the desk in my condo in Cape."

"I'm glad it's sufficient. Not that you have to confine your work to the cottage, of course. My father collected books related to the history of the area, many of them long out of print. You're welcome to borrow any you think may be helpful. You'll find them in the study. I typically work there in the mornings, but now that I've taken on the journal project, I'll work after my post-lunch nap from about one to three. Otherwise, the room is yours to use."

Natalie worked? On what—other than baby afghans?

Since the woman didn't offer any details, and probing would be rude, Cara let the remark pass. "Thank you."

"Not at all. I've also alerted Paul Coleman that you're here and may be in touch. I know you two are acquainted from your previous research."

"Yes. He was very helpful."

"That doesn't surprise me. He lives and breathes Old Mines history. I think he spends every spare minute volunteering at the historical society. That man is a treasure trove of knowledge. We've had many a fine chat about the old days during his frequent visits. In fact, he was here last weekend. Feel free to reach out to him if you need anything from the historical society archives."

"I will."

"As for the rest of our daily schedule, unless you prefer to eat dinner in your cottage or go to town, I thought we'd share our evening meals. I can't promise dinners like tonight's on a regular basis, but if you're satisfied with simple fare, you're welcome to join me."

That was an unexpected bonus. There'd been no discussion about eating together during their prior meetings. Otherwise, she wouldn't have stowed a week's worth of frozen dinners in the fridge in the cottage along with juice, bagels, and lunch fixings.

"I'd enjoy that. I eat alone most nights, except for a monthly meal with my siblings. It would be a welcome change to have company."

"For me as well. In general, dinners have been quiet affairs since my father died."

On impulse, Cara leaned over and touched her hand. "I just want to say again how grateful I am for your generosity and hospitality. The resources and expertise you offered gave me an edge for the fellowship, and I'll never be able to thank you enough. This project will help pave the way toward a full professorship."

"Let's hope so." Natalie patted her hand. "I believe there's worthwhile content from the pages I've skimmed here and there, but I can't guarantee how much of it will be useful to you."

"Primary sources are always valuable. A first-person account will give me a unique glimpse into the world of Old Mines during a transformative era and could offer fresh insights into the history here."

"And as an added bonus, it may also put a family mystery to rest."

Cara cocked her head. "How so?"

"My aunt died on this property. The official ruling was that she fell off the rocky outcrop at the top of the hill on the eastern edge of the land and suffered massive head injuries along with a broken neck. My father never wanted to talk about it, nor did my uncle, but from what I gathered, there were rumors of suicide. Even murder."

"Didn't anyone investigate those?"

"I suppose they did, to whatever extent they deemed feasible. Apparently, there wasn't any obvious evidence of foul play. Her journals weren't discovered until many years later, in a box in the attic of the original house that was on the property, and by then interest in the circumstance of her demise had waned. There also wasn't anyone willing or able to tackle the translation. But I'm thinking we may discover a few clues to her death as we work through them."

"You've just added a touch of intrigue to our project."

Natalie waved that aside. "I'm much too old for intrigue. I'll be happy to learn a bit more about my family history while fulfilling my promise to my father to translate the journals."

"Why didn't he translate them himself? He spoke the language, didn't he?"

"Yes. But his eyes were damaged in World War II, leaving him with compromised vision that would have made working with old, faded handwriting impossible. Besides, he never wrote the language. No one did. My aunt was the rare exception."

"You must be one too."

"No. My father and I used to converse in it often to keep our skills sharp, but I've never written it."

What?

Cara frowned. "Then why did you . . . how can you translate your aunt's journals?"

"I speak standard French, and as you know from your research, Missouri French is an amalgamation of Old Norman French, Native American languages, and frontier English. Some of my translation will be guesswork based on context, but I believe I'll be able to decipher the gist of the text. My

French skills remain quite strong, thanks to my years at the Sorbonne and my continued use of the language."

Cara stared at her as she absorbed that news. "You went to the Sorbonne? In Paris?" Why had her research on the woman not revealed that? As far as she'd been able to determine, Natalie had worked as an administrative assistant her whole life for a lawyer in a nearby small town.

"That would be the one." Natalie leaned back and looked into the distance, a tiny smile playing at her lips. "Oh, I had grand plans for my life, despite the limitations imposed by my bout with polio. I was studying literature, aiming for a PhD and a university teaching career, like yours." A shadow passed across her eyes, and she dropped her gaze. "But that wasn't to be. I became ill near the end of my junior year with a serious case of mono accompanied by debilitating fatigue, and I had to come home. By the time I recovered, Papa had health issues of his own, and he needed me. I never went back."

The poignant note in her inflection even after the passage of decades tightened Cara's throat. "I'm so sorry you didn't get to realize your dream."

"Not every dream is meant to come true. But perhaps I can help someone else realize hers." Natalie sent her a smile, then set her crocheting aside, rose, and gripped her cane. "I believe I'll make this an early night. You'll be all right on your own for the rest of the evening?"

"Yes." Cara stood too. "I'm used to entertaining myself."

"No young man in the picture back in Cape?"

Cara blinked.

That had come out of nowhere.

"No."

Natalie exhaled. "Men can be very foolish—and short-sighted."

"It sounds as if there's a story there." The comment popped

out before Cara could stop it, and she cringed. "Sorry. I didn't mean to pry."

"Don't apologize. I asked you a nosy question, and turnabout is fair play. But no, there's no unrequited love in my past. My physical issues were off-putting, as were my face and figure. Men don't tend to be attracted to homely, big-boned women who limp."

"I'm sorry." What else could she say in response to such a starkly honest statement? "And I do understand what you're saying about the difficulty of appealing to the opposite sex."

Natalie's features softened, and she touched her arm. "Not the homely part. You're a beautiful woman."

If she was, her limited dating history would suggest that her appearance wasn't sufficient to compensate for her other issues.

"Thank you."

At her perfunctory reply, Natalie smiled. "Your time will come. I have a sixth sense about these things. Just focus on your career for now and let nature take its course." She started for the door. "There's a flashlight on the kitchen counter to use for your walk back to the cottage, since our dinner was delayed tonight thanks to all the excitement. The path can be rather dark. Good night."

Cara returned the sentiment as her hostess disappeared through the door, still digesting their unexpected and enlightening exchange.

Who would have guessed that a woman who'd spent most of her life deep in rural Missouri had gone to the Sorbonne, spoke fluent French, and had journals that potentially held not only useful anthropological information but also family secrets?

And what had Natalie meant about her continued use of standard French?

This project was becoming more fascinating by the minute.

Cara wandered into the kitchen, picked up the flashlight, and pulled out the key ring Natalie had given her. After exiting onto the galérie that encircled the house, she flicked on the light and followed the winding stone path toward the compact guest cottage tucked among the trees fifty yards away.

Thank goodness she had the flashlight. Otherwise, she'd have been feeling her way. Who knew nighttime in the country meant utter and absolute darkness? Not this city girl. But the stars were unbelievable.

She stopped, lowered her beam until it pointed toward the ground, and gaped at the diamond-strewn heavens. The stars in Cape were a pale facsimile to this glittering display. It was a shame she didn't know more about astronomy. It would be fun to identify—

A sudden flash of light, much closer to earth, redirected her attention, and she peered into the dark woods ahead.

Nothing.

Had she imagined that momentary bright flicker?

Maybe.

But the sudden shiver that rippled through her despite the lingering heat of day wasn't reassuring.

Aiming her flashlight at the path ahead, she picked up her pace and tamped down her feeling of unease. Logically, there was nothing to fear here. Natalie had lived on this land for decades with nary a problem. If the light had been real, it was probably the groundskeeper she'd mentioned—though why he'd be roaming around in the dark was a mystery.

Whatever the explanation for that terrestrial light, however, she could avoid future unsettling sights by going back to the cottage before nightfall.

She stopped at the door, key in hand, and scanned her surroundings. All appeared calm.

After slipping inside and sliding the lock into place, she flipped on a light in the single-room structure and surveyed the furnishings. A queen-sized bed with what appeared to be a handmade quilt. A tiny kitchenette and café table. A comfortable reading chair, with a lamp beside it. And the generous desk Natalie had once used. All more than adequate for her needs as she and her hostess dived into the journals that would hopefully offer her a unique peek into the culture that had flourished in this remote, isolated area for almost two centuries, until the world intruded.

A surge of excitement set off a tingle in her nerve endings, and her mouth bowed as she crossed the room and pulled her sleep shirt out of the dresser. Only a historical anthropologist would get pumped at the prospect of spending a fall delving into old journals.

One thing for sure. Her work here would never be great fodder for scintillating, date-worthy conversation, even if a dating prospect was on the horizon.

An image of the sheriff appeared unbidden in her mind, and she huffed out a breath. Thinking about him in dating terms was silly. In all likelihood, the man had a significant other. And she wasn't here to date, anyway.

Nevertheless, meeting a handsome man in the first few minutes of her stay had been a pleasant surprise.

And Natalie's revelation about her background had been fascinating, capping off an unexpectedly eventful day.

All of which led her to ponder one question as she prepared for bed.

What other surprises lay in store for her during a research trip that was shaping up to be not only a career booster but an adventure?

THREE

NATALIE WAS LATE.

As the clock on the study wall inched toward nine ten on Thursday morning, Cara rose from her seat, crossed to the doorway, and peeked down the hall.

No sign of life.

Could the older woman have overslept?

Maybe . . . but she'd been punctual, down to the minute, for their journal session and shared dinner yesterday.

Would a knock on the door be too pushy?

Hard to tell. Natalie had been open about many things, but it was clear she valued and guarded her privacy and independence.

Yet in light of what had happened Tuesday, investigating her tardiness seemed prudent.

Taking a deep breath, Cara walked down the hall, stopped in front of the master suite, and gave a soft knock on the door. "Natalie? Are you all right?"

No response.

Pulse picking up, she knocked harder. "Natalie? Do you need any help?"

Muffled sounds came from inside the room, but they were impossible to identify.

"Natalie, I'm opening the door." Without waiting for a reply, Cara twisted the knob and peeked in.

The older woman was sitting on the edge of her bed, a robe thrown over her shoulders, the white hair she wore in a neat chignon mussed from sleep.

"Cara?" Natalie peered toward her, though the woman had her glasses on and the light in the room was more than sufficient to offer a clear view.

"Yes."

"What time is it?"

"About nine fifteen."

She exhaled. "I knew I was running late by the brightness in the room. I'm sorry to keep you waiting."

"No worries. Did you oversleep?"

"Yes. And that's most unusual. I got up at once when I awakened, but I felt lightheaded and decided to sit here until I was steadier. The episode wasn't as bad as Tuesday's, but it's taking longer than I expected to go away."

Two dizzy spells within two days?

That was unsettling.

"Does this happen often, Natalie?"

"Never before this week. It's very annoying."

And perhaps a sign of something more serious afoot health-wise.

"Do you think it would be wise to have your doctor check you out?"

"No. I'm feeling more clear-headed and clear-eyed by the minute." She glanced at an empty wine glass on her nightstand. "I wonder if that could be the culprit. I learned to appreciate wine while I lived in Paris, and I often indulge in a small glass before I nap or go to bed for the night. I finished a bottle last night, as a matter of fact. It's quite relaxing to sip a fine vintage." She shook her head. "I've never had any side effects in the past, but what else could be causing the issue?"

A medical problem of some sort? One that might become serious if left untreated? Perhaps it was even a result of her fall. As the sheriff had pointed out, injuries didn't always manifest themselves immediately at Natalie's age.

"I don't know, but would it hurt to have your doctor weigh in? Falls can be dangerous, and I'd hate for that to happen again. You were lucky on Tuesday."

The older woman sighed. "Steven told me that too during our phone chat Tuesday night. The poor boy is forever driving down from St. Louis to keep tabs on me. A visit to the doctor might help put his mind at ease. And I wouldn't want anything to stand in the way of the work we have to do, either." She leaned over and picked up her phone from the nightstand. "I'll call the office and see if they can squeeze me in. Then I'll get dressed and meet you in the study."

"Would you, uh, like me to help you?"

Natalie dismissed the offer with a wave. "Thank you, but I'm perfectly capable of dressing myself. The dizziness has passed, and I feel fine."

"Can I at least fix you breakfast?"

"I'm not in the habit of eating much early in the day, but if you'd like to brew me a cup of English breakfast tea and warm up a scone, that will help us get started on our work faster. You'll find everything on the counter. There's jam for the scone in the fridge."

"I'll be happy to do that." Cara retraced her steps to the door but paused on the threshold. "You know, we could defer our session until later today. Or pick up again tomorrow, if you'd prefer."

"This morning is fine. I'll meet you in fifteen minutes." Natalie shooed her out.

Bowing to her hostess's wishes, she left the room and headed for the kitchen.

Everything was where Natalie had said it would be, and when the older woman joined her in the study, Cara had a tray waiting, a rose she'd clipped from a bush in back beside the plate.

"Lovely touch." Natalie fingered the petals as she took her seat across the small table they'd decided to use for their sessions. "Thank you."

"It was my pleasure. Did you reach the doctor?"

"Yes. They're going to fit me in at two o'clock."

"Would you like me to drive you into town?"

Brow puckered, Natalie took a sip of tea. "It's not far, and I drove that route to work for many years. I still drive it often. But the road *is* a bit winding. And in light of these dizzy spells . . ."

"Let me take you. I wouldn't mind strolling around for half an hour while you're in the doctor's office. It will give me a chance to get familiar with the town."

"If you're certain you don't mind, I'd appreciate it." Natalie spread jam on her scone, wiped her fingers on the napkin, and opened the first journal to the page where they'd stopped yesterday. "I'll eat while I translate. Ready?"

Cara positioned her fingers on the keys of her laptop. "All set."

For the next hour, they worked through several pages of the journal. It was a painstaking process, with Natalie often resorting to a magnifying glass as she tried to decipher certain faded words. For the most part, however, she was able to make sense of the narrative that had been written by sixteen-year-old Marie Boyer in 1924.

After a particularly thorny passage, Natalie looked over at her. "Are you finding this helpful?"

"Very." Cara finished typing the last phrase. "Marie was on

the front lines when big changes began to happen here, and the first-person glimpses she offers are invaluable."

"That era *was* a pivotal time. Papa often talked about how the highway that was constructed between Old Mines and St. Louis in the 1920s brought the outside world to this very isolated community and changed everything. And of course, after mining dried up, many residents ventured farther afield to find work too. It's interesting to hear the reaction of someone who lived through that."

"How old was she when she died?"

"Twenty-seven. My father would have been fifteen. Four years later, he and his older brother enlisted and went to war." She shook her head. "I can't imagine Papa carrying a gun. He was such a gentle soul. But the one positive to come out of his experience was that he met my mother at a USO in St. Louis."

"Did he bring her back here?"

"No. She died very young of the flu. Not long after that, he built this house and moved back with me."

"How old were you?"

"Two."

"So you were living here when you got polio?"

"Yes, but that's a tale for another day." Natalie tapped the journal in front of her. "Back to Marie's story."

Tempted as Cara was to ask more questions about Natalie's experience growing up on this remote estate, pushing would be a mistake. If the woman wanted to reveal more, she would.

Cara switched gears. "So far Marie hasn't offered us any hints about the mystery you referenced."

"I expect those will come closer to the end. The journals continued until she died. We may begin to pick up clues as we get farther along."

Natalie went back to translating, and Cara resumed typing.

The insights Marie was providing into the Old Mines culture would form an excellent basis for her research project.

But almost as fascinating?

The history of the woman doing the transcribing, along with the intrigue that might lay in the pages yet to come in the journals.

And wouldn't it be amazing if in the process of doing this project, she and Natalie also uncovered the solution to a century-old mystery?

WAS THAT CARA TUCKER?

Brad jolted to a stop as he pushed through the door of the courthouse into the humid air.

Shading his eyes, he squinted toward the dark-haired woman who was strolling down the sidewalk on the other side of the street.

Yeah. It was her.

At the sudden uptick in his pulse, he frowned.

Was that little jolt . . . attraction?

No way.

Elizabeth had been the only woman for him. His once-in-a-lifetime love. The historical anthropologist who'd taken up residence at Natalie Boyer's place had just happened to come into his life at the wrong time. The sad anniversary looming in the immediate future, which had caused all his grief and loneliness to bubble close to the surface, had also left him vulnerable—and yearning for things he could never have again.

Things he didn't deserve to have again.

A wave of pain crashed over him, leaving futile longing in its wake.

And putting himself in close proximity to a woman who made him wish for the impossible was foolish.

He had to get out of here.

But as he started to turn away, Cara angled his direction.

She froze the instant she spotted him, then slowly lifted a hand in greeting.

He hesitated.

The wisest plan was to wave back and walk away.

Instead, his feet seemed to have a mind of their own.

Without any conscious decision to do so, he found himself walking toward the woman who'd been on his mind far too often over the past two days.

She remained where she was, her eyes hidden behind sunglasses, watching him approach.

"Afternoon." He slipped on his own shades as he stopped beside her. "I didn't expect to run into you again this soon, but I'm glad I did. How's Ms. Boyer?"

"She's why we're in town. She had another dizzy spell this morning, and I convinced her to pay a visit to her doctor."

"I'm sorry to hear she's still having issues."

"She doesn't seem too concerned about it, and she's been fine the rest of the day. But it's hard to dismiss two episodes so close together. Especially since she said it's never happened before."

"She told us that too. I'm glad you were able to—"

"Cara? I thought that was you. Natalie told me you were staying with her this fall. Nice to see you again." Paul Coleman strode toward them down the sidewalk and extended his hand.

"Nice to see you too." She returned his clasp.

"Hi, Brad." The midfiftyish man shifted toward him. "Sorry to interrupt."

"No problem."

He redirected his attention to Cara. "How goes the project with Natalie? I imagine translating those journals is a challenge."

"It is. Natalie's been able to ferret out the gist of the entries so far, but it's slow going. I'm hoping we can get through all of them in the weeks we'll have together."

"Put in a good word for the historical society while you're working with her, if you don't mind. Those journals are a treasure that should be preserved for future generations—along with her translation. The two together could help keep Paw Paw French from dying with the last speaker of the language."

"I'll do what I can."

"I hope there were no aftereffects from her fall."

A beat passed. "She says she feels fine."

Brad studied Cara.

The lady was astute.

From what he knew of Natalie, she'd prefer to keep her health issues private. Cara had obviously picked that up too and was respecting her wishes.

"Glad to hear it. Please tell her I said hello."

"I'll be happy to."

"Take care, Brad." With a wave, Paul continued down the street.

Cara watched him leave, faint furrows denting her brow. "Maybe I should have told him about Natalie's latest dizzy spell. I know they're longtime friends."

"If you want my opinion, you made the right choice. Natalie can tell him herself if she chooses to."

The creases on her forehead smoothed out. "Thanks for the validation."

A gust of wind whipped past as the dark clouds that had been massing on the horizon surged across the blue sky, dimming the sun and casting a shadow over the landscape.

Brad shifted around to scan the heavens. "It appears we may be in for a storm. Did you bring an umbrella?" When she didn't respond, he turned back to her. "If you didn't, I have one in my car you can borrow."

She gave him a puzzled look. "One what?"

Huh.

Had she zoned out while he was talking?

That wasn't consistent with the intense focus he'd picked up on Tuesday, but she could be distracted by Natalie's health issue.

"An umbrella. The weather's changing." He swept a hand over the sky.

"Oh." She inspected the expanse of menacing clouds. "I think we'll be fine. Natalie should be finishing up, and we ought to be able to beat the—"

Another gust of wind pummeled Cara head on, sending her dark locks flying behind her.

But the blast of air did more than tousle her hair. It also revealed a beige device hooked behind each ear, with an attached wire that disappeared into the wavy strands.

He did a double take.

Those had to be hearing aids.

Meaning Cara was deaf to some degree in both ears. And she hadn't been inattentive moments ago. She just hadn't heard him.

Compromised hearing could also explain the unique nuance in her speech, especially if the issue was longstanding.

Before he could fully digest his discovery, she reached up and touched one of the exposed devices. The one he was staring at.

Heat crept up his neck, and he redirected his gaze to her face.

"I'm sorry if I've missed anything you said. As you can see, I'm deaf. The cochlear implants are a godsend, but I don't always pick up everything. It's easier for me to comprehend words when I can watch the other person's lips."

Ah. That explained her singular focus in conversations.

"I had no idea until the wind revealed your secret."

She shrugged. "My deafness isn't a secret, but there's usually no reason to bring it up in brief exchanges." She flashed him a tiny smile and checked her watch. "I appreciate the offer of an umbrella, but we'll be in the car soon. It was a pleasure to see you again."

"Likewise."

"Enjoy the rest of your day—and stay dry."

With that, she strode away, her carriage fluid, graceful, and elegant.

He watched until she disappeared around the corner, then wandered back across the street to the squad car.

What he knew about cochlear implants would fill a thimble.

But hadn't he read somewhere that they were a last resort, after hearing aids failed to be of use?

If that was the case, she must have profound hearing loss in both ears.

Questions tumbled around his mind as he slid behind the wheel.

Could her hearing loss have been congenital? If not, when had she lost the ability to hear? How had she lost it? How did she manage the day-to-day challenges of living with devices that assisted her hearing but didn't fully capture everything going on around her? How had the loss affected her life?

A swell of thunder rumbled overhead.

Could Cara hear that?

One more unanswered question.

And his curiosity wasn't likely to be satisfied unless he found an excuse to pay another visit to the Boyer house and engage her in more than the sort of brief exchange she'd mentioned.

Any summons, however, would involve trouble on the property. Like another health scare for Natalie. But he didn't wish any more problems on the older woman—and what else could happen out in the quiet countryside that would require the presence of law enforcement?

The thunder reverberated through the still air again, and he started the engine.

Hopefully Cara and Natalie would get home before the skies opened.

Because unless he was misreading the situation, a major storm was barreling in.

"HEY, LYDIA! Grab me another beer!"

As her brother's command boomed from the recliner in the living room where he sat, as usual, with his feet up while he watched *Jeopardy*, Lydia dried her hands with a dish towel and counted to three.

The sooner she could ditch this place the better.

She yanked a beer from the fridge, marched into the next room, and slammed it on the table beside his chair.

"Hey." He scowled at her. "You want foam spewing all over the place when I open it?"

"If you don't like the service, you can get your own beer from now on."

He twisted off the cap, eyeing her. "What's with you tonight?"

"I'm tired, okay? I clean houses all day. It's hard work."

"So is working at the mill. Do you hear me complaining?"

"Why should you? All you have to do after you come home is sit down to a dinner I cooked and a house I cleaned and put your feet up while you watch TV."

"Boy, has your tune changed. When I gave you a place to live two years ago after that no-account you married cashed out your bank account, ran off with the money, and left you in debt, you couldn't do enough for me."

"I repaid you long ago. And I've been paying you rent for months."

"Cheap rent."

"Not if it includes a cook and housekeeper."

"Whatever." He took a swig of beer. "Speaking of rent . . . are you having any luck finding a new place to live? Ashley's getting antsy to move in."

She snorted. "Your so-called girlfriend is antsy for a free place to crash. She's playing you for a sucker, Randy Politte, and you're too stupid to see it."

His complexion reddened. "That's not true. She wants to get married."

"And in six months she'll run off for greener pastures and you'll owe her alimony for the rest of your life."

"You're just bitter because of what Wade did to you."

"No. I'm smarter. The rose-colored glasses are off." She scrubbed at her forehead, where a headache was beginning to throb. "I'm going to bed. You can put away the dishes and fold your own laundry after you finish your beer. I'm done for today."

"It's too early to go to bed."

"Not if you're tired."

She swiveled away and trudged down the hall. Once inside the tiny room he'd given her after she'd come slinking back penniless, unemployed, and disillusioned, she shut the door. Leaned back against it as she examined the frayed carpeting and stained walls.

Staying in the dive he called home had never been in her long-term plans, but what else could she do? Jobs were scarce for people with limited qualifications. At least cleaning didn't require a diploma or any special experience. Still, it had taken months to build up a regular clientele.

The income was steady now, thank goodness, but the work was exhausting. The residential jobs weren't bad, but cleaning offices after hours stunk—even if those clients were more reliable. No one her age should have to do hard physical labor until midnight. Forty-seven wasn't ancient, but it was too old for backbreaking work, day after day, night after night.

That's why she'd put together an escape plan.

She sat on the edge of the bed, massaged her lower back, and arched her spine.

Fortunately, everything was falling into place with minimal effort. If Natalie Boyer continued to have dizzy spells, it shouldn't be too difficult to convince her she needed a live-in housekeeper who could watch over her. Moving into that large, lovely home would be like taking up residence in a palace after Randy's dump.

Plus, the house held rare, valuable merchandise.

How providential that she'd overheard Ms. Boyer and Paul Coleman talking about it a month ago. Certain people would pay a pretty penny to get their hands on such a find, even if it fell into the one-man's-trash, another-man's-treasure category as far as she was concerned. People could get excited about the strangest stuff.

But assuming all went as planned, she might very well end up with first-class accommodations and a sizable chunk of change in the bank.

She stretched out on the bed and stared at the crack in the ceiling that got bigger every day.

The only fly in the ointment was that professor. With her on site, Natalie had a built-in companion who could keep watch over her until the end of the semester. For the plan to provide a fast escape route from her brother's, Cara Tucker had to go.

The question was, how best to achieve that goal?

A subject worth pondering while the thunder rumbled, the lightning flashed, and the crack in the ceiling widened yet again as the walls shook from the fury of the storm.

FOUR

"**TO USE A SHOWBIZ TERM,** I believe that's a wrap for this week." Natalie closed Marie's journal. "I'd say our work is off to an excellent start."

"I agree." Cara saved the Word document of Natalie's translation and closed her laptop. "I'm glad your doctor didn't find anything alarming yesterday and gave you full approval to carry on with your usual schedule."

"That makes two of us." Natalie folded her hands on top of the first volume in the set of journals. "When are you going back to Cape for the weekend?"

"Early afternoon. I want to spend an hour or two in the cottage first with one of the books I borrowed from your father's collection. This is a treasure trove." She swept a hand over the shelves that lined the walls of the study.

"I know. Paul's like a kid in a candy store whenever I let him pick a book to borrow for a week. I believe he knows more about Old Mines history than any other living soul."

"I wouldn't be surprised. He was very helpful to me with the preliminary research I did for my fellowship application."

"He's a dear man. I'm fortunate to count him as a friend. He's coming by Sunday, as a matter of fact. I expect he'll be gone before you get back, but I may have an opportunity to introduce you to my worrywart cousin. I tried to talk Steven out of driving down and spending his whole weekend with me, but he insisted he wanted to see for himself that I'm all right. You'd enjoy meeting him."

"You're lucky to have such a devoted relative." Cara slid her laptop into its case.

"I am indeed. Any exciting weekend plans on your schedule?"

She gave Natalie a wry grin. "Not unless bill paying, condo cleaning, and a quick stop at my campus office to meet with a graduate student I'm mentoring qualify as exciting."

"Remember, all work and no play . . ."

"I know. I'll squeeze in some fun too. My brother and sister are coming down from St. Louis for brunch on Sunday for our monthly get-together, and that's always enjoyable."

"You're fortunate to have siblings. Growing up in this isolated place was often quite lonely."

"Didn't you attend the local school?"

"Not for long. Polio delayed my enrollment, and once I did go, I was bullied because I was older than all the other children in my grade and I limped. Plus, as you know from your research, by then Paw Paw French had become associated with poverty and backwardness, so it was forbidden on school property. My father didn't take kindly to that, or to the bullying. He pulled me out, homeschooled me, and taught me the language. It was all we spoke around the house."

"No wonder you're proficient at it."

"I'm a bit rusty now, but it's coming back as we work on the journals." She looked toward the door as Lydia opened it and peeked in. "Are we keeping you from cleaning in here?"

"I can do it later."

"No need to delay. We're finished for the day and were just chatting." Natalie stood, bracing herself for a moment on the edge of the table. Then she carried the journal over to the large desk and slid it into a drawer with its companions. "You'll have the room to yourself until I come back here to work after my nap."

"I'll be done by then." Lydia retreated.

As Natalie started toward the door, Cara stood and followed behind.

What sort of work did Natalie do in here, sequestered away, each day? Though she'd referred to it in passing on several occasions, she'd never offered any details.

Tempted as Cara was to ask a few questions, respecting boundaries was important. What her benefactor did in the hours outside their project was none of her business.

But it was curious nonetheless—and one more mystery that would perhaps be solved before her sojourn here ended.

She and Natalie parted in the hall, and Cara continued through the kitchen, out the back door, and down the path toward the cottage, scanning the sky as she walked.

The rain that had accompanied yesterday's storm had passed, but the skies remained leaden gray, suggesting another storm was imminent. While the parched earth could use the moisture, driving all the way to Cape in a downpour wouldn't be—

She halted as the cottage came into sight around the curve in the path.

Had something just darted into the forest at the back corner? A deer, perhaps?

That was possible. They were abundant in the area.

Yet somehow that explanation didn't feel right.

She continued forward slowly, peering into the woods.

At first, only leaves registered. But at a sudden glint, she homed in on the source.

Halted again.

A shaggy-haired man of indeterminate age stood in the shadows, an ax in his hand.

Her heart stuttered, and she took an involuntary step back.

In the next instant, the man melted into the woods and disappeared.

She, on the other hand, remained frozen in place.

Could that be Micah, the antisocial groundskeeper Natalie had mentioned?

It must be. Who else would be wandering about the premises with an ax?

A shiver rippled through her despite the warmth in the air, and she rubbed her upper arms.

What was his story? Why did he avoid people?

Could he even be . . . dangerous?

No.

Natalie was too levelheaded to keep anyone of dubious character on the premises.

Wasn't she?

Wiping her palms down her capris, Cara continued toward the cottage, keeping tabs on her surroundings.

Though the man had disappeared, she didn't linger at the door. She let herself in and slid the bolt into place behind her.

Another mystery to add to the growing list on this isolated property.

But this was one she'd solve sooner rather than later. Come Monday morning, when she and Natalie sat down to begin work for the week, she was going to straight out ask about the man who'd been hovering in the shadows by the cottage.

Because receptive as she was to this off-the-beaten-track adventure and its unexpectedly intriguing nuances, she wasn't in the market for hazardous duty.

"I WONDERED WHERE YOU WERE."

As his wife slipped out the back door and joined him on the porch, Paul closed the book he was reading. "I decided to take advantage of the cooler weather after the rain this morning."

"It did take the edge off the heat." Becky sat in the wicker chair beside him and held out a frosty glass. "Fresh-squeezed lemonade. Can I tempt you?"

He smiled. "Always."

The dimple he loved appeared in her cheek. "You're a sweet talker, Paul Coleman. Are you certain you don't have a touch of blarney somewhere in your DNA?"

"I might—on my father's side. But thanks to the French heritage I have from my mother, I know how to recognize—and appreciate—a pretty woman."

She reached for his hand. Gave it a squeeze. "I'm glad you still see me that way after all these years."

"Beauty, like a fine wine, only becomes better with time."

"Thank you." She lifted her glass toward him, leaned back in her chair, and motioned toward the volume on his lap. "Another book Natalie loaned you?"

"Yes. Due back tomorrow. I was hoping to finish it this afternoon."

"She has quite a collection." Becky sipped her lemonade. "I imagine the professor who's visiting for the semester is in seventh heaven."

"I would be, in her shoes."

"You think Natalie will donate the journals to the historical society after they finish their project?"

"I hope so . . . *if* they finish. Sounds like it's slow going."

"I'm not surprised. Speaking Paw Paw is rare enough these days. I can't imagine trying to decipher the written word. The girl who wrote those journals had to be making it up as she went along."

"That's why the journals and the translation are so valuable." And dangerous.

He took a long swallow of his lemonade.

Becky didn't need to worry about that, though. Not yet. Not while he was still hopeful he could avert a crisis.

All he had to do was get the journals into his hands before Natalie and the professor got too close to the end. And given their slow pace, he should have a window to get that done.

Natalie's dizzy spells were also working to his advantage. Every delay and distraction had the potential to slow down the translation process.

"I'm sure Natalie will follow through on her promise to donate them." Becky swirled the ice in her glass. "It was her father's wish, and from what I've heard about her, she always honors her promises."

"That's true."

But the donation would have happened by now if that professor hadn't come along and messed up all the groundwork he'd begun laying months ago. Natalie had been on the verge of letting him put the volumes in a climate-controlled environment until she was ready to translate them.

Then Cara Tucker had entered the picture.

The best he could do at this point was convince Natalie to let him store the later journals until she and the professor were ready for them. Hopefully, they never would be if the translation project hit enough snags.

And down the road, no one who would care about any secrets they held. Secrets *he* wouldn't care about under normal circumstances. What was past was past . . . except in certain realms, where the past could be exploited and used against an opponent.

It was a dirty way to play, but it was all part of the game these days.

"What time did Dan say he was going to call?"

At Becky's question, he refocused. "About four if he can manage it. He's got another dinner to attend tonight, and he expected it to run too late for him to call afterward. At this rate, our grandchildren are going to forget what their father looks like."

"I know. He's been meeting himself coming and going lately."

"Goes with the territory. It's in his genes."

"It wasn't in yours. Not that you don't work hard, but you had different aspirations."

"That particular gene must have skipped a generation."

"Can I say I'm glad?"

"Yes. And I am too." Especially now. "But if that's what Dan wants, we have to help and support him."

"I know. Including that interview he wants us to do with the St. Louis paper." Becky wrinkled her nose.

"It may not be too bad." Certainly not as bad as trying to deal with what could turn out to be explosive secrets.

It was a shame he couldn't just be upfront with Natalie. Explain his concerns. They were friends, and she'd always been the soul of discretion.

Yet she *had* promised her father she'd translate the journals, and she wasn't going to let this opportunity with the professor slip away. Not that she would tell the world about whatever they found. But Cara Tucker was a wild card. Who knew what she would do with any damaging information they might come across?

"That's not what your expression says." Becky leaned over and twined her fingers with his. "You're as nervous about the interview as I am, aren't you?"

"I'll admit I'd rather not do it."

"What if we say something wrong?"

"There's nothing wrong to say. Dan is a fine young man. There are no dark secrets in his life."

That's why no dark secrets from the past should be used to sully his background and reputation.

Nor would they be.

All he had to do was convince Natalie to let him take the last few journals for safekeeping so she and the professor couldn't peek ahead. And before they got to those—*if* they got to them—maybe those final journals would mysteriously disappear. Or have water or fire damage. A regrettable loss to be sure, but not sufficient to undermine the value of the work Natalie and the professor were doing to preserve Paw Paw French.

Paul took a slow sip of his lemonade, the peaceful view at odds with the roiling in his stomach.

He liked Natalie, and the professor appeared to be a nice person too. He meant no one any ill will.

But in the end, his son came first.

AS HIS CELL VIBRATED in his pocket, Brad eased onto the edge of the narrow road, pulled out the phone, and skimmed the screen.

Brian.

No surprise. His brother would never let this day pass without reaching out, as Mom and Dad had earlier.

He set the brake and pressed talk. "Hey. Mom and Dad beat you this year." He tried without much success to inject a teasing note into his voice.

"They've always been one step ahead of me. You too. Remember when we were about nine and made a very bad decision to try jumping our bikes over the ditch behind the vacant lot down the street? I never did figure out how Dad got wind of that and showed up in the nick of time."

"I guess parents have a sixth sense that alerts them when their offspring are in danger."

At least most of them did.

His stomach knotted.

"I hear you. The folks okay?"

"As far as I could tell. I wish they lived closer, but I get why they moved to a warmer climate after Dad retired. Florida seems to suit them."

"I agree. Tell me how *you're* doing."

"Hanging in." He rolled down his window and rested his elbow on the edge.

"You working today?"

"No. One of the perks of being the boss is that I don't usually have to clock in on Sunday unless we have a hot case."

"What's on your agenda for the rest of the day?"

"Nothing special."

"Why don't you meet up with a friend for coffee? Or dinner?"

"I'm not in a socializing mood."

A beat ticked by, and when his brother continued, his tone was more somber. "I don't like you being by yourself on such a hard day. You're not sitting at home with the shades drawn, are you?"

Brad drew a deep breath of the fresh air wafting in the window. "No. I'm outside." Close enough. "It's sunny here. The heat's let up a little."

"I'm glad to hear that. You doing any gardening these days? You used to enjoy digging in the dirt, making things grow."

Yeah, he had. Once upon a time.

He glanced at the bouquet on the seat beside him. "Not much. The gardens are pretty ragged, but I do plan to deal with a few flowers today."

"That would be good for you and for them." Several seconds passed. "I wish I could have been there today."

"It's a long commute from upstate New York."

"Tell me about it. But you know I'm there in spirit, right?"

Brad's throat clogged. "I know, and I appreciate it."

"Do me a favor. Stay outside in the sun. Go somewhere quiet and peaceful. Maybe take a walk or drop in on someone you know. Would you do that?"

He gave the scene out the window a sweep.

It didn't get much more peaceful and quiet than this large green expanse dotted with headstones. And he was about to visit people he knew.

"I can do that."

"Good. I'll call again in a week or two."

"Sounds great. Tell everyone I said hi—and thanks for remembering."

"Always. Love ya, bro." Brian's voice choked as he ended the call.

Vision misting, Brad picked up the bouquet beside him, slid from behind the wheel, and pocketed his keys.

And as he slowly crossed the lawn . . . as memories of the tragedy from three years ago played again through his mind . . . a tsunami of guilt and grief and loneliness crashed over him, leaving him feeling as lost as he had on a backcountry hiking trip during his college days after his compass went missing.

It also left him with the disquieting question that had been surfacing with increasing regularity in recent months.

Where did he go from here?

FIVE

AT THE SUMMONS FROM HER DOORBELL, Cara smiled, set her oven mitts on the counter, and headed down the hall.

Her siblings were punctual, as usual.

When she opened the door, Jack held up a plastic-wrap-covered plate. "We come bearing gifts."

Cara reached for the offering. "You made Mom's mint squares! I'm drooling already."

"I promised to bring dessert, and what can top these? But they can't compete with Bri's gift. From Paris, no less." He shifted toward their sister. "Let me tell you, your new husband set a high standard for honeymoons. And my fiancée noticed."

"You'll come up with a location Lindsey will like. Just think romantic—if you have it in you." Bri smirked and shoulder-butted him.

He put on his innocent face. "Would Branson qualify?"

Bri rolled her eyes. "Branson and the City of Lights aren't even in the same galaxy. But speaking of Paris . . ." She lifted her hand and dangled a gift bag. "I did pick up a little present for my favorite sister while Marc and I were strolling down the Champs-Élysées."

"A gift from Paris will be the highlight of my day—aside from a visit with my favorite siblings, of course. Come in, both of you." Cara pulled the door wide. "Let me put the dessert in the kitchen before I dig into that bag."

They followed her to the back of her condo and made themselves at home. As usual.

While Jack slid onto a stool at the small island, Bri propped a hip against the counter and folded her arms. "I wanted to bring you macarons from Ladurée, which were to die for, but Marc convinced me they were too fragile to survive the trip home."

Cara took the bag, pulled the tissue from the top, and removed a flat box of dark chocolate truffles from La Maison du Chocolat.

"I think I'm in heaven." Cara hugged the box to her chest.

"Those happen to be from one of the premier chocolate shops in Paris. And I can vouch for the quality. Marc and I sampled them while we were in the store. One word: bliss."

"Gee, it's kind of hard for my mint squares to compete with those." Jack arched his eyebrows at Bri.

"No, it's not. I'm tucking these away for future consumption." Cara set the box off to the side of the counter. "Your mint squares will take center stage after we eat."

"You mean I don't get to try one of those?" He motioned toward the box.

"No, you do not. Those are for Cara." Bri walked over to the island and helped herself to a handful of peanuts from the small bowl. "You could always take Lindsey to Paris for *your* honeymoon and buy your own."

"Let's not get carried away." He took a few peanuts too. "Speaking of food—what's on the menu today?"

Cara plucked a nut from the bowl and popped it in her mouth. "Per your request, mushroom omelets and my cheesy potato casserole. I have salad too."

"Works for me." Jack gave her a thumbs-up. "Okay, Bri, we've been waiting with bated breath to hear all the details of your over-the-top honeymoon. Lay them on us."

"I don't intend to share *all* the details, but I'll tell you about some of the incredible sights we saw."

As Cara put the omelets together and they all sat down to enjoy their brunch, Bri kept them entertained with stories about Paris and the forays she and Marc had taken into the surrounding countryside. She didn't wind down until the meal was almost over.

"It sounds magical." Cara rested her elbow on the table and propped her chin in her palm.

"The perfect word."

"Are you sure Marc didn't mind you taking off for most of a Sunday to come down here on the heels of your honeymoon?"

"No worries on that score. He knows our monthly sibling gatherings are sacrosanct. Lindsey's on board with that too, right?" Bri directed the question to Marc.

"One hundred percent. And remember that when you meet Mr. Right, Cara. He gets a thumbs-down if he balks about you giving us one Sunday afternoon a month."

"I'll pass that on if Mr. Right ever comes along. A big if. There aren't a lot of Marcs in the world—present company excepted."

"True. But there are some hot guys in the fire investigation world, pardon the pun." Bri grinned. "And while I may be biased, my ATF agent husband is a scorcher. Your day is coming, though."

"Probably not anytime soon." Jack finished the last bite of his potatoes. "I doubt she'll meet any eligible men while she's holed up in the middle of nowhere with an older woman who speaks a dying language."

As an image of Brad Mitchell flashed through her mind, Cara picked up her glass. Took a sip of the cold water.

While his eligibility was a question mark, he could hold his own with Bri's new husband in the hot category.

"Or maybe she has."

At her sister's comment, Cara refocused on her siblings.

Jack stopped chewing. "What do you mean?"

"She disappeared into la-la land for a minute."

As her brother and sister scrutinized her, she squirmed. "You guys are nuts. Like Jack said, I'm living off the beaten path this semester."

"Yeah?" He studied her. "You look funny."

"Put away your police detective badge, dear brother. If I ever meet anyone with serious potential, you will both be the first to know."

"Is that a promise?" Bri collected their empty plates and stood.

"Cross my heart."

"So how goes it out in the hinterland?" Jack lifted a corner of the plastic wrap on the plate of mint squares and took one.

"Natalie's place isn't *that* far from town. It's not like I've left civilization behind."

"Have you seen a Starbucks since you've been there?" Jack bit into the rich dessert.

"No."

"I rest my case."

"Starbucks isn't the defining element of civilization." Bri sat back down and took a mint square too. "So how is the project going?"

Cara gave them a quick rundown, including Natalie's mention of the mystery surrounding Marie's death. That would be of far more interest to the investigative duo at her table than the picture of daily life beginning to emerge from the journals.

"Sounds like a cold case waiting to happen." Jack took a second mint square.

"It would be hard to reconstruct what happened a hundred years ago, though." Bri scrubbed a smear of chocolate off her fingers with her napkin. "Does your hostess have any theories?"

"No. She said her father never wanted to talk about it."

"And he's gone too, so dead end. My turn for a pun." Jack grinned and swigged his water. "Anyone else on the premises other than you two?"

"A housekeeper comes two days a week, and a groundskeeper lives on site."

"So he's close by to lend a hand if anything comes up."

"In theory."

Jack frowned. "What does that mean?"

Oops.

Leave it to her detective brother to home in on an ambiguous answer.

"I haven't seen much of him."

"Why not?"

"I guess he's busy keeping the grounds. Natalie has a fair amount of land." No need to mention the sheriff's comment about the man having issues. That would only activate Jack's overdeveloped protective instincts. "So tell us when you're leaving for the FBI National Academy. I'm beyond thrilled you got one of the coveted spots after County nominated you."

"Me too. We start October 1. It's going to be tough to be gone from Lindsey for ten weeks, but she knows it's a once-in-a-lifetime opportunity and is fully on board."

"Good woman." Bri lifted her glass in salute.

"Tell me something I don't know."

They continued to chitchat for another hour after relocating to the living room, but finally Jack looked at his watch. "We have to drive back to St. Louis, and you have to drive back to the hinterland." He nudged Bri's shoulder as they sat side by side on the couch. "You ready to go?"

"Yeah. I suppose it's time to break up this gab fest. We'll miss you while you're in Quantico." Bri nudged him back.

"But think of all the great stories I'll have to tell at our future get-togethers. We may have to schedule an extra one to catch up."

"I'm game if the spouse and fiancée are." Cara stood. "Let me get your plate."

They were waiting for her at the door after her detour to the kitchen.

"Just because our brother here is taking off doesn't mean we can't meet up while he's gone." Bri hugged her.

"That's true. And we have our every-Saturday-morning phone calls too."

Jack gave her a squeeze. "It's not like I can't stay in touch. Watch for texts from me on a regular basis."

"I'll hold you to that."

"You may."

She waited at the door until they drove off, then wandered back to the kitchen. As usual, they'd pitched in with cleanup after eating, leaving her with nothing to tidy up in the spotless space.

Meaning she had time to stop in at the studio for an hour before she drove back to Natalie's. After yesterday's class, it was clear even a week off from her routine had a noticeable impact. She'd have to clear a space in the cottage for a daily stretching session and build a strenuous walk into her schedule.

And hope Micah—or whoever had been lurking around her cottage on Friday—kept his distance in the future.

"HEY, LYDIA! When are you cooking dinner?"

As her brother banged on the door of her bedroom, Lydia tipped down the screen of her laptop. "I don't know."

"We always eat on Sundays at two."

"Not today. I'm busy."

"I'm hungry."

"Why don't you go over to Ashley's? Let her feed you?"

A beat passed. "I'm going over later. But she doesn't cook like you do. You could be a chef."

Compliments would get him nowhere.

"Better get used to her food if you're going to let her move in here."

"Oh, come on." He switched to a cajoling tone. "Make dinner for us."

"Sorry. I'm working on a plan to get out of your house, like you asked."

"You could take a break from that on Sunday."

"Ashley might not appreciate me slacking off. She wants me gone, remember?"

"I'll talk to her. So will you cook?"

"Nope."

An aggravated sigh came through the door. "What are *you* going to do about dinner?"

"I may go out."

"Since when has there been room in your budget for restaurant meals?"

She picked up her phone and called up the photos she'd taken at Natalie's house on Friday. Smiled. "Everyone deserves to splurge once in a while." Especially if there was a source of funding for indulgences on the horizon.

"Are you saying I'm on my own for food today?"

"Yep."

He mumbled an ear-burning comment and stomped back down the hall.

Good riddance.

Yeah, he'd let her move back in two years ago, but it had always been about Randy and what was best for him. He was the same self-centered little boy he'd once been, living in a grown-up body. It had cost him nothing to offer her this empty room, and he'd gotten a cook and house cleaner in the bargain. Plus, she'd ended up paying rent.

Sweet deal for him.

One he was willing to forfeit for a flashy blonde who'd use him and lose him.

But that was his issue. She had her own future to think about.

She raised the laptop screen again and leaned closer to scan the new information she'd pulled up. Amazing how buyers could be found for almost anything. And now that she had photos to share of the merchandise, she ought to be able to get a bidding war going.

First things first, however. She had to get a handle on fair pricing. Otherwise, someone could cheat her. Meaning she had to learn more about the rare product she would soon be selling.

As for the second part of her plan—she reached into her pocket and fingered the keys to Natalie's house. The groundwork she was laying for moving in there was coming along too. Not as fast as she'd like, thanks to that professor's presence. But Cara Tucker wasn't there on weekends, and if Natalie needed assistance then, who would be around to help her?

A question she intended to pose to her client should any more . . . problems . . . arise at the house that could make her uncomfortable about being alone. Because Micah Reeves couldn't be relied upon to come to her aid. That man was downright creepy. If trouble did arise, he'd probably vanish into the woods like he did whenever she spotted him on her treks to clean the cottage.

Yes, Natalie would benefit from a live-in housekeeper.

As would the housekeeper.

Lydia went back to scrolling through the internet and compiling her research. For both parts of her plan to succeed, she had to be buttoned up and thorough. Think through every contingency. Be ready to step in when opportunity presented itself.

And it wouldn't hurt to make an effort to convince Cara Tucker that hanging around Natalie's remote estate might not be in her best interest if she valued her safety.

SIX

AS A CAR CAME INTO SIGHT in front of Natalie's house, Cara eased back on the accelerator.

Steven must not have left yet.

Shoot.

Could she park, circle the house, and escape to her cottage?

A definite temptation after the long drive.

But that would be rude. Natalie had mentioned that her cousin might still be here, had intimated she'd like to introduce them.

What would a five-minute meet-and-greet hurt?

Cara inspected the late-model BMW as she pulled in behind it. Whatever Steven did for a living must bring in a generous income if he could afford a vehicle like that. Unlike the salaries earned by associate professors, which lent themselves more to older but trusty models.

She set her brake and patted the dash of her Accord. "Don't get an inferiority complex. Reliability counts more in my book than a high price tag."

After fishing out the keychain Natalie had given her with the instruction to come and go as she pleased in the main house, Cara let herself in.

Her hostess was seated in the living room, a teapot and two cups on the table in front of her, along with a crumb-littered plate.

As the man in the chair across from her rose, Cara did a double take.

This tall, fortysomething jeans-clad guy with striking good looks and a warm smile was Natalie's cousin?

But . . . weren't most cousins somewhat similar in age? Natalie could almost be this man's grandmother.

"Cara, my dear, welcome back. I trust you had a pleasant and uneventful drive."

As Natalie spoke, she focused on the older woman. "Yes, I did. I'm sorry to interrupt your conversation."

"Not at all. I was just telling Steven that I hoped you'd return before he left. And here you are."

As she did the introductions, Steven walked over and extended his hand, eyes twinkling. "You were expecting someone older, weren't you?"

Drat.

Was she that easy to read?

"Hey. No worries." His grin broadened. "I've seen that expression on many occasions after Natalie introduces me. I'm actually a first cousin once removed. My dad was Natalie's first cousin."

"A cousin is a cousin." Natalie dismissed the distinction with a wave.

"I must admit I had you pegged as an older man. But it's a pleasure to meet you." She returned his firm clasp. "It was kind of you to drive down from St. Louis to check on Natalie."

"I like to keep tabs on my favorite cousin."

"Flattery will get you everywhere, young man." Lips twitching, Natalie rose and joined them. "Cara, would you like to share another pot of tea with us? It wouldn't take me long to brew more."

"Thank you, but I splurged on an espresso earlier. That gave me my caffeine fix for the day. Besides, I don't want to interfere with your visit."

"You aren't. We were wrapping up anyway." Natalie turned to her cousin. "Steven, if you can spare half an hour, why don't you give Cara a tour of the property, show her the trails?" Natalie angled toward her. "Unless you've already gone exploring on your own?"

"No." Nor would she until she talked to Natalie about Micah and got a better handle on the man. Even if her hostess assuaged her concerns, however, the company of an able-bodied man on her first foray would be welcome. "I don't want to delay your cousin, though." Nevertheless, she sent him a hopeful look.

He picked up the cue. "I'm happy to oblige. I don't often get to play the role of tour guide, and I'm in no hurry to get back to the city. This will be fun."

"In that case, I accept. I assume jeans and sport shoes are acceptable for a hike around the property?"

"Perfect. Micah keeps the walking trails groomed, so we won't need our machetes." Steven leaned over and kissed Natalie's forehead. "But send out a rescue party if we aren't back by sunset."

"Ha-ha." She gave his arm a pat. "Cara, you're in excellent hands. Steven knows this property inside and out. I can't imagine how many miles he's logged during his visits."

"Blame that on all the sweet treats you feed me while I'm here." He winked at her and motioned to the empty plate beside the teapot. "And I'd rather shed them walking this beautiful property than working out in a gym."

"Well, you two have at it. I'll crochet a few more rows on my current project while you're gone."

"Shall we?" Steven motioned toward the back of the house.

Cara took the lead, but once they exited the house, he drew up beside her.

"I've been wanting to explore the property." She slipped on her sunglasses. "Thanks for offering to show me around. One caveat, though. I have cochlear implants, so I may occasionally have to ask you to repeat yourself if there's too much extraneous noise in the woods."

"Thanks for the heads-up. I'll do my best to enunciate. And showing you around will be my pleasure. The path starts behind the cottage and follows a loop that has a couple of forks, but they all lead back to the main route. You wouldn't have gotten lost if you'd struck out on your own."

"I considered doing that, but . . ." How much should she say about Micah?

"But what?" Steven prompted as they passed the cottage and veered onto the well-groomed trail.

Cara hesitated—but only for a moment. What would be the harm in getting his read on the groundskeeper? Steven was here on a regular basis, and he seemed like an intelligent man who would have sound judgment. It couldn't hurt to see what he offered.

"But I wasn't certain I wanted to run into Micah."

"Ah. Totally understandable. He can be unnerving. As far as I know, though, he's harmless. Or so Natalie tells me whenever I mention that I've seen him prowling around in the shadows."

"Do you know anything about him?"

"A little." He motioned to a fork in the path up ahead. "That's the first branch-off. It leads to the top of the cliff. There's a beautiful view from there, but the climb can be strenuous on a hot day."

"I'll save that for cooler weather."

"Smart choice." He continued down the main trail. "Back to Micah. He's been here for fifteen, twenty years, I guess. Natalie's father knew Micah's father and hired him as a favor.

Apparently Micah suffered a traumatic brain injury and PTSD while he was serving in the Middle East. From what I gathered, he was homeless for months, and his father was desperate to save him from the streets. He came here and never left."

Though some of his words were a bit garbled as they walked through the woods, she was able to pick up enough to get the gist of his comments.

Cara dodged a pine cone. "Doesn't he have any family?"

"None that I know of. I think his father died years ago. I used to try to talk to him when our paths crossed while I was walking, but I never got more than a dozen words out of him before he hightailed it back into the woods. I gave up after it became obvious he didn't want any social contact."

"What a sad story."

"And what a wasted life—unless you like being a hermit. But he must be content or he wouldn't have stayed all these years."

They rounded a bend, and the lake came into view.

Cara stopped to take in the expanse. "Wow. I can see a piece of this from the cottage, but it's much bigger than I expected."

"It's one of my favorite spots on the property. The trail follows the perimeter."

They struck off again at a brisk pace, but after several minutes Steven stopped and motioned to another, narrower track. "This is a short loop that will bring us back to the main trail. It goes by a limestone cave at the base of the bluff. Want to see the entrance?"

"Sure."

They veered off, and within a handful of minutes they came to a small opening at the bottom of the cliff, partly obscured by vegetation.

"Not too impressive from the outside, but it opens up inside and tunnels back to a huge cavern with other passageways going different directions." Steven stopped beside it.

"Is that knowledge based on personal experience?"

One side of his mouth quirked up. "No. I've peeked inside with a flashlight, but I've never been attracted to caves. In fact, I rarely take this loop. I heard the description of the inside from my dad, who heard it from his father." His lips flattened, and as he stared at the entrance to the cave, twin creases appeared on his brow.

"What's wrong?"

After a moment, he shifted his attention to her. "I was thinking about a story Natalie told me, from while she was growing up here. You know part of this land belonged to her family from way back, right?"

"I thought all of this land had always been in her family."

"No. Only the four acres in the vicinity of the house. After her father moved back here, he bought surrounding properties to create a large estate. But there was a lot of resentment from the locals because he returned a wealthy man, thanks to an inheritance from his wife. Everyone else here was struggling and dirt poor. They didn't want to sell their property, but they needed money, and he made them offers they couldn't refuse."

Interesting as that information was, it would have been more appropriate to hear it from Natalie rather than Steven. Her hostess might prefer to keep that sort of background to herself.

Best to get the conversation back on track.

"So what's the story Natalie told you about the cave?"

"She said there were always rumors it was haunted. Thanks to Marie, I suppose. None of the local people would come anywhere close to it. That makes venturing inside even less appealing."

"I'm with you. Not that I believe in hauntings, but dark, closed-in spaces give me the creeps."

Yet if a haunting were to happen on the property, this would be the place. They had to be standing in the vicinity of the spot where Natalie's aunt had landed after plunging to her death from the cliff above.

A shiver rippled through her.

"They give me the creeps too. Let's continue on to the lake."

"You don't have to ask twice." She started back down the trail.

Once they returned to the main path, he moved beside her again. "You'll see Micah's cabin on the left, in the woods, as we approach the lake. The vegetable garden in the sunny patch in front provides his produce. The rest of his food comes from hunting, trapping, and fishing. And he keeps chickens for eggs. He also has an apple and a peach tree."

"You mean he lives off the land?"

"More or less."

"Doesn't he ever go into town?"

"Not if he can help it. But he does have a motorbike for necessary trips. There he is now." Steven inclined his head toward the lake just as Cara caught a glimpse of the cabin and vegetable garden.

She redirected her attention to the water as they continued walking.

Micah sat in a small rowboat, fishing pole in hand, a deer tucked among the trees on the bank beside him. If he saw them, he gave no indication of it—even when Steven lifted a hand in greeting.

"Not the friendliest guy, that's for sure." She skirted a small branch. "I wonder what he was like before his injuries and the PTSD?"

"I have no idea. Maybe he was always a loner."

"Do you know if anyone ever tried to get him psychological help?"

"If they did, it didn't take. And after all the years he's been here, I doubt he'd be willing to revisit that. The niche he's created appears to suit him."

Cara peeked through the trees toward the water as they began to circle the far side of the lake, which was more heavily forested.

Though Micah appeared to be in the exact same position, frozen in place, she had the oddest feeling he was tracking their movements. The deer certainly was, though it stayed on the bank below as they approached.

"He's definitely a little unsettling." She picked up her pace.

"I know. He used to spook me big time, until I got used to his odd ways. But I don't think he's dangerous. Natalie may be able to give you some insights about him. She knows much more about his history than I do."

"I may ask her a few questions."

"And I expect she'll be happy to answer them. Why don't we switch to a pleasanter topic? Tell me more about the project you two are working on."

She complied while they finished their hike, keeping her comments topline, but the questions he asked suggested he was interested in more than the bare-bones overview she'd provided. Not surprising, since it was part of his family history.

As they approached her cottage, she wrapped up. "The finished translation will not only provide an incredible foundation for my research, it will also be a useful resource in the future that could help save a dying language."

"And perhaps solve a mystery too."

So he knew there were questions surrounding Marie's demise too.

"Natalie suggested that, but those entries would be later in the journals. I don't expect we'll get to the last volumes until closer to the end of my stay."

"All I can say is, I'm glad you're doing the transcribing and not me." He stopped in front of the cottage and held out his hand. "Numbers, not words, are my thing. But good luck with the project."

"Thank you." She took his hand.

"I imagine we'll see each other again. I get down here often. And now I have an incentive to increase the frequency. Maybe we could take another walk on my next visit."

It was impossible to miss his message.

He liked her.

That was a welcome ego boost. Not many handsome, charming, and interested men had peopled her world.

For whatever reason, though, he didn't make her nerve endings tingle like the sheriff did.

Yet.

But it was too soon to close the door he'd opened. You never knew where you might meet Mr. Right, as Bri would point out if she were here.

"I'd enjoy that."

"Wonderful." After a squeeze, he released her fingers. "Now I'm off, after I say goodbye to Natalie."

"Safe travels."

"Thanks." With a lift of his hand, he strolled down the walkway toward the house.

As he disappeared around the bend, Cara let herself into the cottage. Her overnight bag and laptop were still in the car, but she'd wait until he left to fetch them. Since they'd just said goodbye, another encounter would feel awkward.

Yet she'd risk that in a heartbeat if Brad Mitchell were the one leaving.

Rolling her eyes, she dropped onto the edge of the bed.

Jack and Bri were to blame for her sudden fanciful thoughts about the lawman. If they hadn't jumped to all kinds of conclusions at lunch, he wouldn't be top of mind.

Oh, come on, Cara. Give it a break.

She flopped back on the bed.

Fine.

The sheriff would be on her mind, with or without prompts from her siblings.

And now another amiable, attractive man had entered her world in this hinterland, as Jack had called it.

Strange how life worked.

She'd come here to do research, with zero expectation of a single romantic vibe during her stay.

Of course, nothing would likely come of her encounters with either man. But they did add a bit of spice to her project.

And researcher that she was, before she and Natalie broke for the day tomorrow, she'd ask a few discreet questions about the background of the three men who'd entered her orbit.

The handsome cousin, the hot sheriff, and the unsociable groundskeeper.

SEVEN

IT WAS LIKE DÉJÀ VU—except today he was arriving at twilight instead of in bright sunshine.

Brad cut his siren, swung into Natalie's driveway, and took the gravel road as fast as he could safely navigate the loose stones. Spinning out or ending up with a cracked windshield from flying rock would only make his sad Sunday worse.

As the house came into sight, he gave it a quick inspection. No indication of smoke or flames in the dusky light.

That was a positive sign.

Nor was there any activity around the fire truck.

Also encouraging.

He parked next to the other patrol car and slid from behind the wheel as Larry came out the front door of the house.

The senior deputy lifted a hand in greeting and joined him. "Sorry to call you on your day off, boss, but you said to keep you in the loop on any happenings out here."

"Don't apologize for following orders. What's the story?"

"A trash can fire in the kitchen set off a smoke detector. Natalie called 911. Near as the fire crew can piece together, it appears someone threw a burned potholder that was still smoldering in the trash. They found the remnants. The chief says the conditions would have had to be perfect for it to ignite after sitting in the trash can for a while, but stuff like that can happen."

"Anyone hurt?"

"No. Natalie and her houseguest had the fire contained when we arrived. She apologized for calling us, but I told her it was better to be safe than sorry."

"Amen to that. Are the ladies inside?"

"Yes. The fire crew's wrapping up and ought to be out of here soon."

"You get everything you need for a report?"

"Yep." He tapped the notebook in his breast pocket. "Natalie insists she didn't throw a potholder into the trash, but she was the only one who used the kitchen today."

"Who else was in the house in the past few hours?"

"The professor got back late afternoon but only went in for a few minutes. Natalie's cousin was here for the weekend. Paul Coleman stopped by. And her housekeeper, Lydia, dropped off a couple of items Natalie forgot to get at the grocery store on Friday. No one did any cooking in the kitchen besides Natalie, though, so . . ." He shrugged. "I'm guessing she forgot about the potholder. You want me to hang around?"

"No. Sounds like everything's under control. I'll talk to Natalie before I leave."

"You could always come back in the morning, when you're on duty."

"As long as I'm here, I may as well have a conversation." Plus, it gave him an excuse to delay his return to the silent, depressing house that no longer felt like home.

"Whatever works." Larry offered a mock salute and continued to his cruiser.

The volunteer fire crew began trooping out of the house as he approached, and after a brief conversation with the chief, Brad continued to the front door.

Natalie was waiting there, Cara behind her.

"Hello, Sheriff." The older woman's usual composure was a tad ragged around the edges, and wisps of white hair had worked loose from her bun. "You didn't have to come out. Everything's under control. I'm sorry to bother you on a Sunday night."

"It was no bother. I'm glad the outcome wasn't any worse. Evening, Professor." He nodded at Cara. "Ms. Boyer, would you mind if I take a look at the source of the trouble?"

"Not at all." She pulled the door wide. "The kitchen is at the end of the hall, in the back of the house."

A faint haze hung below the ceiling as he walked down the corridor, and the scent of smoke intensified the closer he got to the kitchen.

He paused in the doorway to survey the scene.

The wall above the trash can was scorched, as was the ceramic tile underneath—or what he could see of it beneath the residue from the fire extinguisher. But the damage appeared to be confined to that one area.

"It could have been much worse." Natalie spoke behind him.

"Yes, it could. Opening windows will help the smoke smell dissipate." He crossed to the back wall and raised the two closest to the location of the fire.

"Natalie, would you like me to open a few throughout the house?" Cara touched her arm.

The older woman patted her hand. "I'd appreciate that, my dear. You'll get the job done much faster than I would, and the smell is very annoying."

"I'll be back in a minute."

Cara disappeared down the hall.

Shaking her head, Natalie surveyed the kitchen. "What a mess."

"I can get you the name of a fire remediation company if you like."

"I appreciate the offer, but I don't know if it will be necessary. Micah may be able to handle this. Let me ask him first." She motioned to the kitchen table. "Do you mind if I sit?"

"Not at all." He walked over and pulled out a chair for her.

"Thank you." She lowered herself into it, lines of weariness etching her features. "There has been altogether too much excitement around here of late."

"I hear you." He took a seat at the table. "My deputy says the fire crew thinks a potholder may be the culprit in tonight's incident."

Her brow crinkled. "They told me that too, and it doesn't make sense. I didn't burn a potholder, and I certainly didn't throw one in the trash."

"Is there anyone else who could have done that?"

"I can't imagine who. No one other than me had any reason to use a potholder today." She sighed. "This is most bizarre."

"Yes, it is."

She lasered him with a shrewd look. "You're thinking I did it and don't remember. Like everyone else here tonight, you're assuming I'm forgetful because I'm in my eighties."

That was true—and it wasn't fair. From what he could tell, Natalie's mental acuity hadn't dimmed with age.

He shifted in his seat and backtracked. "I'm sorry if I implied that. The truth is, anyone can have an occasional lapse in memory."

"Admirable attempt at a save." Her mouth curved into a wry twist. "But I know what everyone is thinking. And I'm telling you I did not burn a potholder, and I didn't put one in the trash."

"Then how do you explain the fire?"

"I can't. I'm not a detective. Solving puzzles is your job."

Cara reappeared in the doorway but stopped on the

threshold. "I opened the windows in the living room and study, Natalie. That should be enough to create cross ventilation and move the smell and lingering smoke out."

"Thank you."

"Why don't you join us, Professor Tucker?" Brad stood and motioned to the chair beside Natalie.

After a tiny hesitation, she complied. "Cara is fine. I only use my title on campus, with students."

"Got it." He flashed her a smile as he retook his seat, his pulse ticking up as she tucked her hair behind her ear.

Man, she was a pretty woman. Those large hazel eyes were striking—and were her lush lashes natural or mascara-enhanced? As for her full, slightly parted lips . . .

His mouth went dry.

Why wasn't a smart, attractive woman like Cara married? Or was she?

But there was no ring on her left hand, and what were the odds she'd be spending weeks in this remote spot if she had a husband?

So, assuming she was single, why hadn't some guy *put* a ring on her finger? Were all the men in Cape—

". . . but I don't see how that could be related, do you?"

As the end of Natalie's question registered, he yanked his gaze away from Cara and willed the heat creeping up his neck to stay below his collar. "I'm sorry. What did you say?"

"I said Lydia singed a potholder last week, but I don't see how that could be related to what happened tonight. Do you?"

"No." He spoke to Cara again. "Tell me your version of this evening's events."

"I was walking down the path from the cottage to get my laptop and overnight bag out of my car, and I heard the alarm on the smoke detector going off. I ran up to the back door, unlocked it, and rushed in. I found Natalie struggling to pull the fire extinguisher from the closet. I took over that job while she called 911."

"Did you see anyone else around the house while you were outside?"

"No."

"Who has keys to your house, Ms. Boyer?"

"Other than me, only Lydia, Steven, Cara, and Micah. Not that Micah's ever used his, but he could let someone in the house in case of an emergency."

"Speaking of emergencies." Brad linked his fingers on the table. "Have you ever considered installing a home security system? Those also have a fire alarm component."

"No. Papa always said if anyone came out here and was up to no good, they'd be done and gone long before the police arrived. He thought it would be a waste of money. Same with a fire. He assumed by the time a truck arrived, the house would be too far gone to save."

"While there's a certain amount of truth to that, the emergency coverage in the area is more sophisticated and faster than it used to be. You may want to rethink that decision, especially after tonight's experience."

She exhaled. "You could be right. My father was a clear thinker and always logical, but times change." She lifted a hand to stifle a yawn. "Sheriff, if you don't have any more questions for me, I believe I'll call it a night."

"No more questions. But I'll work on the puzzle about the potholder."

"I'd appreciate it." She stood. "Cara, leave the windows open tonight. It's cooled off quite a bit now that the sun's set, and I'd like to get rid of this smell as soon as possible. We'll keep the kitchen door closed to confine the odor and mess until that's dealt with." She waved a hand toward the charred section of wall and tile.

"Do you want me to see if I can find Micah, let him know

you'd like to talk with him about the repairs?" Brad rose too. It wouldn't hurt to ask the man a few questions, despite the fact Natalie seemed to trust him implicitly.

"No need. We have a system. I leave notes on the back door if there are chores to be done. I'll put one out there before I retire for the night."

"In that case, I'll head out." He could always track down Micah later if necessary.

"And I'll get my bag and laptop from my car." Cara rose too.

"Why don't I walk you to the cottage after that?" Brad pushed in his chair.

"An excellent idea, with a potholder pyromaniac on the loose." Natalie limped over to the counter. "I'll lock up behind you once I write my note to Micah. You two enjoy what's left of the evening."

Brad motioned to the back door. "Shall we?"

"Thanks." Cara started across the room. "Natalie, I'll see you in the morning."

"I'll be in the study as usual. You may want to turn on the light outside beside the door." She waved that direction. "It's grown quite dark."

Brad reached past Cara to pull the back door open as she flipped the switch, inhaling the fresh, subtle fragrance wafting from her hair. It smelled like springtime and hope and—

"Give me a couple of minutes to get the laptop and bag." Cara angled toward him after she exited onto the galérie. "I'll meet you here."

Laptop. Bag. Right.

"I'll, uh, check my messages while I wait." And try to corral his unruly hormones.

Unfortunately, they weren't anywhere near under control when she rounded the corner of the house four minutes later.

"Let me take those for you." He motioned to the items she

was carrying, putting his back to the light to keep his face in shadows. Who knew what his expression looked like?

"I've got the laptop, but if you want to carry the bag, I'd appreciate it." She handed it over.

They descended the steps from the galérie and walked down the path. "So now that we've left Natalie behind, what's your take on the fire?"

Twin furrows creased her forehead, visible despite the darkness closing in around them as the glow from the light beside the door faded. "I don't know what to make of it. From what I've seen during our brief acquaintance, Natalie's not careless in general, and certainly not with anything that could be dangerous. And her mind is as sharp as mine. If she says she didn't burn a potholder and put it in the trash, I'm inclined to believe her."

"She did have two dizzy spells in the past week, though. I wonder if they could have messed with her brain."

"Not that I've seen, and I worked with her for hours last week. To tell you the truth, she's as puzzled by the dizzy spells as she is by the fire. She told me that other than her bout with polio and an illness during her college days, she's always been in excellent health."

"I'll talk with Paul and Lydia, since they were in the house today. I don't have contact information for her cousin."

"I'm sure Natalie would provide it if you asked, but I doubt any of them—" Cara caught her breath as she stumbled on an uneven flagstone.

He grabbed her arm. "Watch your step."

"Thanks." Once she regained her balance, he released her arm and they continued forward. "I usually take a flashlight if I'm out at night. Which I try not to be."

They rounded a bend in the path, and the cottage came into view ahead of them, a dim light burning by the door.

"I don't blame you. It would be easy to fall in the dark."

"I'm not concerned about that. But the criminal element tends to like the dark."

"I don't expect you'll run into anyone out here except Micah. Granted, he's a bit odd, but he's never been involved in any trouble in all the years he's lived on the property. I doubt Natalie would keep him around if she had any worries about his character."

Cara stopped in front of the cottage and pulled out her key. "That's what Steven, her cousin, says. I suppose for a city girl, isolation can breed apprehension."

He pivoted away to scan the surroundings. "Caution is never out of place."

"I'm sorry." She touched his arm. "I missed that."

He swiveled back to her, letting the dim light beside the door illuminate his face as he repeated the comment.

"That's what my brother and sister always tell me." She smiled. "I suppose law enforcement types all think alike."

"You have cops for siblings?"

"No. A detective and a fire investigator."

"That's a lot of law enforcement in one family. Were you tempted to join the ranks too?"

"No. I'm content to spend my days diving into research that would put most people to sleep—including my siblings. They investigate deaths—and other crimes. I investigate dying languages." The corners of her lips tipped up, and she shrugged. "What can I say?"

"I can't speak to your research overall, but I think your current project is very interesting."

"If you're from the area, that's probably because it's a familiar subject. Did you grow up around here?"

"Yes."

"Do you still have a ton of family close by? Everyone seems to, from what I've gathered in my research."

His stomach knotted. "Not anymore. My brother's career

took him to upstate New York, and my parents retired to Florida a few years ago. Mom's people are from Idaho, and Dad was an only child. What about you? Is your family close by?"

"My brother and sister live in St. Louis. Mom and Dad are both gone."

"I'm sorry."

"Me too. They were the salt of the earth." Her voice rasped, and she motioned toward the cottage. "I should go in and let you be on your way. I bet it's past your quitting time."

"As a matter of fact, I'm not on duty today."

Her eyebrows rose. "Then why did you come out here tonight?"

He frowned.

Good question.

There'd been no official obligation to respond to this callout, nor to instruct his deputies to let him know if another SOS came in from Natalie's house.

So why had he?

As the explanation slammed into him, it drove the air from his lungs like a punch to the solar plexus.

He'd asked to be alerted for one simple reason. Another SOS would give him an opportunity to cross paths again with the woman standing in front of him.

And that was wrong, wrong, wrong.

It was also unfair to Elizabeth.

A tsunami of guilt crashed over him, but he fought it back. Cara was waiting for an answer, and he had to come up with a plausible excuse.

"My senior deputy alerted me to the call, and I decided to swing by. Natalie's a fixture in the community, even if she keeps a low profile, and I was concerned about her."

True. Just not the whole story.

Cara gave a slow nod. "I admire your dedication to your job."

"It's not a nine-to-five calling, that's for sure. But it *is* getting late. I should leave." He backed off a few steps. "Let's hope the crisis cluster has passed."

"Amen to that. Thanks for walking me back to the cottage."

"My pleasure. Good night." He turned on his heel and escaped into the darkness.

Yet as he strode away—and despite the guilt pricking his conscience—he admitted the truth. From the moment Cara had appeared on his radar, the darkness he'd been living in for the past three years hadn't felt quite as oppressive.

He'd have to deal with that . . . and the implications.

But not tonight.

Instead, as he circled around to the front of Natalie's house, he refocused on the events of the evening.

While the fire had done no lasting harm, Natalie's insistence that she hadn't used a potholder, let alone burned one, was troubling. Especially since this incident had come on the heels of her dizzy spells.

Yes, people who were older could be prone to health glitches. And yes, accidents like fires in trash cans happened. It was possible Natalie had had a memory lapse despite her insistence to the contrary.

Nevertheless, the condensed timeframe didn't feel right.

He opened the cruiser door and slid behind the wheel.

Maybe he was looking for connections that didn't exist. Maybe everything that had happened was innocent. Maybe this was the last call he'd make out here during Cara's tenure.

Yet deep in his gut, he had a feeling there was more to come.

And that the next incident wouldn't be nearly as innocent.

THINGS COULDN'T BE GOING ANY BETTER. Faster, yes, but the pace would accelerate if problems continued to crop up at Natalie's.

Glass of ice water in hand, I wandered outside, into the darkness. At least the heat had abated somewhat.

I settled into my favorite chair and took a sip of the cold liquid.

Now that the groundwork had been laid for my plan, it was time to begin dropping strong hints to Natalie. Convince her to give my proposition serious consideration. It would be so much easier to get what I wanted—what I needed—if she was cooperative.

If she wasn't?

More persuading might be necessary.

I grimaced.

That wasn't my preference. She was a nice woman who'd never hurt anyone in her life. On the contrary. Everyone knew how she'd taken care of her father in his declining years.

A mosquito landed on my arm, and I slapped at it with my free hand. But not before it pierced my skin.

Muttering an oath, I swigged my water.

Everybody was out for blood these days.

That's why you had to protect your interests. Especially when the stakes were high.

Best case, Natalie would come around. She was a logical person. Even if she didn't want to admit she or her house were vulnerable, it was hard to argue with hard evidence.

The bigger issue could be the professor. As long as she was on the premises, Natalie might not see an urgent need to take any action.

So it was possible Cara Tucker would require some direct convincing to vacate the property.

That would be tougher to pull off but not impossible. I'd have to noodle on the best approach to take with her . . . but I had a few cards up my sleeve that could do the trick.

Another mosquito buzzed me, and I waved it away as I stood and trekked back to the house. I wasn't going to win my battle against the winged marauders on this Sunday night. I was too outnumbered.

I slipped back inside, closed the sliding door behind me, and deposited my glass on the counter.

Froze at the streak of red on my arm.

Blood.

It had to be from the mosquito I'd swatted.

Swallowing past the bile that rose in my throat, I twisted the faucet and scrubbed the stain from my arm.

The red streak disappeared, but the image remained in my mind.

I didn't like blood. Never had. Even that scant streak had been enough to turn my stomach into a blender.

That's why I didn't want anyone to get hurt.

If fate was kind, all would go well and I could accomplish my objective without being forced to take any drastic action. Without causing anyone physical harm.

Ultimately, though, I'd do what I had to do to achieve my goal.

Because sometimes the end justified the means.

EIGHT

WHY WAS THERE a basket of produce next to the back door?

Pausing at the bottom of the steps to Natalie's wraparound galérie, Cara took a quick inventory of the items in the crude woven container. Apples, beans, greens, zucchini, and tomatoes.

Huh.

She swiveled around and gave the woods-rimmed open area behind the house a sweep.

No one was in sight, but who except Micah could have left such an offering? He was the only other person on the premises, and he had a garden and fruit trees.

After cradling her laptop in her arm, Cara fished out her key, ascended the steps, picked up the basket, and let herself into the kitchen.

The stink wasn't quite as potent this morning, but until the mess was cleaned up, the olfactory reminder of yesterday's crisis wasn't going to go away.

As she set the basket on the counter, Natalie pushed through the door from the hall, a mug in her hand.

"Good morning, Cara." The older woman smiled, then wrinkled her nose. "What an awful smell. Did you notice if the note I left on the back door for Micah was there when you came in?"

"I didn't see a note, but I found this." She tapped the handle of the basket.

"Oh, how lovely. I'll have to bake zucchini bread." She crossed to the counter, dug into the basket, and began pulling out moss-wrapped eggs. "Perhaps a Niçoise salad as well, with these and the greens and beans. Such beautiful apples too." She held up one of the glossy pieces of fruit.

"I assume all of this is from Micah? Steven pointed out his garden while we were walking yesterday."

"Yes. He often shares his bounty. And if the note was gone, that must mean he went to fetch his tools. I expect he'll be back soon to sort out the mess in here while we sort out Marie's journals."

"Would you like me to put everything in the fridge for you?"

"Yes, thank you. You can set the basket on the kitchen table for Micah to pick up. As soon as I nuke another cup of tea, we'll be ready to dive into week two of our project. Leave the door unlocked too. I expect he'll be back soon."

While Natalie refilled her mug with water, Cara deposited her laptop on the counter and removed the produce from the basket. Her to-do list today included asking a few questions about the groundskeeper, and there would never be a more opportune moment.

"Steven told me that Micah's been here quite a while." She kept her tone conversational as she tucked the offerings from the man's garden into the produce bin of the fridge. "He's a veteran, right?"

"Yes. I wasn't keen on him coming here at first, but Papa said the poor man was sinking fast in the outside world and needed a quiet place to regroup."

"What happened to him overseas?"

Natalie slid her mug into the microwave. "I don't know any specifics, but it was enough to break his spirit. According to his father, he was a gentle soul with a kind heart and a love for animals before he went into the service. Everyone liked him. But he came home a changed man." She shook her head. "Despite his somewhat intimidating appearance, the gentle nature is still there, though. He nurses injured critters back to health down at his cabin."

A different—and sweet—spin on the reclusive caretaker.

"It was generous of your father to take him in."

"To tell you the truth, I think he recognized a kindred spirit. Papa was a sensitive soul too, and I believe he realized that if he'd had the same experiences as Micah, he could have come out of the war in a similar state." The microwave pinged, and Natalie removed the mug. "I don't think he expected him to stay indefinitely, but it's worked out to everyone's benefit."

Cara tucked the last apple into the bin. "Do you ever . . . worry about him?"

"In what way?" Natalie joined her at the fridge and reached past her to extract the container of half and half.

"Like in terms of safety." Cara leaned back against the counter and wrapped her fingers around the edge.

"Goodness, no. Micah Reeves wouldn't hurt a flea. Why do you ask?"

Cara shrugged. "I'm not used to people who fade into the woods whenever I see them."

"That's just how he is. It's nothing personal. He's not sociable with anyone." Natalie poured a smidgen of cream into her tea and replaced the container in the fridge. "My cousin, on the other hand, is very sociable. Don't you think so?"

At the speculative gleam in her eyes, Cara tried not to squirm. Natalie must have picked up on Steven's interest in a certain professor.

And if that was the case, it wouldn't be prudent to probe for additional information about him, much as she'd like to know more. Questions could add fuel to the fire if Natalie was getting matchmaking ideas.

Keeping her manner casual, Cara pushed off from the counter and moved to the sink to rinse her hands. "Yes. I enjoyed our hike."

"He did too. I got the impression he was quite enamored with you. I think he expected my professor to be a much older woman—like you expected him to be the grandfatherly type."

"It goes to show you should never make assumptions about people."

"Yes. There's a definite lesson there." She took a sip of her tea. "By the way, he's not married. Never has been. Claims he hasn't met the right woman. But he'd be a fine catch. He's smart and personable and has a very successful business as a financial advisor."

While that background answered a couple of her questions about Steven, it also confirmed her benefactor's proclivity to matchmaking.

"Not all men get married, though. I don't think the sheriff has a wife either, does he?" Perhaps shifting the focus to the third man she was curious about would distract Natalie.

Some of the brightness in the other woman's face faded. "Not anymore. Such a sad story. I've only picked up bits and pieces of it since I don't go into town that much and prefer to avoid gossip, but everyone was buzzing about it at the time and—" She set her tea on the counter and pulled out her phone. "Ah. It's Paul."

Quashing her disappointment at the interruption, Cara picked up her laptop and motioned toward the door. "I'll wait for you in the study."

"I won't be long."

While the older woman answered the call, Cara wandered down the hall, let herself into the study, and booted up her laptop.

So Brad Mitchell wasn't married anymore. Why not? And what was the sad story Natalie had referenced?

Maybe she could make a few subtle inquiries about him if the opportunity arose.

As for Steven and Micah, the former sounded like a fine man and the latter appeared to be far from menacing.

Meaning she had no excuse not to add a daily walk to her schedule, along with the stretching routine she'd neglected during her first week here.

Cara scrolled through to the translation document and opened it as Natalie came through the door.

"Sorry for the delay. Paul heard about the fire from the sheriff, who called to ask him a few questions. He wanted to check on me—and continue his campaign to convince me to turn over Marie's journals to the historical society for safekeeping." She limped over to her place on the other side of the table. "After last night, I'm beginning to think his suggestion has merit. I would hate for the journals to be damaged or destroyed. And that's where they're going to end up anyway."

"You're donating them?"

"Yes. It was Papa's wish, after they were translated."

"Which won't be much longer. And after all the decades they've been safely stored on the premises, what are the odds that anything would happen to them while I'm here? The fire was an anomaly."

"I hope so. But I could let Paul have the later journals until we're ready to work on them, on the off chance there are any other strange occurrences."

"I don't see any harm in doing that if it gives you more peace of mind."

"Unless we want to look ahead for some reason as we go. Then it would be most inconvenient." Natalie opened the journal in front of her to the page where they'd left off on Friday. "I'll have to think about this. In the meantime, let's get back to—" Her cell began to trill, and she pulled it out. Scanned the screen. "Steven. Give me one minute?"

"Of course." Cara started to stand. "I can wait in the hall until—"

"No, stay there." Natalie waved her back into her seat. "We've had too many delays this morning. I'll keep this short." She put the phone to her ear. "Good morning, Steven. I didn't expect to hear from you so soon after your visit . . . No, I haven't had any more dizzy spells. I feel fine . . . Oh, I'm sorry. I didn't hear the phone. I went to bed early . . . No, nothing like that. We had a little excitement here."

As Natalie briefed her cousin on the events of the evening and answered his questions, Cara read over the transcription. But it was impossible to tune out the conversation.

"No, I didn't. I may be old, but I'm not careless or absentminded." Natalie's defensive tone softened as she continued. "I know you do, dear boy, and I appreciate your concern . . . Yes, it would be lovely to have you close by, but this has always been my home . . . That's true, but I've never been fond of changes. Why don't we talk more about this on your next visit? . . . You know I'd love that, but I don't want to monopolize your weekends." Her mouth curved up as she listened. "Thank you for that. And if nothing else comes up, I'd love to see you . . . Same to you." Natalie ended the call and set the phone beside her, her upbeat demeanor fading. "He was quite concerned about the fire."

"That's understandable. It could have caused serious damage if we hadn't been able to contain it fast."

"Yes, but he was more concerned about how it started. I think he came to the same conclusion the law enforcement and emergency crew did. That I put the potholder in there and don't remember. He thinks I may be having lapses related to my dizzy spells."

"You could always call your doctor, see what he thinks about that."

"Excellent suggestion. I hope that's not the case, because I'd prefer to live out my days here. However, I've never been one to stick my head in the sand. If I'm beginning to slip, I'll have to consider relocating to St. Louis, like Steven suggested. That would help him keep a closer eye on me." Her irises began to shimmer.

Throat tightening, Cara leaned forward and laid her hand on top of Natalie's. "If it's any consolation, I haven't seen any indication of that. You're sharper than many younger people I know."

"Thank you, my dear." Natalie offered her a tiny smile, patted her hand, and straightened her shoulders. "Let's get back to Marie's journals, shall we?"

Cara didn't argue. They had work to do.

But it grew increasingly difficult to concentrate after noise began to emanate from the vicinity of the kitchen half an hour later.

"Micah must be on the job." Natalie looked up from the journal and adjusted her glasses. "It sounds like he's hammering and sawing. Why don't you close the door and see if that muffles the noise?"

Cara did as she suggested, then retook her seat. "Do you want to continue, or should we wait until the repairs are finished?"

"I'm willing to proceed if you are."

"I'm game. If the background noise gets too distracting or I'm having difficulty understanding you, I'll let you know."

They carried on until eleven, with nothing in Natalie's manner suggesting she was in the least absent-minded or forgetful. On the contrary. Her concentration was intense, and her reasoning as she worked to interpret certain unclear phrases was astute.

The noise continued unabated until they wrapped up, and as Cara shut down her laptop, she motioned toward the front of the house. "I'll leave through that door rather than disturb Micah. Dinner as usual at five thirty?"

"Assuming the kitchen isn't in total disarray—but I expect Micah will clean up after he finishes for the day. He's always been neat and meticulous with the jobs I've asked him to do." Natalie stood, grasped her cane, and walked the journal over to the massive desk where she kept it. "I must admit the noise is beginning to bother me, though. I doubt I'll get much of a nap either, and that won't help my concentration this afternoon. I may have to take a break from work."

Another reference to work.

Why not ask about it? If she was involved in some sort of secret project, she wouldn't keep mentioning it.

"May I ask what sort of work you do in the afternoons? I know about the baby afghans, but I have a feeling that's not what you're talking about."

"No, although that's important work too." She slid the journal into the desk drawer, closed it, and rested a hand atop the large monitor on the credenza behind the desk. "I also do a different type of translation work. I have contacts with publishers from the friends I made while I was in Paris, and I've been doing French translations of English books for many years."

Cara's jaw dropped. What other secrets did this remote estate contain? "I had no idea."

"Few people do. Even my old boss at the law firm didn't know I moonlighted. But it's enjoyable work, and it helps me maintain my language skills. It's important to keep the mind active as we age." A brief shadow passed over her features, but then she brightened. "And I do think the work has kept my brain agile. I'm hopeful the sheriff will get to the bottom of the potholder caper. I'm also hopeful that my dizzy spells are a thing of the past."

"Me too." Yet convinced as she was that Natalie's mind was sharp, the odds that Brad Mitchell would come up with an explanation for the fire yesterday were minuscule. Whatever the cause, it would likely remain a mystery.

"If I can get access to the oven, I'll bake zucchini bread for dessert."

"Sounds delicious." Lifting her hand in farewell, Cara exited into the hall and slipped out the front door. Why disturb a man who preferred to avoid people?

But her plan to steer clear backfired when he came out the rear door as she rounded the corner of the house.

It was hard to tell who was more surprised.

Cara jolted to a stop, but so did he as their gazes met.

He broke eye contact first, snatched a roll of drywall tape from the galérie railing, and bolted back inside.

As the door closed behind him, Cara shook her head.

The man was as skittish as the deer she'd run into on the path from the house to the cottage on occasion.

Suggesting that everyone's take on him was accurate.

He was harmless, and more prone to run from people than to cause them trouble.

Picking up her pace, she continued down the path to the cottage and let herself in. Locked the door behind her. Set the laptop on the desk and changed into her sport shoes. With Micah occupied in the house, this would be an excellent opportunity to take a brisk hike around the lake on the trail Steven had shown her yesterday without having to risk running into the reclusive groundskeeper.

Not that she should worry about such a chance encounter, anyway. Everyone considered him safe.

So the best plan was to trust the opinions of people who knew him far better than she did, focus on her work with

Natalie and the academic paper she was in the early stages of writing . . . and remain vigilant.

Just in case the strange vibes she'd been picking up on occasion here in the hinterland morphed into something more dangerous.

"NATALIE'S BEEN HAVING MORE than her share of problems lately, hasn't she?" Becky turned from the fridge and held out a bowl of potato salad.

Paul took it. "Yes."

"She's lucky that fire wasn't any worse."

"I know." He set the bowl on the table. "What made you bring that up?"

"I saw Micah in town today . . . from a distance." Becky crossed back to the stove. "He was going into the hardware store. I assume he was getting supplies to do repairs at the house."

"There must not have been much damage if he could handle it."

No point in telling Becky that Brad had called him this morning at work with questions about his visit yesterday.

Questions that suggested the sheriff might be buying Natalie's claim that she wasn't the one who'd put the potholder in the trash.

But the odds of him pinning the fire on anything more than an accident were negligible. At Natalie's age, and taking into account her recent dizzy spells, her memory could be unreliable.

"Paul?" Becky stopped stirring the sloppy joe mixture and angled toward him. "Are you listening?"

"Of course." Sort of. "I expect you're right. If the damage was too extensive, she'd have to hire a carpenter or builder to do the repairs." He filled two glasses with water from the dispenser in the fridge. "Sorry if I seem distracted. I'm thinking about the interview tomorrow with the St. Louis paper."

"Me too." She began dishing up the sloppy joes. "I'm not looking forward to it."

"Me neither. But we should be fine. Dan gave us an excellent briefing."

"I wish I had your confidence."

"All we have to do is tell them what a wonderful son he is and brag on all his accomplishments. Talk about how civic-minded he's always been, back to his Eagle Scout days."

"Bragging, I can manage—but what if they ask hard questions?"

"Like what?"

"I don't know. Like . . . what if they dug deep and found out about that fender bender he had when he was seventeen, or the two speeding tickets he got as a teenager?"

"If that's all they can come up with to discredit him, he has an easy ride to victory. The media's been full of stories about how his opponent tried to buy alcohol with a fake ID on more than one occasion before he was legal age, not to mention the more recent rumors of an affair he had with an intern. Dan will be fine."

Especially if the later journals Natalie hadn't yet parted with, which could resurrect a ghost or two best left in the dust of history, were out of the picture.

Another reason to get them in his hands ASAP.

"I hope so." Becky carried their plates to the table and sat beside him. "But I'll be glad when this election is over."

"You'll also be proud when we stand in the audience and watch our son be sworn in as a congressman, though." He took her hand. Gave it a squeeze.

"True. And he'll do a wonderful job for the people of his district. Assuming all goes well with the rest of the campaign."

"It will."

There was only one thing that could potentially derail his trajectory to victory.

A family scandal.

While the sins of a father—or in this case, a great-grandfather—shouldn't be visited on subsequent generations nor used to besmirch another family member's character, politics was an ugly, dirty business.

That's why he had to convince Natalie to relinquish those journals.

And if she didn't agree soon?

He'd have to build on yesterday's kitchen fire and come up with a few more persuasive strategies to convince her that the home she loved might not be as safe as she'd always thought.

NINE

SHE HAD SEEDS TO PLANT with two people today . . . one of them Natalie. And the timing of her employer's appearance was ideal.

Calling up a smile, Lydia paused in the hall as the older woman exited the study. "Good morning, Ms. Boyer."

"Hello, Lydia. Sorry for the mess in the kitchen. Don't worry about cleaning in there until Micah is finished. I expect he'll be done by your next visit on Friday."

"I can work around him. No worries." She summoned up her most solicitous expression. "I heard about the fire from the sheriff. He called me to ask about a potholder."

"I don't suppose you knew anything about that?"

"No, ma'am, but I'm glad you heard the smoke alarm. The damage could have been a lot worse. You could even have been hurt."

"Yes, I was most fortunate. I was also very lucky that Cara appeared when she did. I'm not certain I could have extinguished it without her help."

The perfect opening.

"The sheriff told me she heard the alarm and rushed in to help. But I keep wondering what would have happened if she hadn't been close by—and what could happen once she's gone and you're here all by yourself. Especially after your dizzy spells."

Natalie offered her a strained smile. "You sound like my cousin."

Excellent. If Steven was concerned, perhaps he'd champion the idea she was about to propose.

"We all worry about people who matter to us." She tightened her grip on the handle of the vacuum cleaner beside her, wadded the dust rag in her other hand into a ball, and took the plunge. "Have you ever considered having someone live here with you?"

"I have Micah."

"I can see how that would be a comfort, but he isn't always close by. I was thinking more like a live-in housekeeper."

Natalie cocked her head. "No. I can't say I've ever given such a notion any thought, but I do like that idea better than the one Steven proposed."

Uh-oh.

That wasn't promising.

Lydia tried to keep her features neutral. "What did he suggest?"

"He thinks I should move to St. Louis, closer to him. Buy a condo."

A word she tried not to use in public echoed in her mind.

That wasn't the sort of news she wanted to hear. It would wreak havoc with her plans.

She schooled her features into a look of dismay—which wasn't hard. "I suppose I can see his point. But I can't imagine you not living in this house. It's always been your home."

"I know. I can't imagine leaving here, either." She sighed and leaned more heavily on her cane. "Age is creeping up on me, though. The calendar doesn't lie. One of these days I may require a caretaker."

"Well, if you ever decide you'd like someone to be close at hand, I'd be happy to step in. I'm here two days a week as it is. That might put your cousin's mind at ease. Yours too. I'd hate for you to have to leave this beautiful house unless no other option was available."

Natalie studied her for a minute, with the assessing gaze that was as sharp as it had always been. "I appreciate that, Lydia. You're a hard worker, and you've been very reliable in the years you've been with me. Your idea may be a sensible solution. You don't have any family who would object to you leaving your own place behind to live here?"

Ha.

Randy wouldn't give a rat's patootie where she lived once Ashley moved in.

But cutting ties with him completely wouldn't be smart. It was possible he'd be useful if she needed help with certain parts of her plan. Assuming she dangled an incentive in front of him.

"No, ma'am. I'm living with my brother, but I plan to move soon." Like ASAP.

That's why she had to plant a seed with the professor too, to expedite the process.

"Let me give your idea some thought."

"Of course. If you're finished in the study for now, I'll go ahead and clean in there."

"Yes, we're done. Cara's gone back to the cottage, and I'm going to brave the noise and mess in the kitchen to have a quick lunch before my nap."

"Good luck with the nap." She cringed as a hammer banged.

"I may resort to ear plugs, like I did yesterday. I'll see you on Friday, Lydia."

"I'll be here. Like always. You can count on me."

She moved aside as Natalie left the room and limped down

the hall toward the kitchen, then trundled the vacuum cleaner into the study and closed the door. Exhaled.

While Natalie hadn't jumped at the idea of a permanent housemate, she hadn't nixed it outright, either. On the contrary. She'd appeared to be receptive.

The groundwork for the relocation had been laid.

Now on to a bit of recon here in the study.

Wiping her palms down her slacks, she crossed to the desk. After casting a glance back toward the door, she quietly opened the drawer. Pulled out the treasure. Snapped several fast photos with her phone as proof the merchandise existed. Then she returned it to its spot, stowed her cell, and went back to the vacuum cleaner.

Important as it was to have photos, they might not be needed that soon. If Natalie agreed to her plan to move in here, there wasn't as much urgency to deal with the merchandise. In fact, it would be smart to wait until the professor was gone and the project she and Natalie were working on was finished. There was too much activity in those desk drawers at the moment.

She flipped on the vacuum and began running it in rhythmic sweeps over the large area rug, leaving a meticulous pattern behind in the nap.

If she could expedite the professor's departure, that would speed up both aspects of her plan.

So as soon as she finished cleaning in here, she'd plant seed number two.

CARA TIED HER SPORT SHOE, rose, and picked up her sunglasses.

Time for her post-lunch walk.

And with Micah still hammering in the kitchen, there was no chance she'd come upon him suddenly in the woods and startle both of them.

She took a swig from her bottle of water and—

At a sudden knock, she jerked. Coughed. Spun toward the door.

A muffled voice spoke, but she couldn't decipher the words.

"Hold on a minute." She hacked again. Took a slow, calming breath as she walked across the room. Pulled the door open.

Lydia stood on the other side.

"I'm sorry to bother you, Professor." A bucket of cleaning supplies hung on one arm, and she held folded sheets and towels in the other. "I try to get the cottage done while you and Ms. Boyer are working, but the house took me longer today, what with the mess in the kitchen. Is this a bad time to clean?"

"First of all, it's Cara. And now is fine." Her pulse began to moderate. "I was about to take a walk around the lake, so I won't be in your way."

The housekeeper frowned. "You're going walking alone?"

Cara's antennas went up. "Yes. Is there any reason I shouldn't?"

She shifted from one foot to the other. "No. I mean . . . Micah's in the house working. He shouldn't be out and about."

"Would it be a problem if he were?" It was possible Lydia knew more about the man than Natalie or Brad or Steven did.

"Well . . . I guess not. He's never been in any trouble that I know of. But he kind of creeps me out. I don't know if I'd feel comfortable walking around in the woods with him roaming about. That could just be me, though. Ms. Boyer doesn't seem to have any worries about him."

No, she didn't, and she'd had plenty of opportunities to observe him in the years he'd lived on the property.

Nevertheless, Lydia's concerns were disconcerting.

Not that there was any reason to admit that.

"I'm sure I'll be fine." She forced up the corners of her mouth and patted the pocket in her sweatpants. "Besides, I have my pepper gel with me. Comes from city living, I suppose."

"I think that's smart. It always pays to be prepared. And Micah is probably harmless." Her tone, however, suggested she didn't believe that. "Are you certain you don't mind me cleaning now?"

"Absolutely. Come in."

The woman slipped past her. "Enjoy your walk."

"Thanks."

But despite her perfunctory response, the truth was she wouldn't find the trek as relaxing now that it was obvious someone who knew Micah had reservations about him.

She did have her pepper gel, though, and as she struck off down the path, she pulled it out. Keeping it at the ready would help calm her nerves.

And once she came back, thirty minutes of stretching should help diffuse any residual tension and set her up for a productive afternoon of research and writing.

Tomorrow, she'd rinse and repeat.

Because she wasn't going to let vague, groundless fears keep her cottage-bound.

Especially since Brad Mitchell hadn't seemed too concerned about Micah. The sheriff came across as a smart man with sound judgment, and he hadn't issued any warnings. And while they were new acquaintances, she was inclined to trust his instincts.

Even if Lydia's wariness about the groundskeeper undermined her confidence in those instincts a tiny little bit.

"YOU EVER FIGURE OUT the potholder puzzle?"

At the question, Brad swiveled in his chair to face his senior deputy, who'd propped a shoulder against the office doorway.

"No. I talked to the housekeeper and Paul. Neither claimed to have any knowledge of a burned potholder. I haven't talked to the cousin who was there."

"Are you planning to?"

"I don't know."

"You starting to come to the same conclusion we did? That Ms. Boyer threw it in the trash and doesn't remember?"

Brad leaned back, rested his elbows on the arms of his chair, and steepled his fingers. "She's adamant she didn't, and in my encounters with her over the past week, I didn't pick up anything to indicate she's lost one iota of mental acuity or become forgetful."

"Sometimes that sort of thing can come on suddenly in older people. Plus, it's not like you see enough of her to give you a baseline comparison."

"True. But Cara's spent hours with her, and she said Ms. Boyer is as sharp as she is."

"So it's Cara now." Larry ambled in, speculation sparking in his eyes.

"That's what she told me to call her." He kept his tone conversational. "She says only her students call her professor."

"Uh-huh." Larry dropped into the chair across the desk. "She's a pretty woman."

This wasn't a conversational tangent he wanted to follow.

But changing the subject too abruptly would only feed his deputy's interest.

Best plan? Play this low key and casual.

"Yes, she is."

"She married?"

"That hasn't come up in our conversations." But he'd bet a week's salary she wasn't.

"You could find out."

Brad stifled a groan.

For months now, Larry had been dropping subtle and not-so-subtle hints that he should reenter the dating scene. And nothing so far had dissuaded him from his mission to beef up his boss's social life.

Brad mulled over his strategy.

Maybe he needed to be more direct instead of brushing off these types of comments with a simple "not interested."

He rocked forward and linked his fingers on the desk. "For the record, I'm not planning to take another walk down the aisle. Ever. I'd appreciate it if you'd stop trying to nudge me that direction."

Larry considered him. "Can I be honest?"

"Depends on how much you value your job." He was only half joking.

"I'll take the risk." Larry crossed an ankle over a knee, his relaxed posture at odds with the intensity in his eyes. "The truth is, Elizabeth wouldn't want you to spend the rest of your life alone, mourning her. I knew her. She wasn't like that. She was full of life and joy and believed in living each moment as fully as possible. Nor would she want you to blame yourself for what happened that night."

Stomach knotting, Brad clenched his fingers tighter.

He couldn't argue with anything Larry had said.

But there was more to the story.

"I'm not going to disagree with your take on Elizabeth—but what happened that night *was* my fault."

"Sorry. Not buying."

Anger coiled up inside him. "How can you say that? You weren't there. I was. I know every detail."

"You weren't there at the moment it happened. So you can't know every detail." Larry uncrossed his legs and leaned forward. "But I know you—and I know how much you loved Elizabeth and Jonathan. I also know that wallowing in guilt and punishing yourself for the rest of your life isn't going to bring them back. If you have amends to make, make them with God and let the past go. Focus on today. Elizabeth would want you to make it count . . . and to fill it with joy." He stood. "Here's my two cents. If the opportunity comes along to find love again, don't add passing it by to your list of regrets. See you on patrol." He gave a mock salute and disappeared out the door.

Brad remained in his chair, staring at the blank wall across from his desk.

The wall that used to hold a photo of him and Elizabeth and Jonathan . . . until looking at it every day became too painful and he'd relegated the beaming trio to a closet at home.

An exercise in futility.

It hadn't lessened the ache in his heart. Nothing had.

At last, he stood and trudged over to the window. Shoved his hands into his pockets and lifted his face toward the heavens.

Larry may have stepped a mite too far into personal territory today, but they knew each other well. And his deputy was right.

Elizabeth wouldn't want him to grieve forever. Nor would she hold the mistake he'd made that night against him. She'd want him to move on. To love again, if the opportunity arose.

In his head, he knew that. But his heart wasn't on board yet. Nor would it be until he could put his guilt to rest and stop what-iffing.

A monumental task he'd backburnered for years, but which had suddenly become a high priority.

Expelling a breath, Brad massaged his temple, where a dull pounding kept tempo with the beat of his heart.

Maybe Larry's advice on the guilt front was sound too. Maybe he ought to seek forgiveness from the highest source. While his trips to church had been sporadic since that terrible night, despite Father Johnson's attempts to reach out to him, he'd be welcomed back to the fold with open arms if he chose to return. Offered absolution.

All he had to do was open the door . . . to God and the future.

A future that beckoned with a touch of brightness for the first time in three long, lonely years.

Thanks to an encounter with a lovely professor who'd brought something back to his life that had been absent since that cold, rainy night when his world came crashing down.

Hope.

TEN

AS SHE APPROACHED THE LAKE, pepper gel in hand, Cara surveyed Micah's cabin tucked back among the trees.

The man was nowhere in sight.

Nor had she spotted him on any of the walks she'd taken over the past two weeks. Natalie's groundskeeper knew how to keep himself scarce. Once he'd finished the kitchen fire repairs, he'd melted back into the shadows of the woods and disappeared.

Fine by her.

The occasional distant light bobbing through the trees at night through her cottage window—evidence of Micah's nocturnal wanderings, no doubt—was disquieting enough.

She continued past the cabin, keeping it in her sights as she hiked at a brisk pace. All appeared quiet. The crude basket Micah used for produce deliveries was in its usual place beside the front door, and the small wooden cage still rested atop the stump of a large tree that must have towered over the cabin at some point. The resident rabbit she'd glimpsed inside had to be one of the injured animals Natalie had said the groundskeeper attended to.

As she left the cabin behind and began to circle the far edge of the lake, Cara raised her face toward the blue sky, letting the warmth of the sun seep into her skin. The high temperatures from the late-summer hot spell had abated, and on this end-of-September afternoon there was a touch of fall in the air.

What a glorious day.

Best of all, the translation work was progressing at a faster pace now that she and Natalie had settled into the groove of working together, and there'd been no more drama on the estate. Her benefactor's dizzy episodes appeared to have been an anomaly, as had the fire.

It seemed the rest of her stay here would be smooth sailing.

Even her social life had picked up, thanks to Steven.

A smile curved her lips as she watched a hawk soar overhead on a wind current.

During her stay, Natalie's cousin had come every weekend to see his older relative, even arriving once late on a Thursday to extend his visit. And he had begun lingering until she got back from Cape on Sunday afternoons. Their hikes around the lake together were always enjoyable, as was the conversation they shared over glasses of iced tea after their return. Conveniently provided by Natalie.

While there was no real zing between them, he was a pleasant man.

Cara rounded the edge of the lake and started down the path that wove among the trees bordering the water on the far side.

The only thing that could have made the past couple of weeks better?

A visit from the sheriff.

Barring another disaster or medical emergency, however, he'd have no excuse to stop by. And Natalie had endured more than her share of those this month.

Cara sidestepped a large rock.

Too bad she hadn't crossed paths with him on her trip to town yesterday—ostensibly to restock her supply of bagels, if anyone had asked. No way would she have admitted that her real motive had been the hope of another chance encounter with the sheriff, like the one she'd enjoyed the day of Natalie's doctor visit.

It was just as well that they hadn't met, though. Letting herself get interested in a man who lived two hours from Cape wouldn't be prudent. He was GU, as her brother had once termed a woman who lived too far away to consider dating. Geographically undesirable.

Steven, on the other hand, was safe. Because much as she enjoyed his company, the lack of sparks between them suggested they had no long-term future. If that happened to—

At a sudden movement a few yards ahead to her right, she jolted to a stop, fingers tightening on her pepper gel.

A nimble doe sprang up onto the narrow path from the steep bank that led down to the water. Stopped. Looked at her.

Odd.

All the deer she'd encountered on the property had bounded away the instant they'd noticed her.

This one didn't move.

And it was blocking the path.

Would taking a step or two forward convince it to bolt?

Worth a try.

She edged forward, but the deer didn't budge.

Huh.

Maybe she should barge ahead and hope the doe would take off.

But what if it didn't? What if this animal with the big, soulful eyes attacked her instead?

Unlikely—but why take the risk?

So unless there was an off-trail option to skirt the deer, she'd have to retrace her entire route or wait for it to leave.

She inspected the hill to her left, which slanted up. Too steep to traverse.

Turning her attention to the right, she peered down the short slope to the water. It wasn't quite as vertical as the incline on the left, but—

Wait.

What was that?

She changed position to get a clearer view between the branches of the trees.

Was that Micah's boat, caught in a tangle of reeds and tall grasses on this shallow edge of the lake?

Yes, it was.

How strange.

Why would he let his boat drift into such a difficult area to access?

At a sudden rustle to her left, she swung back toward the deer.

It was bounding away, up the trail.

That was a plus. She'd be able to finish her walk without backtracking.

Yet instead of continuing on, she looked again at the boat, a shiver of unease rippling through her.

Something didn't feel quite right.

Should she—

Oh!

Cara's heart stuttered as she homed in on a floating object that was peeking past the far side of the boat.

Was that a . . . hand?

She squinted at it.

Dear God.

It *was* a hand.

Pulse pounding, she scrambled down the embankment, clutching at branches and bushes as she half slid to the edge of the lake. Holding on to a tree trunk for balance, she leaned out. Grabbed the edge of the boat. Jockeyed it aside.

And almost lost her lunch.

A man was lying on his stomach in the water.

But she didn't need to see the face to know his identity. The shirt and shaggy hair were familiar.

It was Micah Reeves.

"WHERE IS SHE?" Brad vaulted out of the squad car and tossed the question to Larry, who was standing on Natalie's front galérie.

"The professor?"

"Yes."

"Inside." He motioned behind him. "She stayed by the lake until we arrived, but she was pretty shaken up. I brought her back up here. Alan's with the body."

"Is the coroner en route?"

"Yes."

"I'll go down to the lake after I get a statement. You can stay here to direct the coroner." He took the steps two at a time, gave a perfunctory knock on the door, and let himself in.

The living room was empty, but a soft murmur of voices came from the back of the house.

He strode that direction, stopping on the threshold of the kitchen.

Natalie and Cara sat at the table, a subtle hint of new-paint smell lingering in the air.

Brad gave the fire-damaged area a cursory scan.

It had been restored to pristine condition.

But his main focus was the two women at the table.

While Natalie's complexion was pale, Cara's was pasty. Shock had dulled her eyes, and even from several feet away, he could tell she was trembling.

He moved to the table and sat beside her, calling up every ounce of his willpower to resist the temptation to fold her hand in his. "You okay?"

Her breath hitched, but she nodded.

"Ms. Boyer?" He transferred his attention to the older woman. "How are you?"

"Devastated. I know most people didn't care for Micah, but he and I had an understanding. He took excellent care of the property, and I always felt like he watched out for me in his quiet way. Such a gentle soul, with his love for animals." Her voice caught. "I can't believe he's gone. Do you have any idea what happened?"

"Not yet." He pulled out his notebook and refocused on Cara. "I have to ask a few questions."

"Okay."

"If you don't need me, would you mind if I lie down?" Natalie grasped her cane. "One of my rare headaches is coming on, and if I don't deal with it fast, it will last for hours."

He stood. "I can catch up with you later if necessary. The only question I have at the moment is whether Micah had any next of kin who should be notified."

"If he did, he never shared their names with me. There may be some personal information in his cabin, though."

"I'll swing by there." As she rose, slowly traversed the room, and disappeared down the hall, he turned to Cara. "Would you like a glass of water?"

"No, thanks."

He retook his seat and opened his notebook. "Let's start with what led up to you discovering the body."

With a nod, she launched into her story.

Brad took notes as she talked. Her account was so precise and detailed he didn't have to pose a single question or ask for any clarifications. Not surprising for a woman who spent much of her life doing meticulous research.

"After I called 911, I waited by the lake for someone from law enforcement to arrive." As she concluded, she drew a shuddering breath. "What do you think happened to him?"

He closed his notebook. "We'll have to let the coroner weigh in. A number of factors could have been involved. A heart attack. A fall that knocked him out while he was trying to extricate the boat from the reeds. A cerebral hemorrhage."

"But he was relatively young, and he fished in that lake all the time. Why would he venture into the reeds?"

"Who knows? But accidents—and fatal medical issues—can happen without warning."

Her brow crimped. "I know, but this feels off to me."

"How so?"

"From what I've heard and observed, Micah wasn't sloppy or careless. Case in point." She motioned toward the impeccably repaired wall. "You can't even tell there was a fire, and he cleaned up the kitchen every night while he was working. It was pristine in here. As for health issues . . . I suppose that's possible, but with all the physical work he did, I imagine he was in excellent condition."

True as all that might be, no one was immune from catastrophe . . . as a job in law enforcement verified every day.

"I'll pass all that along to the coroner." He slid his notebook back into his pocket and stood. "I'm going down to the lake. Would you like me to walk you to your cottage?"

She rose too. "No, thanks. I want to get a book from the collection in the study. Besides, with so much law enforcement presence right now, it's not like I have to worry about walking around by myself."

"*Did* you worry about that?"

She lifted one shoulder. "A little. I'm a city girl, remember? Being on an isolated estate can sometimes be a bit unsettling."

"There's nothing wrong with trusting your instincts if you sense danger. It's always safer to be too cautious than not cautious enough."

"I suppose, but—"

"Oh, Sheriff, I'm glad I caught you." Natalie reappeared in

the doorway. "I took a quick look through my father's files to see if he had any information on next of kin for Micah. I found one contact name and a phone number. But it's from many years ago, after Micah's father died, so I'm not certain it's valid anymore." She walked over to him and held out a slip of paper.

He took it. "Thank you. I'll also check the cabin." He started to fold the paper. Paused at the two words written on the back.

Be careful.

He raised his eyebrows. "What's this?" He held it up.

"I wrote the contact information on the back of a note Micah left for me after he finished the repairs in here. Another example of why I always felt he looked out for me."

"What do you think prompted this warning?"

She shrugged. "Coming on the heels of the fire, I imagine it was his way of showing he cared about me. Like his produce and egg deliveries, and the occasional bouquet of wildflowers he picked in the meadow. He was a sweet man." She massaged her temple. "Now I'm going to rest for a bit."

As she once again retreated down the hall, Brad pocketed the note.

"It would be sad to have no family who cared when you died, wouldn't it?"

At Cara's quiet question, he gave her his full attention. Compassion had softened her eyes, the slight shimmer in their depths evidence of her caring nature.

"Yes, it would. But maybe the name on this paper will lead me to a long-lost relative." He tapped the shirt pocket he'd slipped it into.

"What will happen to him if no one claims . . . if there's no one to make arrangements?"

"I'll talk it over with Natalie. She may have some thoughts on the subject."

"That makes sense." She motioned toward the hall. "I'll go on to the study and let you get down to the lake."

Much as he'd like to extend his time with her, duty called.

He crossed to the back door and turned. "I'll keep you and Natalie apprised of the investigation."

"Thanks."

He let himself out, then struck off for the lake, circling counterclockwise to speed up his trip to the location Cara had provided.

It didn't take long to make the short circuit, and the young deputy was waiting for him on the path above the body.

"You take a close look yet?" Brad stopped beside the man.

"Only to confirm he was dead."

Not surprising. Newly minted deputies weren't inclined to get up close and personal with death if they could avoid it.

"Coroner should be here soon. I'm not going to touch much until Rod's done. He always gets first dibs. Hang tight till he shows up."

"Roger."

Brad scrambled down the slope, gave the body a cursory once-over, took several photos, and rejoined Alan to wait for the coroner. Rod's assessment would help guide the investigation, what little of it there was liable to be. Unless he found obvious evidence of foul play, they'd document the scene, then rely on the autopsy to determine cause of death. In all probability, manner would be accidental or natural.

Several minutes later, Larry appeared around a bend in the trail, Rod and his assistant behind him with a stretcher in tow.

After a brief exchange, Brad followed the coroner down to the edge of the lake.

The man took a number of overall photos, then got up close and personal with the body.

"You see the gash on the back of his head?" Rod leaned closer.

"No. I was waiting for you."

"Water washed away the blood. It's not easy to spot with all the hair this guy has." He patted the edge of the boat. "There's a smear of what appears to be blood on this side."

"You think he fell, knocked himself out, and went into the water?"

"Plausible. But that's not my determination to make." He flashed him a grin. "I just rule on cause and manner. You'll have to determine how the deed happened, if the case merits that sort of scrutiny. Let me get a water temperature and sample, take a few more photos, finish my scene work, bag the hands, then we'll transport and leave you to investigate further."

It didn't take long for Rod and his assistant to wrap up, and with Alan lending a hand, they carried the body out.

"I want to take a few photos of the blood on the boat and get a sample." Brad motioned to the satchel Larry was toting. "I assume there are evidence envelopes in there?"

"Yep."

After tugging on latex gloves, Brad didn't waste any time completing that task and giving the area a thorough inspection.

But other than the blood on the boat, there was nothing to see. Certainly nothing that appeared suspicious. While it was possible there was trace evidence in the small craft, nothing was visible to the naked eye.

Just in case, though . . .

"You still have that plastic sheeting in your trunk?"

"Yes."

"Let's take the boat back to Micah's cabin, put it in his shed, and cover it."

His deputy arched an eyebrow. "Are you suggesting we carry it back?"

"Why not?" Brad hiked up the corners of his mouth. "It's not that big, and it's aluminum. It can't weigh much more than a hundred and twenty pounds. I thought you'd gone back to working out with weights."

"I have, but hauling a boat around is different than picking up a barbell."

"Tell you what." Brad fished out one of the paddles that was caught in the reeds. "Why don't you row it back across the lake and I'll meet you near the cabin? Put on gloves and grab the other paddle." He motioned to it, stuck in the reeds farther down. "That work?"

"Yeah. I can handle rowing. You want to ride along?"

"No. I want to walk the path."

After the other paddle was retrieved, Brad steadied the boat while Larry boarded, gave the craft a push, and set off down the trail that wound through the woods—even though the odds of spotting anything suspicious were small.

Securing the boat was probably overkill too, but better safe than sorry.

He pulled his sunglasses out of his shirt pocket, Micah's note to Natalie crinkling as he withdrew them.

Be careful.

Brad frowned as the man's warning strobed again through his mind.

The older woman assumed Micah's cautionary advice had been prompted by the fire, but what if that hadn't been the impetus? What if Micah had been aware of dangerous activity on the estate? Was it possible the fire, and even Natalie's dizzy spells, were somehow related to the warning?

He picked up his pace down the path toward the man's cabin, questions swirling through his mind that would be a stretch under normal circumstances.

Now that Micah had turned up dead, however? Not so much.

In fact, despite the lack of an apparent motive, the previous happenings cast a shadow of suspicion over the man's sudden end.

Nevertheless, he'd wait for the coroner to weigh in and for the autopsy report to be completed before jumping to any conclusions.

And if either generated so much as one smidgen of doubt, he'd dig in deeper.

Because while no one other than Natalie might miss Micah, the man deserved justice.

And if someone up to no good had assumed the demise of a man who preferred animals to people would pass with little fanfare, they were in for a surprise.

ELEVEN

"*PAUL! HOW LOVELY TO SEE YOU.* Come in." Natalie moved back into the hall and pulled the door wide.

He called up a smile and stepped inside. "I hope you don't mind the unexpected visit. I had to run over to the historical society on my lunch hour, and I was so close I decided to drop in. I've been thinking of you ever since I heard the news about what happened to Micah yesterday."

A shadow passed over her face as she slowly shut the door. "I'm still in shock." She motioned toward the living room. "Please, have a seat. I'll make us a pot of tea."

"I can't stay long enough for tea. I have to be back at my desk in half an hour. But I'll sit for five minutes." He followed her in and claimed a chair beside the couch. "I'm more sorry than I can say about Micah. I know how much you counted on him to keep everything around here shipshape."

"Yes, I did." She sighed. "One more reason for me to mull over Steven's suggestion that I sell the place and buy a condo in St. Louis where I wouldn't have to worry about such matters."

That was news.

"I didn't know your cousin was pressing you to move."

"I wouldn't say pressing, but he *is* concerned about me. More than ever, with Micah gone. He's planning to come down later this week and spend a few extra days with me. I imagine we'll discuss my situation."

Paul smoothed out a wrinkle in the upholstered arm of the chair as he mulled over this unexpected turn of events. His main goal had always been to convince Natalie to give him the journals, not leave the area.

"You may be able to find someone else to handle the upkeep chores here."

"Lydia, my housekeeper, proposed that this morning too. She said her brother might be interested in taking over maintenance duties on a part-time basis, which should be sufficient."

"That may be worth considering."

"Yes, I suppose at the very least it could be a solution in the near term. I do want to follow through on my commitment to Cara before I make any major lifestyle changes."

The very subject he wanted to discuss.

"How's the translation coming?"

"Better. We've established a rhythm, and the pace is picking up as I get more accustomed to Marie's penmanship and can decipher it more easily."

Bad news.

"I'm glad to hear that." Somehow he held on to his placid expression as he mouthed the lie. "Have you come across any interesting nuggets?"

"Nothing the average person would find noteworthy, but the glimpses the journals offer into this area during that era are fascinating. Cara is beyond excited."

"I can imagine." He flicked an imaginary speck off his slacks, keeping his manner and tone conversational. "How far along are you?"

"Closing in on the one-third mark. We're on track to finish

by the end of the semester. Perhaps much sooner if our pace keeps accelerating."

Paul's stomach cramped.

What if they got to the end before the election?

What if there was incendiary information in the last journal or two that somehow leaked to the press?

Such a disclosure wouldn't come from Natalie, of course. She was the soul of discretion.

The professor, however, was an unknown. This research project was important to her. She might not intend any harm, but there was a real risk if Natalie had given her carte blanche to use any of the information they uncovered. What if there was enough in the journals to resurrect an old, rumored scandal? Enough to throw suspicion on a certain high-profile person in relation to Marie's death?

The press would gobble that up.

And while the woman's demise was a decades-old cold case, it was possible someone committed to justice would want to dig back in and put it to bed.

Someone like Brad Mitchell.

A person Cara had been having what appeared to be a very friendly conversation with in town soon after her arrival.

Who knew how this would play out if she shared what she found with him?

And Dan didn't need any bombshells close to the election.

Besides, whatever had happened on that long-ago night when Marie died wasn't relevant to a political race decades later.

Nevertheless, the press and the opposition could use it to smear the Coleman name.

Paul tightened his grip on the arms of the chair.

Should he alter his plans? Be upfront with Natalie instead of trying to convince her to give him the journals? Ask her to hold off on—

"Paul?" She reached out and touched his arm, her face creased with concern as she examined his white knuckles. "Are you all right?"

"Yes." He took a deep breath and pried his fingers loose from the chair. Swallowed. "I have a lot on my mind these days. Politics is a stressful business, and Dan is neck-deep in it."

"I've been following his campaign. He appears to be doing quite well."

"He is. But politics is unpredictable, and the opposition can be ruthless."

"Too true in our world today. I expect Dan will be fine, though. I've read up on his opponent. It seems to me he has a few skeletons in his closet that would discourage him from finger pointing or—" She pulled out her phone. "It's the sheriff. He may have an update on Micah. Do you mind if I take this?"

"No." Paul stood, the opportunity to broach his concerns gone for today. "I have to leave anyway. Duty calls. I'll see myself out."

"Come again soon."

"I will."

As she put the cell to her ear and greeted the sheriff, Paul crossed the room, slipped through the front door, and closed his eyes, suppressing a chill as a dark cloud scuttled across the sun and cast a shadow over the scene.

His campaign to put those later journals in cold storage had yielded zip, despite the efforts he'd made to convince Natalie they'd be safer in his hands.

Coming clean about his real motive for wanting to get them in his possession remained an option. One he'd almost exercised. But there was a risk in doing that. Even if he extracted promises from both Natalie and the professor to keep the contents confidential until after the election, they could also be damaging if Dan was elected. Used by those who opposed his agenda as a distraction to undermine his ability to fulfill his campaign promises.

That technique had certainly been employed in politics in the past.

So maybe it was best he hadn't mentioned his concerns today. Maybe he should continue pursuing his original goal to get Natalie to give him the journals. After all, he'd invested a lot of effort trying to convince her they might not be safe here. That danger could lurk within these walls.

It had been an unpalatable task. One that had taken him far outside his comfort zone.

But Dan was his son. Natalie was only a friend.

And family came first.

WELL, SHOOT.

Scanning her cell as Jack's number flashed on the screen, Cara paused in her trek down to the lake.

Had her overprotective brother gotten wind of what had happened here three days ago?

If he had, she was in for a ton of questions. Any suspicious death raised his antennas. More so if a family member was in close proximity.

But delaying this conversation wouldn't change whatever he had to say. And with him leaving for Quantico tomorrow, she owed him a good-luck wish.

Bracing, she pressed talk. "Hi, Jack."

"Hi back. Did I catch you at a bad time?"

"No." She walked over to the edge of the path, set down the small satchel she was toting, and perched on a large rock. "I'm taking a hike around the lake."

"Great day for it."

"Yes, it is." The mild temperature, brilliant sun, and clear blue sky were Missouri autumn in all its glory.

"Can you hear me okay?"

"Yep." Thanks to Bluetooth, which sent the sound directly from her phone to her sound processors. A big improvement over the days when she'd had to rely on the T-coil in her processors to eliminate extraneous noise.

"I just wanted to say ciao and remind you to stay in touch."

So this wasn't about Micah's death.

She exhaled.

"I was going to call you later today to wish you good luck and bon voyage. And I don't intend to bother you much while you're away. They're going to keep you super busy. You don't need any interruptions."

"Your calls are never an interruption."

"Says the man who almost hung up on me the night you had your soon-to-be fiancée over for dinner last month."

"A rare exception. I didn't want the lamb chops to burn."

"Did you say lamb chops?" Though Jack was speaking slowly and distinctly, as he always did during their phone calls, sometimes it was hard to catch unfamiliar words.

"Yes."

"Seriously? How come Bri and I never get lamb chops when you host the sibling Sunday meal?"

"Do you know how much they cost?"

"Oh, so Lindsey's worth the price of lamb chops and sisters aren't. Thanks a lot."

A noise that could be a huff came over the line. "Fine. I'll have lamb chops next time I host."

Cara grinned. It was too easy to needle her brother. "I'm kidding, Jack. We know you love us. You don't have to serve us fancy food to prove that. All we require is a regular infusion of mint squares."

"Those, I can provide. How's the translation coming along?"

"Fine. Picking up momentum."

"I imagine you're getting a ton of work done out in the middle of nowhere, with nothing to distract you."

Nothing to distract her?

Oh no, nothing at all. Just dizzy spells and a kitchen fire and a dead body in the lake.

None of which Jack needed to know.

"Productivity does tend to rise when life is quiet and there aren't any disruptions."

A true statement, even if it didn't characterize her sojourn here up to this point.

"You'll stay in touch?"

"Count on it. Expect occasional dispatches from me to arrive in Quantico. Take care of yourself."

"You too. Love ya, sis."

"Back at you."

After they said their goodbyes, she ended the call, slid the phone into her pocket, and stood to complete her mission of mercy.

The rabbit with the splinted leg in Micah's crude wooden cage required food and water, and who else was there to tend to it? While her knowledge about injured animals was limited, the internet offered a trove of guidance.

She lengthened her stride until the cabin appeared but slowed when Steven came out the door.

What was he doing here?

Natalie's cousin seemed as surprised to see her as she was to see him, but after a moment he smiled and raised a hand in greeting.

She continued toward him, stopping beside the cage containing the rabbit as Steven walked over to join her.

"I didn't expect to see you here." She set her satchel on the ground, a few leaves of lettuce peeking out the top.

"Likewise. I'm guessing you came to play Florence Nightingale." He flicked a glance at the tote and indicated the cage.

"Yes. I spotted him during my walks, and there was no one else to take care of him. At least a neighbor took the chickens. What's your excuse for stopping here? And so early in the afternoon. I thought Natalie said you were coming tonight."

"I left the office at noon. Slow morning. Natalie said the sheriff didn't find any other contact information for Micah down here, and the name she had didn't lead anywhere. I thought I'd take one more look. It's hard to believe there isn't a soul who should be notified."

"Also sad. Did you have any luck?" She motioned toward the cabin.

"No."

Not surprising. Brad would have done a thorough search. If there'd been anything to find, he'd have found it.

"At least he left final instructions."

Steven's eyebrows rose. "I didn't know that."

"Oh. I assumed Natalie had mentioned it to you."

"We haven't talked much about him since Monday. I don't bring him up because it disturbs her."

That was true. While there wasn't any family to mourn Micah's passing, one person was quietly grieving his death.

"Yes, I know. The sheriff found a handwritten note in a box in the cabin, along with a last will and testament bequeathing his modest savings to the local animal shelter. Micah wanted to be cremated, and he asked that his ashes be spread over the lake."

"Is Natalie on board with that?"

"Yes. She said the least she could do was honor his final wish after all the years he worked here."

"When is that going to happen?"

"After the coroner releases the body, I suppose."

"Any word from the sheriff on the results of the autopsy?"

"No. He said he'd let me and Natalie know about the findings, so I assume they haven't come in yet."

Steven slid his fingers into the pockets of his jeans and surveyed the lake, grooves denting his brow. "There's sure been some weird stuff going on here lately."

"Amen to that."

He refocused on her. "May I ask you a question about Natalie?"

"Yes." But she'd weigh her answer carefully, depending on what he wanted to know. While she and the older woman were newer acquaintances, she'd developed a strong protective instinct toward her during her stay on the premises.

"I know she claims she knows nothing about the burned potholder that started the fire, and I know she hasn't had any more dizzy spells, but with Micah gone, I'm more worried than ever about her living out here alone. You're with her now, but not for long. From what you've seen working with her every day, do you think my concerns are justified?"

"No." That was an easy answer to give. "She seems 100 percent fine to me. And from what she said, her doctor didn't express any serious reservations about her health."

"That's good to hear." The tension in his features eased, and the corners of his lips twitched. "But I expect I'll still worry."

"To tell you the truth, I'm glad she *has* someone to worry about her."

"I'll keep that in mind if she starts complaining about me being overprotective." He flashed her a full-out grin, then waved toward the cage. "So what are you going to do with this little guy?"

"Keep giving him food and water until I take him to the vet in town next week."

"It's a shame we're not closer to St. Louis. I know a vet there who could check him out. She does make occasional house calls, but this is way beyond her radius."

She.

A friend? Neighbor? Medical provider for a four-legged companion, perhaps?

Cara kept her tone nonchalant. "Do you have a pet?"

"No. I'm not a cat person, and my long hours on the job wouldn't be fair to a dog. Besides, pets are a big responsibility, and I have too many of those as it is."

There wasn't a single clue in that answer about his relationship with the female vet.

Fine. It wasn't any of her business, anyway.

Cara smiled. "I hear you. Same story here. Well . . . I'll go ahead and take care of Thumper, then finish my circuit around the lake."

"I'd offer to join you, but Natalie's expecting me for lunch."

"No worries. I've got the route down pat."

"Maybe tomorrow, if you'd like some company?"

"I'd enjoy that."

He began to walk away, but turned back after a few steps, his demeanor once more solemn. "Be careful, okay?"

The same warning Micah had written on the note to Natalie after the fire.

A tiny shiver rippled through her at the odd coincidence.

"I will. But I don't think there's anything to worry about."

"I hope not." He looked toward the lake again. "But I have a strange feeling about everything that's been going on here. Natalie could have been injured in the fire, and now Micah's dead. I wouldn't want anyone else to get hurt."

With that, he set off down the trail toward the cottage and the house.

Cara watched until he disappeared from sight, tended to the rabbit, and set off along the path toward the far side of the lake, quashing her sudden case of nerves.

It was silly to be uneasy.

The potholder incident had to have been an accident, even if no one could pin down how it had ended up in the trash. And Micah's death would surely be ruled accidental or natural.

There was no reason to worry about her own safety.

None at all.

Yet as she trod over the withered, fallen leaves on this autumn day, she couldn't shake the feeling that the warnings Micah and Steven had issued were worth heeding. That something not quite kosher was happening on the grounds of this isolated estate, with its legacy of tragedy.

But she wouldn't be here long. Only until the end of the semester. And she had no long-term connection to this place.

So if something untoward *was* happening here, it couldn't possibly affect her.

Could it?

TWELVE

HALFWAY DOWN THE PATH behind Natalie's house, Brad paused.

It wasn't really necessary to visit Cara in her cottage. Natalie could tell her the news he'd shared about Micah.

Maybe he should forget this idea.

"If the opportunity comes along to find love again, don't add passing it by to your list of regrets."

As Larry's counsel replayed through his mind, Brad exhaled.

He wasn't anywhere close to falling in love with Cara. The two of them were just getting acquainted.

But his people instincts had always been sound. That's why he'd known almost from the get-go that Elizabeth was destined to be his wife.

And Cara had triggered that same instinct during their first meeting, even if he'd tried to ignore it at the time.

Acting on that instinct too fast, however, would be out of character for a man who never let emotion overrule logic—a personality trait that had served him well in his work, and would also serve him well with Cara.

Larry was spot-on, though. Ignoring the opportunity that

had appeared, unbidden, on his doorstep would be foolish. He owed it to himself to at least explore the possibilities with the lovely historical anthropologist.

That's why he had to double down on dealing with his guilt. Acknowledge emotionally what he'd begun to accept intellectually. That maybe the burden he'd shouldered for what had happened that night was too heavy. That perhaps his selfishness hadn't been the sole cause of the tragedy.

Taking a deep breath, he put his feet in gear again and continued toward the cottage.

As he approached, he caught a glimpse of Cara through the front window.

Once again, his step faltered.

She was wearing a form-fitting top and yoga pants, one leg elevated behind her in an impossibly high position, a pink, flat-toed ballet slipper visible above her head as she rested one hand on the back of a chair beside her. Then she straightened up, executed a spin, and disappeared from view.

Whoa.

Who would have guessed the professor was also an accomplished ballerina?

Brad hesitated.

Should he backtrack? Leave her to her dancing? Barging in on what felt like a very private ritual seemed somehow too personal.

The decision was taken out of his hands, however, when she twirled back into view and came to a stop facing his direction. Her eyes widened, and she grabbed the back of the chair again.

Unless he wanted her to think he was a voyeur, he'd have to continue to the cottage and tell her the impetus for his visit.

He started forward again.

She pulled the door open as he approached, her cheeks flushed. From exertion—or being caught in ballerina mode?

No way to know.

"Sorry. I didn't mean to invade your—"

"Wait." She held up a finger. "Let me turn off the music."

Music?

The only sound trilling through the quiet air was the chirp of a cardinal in a nearby tree.

Cara vanished but returned seconds later, shrugging into a loose-fitting shirt that covered the skinny straps of her top and the broad expanse of creamy skin it had exposed. "I stream music from my phone directly into my processors. Wireless technology is a godsend for activities like dancing. What were you saying before?"

"Just that I, uh, didn't want to invade your space, but I have news about Micah. I shared it with Natalie, and she can pass it on if you'd rather continue what you were doing."

"I was wrapping up, and I'd like an update." She glanced behind her, brow knitted. "The place is kind of a mess. I push everything aside for my dancing. Would you mind if we sit out here?" She motioned to two plastic patio chairs in front of the cottage.

"That would be fine."

"Give me a minute to change my shoes." She disappeared back inside, closing the door behind her.

He continued forward, claiming one of the chairs.

When she reappeared two minutes later, she was wearing sport shoes. The shirt had also been buttoned and hung long over her hips.

She sat beside him. "I hope you found some answers about Micah."

"A few." He tried to shift gears. Erase the images of her supple movements and long legs and graceful arms.

It wasn't easy.

So despite the fact that his memory needed no prompting, he pulled out his notebook and redirected his attention to the scribbles he'd jotted during his conversation with Rod. "After ruling out any other kind of medical event as a cause of death, the coroner is going with drowning, pending the toxicology results. Best estimate on time of death is sometime between six a.m. and noon on Sunday. Micah had a gash on his head, deep enough to potentially cause unconsciousness. One theory is that he lost his balance and fell backward in the boat, hit his head, tumbled into the water, and drowned."

"One theory? Are there others?"

He flipped the notebook closed as a squirrel scampered past, acorn in mouth, intent on its task to store reserves for the coming winter. No ambiguity there.

If only life were that simple.

"Sorry." Cara leaned toward him a hair. "I didn't mean to put you on the spot. I assume you can't discuss active investigations."

"No apology necessary. And I doubt it will be active for long. The tox screen won't be back for weeks, but I didn't find any evidence of drugs or drinking in Micah's cabin. I expect it will be clean. Accidental drowning may end up being our only theory."

Despite the questions he hadn't been able to answer.

Like, why were Micah and the boat together, on the shallow, marshy side of the lake? The odds that the man had rowed into grass and reeds were small, and while the boat could have drifted there, the body should have sunk wherever Micah fell into the water.

And why had there been a smear rather than rivulets of blood running down the side of the boat where he'd theoretically hit his head? Yes, he could have touched his head before he lost consciousness, groped for the boat as he flailed in the water, but there'd been no blood on the cuff of his long-sleeved shirt to suggest his wrist had come into contact with his head if he'd reached for his wound.

"You seem troubled."

At Cara's comment, he refocused on the conversation. "I was thinking about a few pieces that don't quite fit for me."

"Ones you can discuss?"

"Not at this stage."

"Understood." She didn't appear to be in the least put out by his reticence.

"The coroner did release the body, which means we can proceed with Micah's wishes for his remains. I found a Bible in his cabin, so Natalie is going to read a passage before the ashes are scattered. I have a friend with a golf cart who offered to bring it by, and I'll drive her down to the lake."

Admiration—and perhaps something more—radiated from her. "That's very kind of you."

"It feels like the right thing to do."

"I'm sure Natalie appreciates it. I was planning to attend too. A committal with no witnesses would be sad."

"Yeah." He swallowed. "It's sad enough even when a crowd shows up."

Her eyes softened. "I get the feeling you're speaking from personal experience."

He took a slow, shaky breath.

It would be easy to shut down this conversation. Avoid the hard stuff. All he had to do was stand up, make a generic comment about death always being sad, and use his busy schedule as an excuse to flee.

Instead, he remained seated beside this woman who radiated compassion and quiet understanding. Who was nursing an injured rabbit back to health, according to Natalie. Who planned to show up for the final disposition of a man whose solitary life had touched her heart.

Maybe it was time to tell her his history, and to share with her the grief and angst and guilt that had been his constant companions.

All he had to do was summon up the courage to reveal his secrets—and hope she didn't blame him for ending two lives far too soon, as he'd blamed himself for three long years.

Beside him, Cara started to rise. "Sorry again. I didn't—"

"Wait." Brad reached out to restrain her. If he wasn't willing to talk, she'd walk away. Possibly forever. And he couldn't take that risk. "I was thinking about how to respond to your comment."

After a tiny hesitation, she settled back into her chair. "Sometimes I have a tendency to ask too many questions. Comes with being a researcher, I suppose."

"Or a sheriff." He forced up one side of his mouth.

She played with the hem of her shirt, fingering a loose thread. "In the interest of full disclosure, Natalie mentioned once that you weren't married anymore, and that it was a sad situation. I wondered if you were divorced. Now I'm thinking your story is even sadder than a broken marriage."

He watched two chipmunks dash across the lawn in a game of tag. "Yes, it is. And it's not one I talk about often." Like never.

"I understand if you'd rather—"

"No." He looked over at her. "I'd like to tell you what happened, if you can spare a few more minutes."

"I can spare all afternoon, if that's what you need. I know how important it is to have someone to talk to when you're hurting."

As pain pooled in her irises, his stomach contracted. It seemed he wasn't the only one with heartache in his past.

"It sounds like you have a story of your own."

She toed aside a shriveled, dead leaf. "I do, and it's not a pretty one. Someday I may share it with you. But this afternoon I'm more interested in hearing yours."

Soul baring hadn't been on his agenda today. Yet it was a logical next step if he wanted this relationship to progress beyond the superficial. Plus, if he gave her a peek into his heart, it was possible she'd eventually reciprocate . . . and open the door to deeper sharing.

Transferring his focus to a broken branch off to the side behind her so sound would be directed her way but he could avoid eye contact, he plunged in.

"I had a wife and four-year-old son, Elizabeth and Jonathan. They were my world. Three years ago, after Jonathan came down with flu symptoms, we treated him with all the usual remedies. Or Elizabeth did. I was working a murder case and was busy tracking down suspects. I finally came home to crash after twenty-four hours with no sleep. Jonathan's fever had spiked, and Elizabeth thought we should take him to urgent care. But all I wanted to do was sleep." His voice rasped.

Cara reached out tentatively, as if she was uncertain about how he'd react, and covered the fingers he'd clamped around the arms of the chair with her own.

The comforting gesture gave him the courage to continue.

"Elizabeth tried to convince me to drive them there. She was a city girl, and she never liked navigating the country roads at night. But I didn't feel the same urgency she did about Jonathan's condition. She tended to overreact to illnesses. I told her I needed to sleep, and that we could take him to urgent care in the morning if he hadn't improved. Then I went to bed."

He stopped, the sudden flood of memories squeezing the breath from his lungs.

As if sensing his distress, Cara leaned closer, using body language rather than words to convey her support.

After swallowing past the constriction in his throat, he picked up the story.

"I found the note later that said she didn't feel comfortable waiting and had decided to take Jonathan herself. Except they never got there. Fog had descended, and she missed a curve. I assume she got disoriented."

The cadence of Cara's breathing wobbled.

He forced himself to finish the story. "The car fell fifty feet, into a drainage ditch. She was gone when the paramedics arrived. Jonathan died the next d-day."

As he choked out the last word, he dropped his chin. Fought for control.

And waited for her to retract her hand the instant she came to the same conclusion he had after the accident. That he'd been selfish. That if he'd powered through his fatigue at home as he often did on the job, Elizabeth and Jonathan would still be here. After all, he couldn't expect Cara to absolve him on the spot when it had taken him years to begin to question the extent of his culpability.

Yet as the seconds ticked by, the warmth of Cara's hand continued to seep into his skin.

When he at last looked up, her face reflected sympathy and compassion, not recrimination.

As hope stirred in his heart, he took a steadying breath. May as well give voice to the guilt that dogged his steps. "Ever since the accident, I've been blaming myself for what happened. For putting my own needs before the needs of my family."

"I don't see it that way." She shook her head, no hint of censure in her quiet, firm tone. "You were exhausted. You assessed the situation and did what you felt was appropriate. Your wife did the same. You both made decisions you thought were reasonable. At this stage, there's no way to know who was right or how a different scenario would have played out, or what really happened on the road."

"But I *do* know the outcome. And for years I believed that if I'd been with them, no one would have died. I can drive the roads around here in my sleep. I wouldn't have missed that curve."

"You can't know that for sure." She leaned toward him, posture intent, demeanor earnest. "Maybe your wife didn't get disoriented. It's possible a deer darted in front of her and she tried to avoid it. The same could have happened if you were behind the wheel. If fatigue had dulled your reflexes, you could have ended up in the ditch too. It's all second-guessing at this point." She gentled her voice. "Besides, blaming yourself for what happened won't bring them back."

He swallowed. Rubbed the back of his neck. "I've been slowly coming to the same conclusion. And I heard a similar message from my chief deputy not long ago. But he didn't know all the details I told you. No one does."

The pressure of her hand increased, confirming she'd grasped the significance of his admission. "I'm honored you shared them with me."

"Can I be honest? I almost didn't. I was afraid you might be shocked and want nothing more to do with me."

"Do you *want* me to have more to do with you?"

At her direct question, he did a double take.

A wry smile curved her lips. "See? There I go again, being too direct. I suppose that could be one of the reasons I have very few dates."

"I can't speak for other guys, but I prefer a woman who's upfront and doesn't play games. The answer to your question is—"

"Sorry to interrupt, Sheriff."

As Natalie's cousin spoke, Brad angled toward the path.

Could the man's timing have been any worse?

Steven's gaze flicked to their connected hands, and Cara retracted hers.

"No problem." Brad rose as Steven approached.

"Natalie asked if you'd stop in again before you leave. I believe she has a question about the golf cart you're arranging."

"I have to get back to work anyway." Cara stood and edged

toward the door of the cottage. "Why don't you walk back to the house with Steven?"

He couldn't fault her suggestion. There was no justification to linger.

But he didn't intend to leave with her question hanging in the air between them.

"That works." First, though, he turned to face her. He wasn't taking any chances she'd miss his response. "The answer is yes."

A becoming flush rose on her cheeks, and she gave him a smile as warm as a toasty fire on a cold winter day.

Then she slipped inside and shut the door.

After a moment, he pivoted and walked with Steven back to the house, responding to the man's chitchat on autopilot, his heart lighter than it had been in a very long while.

There was no guarantee the new, tentative relationship he was building with Cara would go anywhere, of course.

If nothing else, however, her presence in his life right now was like a bright ray of sun, illuminating the darkest corners of his soul. Nudging him to deal once and for all with the guilt he'd been slowly working through.

And he no longer had to manufacture a pretext to drop by to see her, with all that had happened on this property—especially if the questions about Micah's death continued to gnaw at him.

Perhaps the groundskeeper's demise had, indeed, been innocent. An accident.

But he wasn't yet ready to put this one to bed, as he'd told Natalie before he stopped in to see Cara. Not until the tox screen came back and he poked around for more clues that might help explain the anomalies continuing to raise red flags.

Because if there was more to Micah's death than the investigation had revealed to date, a very bad person who should be behind bars was walking around free.

And nobody got away with manslaughter—or murder—on his watch.

THIS HADN'T BEEN PART OF HER PLAN.

Lips mashed together, Lydia flipped off the vacuum cleaner and pushed it toward Natalie's utility closet.

The mere notion of having her brother hanging around here stunk. But she needed more time to convince Natalie that a live-in housekeeper was a smart idea—and Micah's death had given her an ideal bargaining chip.

Suggesting to Randy that he could pick up some easy money doing handyman chores if she put in a good word for him had been the perfect carrot to dangle. The opportunistic blond floozy he'd fallen for had agreed to hold off on moving in while he earned extra bucks to put toward a bigger rock in her engagement ring.

Lydia stashed the vacuum and rolled her eyes.

Like a third of a carat was such an improvement over a fourth.

Nevertheless, the ploy had bought her a bit of breathing space.

But the faster she could vacate Randy's revolting dump, the better.

Meaning she'd have to beef up her efforts to convince Natalie it would be in her best interest to stay in her home with a live-in housekeeper rather than move to St. Louis, like her cousin was recommending.

Planting a seed of danger with the professor had also been smart. Now that Micah had turned up dead on the heels of the fire, that seed could begin to sprout—with a little careful nurturing.

Lydia pulled a dust mop out of the closet. Picked up a rag from the stack and slung it over her shoulder.

Maybe she ought to spike Natalie's wine with Ambien again. That had worked like a charm. The two back-to-back dizzy spells had helped build a strong case for a live-in housekeeper.

But Ambien came with risks. What if Natalie fell and injured herself, was forced to leave the property? Another fall would also add fuel to Steven's attempts to persuade her to move to St. Louis. The man had brought that idea up to her no less than twice today.

Knowledge she'd gleaned through a bit of judicious eavesdropping.

The back door rattled. Clicked shut. Male voices rumbled in the kitchen, along with Natalie's.

". . . a cup of tea, Sheriff?"

"No, thank you. I have to be going. Steven said you had a question about the golf cart?"

Lydia eased closer, ear cocked toward the closed door that separated the kitchen and hall.

"Yes. I appreciate your efforts to arrange that, but I know it goes above and beyond the scope of your job. I'd like to compensate you and the friend who is providing it."

"That's not necessary, Ms. Boyer. Both of us are glad to lend a hand."

"Well . . . in that case, I'm most grateful. Let me walk you out."

Before Lydia could scurry away, Steven opened the door from the kitchen and stepped aside as Natalie walked through.

"Oh, Lydia. We were just talking about Micah's service at the lake. It will be one day next week. You're welcome to attend if you like."

She curbed an eye roll.

As if she cared about the strange man who'd always given her the creeps. Good riddance, as far as she was concerned.

But she pasted on a suitably somber expression. "Thank

you. If you'll let me know the exact day and time, I'll check my schedule." And make her excuses after finding something else to be doing then.

"I'll pass that along as soon as all the arrangements are finalized. If would be nice if a few people who were acquainted with him attended."

Which would be almost nobody beyond the people gathered in this room.

That's why his passing was of little consequence—except it had given her plan a boost by illustrating the danger of living alone. Like, what if Natalie got hurt and no one found her for hours . . . or days?

A thought she'd pass on as soon as she got the chance.

"Yes, it would. If you're finished in the kitchen, I'll clean in there now."

"It's all yours."

She skirted the small group gathered in the hall and continued to the back of the house.

As she closed the door behind her, her phone began to vibrate. After pulling it out, she grimaced.

Randy again. Probably wanting to know if she'd set up an interview for him with Natalie yet.

That wasn't a high priority.

The longer she could delay a meeting between the two of them, the longer it would be before Ashley got on his case again about kicking out his third-wheel sister so she could move in.

Lydia let the phone roll to voicemail. She'd deal with her brother later.

In the meantime, she'd have to consider spiking another half-empty bottle of wine with perhaps a lesser amount of Ambien. Just enough to keep Natalie off balance—literally.

As for the professor . . . a few more hints about danger wouldn't be a bad idea.

Because in truth, that danger might come to pass.

THIRTEEN

"THE LORD IS MY SHEPHERD; I shall not want. He maketh me to lie down in green pastures: he leadeth me beside the still waters. He restoreth my soul."

As Natalie read the twenty-third psalm, Cara looked out over the lake, where Brad sat in Micah's boat, the biodegradable box of ashes resting on the seat beside him.

No one else had attended the simple ceremony.

No other human, anyway.

But on the far side of the lake, two deer stood unmoving, watching the proceedings. High above, a hawk circled, riding the wind currents. Closer by, tucked among the scrubby brush at the edge of the water, three raccoons huddled together. Rabbits, squirrels, and chipmunks were also in attendance, all strangely motionless as Natalie finished the psalm and closed the book.

"And now we commend you to God, Micah Reeves, with gratitude for your service and your kindness. May your new life in the heavenly kingdom be filled with peace and love."

At her signal, Brad set the box on the ripples and waited until it sank out of sight as the late-afternoon light gilded the lake.

While he rowed back, Cara bent down to Thumper's cage, where it had rested beside her during the brief service. Since the vet had removed the splint and pronounced the bunny healed yesterday, Natalie had agreed it would be fitting to release it back to the wild at the end of the ceremony.

She opened the latch and lifted the door.

For a moment, the rabbit didn't move. Then, inch by inch, it crept out of the cage. Sniffed the air. Hopped down to the lake. It paused there for a few seconds before disappearing in the tall grass and bounding toward the woods.

"I hope Micah is happy now. And healed."

At Natalie's tear-laced comment, Cara stood and placed an arm around her shoulders. "I'm sure he is. I think God has a special love for gentle spirits who appreciate and nurture his creation."

"A beautiful sentiment, my dear." Natalie patted her hand.

Brad reached the shore, jumped out of the boat, and secured it to the post on the tiny dock. On the far bank, the deer melted back into the shadows as the hawk dipped over the lake in a graceful arc and flew off.

It was almost as if the wild creatures had come to pay their respects to the man who'd lived among them.

A fanciful thought, perhaps, but oddly comforting.

"Thank you for doing that, Sheriff." Natalie grasped Brad's hand when he joined them. "Dinner is waiting at the house. You haven't changed your mind about joining us, have you?"

"No, ma'am. And please call me Brad. I'm not here today on official business."

"In that case, you must call me Natalie. I believe we've become friends over the past few weeks through unfortunate circumstances. But every cloud has a silver lining, as they say, and I would certainly put a new friend in that category. May I take your arm as we walk back to the golf cart?"

"At your service." He crooked his elbow.

Cara followed them, claiming the rear-facing seat for the short drive back.

Once at the house, Natalie put them both to work helping her dish up the dinner, and she proved to be her usual adept conversationalist while they ate. She also entertained them with stories about her escapades during her years at the Sorbonne.

Only when dessert was served did the exchange return to the events of the day.

As Natalie sliced a lemon cake, the corners of her mouth rose in a melancholy smile. "Micah had quite the sweet tooth, you know. I used to leave little bags of cookies and brownies and other treats for him on the back galérie whenever I got in a baking mood. And I made one of these cakes for him every Christmas. I thought it was fitting to serve it in his memory." She gave them each a generous portion and retook her seat. "You know, I'm still shocked by how he died. I suppose we have to accept the coroner's ruling, but it doesn't feel right."

"How so, Natalie?"

At Brad's question, Cara scrutinized him. His tone was relaxed, but she'd been around him enough to pick up an underlying gravity that suggested there was more to his query than simple chitchat.

"I can't explain it." Natalie cut off a bite of her cake with the edge of her fork, twin creases denting her forehead. "Like I can't explain the potholder in the trash or my dizzy spells. It's just that so many odd things happening close together seems rather too coincidental to me. I suppose that sounds paranoid."

"Not to those of us in law enforcement. Suspicion is our middle name." Brad's lips quirked, but then he grew more serious. "To tell you the truth, I'm not much of a believer in coincidence either. That's one of the reasons I revisited the scene the next day and also went over Micah's boat with a fine-tooth comb."

Ah.

That would explain why it had been stowed in the open shed beside the cabin for several days, shrouded in plastic, instead of tied by the dock.

"Did you find anything helpful?" Cara picked up her coffee cup as she directed her question to him.

He shifted his attention to her at once, a white-hot sizzle of current arcing between them across the table. As it had been doing during the entire dinner.

This dining room was a virtual electrical storm.

Did Brad feel it as much as she did?

The intensity of his gaze suggested he did, but it was possible she was over—

At the sudden clearing of a throat from the head of the table, Cara glanced at their hostess. There was a speculative gleam in her eyes as she looked between her two guests.

"I'm curious about that myself." Natalie ate a bite of cake, a twinkle in her irises.

Cara peeked at Brad over the rim of her cup as she took a sip.

The sudden flush on his face suggested he'd been as caught up in the storm as she had. "I'm sorry. I lost the thread of the conversation for a minute."

"Cara asked if you'd found anything helpful on Micah's boat."

"Oh. Right." He patted his mouth with his napkin. "No. I didn't."

"So where do you go from here?"

"Nowhere, I'm afraid, unless the tox screen provides new information or another piece of evidence turns up. You're sure you didn't see anyone on the premises Sunday morning?"

"No. I don't go wandering about anymore. If Steven had been here, he might have spotted someone on one of his hikes, but he left Saturday night to deal with an urgent business matter back in St. Louis. The price of success, I suppose."

"Well, I intend to keep my ear to the ground."

"Hmm." Natalie tapped a finger on the table. "You know, in some ways this reminds me of the mystery about Marie."

Brad frowned. "Who?"

"A long-ago relative." She gave him a quick recap of her tragic end. "Cara and I are hoping to find a clue in her journals about what happened. I don't think my father ever believed her death was an accident."

"Why haven't I ever heard that story?"

"It happened long ago, and time moves on. People forget. It was eventually consigned to family lore."

"Do you know if the death was investigated?"

"I expect it was, with whatever techniques were available in those days in this backwater part of the world. But I doubt they were very sophisticated. However, the journals may shed a ray of light on the matter."

"If you find anything that might provide better closure on her case, please let me know. It's never too late to set a record straight."

"I'll keep that in mind. Would you like more coffee or cake?" Natalie encompassed both of them with the question.

"No, thank you. That was a delicious meal." Brad set his napkin on the table.

"I couldn't eat or drink another bite, either." Cara smiled and stood. "I'll handle cleanup, as usual."

"*We'll* handle cleanup." Brad rose too and picked up his plate.

"But you're my guest." Natalie grasped the cane beside her chair. "I never ask guests to do their own dishes."

"You didn't ask. I offered." He rose and pulled out her chair. "Many hands and all that."

Natalie stood and gave them both another once-over. "Well, if you insist, I'll relent. To tell you the truth, I wouldn't mind sitting in bed with my latest book and making this an early night." She touched Brad's arm. "You'll walk Cara to her cottage before you leave?"

"That was my plan."

"Excellent. Cara, I'll see you in the morning at nine o'clock sharp. Good night to you both."

They returned the sentiment, and as she disappeared down the hall, Cara began to clear the table. "Honestly, you don't have to help with the dishes. That's a bargain Natalie and I made. You've already given up a big part of your day to help her honor Micah's wishes."

"I didn't mind. Besides, I not only got a fine meal in the bargain, I also got a chance to spend a few hours with you."

The voltage in the room spiked again.

Whew.

"You know . . . talk like that could turn a girl's head."

"I'm hoping it also touches her heart."

O-kay.

His response to her question at the cottage about whether he wanted her to have more to do with him had obviously been sincere.

This wasn't a man who played games in the relationship arena.

But much as she liked him, there were still barriers to serious involvement. And since he was being clear about his interest, she may as well put those on the table.

"I'd like to comment on that, but why don't we clear the table and relocate to the kitchen first?" She inclined her head toward the hallway. Natalie wasn't the type to eavesdrop, but voices could carry in this house. And while it was apparent the woman had picked up on the chemistry between her dinner guests, a private conversation like the one she and Brad were about to have should remain private.

"Okay." He began to gather up the dishes, faint puckers marring his brow. As if he was worried she was about to tell him to take a hike.

Not even close.

Men like Brad didn't come along every day, and she'd be a

fool to let logistical and personal challenges derail a budding romance—assuming they could be overcome.

They worked in silence until the dishwasher was loaded and humming away. Then Cara motioned toward the table. "Let's sit."

In silence, he crossed to a chair and pulled it out for her.

After she sat, he joined her, folding his hands on the table. "I'm thinking an apology may be in order. Maybe I read too much into what you asked me last Friday."

"No, you didn't. But there are challenges."

"There always are in any relationship."

"More in some than others."

"What specific challenges are you thinking about in terms of us?"

Us.

What a beautiful and hopeful word.

But getting to an *us* would require work.

"Location, for one. My work is in Cape. Yours is here."

"I can live anywhere in this county."

"Even if you moved to the most southeastern part, the commute for me would still be crazy long."

"There are other counties in Missouri that need sheriffs and deputies."

She blinked.

"But . . . this is your home."

A shadow passed across his face. "It *was* my home. Now there's nothing holding me here. Everyone in my family has relocated. Besides, geography would never trump love for me, if that's where this leads."

Wow.

Was this man for real?

"You mean you'd give up your career for a woman?"

"Not my career. But for the right woman, I'd change my job, if that's what it took." His voice was steady. Certain. Resolute.

Double wow.

"Can I say I'm impressed?"

"I'd be happier if you said you were interested."

"I'm interested." An understatement if ever there was one. "What I can't figure out is why *you* are."

He squinted at her. "Why wouldn't I be? You're beautiful and smart and caring. Not to mention accomplished, talented, and a great conversationalist. You seem to have your act together, and you have strong family ties, which says a lot. What's not to like?"

She tried not to let his compliments go to her head.

But she couldn't stop them from going straight to her heart.

Still, he needed to be aware of what he was getting into with her.

"Maybe the fact that I resemble a space alien?" She lifted her hair to expose the transmitting coil held in place on the side of her head by a magnet, along with the sound processor and microphone hooked behind her ear. "I also don't speak with a normal cadence. Sometimes I can't communicate well. All of that can be off-putting, and it makes socializing hard. Most guys don't want to deal with the extra effort dating me requires."

"Their loss."

His comeback was quick, decisive—and heartening.

"I appreciate that more than I can say. But dealing with my issues can be wearing in the long run. The couple of men I dated for more than a handful of times eventually gave up."

"I repeat. Their loss. For the record, I'm not the kind of guy who gives up on something—or someone—worth having."

She didn't doubt that. Not from what she'd seen of him so far.

But there was more to her story.

The question was, how much of it did she want to share?

FOURTEEN

HE'D OVERSTEPPED.
Brad could see it in Cara's sudden, subtle withdrawal. In the creases on her brow. In the lower lip caught between her teeth as she traced an irregular grain in the wooden tabletop with a finger that wasn't quite steady.

He was rushing her, and this wasn't a woman who'd tolerate being rushed. Every instinct in his body told him that.

The strangest part of all this?

He'd never had any intention of rushing her. Or himself. His plan had been to let her know he was interested but keep it low key. For his sake as well as hers while he tried to come to grips with the notion of a new romantic relationship.

"Hey." He touched the back of her hand, waiting until he had her attention to continue. "I'm sorry if I came on too strong."

She studied him for a moment. "Sorry for yourself, or for me?"

A direct question, in keeping with her admission that she tended to be blunt. And it deserved an honest answer.

"Let me clarify. I'm sorry if I spooked you by being too candid about my feelings. In terms of myself, I'm more surprised than sorry. I never planned to get involved with another woman, and I'm still feeling my way. I intended to be more discreet while I sorted through this unexpected change in plans, but when I'm with you, my mouth has a mind of its own. It says stuff I normally would keep closer to the vest."

"Is that bad?"

"You tell me."

Several beats passed as she considered him.

"I guess not. It's just that . . ." She knitted her fingers together on the table. "Much as I appreciate your implication that I might be someone you wouldn't give up on, my physical idiosyncrasies probably aren't the only reason the men I've dated bailed."

Was she opening a door to sharing more confidences?

Only one way to find out.

"Does this relate to the not-pretty story you referenced the day I told you about Elizabeth and Jonathan?"

After a moment, she gave a slow nod. "It's from my early childhood."

"How early?"

"As far back as I can remember." She swallowed. "I don't talk much about those years. No one but my adoptive parents ever knew all the details. I've tried hard not to let what happened to me as a child affect my adult life, but the truth is, I have lingering trust issues. It could be *my* fault the guys I've dated lost interest. It's possible I was sending subliminal back-off messages."

"I haven't picked up many of those."

"You may be the rare exception." After giving him a tiny smile, she grew more serious again. "But my trust issues could rear their ugly head at some point. It's happened with other men."

She had trust issues with men, specifically?

He wasn't liking the sound of that.

Trying hard to maintain a calm tone despite the sudden tension thrumming through him, he kept his question as general as possible. "What's the source of the trust issues?"

"Not what you're thinking. No one ever physically abused me."

Thank God for that.

Yet something very traumatic had happened if it had left her cautious around men after all these years.

"Do you want to tell me about it?"

"The truth? No. I'd rather not think about it ever again."

"Then don't. I won't push you." Even if he was tempted to. "I understand how hard it can be to talk about painful experiences."

"But you told me about yours."

"It felt right to share them with you." He left it at that. If she decided to trust him with her story, that choice had to come from within. And if she opted not to tell him today, that didn't mean someday in the future she wouldn't—

"Do you have a few more minutes?"

Apparently today was the day after all.

The knot in his stomach began to unwind.

"Yes."

"Okay. I'll try to give you the short version." She focused on her linked fingers. "When I was three and a half, I got the measles. That led to ear infections, which resulted in severe hearing loss. Deafness can be a complication in up to 10 percent of measles cases, and I was in that unlucky percentage. My verbal development had been normal up to that stage, but after the hearing loss my speech suffered and my father . . . he started making fun of me."

Though her tone was dispassionate, the hurt in her eyes was almost palatable.

Brad's gut clenched.

How could a father belittle a vulnerable child who'd been

thrust into a sound-deprived world and was floundering to cope?

No wonder she didn't trust men, if the man who was supposed to love and support her had mocked her instead.

Brad reached over and stroked a finger down the back of her hand.

She lifted her chin, irises shimmering. "It shouldn't hurt this much anymore. I shouldn't *let* it hurt."

"It's not easy to erase hurts." As he knew too well. "Where was your mom during all of this?"

"Doing her best to shield me from his ridicule, as far as I can remember, but she worked long hours during the day as a waitress and wasn't around much. My father was a shelf stocker at night in a warehouse. He was gone while I was sleeping. I've often thought how different it might have been if their jobs had been reversed." She sighed. "But it didn't matter in the long run. Mom died when I was five, and after that there was no one to protect me. I finally stopped speaking altogether."

"And no one in your world noticed this? What about the person who took care of you while your father was at work?"

"He put me to bed before he left for his shift, and I stayed there until he got home. A neighbor's daughter slept at the house while he was gone for the first year. I never interacted with her."

"What about after that?"

"I was by myself."

A wave of shock ricocheted through him. "You mean he left a six-year-old alone all night?"

"Yes, but it was okay. I was happier when he wasn't there, and I'd learned to be self-sufficient."

Anger bubbled up inside him.

That was a lesson no six-year-old should ever have to learn.

"How did you end up in the foster system?"

"My father had always been a drinker, but after my mother died, he hit the bottle harder. He was killed in a DUI when I was six and a half. I didn't have any relatives—or none who wanted to take me—so I entered the foster system. Several months later, Mom and Dad took me in, God bless them." She blinked, as if to clear her vision. "Do you have good parents, Brad?"

"The best."

"Then you know about the power of that kind of love." She glanced at his hand atop hers. "I wouldn't have blamed them if they'd given up on me in those first months. They were already caring for two foster children from troubled backgrounds—my sister and brother, Bri and Jack—and taking on a child who didn't communicate had to have been a huge leap."

"I assume they called in pros to help?"

"Yes. They arranged for therapists to work with me on speech, since I wasn't verbal at all. They also got me a cochlear implant in one ear and a hearing aid for the ear that had a tiny bit of hearing. I went through months of auditory rehab after the implant, learning how to hear in a new way. Mom and Dad worked with me hours on end too. The second cochlear implant didn't come until later, after the hearing in that ear failed too. But the whole process was a slow slog until Mom came up with the idea of enrolling me in ballet lessons."

"I'm surprised she thought of that. It seems like a stretch for someone with hearing issues."

Cara's lips flexed. "Mom was all about thinking outside the box, especially where her kids were concerned. And she and Dad didn't want any limits imposed on us—by society or by ourselves."

"An admirable attitude. But she definitely pushed the boundaries with ballet."

"Tell me about it. In the end, though, it proved to be an

inspired idea. I could pick up the musical beats far better than I could hear voices, and ballet opened a whole new world to me. I discovered I could express all the feelings I'd been bottling up inside through movement and music. It was freeing and an absolute breakthrough. It became my lifeline. In some ways, it still is. My Saturday morning lessons are sacrosanct."

"And you dance in between too."

"Every day—but usually not for an audience." She flashed him a smile. "Anyway, ballet was the turning point. I began to speak more and to open up to people who'd earned my trust. All thanks to Mom and Dad. If it wasn't for them, I don't know where I'd be. Certainly not a professor of historical anthropology who gets up in front of large groups and lectures about the forces that shape people and cultures."

As Cara concluded, one word strobed through Brad's mind. Amazing.

There was no other way to describe this woman, who'd turned out so grounded despite all the bad things that had happened to her.

"To borrow your earlier comment to me, I'm impressed. Not only by all your accomplishments, but by your resilience."

"I had excellent role models in Bri and Jack. The three of us formed an incredible bond. Stronger than the one shared by many siblings related by blood. Again, thanks to Mom and Dad." She exhaled. "So now you know my history—and why I come with challenges."

He left his hand over hers and locked onto her gaze. "I'm not afraid of challenges."

Hope kindled in her eyes, warring with caution. "I don't want to get hurt, Brad."

"Neither do I." That was the truth. He'd had enough heartache and loss to last two lifetimes. "So why don't we take it slow and easy, see what develops? Play it safe?"

"I'm not certain safe is part of the equation in any relationship." She took a deep breath. "But I'm willing to take a chance with you."

Pressure built in his throat. "Thank you."

"Thank *you*. For your interest and your honesty." She eased her hand free and checked her watch. "I suppose we should call it a night."

"I'll walk you back to the cottage."

"You don't have to do that. I'm used to making the trip alone."

"I promised Natalie I would. And I always keep my promises."

"Nice to know." Her lips bowed as she pushed back her chair.

He rose too, followed her out the door, and waited while she locked up. When she turned, he reached for her hand and wove his fingers through hers. "This isn't too fast, is it?"

"No." A dimple appeared in her cheek. "I'd have been disappointed if you hadn't done that."

The walk back to the cottage in the quiet night was much too short, and all too soon she was unlocking the door.

He couldn't leave, though, without a plan in place to see her again.

"There's a great restaurant not far from here, if I could interest you in dinner one night next week."

"Sold."

He hitched up one side of his mouth. "That was easy."

"Should I play hard to get?"

"No. I'm not into game playing. Why don't I call you over the weekend to arrange a day and time?" A flimsy excuse to hear her voice between now and their date, since there was no reason they couldn't finalize their plans tonight, but if she caught on to his ploy, she let it pass.

"My calendar is wide open in the evenings. Whatever works for you will be fine with me."

"Good."

Silence, broken only by the chirp of serenading crickets.

There was no excuse to linger. He should go.

But as Cara's eyes suddenly filled with yearning . . . as the air around them began to crackle . . . as longing pulsed between them . . . a powerful temptation to kiss her chipped away at his resolve to confine expressions of affection tonight to hand-holding.

He had to get out of here.

Fast.

If he didn't, he was going to—

All at once, Cara rose on tiptoes and pressed her lips against his. Then, with a whispered, puff-of-warm-breath "good night" that caressed his cheek, she slipped through the door and closed it behind her.

Heart thudding, he groped for the chair beside him and held on tight.

It seemed his definition of slow was different than Cara's.

Yet by her own admission, she was a woman who didn't beat around the bush. Who communicated what was on her mind.

Since kissing had apparently been front and center, she'd taken the initiative and set the stage for more—whenever he was ready.

Which might be a lot sooner than he'd expected, given the buzz radiating all the way to the tips of his tingling fingers.

At last he turned and walked back down the path, pausing to cast one last final look at the cottage before he rounded the house to return to his car.

A soft, uplifting glow emanated from the windows.

But it was nothing compared to the glow in his heart.

So barring any unforeseen complications, his top off-duty priority was about to become the beautiful historical anthropologist whose life had fortuitously intersected with his.

THE DIZZY SPELLS had been a perfect prelude—and catalyst.

The potholder incident had moved me closer to my goal.

It had seemed, for a while, that it was going to be far simpler to carry out my plans than I'd expected.

Until Micah had gotten in the way,

I gulped down the dregs of my second scotch, the mild, malty sweetness tempering the sour taste in my mouth.

Now, to make matters worse, the sheriff was questioning his death.

Why?

What had happened to instill doubt in his mind about what should have been a logical conclusion—that it was an accident?

Would he dig deeper for answers or eventually let the case go for lack of evidence? After all, doubts didn't lead to proof—or convictions. And a rural sheriff had limited staff and time to devote to investigations if he had nothing more to go on than suspicion.

Unless he *did* have more to go on.

Was it possible he'd found proof of a crime?

Maybe.

Mistakes could happen if you were forced to fix a problem with limited opportunity to prepare.

But proof a crime had been committed didn't always lead to the perpetrator.

The ice in my glass began to rattle, and I set it on the counter. Examined my quivering hand.

It was shaking just like it had the first morning Micah had materialized out of the woods while I was heading toward my destination. Watching me as he cradled some small critter in his arms. Creeping me out with those penetrating eyes of his.

A scenario that had been repeated on several occasions.

In all the years I'd known him, he'd avoided eye contact

like the plague and skulked about in the shadows. His sudden inclination to not only make his presence known but stare at me had been more than intimidating.

It had felt almost like a warning.

But how much could he know? My clandestine activities took place out of sight.

Nevertheless, confining my subsequent forays to after dark had seemed prudent.

Still, if he suspected I was involved in shady activity and had shared that with Natalie, my plans could have been ruined.

So what choice had there been except to eliminate him as a threat?

Bile rose in my throat, and I closed my eyes. Swallowed.

Considering my fast track to get the job done, everything had gone as well as could be expected. But the task had been distasteful, and the blood . . .

My stomach began to roil, as it had that morning.

The ski cap that kept the blood contained during the maneuver to get him into the boat had been a smart idea. But it was unfortunate that dumping him in the middle of the lake had proven impossible. Who knew that trying to jockey a limp body over the edge without capsizing the boat would be so tricky?

Moving to the reeds hadn't been ideal, although the boat had rocked less. And situating it there had made it possible to escape to shore without getting too wet.

After I'd smeared blood on the side of the boat.

That's when I'd lost my breakfast in the lake.

I poured another scotch.

Drinking wasn't smart. I knew that. And I wouldn't do it again. I had more work to do at Natalie's, and I needed a clear head to finish my mission.

ASAP.

Because the longer this took, the higher the risk.

Micah might be out of the picture, but the professor was still on the premises—and she'd taken to wandering about too.

That was dicey.

What if she saw me somewhere I shouldn't be and got suspicious? Mentioned it to the sheriff, with whom she appeared to be cozy?

The odds were low that he'd find anything to pin on me, but he seemed sharp. Tenacious. The type who'd stick with a case that bothered him until he had answers.

That could be bad news.

So I'd have to watch Cara Tucker and hope she didn't get in my way, as Micah had.

But if she did, she might end up just as dead as Natalie's enigmatic groundskeeper.

FIFTEEN

"I BELIEVE THESE OLD EYES NEED A BRIEF REST." Natalie set Marie's journal down on the table and removed her glasses. "But we're making fine progress."

"Yes, we are." Cara lifted her fingers from the keys of her laptop and leaned back in her chair. "We're definitely picking up speed now that we're becoming more familiar with Marie's writing style."

"I'd say familiarity is helping other things pick up speed too. Like friendship with a rural sheriff."

Cara stifled a groan.

Of course Natalie had noticed the high-voltage current zipping between her two dinner guests last night. She was as sharp and perceptive as someone half her age.

"I've enjoyed getting to know him, but I'm, uh, not planning to rush into anything more serious than friendship."

"Very wise. However, I was talking about *my* friendship with him." The woman's eyes began to twinkle.

"Oh." What else could she say? She'd walked straight into that one.

"Nevertheless . . . the sparks between the two of you last

night were a force to be reckoned with. I thought I'd have to pull out the fire extinguisher again."

She could punt—but denying the obvious would be disingenuous.

"To tell you the truth, they kind of came out of nowhere. I never expected to meet any interesting men while I was here."

"Then two of them came along. Steven seems quite taken with you as well."

Uh-oh.

Was Natalie going to be disappointed if nothing happened between her cousin and her houseguest?

"He's a very nice man too." She shifted in her seat. "It's just that—"

"Cara." Natalie held up a hand. "No explanation necessary. Sparks happen, or they don't. Attraction can't be forced. I'd be delighted if this trip produces more for you than a translated journal you can use as background for your paper, should someone catch your fancy. The notion of these tucked-away acres being the catalyst for true love appeals to the romantic in me." She winked and motioned to the journal. "Shall we get back to work?"

"Whenever you're ready."

They plowed through several more pages during the remainder of their session without any glitches, until Natalie paused near the end.

Cara looked up from her typing. "Did you come across a difficult passage?"

"No, not at all. It's clear as a bell. I think we may have run across the first clue in our quest to discover what happened to Marie. It's certainly a mysterious entry."

"I'm all ears."

Natalie picked up the journal and began to read, translating as she went. "'I met the most charming man today. Of course, I already knew who he was. Everyone in town does. And I have seen him about now and then. But tonight, we talked for the first time, and it was wonderful! He was attentive and gracious, and I was so flattered. I dare not record his name on these pages, though. That would ruin the magic and break the spell. Instead, I shall call him MSL—my secret love—and dream about him. Because that is all I can ever do, even if I would wish for so much more.'"

As Natalie concluded, Cara stopped typing. "You think this mystery man is the key to Marie's demise?"

"We'll have to see if he turns up again, I suppose. Marie would have been twenty-five when this was written, and there are several journals still to go through. It's possible she'll never mention him again."

"Whoever he was, he certainly made an impression on her. I wonder what she meant about only being able to dream about him?"

"Perhaps we'll discover that too, as we go along. And now we should wrap up. Lydia is bringing her brother by to introduce us and give me an opportunity to see if I think he'd be an acceptable part-time groundskeeper. That's all I need, I suppose, but it won't be like having someone on the premises 24/7. I didn't see much of Micah, but I always knew he was close by. Of course, I have you with me until the end of the semester." Her mouth curved into a wistful smile. "I've enjoyed your companionship."

"The feeling is mutual." Cara set her elbow on the table and rested her chin in her palm. "You know . . . maybe you could rent out the cottage after I'm gone. I could see a retired couple or newlyweds living here, if the price was reasonable. They might even be willing to do minor chores for you."

Natalie's face lit up. "What a brilliant idea. I expect I'd have to expand the cottage beyond a studio. Add a bedroom, perhaps, and beef up the kitchen to make it suitable as a full-time residence. But that should be doable. I'll run this by

Steven, get his take. He's smart about those sorts of business questions." She closed the journal. "I'd say we had a productive session today on several fronts."

"I agree." Cara saved the transcript and powered down her laptop.

The doorbell rang, and Natalie grasped her cane. "That must be Lydia and her brother."

"I'll let myself out the back way." Cara shut the lid of the laptop.

"Dinner together, as usual?"

"Of course." She stood. "Although I may have to beg off one night next week. Brad suggested that we, uh, go out for dinner together."

"Never pass up an invitation from a charming, handsome man. Especially one who also appears to have integrity and honor." Natalie rose and started toward the door.

Cara followed, turning to the right in the hall as Natalie went left, toward the front door.

After strolling back to the cottage, she set her laptop on the desk, ate a quick lunch of fruit and yogurt, then sat down to work.

Except her lined, legal-size tablet was missing.

Drat.

She must have left it in the study. And she needed the research prompts she'd jotted about the entries from today's translation.

At least it wasn't a long trek back to the house.

She retraced her steps down the path, opened the door, and quietly let herself into the kitchen. In all likelihood Natalie was still talking to Lydia and her brother in the living room. The best plan was to get in and out fast, without interrupting.

Tiptoeing down the hall, she picked up noise that was likely the rumble of conversation, confirming her suspicion that the interview wasn't over.

Good.

If they were still talking, she ought to have plenty of time to grab her notes and escape unnoticed.

She picked up her pace . . . but came to an abrupt halt in the study doorway.

Why was Lydia standing behind the desk, leaning down on the side containing the drawer holding Marie's journals, intent on whatever she was looking at?

All at once, as if sensing her presence, the housekeeper glanced over. Paled. A noise sounded—a slam?—and she jerked upright.

Before Cara could think of anything to say, the other woman spoke.

"I, uh, was waiting in here while Ms. Boyer finishes up with Randy alone. I, uh, noticed this drawer was open and decided to close it. Ms. Boyer likes everything neat, you know." The smile Lydia offered looked forced. "But there was, uh, something stuck, and it took me a minute to get it shut. If you want to use this room, I can, uh, wait in the kitchen."

"I won't be long." Cara motioned to the worktable, debating her next move. "I left my tablet here and came back for it. I also have to get a couple of research books."

Not true. But there was a definite ring of deceit to Lydia's explanation, and leaving her alone in here felt wrong.

"I'll wait in the kitchen." Lydia sidled out from behind the desk. "I wanted some water anyway."

As she hurried across the room, Cara shifted aside to clear the exit. Lydia edged past, continued down the hall, and disappeared into the kitchen.

Cara stared after her.

That had been weird.

And the odd vibes swirling through the air were disturbing.

It was possible, of course, that her instincts were off. That Lydia's presence behind the desk had been innocent.

But what if it wasn't?

Should she tell Natalie what had happened?

Yes.

If the situation had been reversed, Cara would want to be informed. The decision about how to handle this should be up to Natalie.

After selecting a random book from the shelf, Cara sank into one of the upholstered chairs in the study to wait for the interview to end.

Ten minutes later, noise from the hallway suggested someone was moving about.

Shortly after that, Natalie appeared in the doorway, eyebrows arching when she spotted the unexpected occupant. "Cara! I thought you'd gone back to the cottage."

"I did, but I realized I'd forgotten my tablet." She lifted it. "Lydia's in the kitchen. After they're gone, may I speak to you for a few minutes?"

"Of course. I'll be back soon."

She disappeared down the hall, reappearing less than a minute later with Lydia in her wake as she passed the doorway.

The housekeeper glanced into the study as she passed, forehead creased.

It would be interesting to see if she mentioned their encounter to Natalie.

Three minutes later, as Cara replaced the book she'd pulled from the shelf, the older woman rejoined her. "What did you want to talk about?"

Cara wiped her palm down her leggings.

Playing tattletale was never fun, but in this situation it felt like the prudent course.

"Is anything wrong?" Natalie crossed to her, concern tightening her features.

"I hope not. Did Lydia say anything to you before she left about me finding her in here today?"

"No. After the three of us chatted for about five minutes,

I asked her if she'd mind letting me talk to her brother one-on-one. She offered to wait in here. She never mentioned you. Why?"

Cara gripped her notes tighter. "When I came in, she was behind the desk, looking in one of the drawers."

"Oh my." Natalie's brow crimped. "That's disturbing. Did she offer an explanation?"

"Yes." Cara passed it on.

"That doesn't quite ring true, does it?" Natalie walked toward the desk. "Which drawer was it?"

"I couldn't tell from the doorway, but it was on the right side." She followed the woman over.

Natalie circled the desk. Opened the top drawer, where the journals were stored. Ran her finger down the spines of the stack.

"They're all here, exactly as I left them. I don't know why Lydia would have an interest in these, anyway, since no one but me can read them." She closed that drawer and leaned farther down to pull out the one below. "Hmm."

"What's wrong?" Cara edged closer and peeked into the drawer. It contained what appeared to be albums of some sort. Two of them.

"These have been disturbed."

"What are they?"

"My father's stamp collection. He was an avid philatelist. Made quite a study of the subject. Through the years he amassed an enviable collection. I never had much interest in the hobby, but since his stamps meant a great deal to him, I've left them in his desk all these years. On occasion, when I'm missing him, I take one out and page through it. I always feel as if he's watching over my shoulder when I do that." She stroked a gentle hand across the cover of the first one, where the name Robert Boyer was embossed in gold.

"How do you know they've been disturbed?"

"The stamp tongs and magnifying glass are out of position. They've fallen down beside the albums. I always leave them on top, as Papa did." She removed the albums one by one and set them on the desk. "I'll look through these. I'm not suspicious by nature, but I also don't believe in turning a blind eye to behavior that raises red flags. Thank you for alerting me to this, Cara."

"I hope it comes to nothing."

"I do too. Lydia's been a reliable housekeeper for several years."

"What did you think about her brother, if I may ask?"

Natalie shrugged. "I wasn't impressed. He may be a hard worker, but he didn't strike me as a go-getter, or the sort of person I'd want to call a friend. An interim fix at best, I'd say." She rested a hand on the albums. "I do hope I don't find anything amiss inside."

"Me too." Cara lifted her tablet. "Now it's back to work for me."

"I'll see you at dinner, my dear." The woman settled behind the desk.

When Cara looked back from the doorway, Natalie's head was bent over the first album.

She continued down the hall and out the door, locking it behind her.

It was Natalie's decision, of course, but in her benefactor's shoes she'd be nervous about keeping someone around who snooped into private areas.

And despite Lydia's excuse, she *had* been snooping. Cara knew that as surely as she knew the cold days of winter would soon follow this lingering interlude of fall warmth.

Strange how she'd initially been concerned about Micah, who'd turned out to be a gentle soul with a soft spot for animals, when someone who'd seemed far more innocuous might end up being much less trustworthy.

Or not.

Depending on what Natalie found—or didn't find—in the albums.

"I THOUGHT IT WENT WELL. What do you think?"

As her brother maneuvered his truck down the long gravel drive from Natalie's house back to the road, Lydia curled her fingers into a ball on her lap.

No, it had not gone well.

Just the opposite.

In fact, unless Lady Luck decided to smile on her, all of her plans may just have gone up in smoke.

Why, oh why, had the professor forgotten her tablet today of all days? And why had she come into the study at the exact wrong moment?

Lydia mashed her lips together.

Half a minute later, the drawer would have been shut and she'd have been sitting on the couch, the stamp tucked in her purse, no one the wiser.

Instead, Cara Tucker had shown up seconds after she'd stashed the prize and was putting the album back.

If only the gift of a silver tongue hadn't passed her by. It was obvious the professor hadn't bought her stumbling attempt to—

"Hey. Are you listening to me?" Randy sent her an annoyed glance and turned on the radio.

A country-western tune blasted through the cab.

Her head began to pound, and she reached over and punched the dial.

Blessed silence descended.

"What's with you?" Randy glared at her.

"I have a headache, okay?"

"You were fine on the drive out here."

Not exactly fine, since she'd been less than thrilled about the idea of him working here even part-time. But if that bought her another week or two to wheedle her way into a live-in position with Natalie, she'd have sucked it up.

However, the incident in the study aside, the brief exchange she'd witnessed between him and Natalie before Natalie asked to speak with him alone hadn't been promising. As far as she was concerned, her brother had bombed the interview with his tendency to brag and blow his own horn. Natalie would have seen through all that, and she wouldn't have been impressed.

Bottom line, his chances of getting the job were lower than a snake's belly.

And at this point, so were her chances of keeping the job she had.

Lydia closed her eyes. Swallowed.

Her one foray into a life of crime, and this was how it ended.

"Are you sick?" Randy actually sounded concerned.

"Yeah. Maybe." Sick at heart, if nothing else.

"Roll down your window." He opened his as he spoke.

"Why?"

"We gotta let the germs out. I can't afford to get sick. I don't have any sick days left for this year."

So his concern was self-centered.

Surprise, surprise.

She lowered her window, leaned back against the seat, and angled her head to watch the passing scenery.

Nothing much to see except trees with heat-parched leaves that were waiting to drop at the first sign of frost. Spent and hanging on by a thread.

Kind of like she was, with all her plans to leave Randy's place for cushier digs collapsing around her.

Because Natalie would discover the missing stamp. If not today, soon.

And there would be only one suspect.

Of course, admitting the theft would be stupid. Just like it would be stupid to admit she'd spiked Natalie's wine with Ambien. And Lydia Foster wasn't stupid. No one would ever be able to prove she'd done either of those things.

Unless the sheriff checked the stamp album for fingerprints.

Her stomach kinked.

Would he do that?

Maybe, if Natalie reported the stamp missing and the professor said she'd seen the housekeeper looking in the desk.

She'd have to get rid of the fingerprints. Fast.

But that wouldn't erase the suspicion.

Meaning that come tomorrow, she might not have a job or a place to live. All she'd have was the two grand that had been bid on the stamp in her purse. But that would be a one-off. The stamp well had dried up.

The scene before her blurred, and she sniffed. Swiped at her lashes with the back of her hand.

Her life was a train wreck.

"Are you getting a cold?" Her brother scowled at her. "I told you, I don't want no germs."

"No, I'm not getting a cold."

But a cold would be much, much easier to deal with than the mess she'd made of her life.

Unless she could figure a way out of her bleak situation before tomorrow.

SIXTEEN

"I HAVE A PUZZLE FOR YOU."

As Rod's comment crackled over the phone line, Brad glanced at his chief deputy and slid into his patrol car, cell to his ear. Larry had the graffiti situation in hand, and it didn't take two law enforcement officers to listen to the owner rant about his barn being defaced.

"Lay it on me."

"It's about Micah Reeves's death."

Brad's ears perked up. "I'm listening."

"During the autopsy, I found a small amount of caked matter on the back of his shirt. It bothered me."

"Why?"

"I'm not sure. It could have been poop from a passing bird, for all I knew. He'd been lying there awhile. But I decided to send it out for testing. It wasn't bird poop."

Silence.

Naturally.

The coroner loved milking juicy tidbits for all they were worth.

Brad played along. "What was it?"

"The report says it contained food-derived proteins and a multitude of peptide digests."

"Can you translate that to English?"

"Vomit."

Brad frowned. "Are you saying Micah threw up?"

"Onto the back of his shirt?"

Oh yeah. That didn't fit.

"Did you run DNA on it?"

"I did. It's not Micah's, as we already concluded. There were no matches in the databases."

So someone had thrown up on him.

It wasn't Cara. She would have told him about that. And no one else had come forward to report the body.

Of course, if a trespasser had spotted Micah, they may have been reluctant to admit they'd been on the premises. They could have gone over to investigate, puked, then hightailed it off the property.

But a killer who didn't have the stomach for murder wouldn't report a body, either.

Brad's pulse picked up. "You may want to put a temporary hold on your manner of death ruling."

"We're tracking the same direction. Good luck figuring this one out."

"Thanks."

Brad ended the call, slid his cell into his pocket, and started the engine.

From the beginning, this death hadn't felt as innocent as it seemed. The lack of blood in the boat, and the odd smear on the side. The location of the small skiff and the body. Now this.

Each new fact increased the possibility that foul play could have been involved.

He tapped his finger on the wheel.

The question was, why would anyone want to kill Micah?

The man hadn't appeared to have any friends—other than Natalie—let alone enemies.

Yet if murder was involved, someone had wanted him gone for a reason.

The challenge was to figure out who and why . . . and to determine if all the other strange happenings on Natalie's property could somehow be related.

A daunting task on this early October day.

Because if someone had taken Micah's life, they'd left law enforcement very little to work with. And the case was getting colder by the day.

So unless he got a major break or the perpetrator made a serious mistake, it was possible justice would never be done.

He scowled as he put the car in gear and drove forward.

That didn't sit well.

Neither did the fact that if, indeed, all the strange incidents on the Boyer property were somehow tied together, the danger there might still be present.

Meaning Cara could be in the thick of it.

She was an outsider, though. A temporary resident. She had no connection to the Boyer estate, no vested interest in the place. She wasn't a threat to anyone.

But Micah hadn't been, either, based on current intel.

A chill snaked through him as he drove through the early morning light, two things clear in his mind.

Collateral damage could happen if you were in the wrong place at the wrong time.

And more and more, Natalie's property was looking like a very wrong place to be.

MAYBE NATALIE HADN'T NOTICED the missing stamp yet.

Lydia checked her watch as she dusted the living room. She'd been here all morning, and the woman hadn't said a word.

Then again, her boss and the professor had been locked away in the study working on that stupid journal. Hard to believe they paid people to dig into ancient history. Who cared what had happened in this godforsaken area a hundred years ago?

She was much more interested in current events.

Like how to find a way out of her brother's house that didn't exchange one dump for another, now that her odds of convincing Natalie to be her ticket to a cushier life were in the toilet.

Getting greedy had been a mistake. Sure, those old stamps were just sitting there gathering dust, of no benefit to anyone, but she should have focused first on wrangling an invitation to live here instead of letting the temptation to pick up what had seemed like easy money mess with her priorities.

She swiped at the film of dust on the antique hall table. Keeping this place clean was a constant battle, and the gravel drive didn't help matters. Natalie ought to pave it and—

". . . see you at dinner." Cara Tucker opened the door to the study, aiming the remark over her shoulder.

"I'll look forward to it."

The two women emerged from the room.

Cara greeted her but didn't linger. It was hard to tell from her expression if she'd shared the desk incident with Natalie.

As Cara disappeared toward the back of the house, Natalie smiled. "I appreciate your offer to pick up blackberries at the market for me, Lydia. They didn't have any when I was there earlier in the week."

"It was no problem, ma'am. I know how much you like them. I put them in your fridge."

"Excellent." She waited a few beats. "I believe I'll have my lunch."

"Yes, ma'am."

Several more seconds passed, but Natalie didn't move. She just stood there, as if she was waiting for . . . what? A confession?

It would be a long wait.

No one could pin anything on her, even if Natalie called the sheriff. Not after she'd arrived extra early today and cleaned in the study first. Including a major wipe down of the items in the bottom right-hand drawer of the desk.

There were no incriminating fingerprints to find on that stamp collection.

Putting back the stamp tucked in her pocket had been an option, of course. One she'd mulled over. Yet in the end she'd held on to it. If she was going to get fired, she needed the money it would provide for a deposit on an apartment somewhere.

"You know, I'm a great believer in second chances." Natalie set her cane in front of her and rested both hands on top, her tone conversational. But as the silence between them stretched, there was a subtle shift in her posture. "I understand you were looking in the desk in the study yesterday, Lydia. Last night I discovered a stamp missing from my father's collection. Do you know anything about that?"

Lydia wadded the dust rag in her fingers, wavering.

If she confessed and offered to return the stamp, would Natalie really give her another chance, as she'd implied?

But what if she didn't? What if she called the sheriff instead and asked him to press charges?

It would be safer to play dumb. The sheriff wouldn't find anything if he investigated. She'd covered her tracks, despite the circumstantial evidence that put her in the bull's-eye. And if she admitted her guilt, Natalie would never trust her again. No matter what the woman said.

Second chances didn't happen in real life.

"No, ma'am."

Natalie let out a long, slow breath. "I think we both know that's not true, Lydia. You've been a reliable worker, and I'm sorry to have to do this, but I can't have people in my house who aren't honest and who won't own up to wrong behavior.

I'll send you a check for the work you've done, but I'll have to ask you to leave. Now."

Her throat pinched, and bitterness washed over her. The outcome was no surprise. She never got any breaks.

"I'm sorry it didn't work out, Ms. Boyer."

"I am too, Lydia. And please let your brother know I won't be needing his services, either."

"I will." But not until she lined up somewhere else to live. "I'll get my things."

She retreated to the kitchen, where she'd left her purse and sweater.

When she returned to the hall, Natalie was standing by the front door. As if she couldn't wait to kick her out.

"I wish you well, Lydia. I'll pray for you." There was no anger or recrimination on her face. Instead, she looked sort of sad.

Lydia bit back the sharp retort hovering on the tip of her tongue. No sense creating any more hard feelings with her employer. Or rather, former employer.

But the truth was, prayers wouldn't help her. God didn't care about people like her. If he did, she wouldn't be in this mess—divorced, barely making ends meet, bounced from a cushy job, and soon to be kicked out of her brother's house.

It wasn't fair.

Slinking away, however, would be too humiliating.

So she straightened her shoulders, gripped her purse, and walked past Natalie.

Only after the soft click of the door sounded behind her did her posture sag and her step falter.

For the door to Natalie's home wasn't the only one that had closed for her today.

It appeared the time had come to leave this place behind. Use the funds the stamp generated to start over somewhere else. Someplace where no one knew her.

And this go-round, she'd steer clear of men, substitute waiting tables for cleaning, and stay far away from anything that reeked of ill-gotten gain.

If nothing else, she'd learned one valuable lesson from this fiasco.

She wasn't cut out for a life of crime.

WHO COULD BE CALLING HER at such an ungodly hour?

Cara blinked to clear the sleep from her eyes and peered at her phone on the nightstand in her condo as her vibrating smartwatch alerted her to an incoming call.

Oh.

Nine o'clock wasn't all that early. Unless you were a night owl who considered sleeping in every Saturday an indispensable indulgence.

She groped for the phone and squinted at the screen.

Bri.

She huffed out a breath.

Her sister knew better than to call her at this hour on the weekend.

Cara scooted up in bed, pressed talk, and put the cell to her ear. "Morning. Hold for a minute." After putting on her hearing gear, she picked up the conversation. "Sorry. I had to get my ears in place. All set."

"Did I wake you up?"

"Is it Saturday before ten?"

"I'll take that as a yes. Sorry. I'm en route to a fire scene and this may be the only opportunity I have all day to squeeze in a call to my favorite sister. You want me to hang up?"

"No. I'm awake now. Sort of." Cara yawned. "What's going on?"

"Same old, same old."

"Ha. Says the new bride. How's married life?"

A contented sigh came over the line. "Bliss. Any prospects on your end?"

An image of Brad materialized in her mind, and Cara's lips curved up.

But it was too soon to say anything to her siblings. What if the first date fizzled?

"No news to report."

"Bummer. But hang in there. Once you're back in civilization, the pool of possibilities will expand."

"I'll hold that thought."

"You hear anything from Jack?"

"Not much. A couple of quick texts. What about you?"

"Same here. I think he's directing the bulk of his communication to Lindsey."

"Fiancées get first priority."

"Remember that when your time comes."

"*If* it comes."

"It will. I have great confidence. What's new on your end? Is all quiet on the southwestern front—or, as Jack would say, in the hinterland?"

Hardly.

In addition to all the other strange happenings, there was now a stamp-stealing ex-housekeeper in the mix. Lydia may not have confessed to Natalie, but according to the older woman at dinner last night, she'd had guilt written all over her during their hallway talk yesterday.

The question was how much to tell her siblings.

Other than Micah, none of the incidents that had occurred during her tenure were newsworthy. His death, however, could cross their radar, and if they connected the dots, they'd be upset she hadn't said anything.

It might be best to give Bri a topline in case they got wind of that situation.

"Quiet for the most part, but there was a sad event on the

property." She kept her voice as neutral as possible. "Natalie's groundskeeper died."

"Oh, I'm sorry. What happened?"

"It appears he fell out of his boat on the lake, hit his head, and drowned."

"That *is* sad. Did he have a family?"

"No."

"I suppose that's a blessing. Losing someone in such a tragic manner would be hard for the people left behind."

"Natalie's upset, though. She's counted on him for years."

"I can imagine. No chance there was any funny business about his death, is there?"

Leave it to Bri to ask questions about a death rather than accept the news at face value.

Kind of like Brad, come to think of it.

"I don't think so. The sheriff is looking into it, but as far as I know, the investigation is more a formality than anything else." Unless he'd found some basis for the suspicions he'd hinted at during dinner the night of Micah's service, when he'd said he planned to keep his ear to the ground.

"Watch your step just the same. I don't like you in the vicinity of odd deaths. And let me know if anything else unusual happens on the property."

"Why? This is way out of your jurisdiction."

"I have connections. I could always ask someone to have a chat with the sheriff, since my sister is peripherally connected to the event. Not all small-town types are as diligent as they could be."

"This one is."

"How do you know?"

Whoops.

"I've, uh, met him. He came by to see Natalie twice, and I also ran into him in town." She wadded the sheet in her fist and braced. "As a matter of fact, I'm also the one who found the groundskeeper's body during one of my daily walks."

"Cara! You waited until now to tell me that?"

"I would have gotten around to it." Maybe. But at least that piece of information ought to distract Bri from asking any more questions about her younger sister's interactions with the sheriff.

"Are you okay with that?"

"It didn't give me nightmares or anything, if that's what you mean."

"Listen . . . you want me to run down there a night next week? If there's a Thai restaurant in the area, we could indulge in that spicy food you like."

Pressure built behind her eyes at her sister's kindhearted gesture. It was classic Bri. "I appreciate the offer, but it's too long of a drive after a full day of work. Especially since you're not a fan of Thai cuisine."

"I could suffer through it for the sake of my little sister."

"You're barely a year older than me."

"Once a little sister, always a little sister. The offer's on the table if you change your mind." In the background, a siren sounded. "Gotta run. I'm at the scene. Let me know if you need me. Otherwise, we'll talk next Saturday. And I promise I won't call this early."

"No worries. I should get up anyway. I have to run to my office on campus, and I don't want to be late for my ballet class."

"Enjoy."

"Always."

They rang off, and Cara swung her legs to the floor. Stood. Stretched.

Dinner with Bri next week would have been fun if the drive wasn't so long.

But she did have dinner with Brad on her calendar.

And much as she loved her sister, a date with the handsome sheriff would be even better than a chatty meal with Bri.

Because not only was she eager to enjoy his company in an unofficial capacity, she was curious to find out if keeping his ear to the ground in the Micah case had produced any new leads.

A long shot, no doubt. Brad himself had admitted as much.

Yet Natalie seemed unconvinced the man's death had been an accident.

In all honesty, she didn't have positive vibes about that herself.

Furrowing her brow, Cara pulled her dance clothes from the closet.

Trouble was, if natural causes or an accident hadn't ended his life, that meant someone had killed him.

Someone who was still out there.

A shiver rippled through her.

Not the cheeriest thought on this Saturday morning.

So she'd try to put it aside. Leave all crime-related matters in Brad's capable hands. If there was anything to worry about, he'd tell her.

Nevertheless, it wouldn't hurt to watch her back from now on.

Just in case someone much more menacing than gentle-natured Micah was lurking about the premises for purposes they alone were privy to, waiting to wreak more havoc.

SEVENTEEN

PAUL TOOK A STEADYING BREATH as he ascended the steps to Natalie's galérie.

This was the last place he wanted to be late on a Sunday afternoon, and the task ahead was the last thing he wanted to do.

But this was the only way forward.

And since there were no cars parked in front of Natalie's house, suggesting her cousin had left after his weekend visit and the professor wasn't yet back from Cape, he couldn't ask for a more ideal window to get the job done.

Mustering every ounce of grit he could dredge up, he leaned forward and pressed the bell.

Three minutes later, the front door swung open.

"Paul!" Natalie's eyebrows rose, and her lips tipped up in welcome. "What a lovely surprise. Come in." She stepped back and pulled the door wide.

"I hope I'm not interrupting anything." He crossed the threshold on stiff legs and moved into the foyer.

"Not at all. Steven's gone back to St. Louis and I had an early dinner. My activities for the remainder of the day consist of reading and crocheting. I'd welcome a bit of conversation."

She motioned toward the living room. "Have a seat. May I offer you a cup of tea?"

"No, thank you. I can't stay long."

She followed him in and claimed a chair while he perched on the edge of the couch. "What brings you out to my neck of the woods? Were you at the historical society?"

His heart began to pound.

This was it.

Sweat broke out on his upper lip as a sudden barrage of doubts assailed him.

Maybe he should change course. It wasn't too late. He could come up with some excuse for this visit, chat for a few minutes about inconsequential matters, and walk out the door.

Because what he was about to do was risky, and once he stepped over the line, there was no going back. If he made a mistake, it could come back to haunt him—and Dan—forever.

"Paul?" Natalie leaned forward, brow bunching. "You seem quite distressed."

Not surprising, given the churning in his stomach.

"I am." He twisted his fingers together.

Just do it, Coleman. Get the distasteful task over with. If you ever want to have a decent night's sleep again, you know you have to fix this problem.

"Is Becky all right?"

"Yes."

"And Dan?"

That was his opening.

Paul wiped a hand down his face and tried to fill his lungs, but they refused to inflate.

"Heavens, Paul, are you ill?" Natalie touched his arm, alarm tightening her features.

Yes, he was, but it wasn't a physical ailment.

This sickness was in his heart.

And there was only one remedy for that.

He had to follow through on his plan.

"I'm not ill, Natalie. Not in the way you mean. But I do have . . . I have a confession to make."

"A confession?" Her eyebrows peaked again. "What sort of confession?"

Much as he wanted to look away, he forced himself to maintain eye contact. "The fire in your kitchen was my fault."

Shock flattened her features. "What are you talking about?"

"I started it—but I didn't mean for it to get out of control. That was never my intent."

A few beats ticked by as she stared at him. "I'm sorry. This isn't making sense. The fire didn't start until after you were gone."

"I know, but I burned that potholder on purpose when I went to the kitchen to get some extra napkins after I spilled my tea. I put it in the trash with embers still glowing, expecting it to catch fire fast. I knew the detector in the kitchen would go off at the first hint of smoke, and I was going to help you put the fire out. I didn't think it would cause any real damage, since it was contained in the trash can. When nothing happened, I assumed the embers had been snuffed out. I had no idea there were any active sparks that would ignite later. The odds of combustion after such a long delay have to be minuscule."

Her face was a study in bewilderment. "But . . . I don't understand. Why would you do such a thing?"

"I hoped it might add weight to my argument that Marie's journals would be safer with me."

She blinked. "You did all that just to protect the journals?"

Untwisting his fingers, he flexed his blanched knuckles and dipped his chin. "There was more to it than that."

"I'd like to hear about it."

"It has to do with Dan."

"Go on." Her voice was steady.

"You know how dirty politics is these days. I was afraid there would be information in the journals that could be used to smear the Coleman name."

"What kind of information?"

Paul swallowed. "You know there were rumors about Marie's death."

"Yes. I also know my father never believed the accidental ruling was accurate. Do you have information to suggest it was more than that?"

"Nothing concrete. Only family lore that was passed down to me by my father. The story was that my grandfather, who was also in politics, had a long-running affair with a local woman whenever he was in town. My father heard his parents arguing about it once. After Marie died in such a tragic way, my father overheard another row between his parents. According to him, my grandfather denied having anything to do with her death, but my father wasn't certain my grandmother ever believed that. They stayed together for propriety's sake, but their marriage was over except in name."

"Was any of this shared with the authorities at the time?"

"Not that I know of. I first heard the story a few years ago, while my father was in his final days in hospice, and he didn't offer anything more than what I've told you. But there may be clues in Marie's journals that would implicate my grandfather in her death. If that information is shared with the wrong people, it could be used to smear the family name. I don't care for myself, but Dan doesn't deserve to have his career ruined by the misdeeds of long-dead relatives. He's worked hard all his life, and he'll be a fine congressman. I did what I did to protect him, but in hindsight I realize I made bad choices."

Natalie took a deep breath. Leaned back in her chair. Studied him. "Does Dan know about any of this? Or Becky?"

"Not yet. I went to see Father Johnson before I came here, and we had a long talk about the situation. I do plan to tell Becky tonight." He massaged the bridge of his nose. "I'm here to ask your forgiveness for the fire and for my attempts to convince you to give me the journals. Instead of taking matters into my own hands, I should have asked you and the professor to keep any damaging information confidential."

"And I would have. You know me well enough, Paul, to know I would never share personal information with anyone. I feel confident you can trust Cara too. She's a woman of integrity, discretion, and high standards."

There was no recrimination in her tone, but the truth of her response stung nonetheless. He should have trusted her.

What a fool he'd been.

"I'm sorry, Natalie. For everything I did, and for ruining a friendship I've cherished." He stared at the carpet beneath his feet, fighting to get the words past the constriction in his throat. "If you want me to call the sheriff and turn myself in for the fire, I will. I'll also pay the cost of any damages. I'll do whatever it takes to make amends. All I ask is that you give me this evening to talk with Becky."

Five seconds ticked by.

Ten.

Fifteen.

Finally, he looked up.

At the compassion softening Natalie's features, his pulse stuttered.

Where was the righteous anger? The indignation? The disgust?

"I'm not going to press charges, Paul."

His jaw dropped. "Why not?"

"It took a lot of courage for you to come here tonight and

admit your guilt, to tell me about your family history, and I don't believe in punishing people who have sincere remorse and the courage to acknowledge culpability. I also understand that what you did was motivated by love for your son. Your attempt to protect him was admirable, if ill-advised."

At her gracious generosity, his vision blurred.

"I don't deserve your forgiveness." Somehow he choked out the words as he extended a shaky hand. "But I'll be forever grateful."

She clasped his fingers and squeezed before releasing them. "I'll talk to Cara about the journals. I believe you'll be able to count on both of us to be extra cautious in our use of the contents. And I'll keep you informed about any information we find that may be pertinent to your family history."

"I'd appreciate that." He stood. "May I take a raincheck on the tea you offered earlier?"

"You may indeed. Anytime." She rose and gripped her cane. "I'll walk you out."

He followed her to the door. "I wish I could do more than say thank you."

"You could give me a hug. I don't believe you've ever done that." She held out her arms.

Without hesitation, he stepped into them. "I'm always happy to dispense hugs."

"I'll remember that in the future." After a moment, she released him, the kindness in her eyes a balm to his soul. "We've been friends for many years, Paul. I don't want to lose that. I don't condone what you did, but I respect that you came forward to confess. And I believe in living Ephesians 4:32. Drive safe going home."

"I will." He lifted a hand and returned to his car as an older-model Accord appeared in the distance on the drive.

The professor was back.

Hopefully she was as circumspect and honorable as Natalie believed.

But this was in God's hands now. He was done trying to orchestrate outcomes. If he'd ever wondered whether he was cut out for subterfuge, this experience had given him his answer.

A resounding no.

And as he crunched down the driveway, waving at Cara when they passed, he gave thanks for Natalie's kindness and forgiveness.

Then he added a silent prayer that whatever she and Cara found in Marie's journals would provide answers to a long-standing mystery and allow both families to close the door on that page of ancestral history.

IT WAS TIME to formalize their date—and end his weekend with a Cara fix.

Lips bowing, Brad tossed the container from his microwave dinner into the trash, picked up his phone, and wandered over to the back window as he scrolled to her number and placed the call.

She picked up on the third ring, her greeting a tad breathless.

"Did I catch you at a bad time?"

"No. I just finished my walk around the lake. Give me a sec to go inside." A scuffling noise came over the line, followed by a door opening and closing. "Sorry for the delay."

"No problem. How was your weekend?"

"Full. A little work at my office, a ballet class, a call from my sister, church this morning. How about yours?"

"Low key. I did have a long chat with my parents. And I went to church too." A long overdue return that had lifted his spirits. "I also spent a fair amount of the weekend thinking about you."

"Can I admit I thought about you too? Or should I be more coy?"

"I prefer people who are straightforward."

"In that case, I thought about you a *lot*. Also about our dinner this week."

His smile morphed into a flat-out grin. "Same here. That's why I called. Would Thursday night work? The restaurant I have in mind is closed on Monday, I have a presentation at the city council meeting in Potosi on Tuesday night, and I'm on duty Wednesday until late."

"You're one busy guy."

"It keeps me out of trouble." And too occupied to mope around.

"Busyness can also help keep unhappy memories at bay."

At her soft comment, he leaned a shoulder against the wall and watched a male and female cardinal sail onto a branch and nestle up side by side in the twilight.

Professor Cara Tucker's intuitive abilities were impressive.

"Yeah. That too." May as well admit the truth, after everything else they'd shared.

"Been there, done that. Let's hope dinner together will accomplish the same end and create new, happy memories in the process."

"I think that's a given. May I pick you up at five thirty?"

"I'll be ready."

With the date set, his excuse for calling was gone. But he wasn't ready to hang up.

"How's Natalie doing?"

"Healthwise, fine. She lost her housekeeper, though, which was upsetting."

That was news. As far as he knew, the woman had been with her for years.

"Why would she quit?"

"She didn't. Natalie let her go."

"Out of the blue?" That didn't sound like the Natalie he'd come to know. She seemed like a measured, thoughtful, level-headed person who wasn't prone to rash decisions.

A few seconds ticked by. "Can I tell you this in confidence?"

"Yes."

"She has pretty solid circumstantial evidence that Lydia stole a valuable stamp from one of her father's albums."

Brad frowned. "Do you know why she didn't contact me to report it?"

"She said she didn't want to make a big issue out of it because only one stamp was missing and it appeared Lydia had a hard enough life as it was. I honestly think she would have let her stay on if Lydia had admitted the theft when Natalie gave her the chance, but she didn't."

What a missed opportunity for the housekeeper.

But who knew what had happened in the woman's life to shape her character? From what he'd heard, the brother she lived with was no great shakes, and her husband had dumped her. Someone like that could have difficulty with trust—and with believing in the goodness of others.

Sad.

"Does Natalie have someone else lined up?"

"No, and I know that worries her."

"I wonder if she'd be interested in the woman who cleans for me. I think she's in the market for another client or two."

"My guess is yes."

"I'll find a way to pass on her name without breaking your confidence."

"Thanks. Any news on Micah's investigation?"

"There've been a couple of developments, but so far they haven't led to any conclusive evidence that his death was more than an accident."

"If there *was* more involved, I hate to think that person is roaming around free and poised to get away with murder."

"You and me both." Especially since he had no clue about the motive.

Not to mention the fact that Cara was still taking walks around the lake. Alone.

"But why would someone hurt Micah?"

"I can't answer that yet. And until this is resolved, you may want to be extra cautious."

She didn't respond for several seconds, and when she did, a thread of trepidation wove through her question. "Are you suggesting I could be in danger?"

"I wouldn't go that far. But as I said the night you and I and Natalie had dinner, I don't like coincidences."

"I think Natalie figured out one of the coincidences, if that makes any difference."

"Which one?"

"The kitchen fire. While we were working today, she told me she'd solved that mystery."

"What's the story?"

"I don't know. All she said was that it had been a silly mistake."

Be that as it may, taking that off the table didn't alleviate his suspicions about Micah's death.

"Even if there's an explanation for that incident, a few elements of the crime scene bother me. I'm not letting this go yet."

"I admire your perseverance."

"We'll see where it leads." But at the very least he could talk to people who had a connection to Natalie or were regular visitors to her place, check alibis for the time-of-death window Rod had identified. Paul Coleman, the housekeeper, Steven, and anyone else Natalie saw on a consistent basis. Even Cara, to cover all the bases.

But he'd start with the others. The woman he was talking to was definitely not a killer.

"In terms of using caution, do you think I should stop taking my walks around the lake? I do carry pepper gel, and I stay alert to my surroundings."

"To be honest, I'd prefer that. But I'm not going to tell you what to do. It's your call."

"I appreciate that. If Jack were here, he'd be much more heavy-handed."

At her wry tone, his mouth flexed. "Are you saying you have an overprotective brother?"

She snorted. "Is the pope Catholic?"

A chuckle rumbled up inside him. "I like him already."

"Fair warning—that won't win you brownie points from me if you follow in his footsteps. I have to rein him in on a regular basis. Bri does too. From what I heard, her future husband and Jack had quite an altercation at their first meeting."

"Duly noted."

"However, I do appreciate your concern. And for whatever reason, protectiveness from you doesn't rankle me like it does from Jack."

"I'll take that as a positive sign." He was out of excuses to extend the conversation. "I'll call you before Thursday." Or drop in for a visit if he came up with a way to give Natalie his housekeeper's contact information without telling her he and Cara had discussed it.

"I'd like that. See you soon."

As they rang off, he watched through the window as a stray hummingbird zipped over to a patch of late-blooming goldenrod at the edge of the yard, where it flitted among the flowers in search of nectar to help sustain it during its long, tardy journey south for the winter. If it didn't leave soon for warmer climes, it would be in big trouble. Hummingbirds weren't designed to live in a cold environment.

Neither were humans.

Happily, his world had warmed into the balmy range, thanks

to the historical anthropologist who'd begun to dominate not only his waking thoughts but his dreams.

Another incentive to get answers in Micah's case.

Cara's safety had become a top priority, and peace of mind on that score would be elusive as long as doubts plagued him about the man's death. If a murderer was on the loose, who knew when—or why—they might strike again?

He expelled a breath and turned away from the lengthening shadows outside as dusk succumbed to the encroaching darkness.

One thing for sure.

If someone had killed once, they'd kill again.

Meaning anyone who got in their way would be in deadly danger.

EIGHTEEN

ALL DRESSED UP AND NO PLACE TO GO.
What a bummer.
Expelling a breath, Cara made a face at her phone. Set it on the desk in the cottage.
Brad had been super apologetic, but when two young children went missing in your jurisdiction and the state patrol was called in to assist, duty took precedence over a date.
Totally understandable.
Also totally disappointing.
But finding those kids was way more important than a cozy dinner for two. And Brad had promised to reschedule ASAP.
Cara wandered over to the fridge in the cottage and opened the door. Surveyed the freezer compartment. Her initial stash of microwave dinners stared back at her, untouched, thanks to Natalie's generous invitation to join her for evening meals.
If Steven hadn't arrived for his weekend visit a day early, she'd mosey over to the house and suggest treating her hostess to dinner at the diner in town, as she had on a couple of previous occasions.
Or she could knock on the door, tell Natalie about the canceled date, and ask to borrow two eggs. Knowing her bene-

factor, an invitation to join her and Steven for dinner would follow.

But much as she enjoyed the company of Natalie's cousin, she was too geared up for a date with Brad to socialize with a different man, no matter how charming and handsome he was.

A frozen meal would have to suffice.

After selecting one of the dinners, she put it in the microwave and set the timer. Then she stepped out of her heels, padded across the floor to her closet, and pulled out her most comfortable pair of sweatpants and a sweatshirt. No need to impress anyone tonight with a chic ensemble.

It didn't take long to eat her dinner once the microwave pinged, leaving the whole empty evening to fill.

May as well work.

She moved to the desk chair, booted up her laptop, and dug in.

Three hours of intensive research and writing later, her brain finally balked.

No surprise.

She'd been at it since nine o'clock this morning, beginning with a two-hour translation session followed by an afternoon of more research and writing.

Maybe she'd cuddle up in bed with her laptop and read through Marie's journal. Their daily word-by-word translations were more about sentence integrity than overall flow, and it would be helpful to read it in one fell swoop for continuity.

After taking care of her nightly bedtime routine, she flipped off the lights in the cottage and retreated to the bed. The screen would provide sufficient illumination for her purposes.

Once she'd stacked the pillows behind her, she began on page one and went straight through the journal, lingering over the entries from this week. More and more, Marie's jottings were filled with mentions of the mysterious man—who could be Paul Coleman's grandfather, according to the story Natalie had told her on Monday morning. A prominent politician in his day, known throughout the state and in Washington.

Also very married, with a son.

Marie's reluctance to use his name suggested he could, indeed, be the man who'd turned her head with pretty talk and made her dream of a life he never intended to offer her.

So far, however, their dalliance seemed to be comprised of stolen moments of conversation, nothing more.

Whether that changed remained to be seen.

She could always suggest that they look ahead, skip to the final entries, and translate those. Surely they'd contain answers.

But Natalie had said from day one that she preferred to go through the journals in the order they were written, and she was the boss.

Whatever they found, though, Cara agreed with Natalie. Telling the world about any scandal that may have occurred almost a hundred years ago would serve no purpose. If a crime had been committed, it was too late to prosecute anyone. Why ruin lives in the present for sins in the past? The best outcome would be to find answers for the ancestors about a death that had left questions with both families.

Cara tipped down the screen of the laptop and leaned her head back against the pillows. Yawned. After she rested her eyes for a minute, she'd power down for the night and indulge in her secret addiction.

Reading romance novels.

The brand-new release she'd picked up in Cape last weekend was calling to her.

That wasn't a pastime most people would attribute to a university professor, perhaps, but as far as she was concerned, reading uplifting stories about people who overcame daunting odds to find their happy ending was soul soothing.

Of course, it was even better when happy endings occurred in real life.

An image of Brad filled her mind, and she sighed, letting her eyelids flutter closed. Now there was a man worthy to be a hero in any romance novel.

The world around her melted away as sleep tugged her into dreamland, and she let herself drift off. How could she resist being swept away to a fantasy world dominated by a sheriff who might be destined to play a starring role not only in her dreams but in her life?

When Cara's eyes at last flickered open, she clung to the sweet dream as long as she could. But as it faded away, she flipped up the laptop screen beside her and checked the time.

Eleven forty-five? She'd been asleep for more than two hours?

It was definitely bedtime.

She powered down, swung her legs to the floor, and carried the laptop back to the desk, the dim nightlight in one corner of the room the sole source of illumination.

As she returned to the bed, she detoured to close one of the curtains that was partially open.

Froze at the window.

Was that a light in the distance, flickering through the woods?

She sidled to the side of the glass, out of sight, and squinted through the darkness.

Yes, it was a light. And it was moving. Like the occasional lights she'd seen bobbing at night in the past that she'd assumed were evidence of Micah's nighttime forays.

But Micah was dead.

So who was wandering about at this hour?

A ripple of unease quivered through her, and she pulled the curtain shut. Took a step back.

Should she call Brad and alert him?

No. It was too late.

If he was still working the missing children case, he had other priorities. If he'd made it home and crashed, he didn't need to be interrupted. This could wait until tomorrow. Whoever was out there would disappear into the shadows if law enforcement showed up and began prowling around.

Before alerting Brad, she'd also bring it up to Natalie in case she happened to have an inkling of who might be roaming around her property at night.

Even if she didn't, it was possible the intruder had no ill intent, nor any connection to Micah's demise. It could be someone engaged in illegal trapping, or taking a shortcut, or meeting up with a partner for a clandestine tryst. There were all kinds of explanations for the presence of a stranger on the property that didn't necessarily involve serious criminal activity.

Nevertheless, Cara double-checked the locks on all the windows and the door, set her phone on the nightstand, and put her pepper gel within reach as she climbed into bed.

It never hurt to take precautions.

Especially when her instincts were telling her that whatever activity was taking place on Natalie's property in the dark of night was far from innocent.

"GOOD MORNING, CARA. Did you sleep well?"

As Natalie greeted her the next morning in the study, Cara closed the door behind her and joined the older woman at their worktable.

"To be honest, no. I tossed and turned a lot."

"I'm sorry to hear that. Didn't you enjoy your evening with Brad?"

"Unfortunately, he had to cancel." She explained the circumstances.

"I had no idea you were here. Steven and I were in the basement for about an hour around dinnertime. He was helping me look for a box of my mother's personal items that I wanted to go through. Otherwise, I would have realized no car pulled in. You should have joined the two of us for dinner."

"You weren't expecting me, and I have food in the cottage." Sort of. A frozen dinner was nothing like the delicious food Natalie prepared, but it had sufficed for one night.

"I imagine you were disappointed about the dinner. That was probably on your mind." Natalie gave a sympathetic nod. "But I have no doubt Brad will reschedule."

"He said he would. The broken date isn't why I had trouble sleeping, though." She flipped up the lid of her laptop, keeping her tone conversational to avoid creating undue alarm. "Actually, I saw a light in the woods late last night from the cottage window."

Natalie's mug of tea froze halfway to her mouth. "Near the house?"

"No. Deeper into the woods, in the direction of the lake. I thought you might have a clue who it could be."

Natalie set the mug back down. "No, I don't. No one should be roaming about on this property."

"Could it have been a neighbor, by any chance?"

"I doubt it. I don't see them much, but we do chat on occasion. If one of them had a reason to come onto my land, they'd ask. Are you certain you saw a light?"

"Yes. It was like the ones I saw once in a while when Micah was still here. I always assumed it was him."

"Late at night?"

"Yes."

Natalie shook her head. "I doubt that was him. He didn't like the dark and tried to avoid being outside at night whenever possible."

"How do you know?"

"He told me, after I mentioned once that I was concerned about what I'd do if I ever needed help at night. He also said anytime I wanted him, all I had to do was come out on the back galérie and bang a pot with a metal spoon, and he'd hear me—day or night, because he slept with the window cracked.

Sound does carry a long distance out here, and since he was tuned in to the environment, I felt confident in that plan."

"In that case, who's been wandering around on your property?"

"I have no idea."

"Do you think Steven may have noticed lights during any of his visits?"

"It's possible. He does stay up later than I do. But he holes up in his room to answer emails and read financial reports. My cousin lives to work." She wrinkled her nose. "We can ask him about the lights during our break, though. He'll be up by then."

Her cousin slept until almost ten?

Natalie must have read the surprise on her face because she chuckled. "Steven tends to be a night owl. He has to get up early in St. Louis, so he likes to sleep in whenever he's here."

Ah.

A kindred spirit.

"I can relate. My siblings are always teasing me about *my* night-owl tendencies."

"Perhaps you two have more in common than you thought."

She let that pass.

"After we ask Steven about the lights, I'd like to let Brad know what I saw, especially given what happened to Micah."

"By all means. If there's nefarious activity happening on this land, I want it fully investigated." She adjusted her glasses. "Shall we dive into the journal?"

"Yes."

They worked steadily for an hour, and Steven was, indeed, up and in the kitchen eating a piece of toast when Cara went to get Natalie a second cup of tea and replenish her coffee.

"Morning." He greeted her with a smile and started to stand.

"Stay put. I'm here for refills during our break." She held up their mugs. "I do have a question for you, though."

"Ask away."

As she filled Natalie's mug with water and put it in the microwave, she repeated the story she'd told the older woman.

By the time she finished, deep grooves dented his forehead. "That's disturbing."

"I take it you don't have any idea who it could be."

"No—but whoever it is, they're trespassing."

"At the very least." She removed Natalie's mug and put a teabag in the steaming water.

"What do you mean?"

"I'm wondering if they may have some connection to Micah's death."

"I thought the sheriff had decided that was an accident."

She added more java to her mug from the coffeemaker on the counter. "That's the obvious answer. But there are a few things about the death that bother him, so he's digging deeper."

"Huh. I wonder what he found that raised a red flag."

"I don't know. He didn't share any details with me."

Steven sipped his coffee, his expression dubious. "It's hard to imagine anyone targeting Micah. I can't believe he had any enemies."

"I know. It's strange."

"Well, if there's anything dangerous happening around here, you may want to forgo your solo treks around the property."

She sent him a rueful grin. "The sheriff gave me the same advice, so I've confined my walks to this area and the driveway. But I miss hiking around the lake."

"Whenever I'm here, we can hike around the lake together. Safety in numbers, as they say."

"That would be great."

"Shall we meet up today after you finish with Natalie?"

"Yes. I'll drop my laptop off at the cottage, change shoes, and wait for you by the path. Eleven fifteen?"

"I'll be there." He winked and raised his mug.

She smiled, then headed back to the study, a mug in each hand.

But as she walked down the hall, her lips flattened.

Since neither Natalie or Steven could think of any legitimate explanation for someone to be on the property at night, it appeared that whoever was wandering about was here for illicit purposes.

Whether their presence had anything to do with Micah's death remained a question. One Brad would want to address.

She'd have to let him know about this new development ASAP.

So the minute she and Natalie finished for the day, she'd head back to the cottage and call him while she waited for Steven to come by for their walk.

And with warnings from both of the men who'd entered her life echoing in her mind, she was definitely going to avoid the path that led to the lake in the future unless she had company.

Because with compromised hearing, she was an easy target for someone who wanted to sneak up on her undetected. While her implants were a godsend, it wasn't always possible to distinguish and identify stray noises.

Besides, the sounds of nature during her walks often resulted in a cacophony of clatter unless she turned down the volume on her processors, and if she did that, she'd be even more vulnerable.

So this girl was playing it safe from here on out.

Until Brad found all the pieces to Micah's puzzle, she'd hunker down in the house or her cottage and confine her walks to circuits of the yard or treks with Steven whenever he was around.

And as long as she followed that prudent plan, what could possibly go wrong?

NINETEEN

BRAD CAME TO AN ABRUPT HALT on the path that led from Natalie's house to the guest cottage.

Watching Cara and Steven laugh together as they emerged from the woods on the trail behind the structure didn't make this a candidate for his best-Friday-ever list.

On the contrary.

The cozy scene pushed it down darn near the bottom.

But he *had* canceled their date last night, and if she wanted to take a hike with Natalie's cousin, he had no right to be upset.

Heck, he ought to be glad she'd found someone to go with instead of striking out on her own.

Except he wasn't.

Which made no sense, if he cared about her safety.

Unless . . .

Could he be . . . jealous?

That unexpected notion smacked him in the face.

Jealousy wasn't an emotion that had raised its ugly head in his life for more years than he could remember, yet the unpleasant sensation was as fresh as if he'd experienced it yesterday.

Yeah, he was jealous. The man who'd never expected to get involved with another woman was face-to-face with the green-eyed monster.

And it didn't feel good.

"Brad!" Cara caught sight of him and waved.

He hoisted up the corners of his mouth and lifted a hand in response.

The smile she'd been sharing with Steven warmed significantly as she beamed it toward him, and the tightness in his shoulders eased.

Maybe he didn't have anything to be jealous about after all.

"Were you looking for me?" She continued toward him, Steven half a step behind her.

"Yes. I got your voicemail. I was tied up with the state patrol when you called."

Her expression sobered. "Did you find the missing children?"

"Yes. Their father took them to get back at his ex-wife for having a restraining order issued against him. The kids are safe. He's locked up."

"I'm glad the outcome was positive."

"Me too. It could have gone downhill fast. I've seen that happen." He transferred his attention to her companion. "Hello, Steven. If you'll be available in a few minutes, I'd like to talk with you."

"Sure. Just knock on the back door. I'll be working in the kitchen." He turned to Cara. "Have a safe drive back to Cape, and enjoy your weekend."

"Thanks."

He circled around them and strolled down the path toward the house.

Brad shifted his attention to Cara. "Sorry to interrupt, but I'm glad I caught you before you left. It sounded as if you had something important to tell me, and since I had other business in this area anyway, I swung by."

"I do have news. But first, in case you were wondering, there was nothing to interrupt. I've been heeding your advice about sticking close to the house instead of taking my daily walks around the lake. When Steven offered to go with me today, I jumped at the chance to stretch my legs. It was all about safety in numbers, nothing more."

Her people-reading skills were remarkable.

"Can I admit that relieves my mind, without sounding too possessive?"

"You can. And you can also put any worries to rest. There's only one man on this property who interests me in anything beyond friendship."

"Nice to know."

"Now that we've cleared up your concern, what's in the bag?" She motioned to the white sack in his hand.

"A peace offering for the canceled date." He lifted it. "There's a Mennonite bakery not far from here that has the best chocolate chip cookies on the planet, baked fresh every day. I picked some up en route. I thought we could share them while you tell me why you called."

"Mm. Much tastier than my usual fruit-and-yogurt lunch. Let me get a couple of waters." She pivoted and jogged toward the door.

As she disappeared inside, he took the same chair he'd claimed for their previous chat in front of the cottage.

She reappeared less than a minute later.

"That was quick." He took the bottle she handed him.

"I move fast if homemade chocolate chip cookies are in the offing." She sank into the other chair. "I don't bake often, so this will be a treat."

"No time, or no inclination?"

"Both." She twisted off the cap of her water. Studied him for a moment. Sighed. "If the way to a man's heart is through his stomach, I'm not certain I should tell you this yet . . . but in the interest of full disclosure, I'm not much of a cook. Jack's the chef among the siblings."

"A culinary degree isn't a top priority for me in a relationship."

Her lips scrunched into a rueful twist. "I don't even do the basics well. Cooking Chuck's simple fare at the diner would be gourmet for me."

"So what do you eat?"

"A lot of salad. But I do make a mean omelet and a great potato casserole. Ever since Jack claimed he almost broke a tooth on my barbecued ribs, my siblings always request those two items when it's my turn to host our monthly meal."

"I like salad, and my meatloaf and chili are decent. I'm also proficient on the grill. If I want fancier food, I go to a restaurant. In terms of dessert, it's hard to beat these." He lifted the bag again. "Besides, it isn't fair to expect a woman to handle all the cooking chores."

She grinned. "I like how you think. And I'm ready to try one of those cookies whenever you are."

He set his water down, opened the bag, and held it out.

Cara reached in and took a cookie. Bit into it while he pulled one out for himself. Closed her eyes.

"See what I mean?" He started on his.

"These are incredible." She chewed slowly, as if savoring every burst of flavor from the crumbly goodness.

"Help yourself to another one." He picked up the bag again.

She didn't hesitate to accept the invitation. "You can ply me with these anytime."

"I'll keep that in mind." He finished off his cookie and swigged his water. "Now tell me why you called earlier."

As soon as she finished chewing, she launched into her story.

He listened without interrupting, the red flags that had

continued to flutter in his mind about Micah's death waving harder with every sentence.

The groundskeeper's dislike of the dark, along with the fact that someone had been wandering about on Natalie's property at odd hours, helped justify further investigation.

"So what do you think?" Cara moved on to her second cookie.

"I think I'm going to take a walk around the property in the vicinity of where you think you saw the lights last night."

"It would be hard to pinpoint the spot. I couldn't gauge distance very well."

"I'm still going to walk around the general area."

"What happens if you don't find anything suspicious?"

Excellent question, given that was the probable outcome without an exact location to search.

"It would be helpful to have eyes on the place at night, but we don't have the manpower for that, and I doubt Natalie would want to incur the cost of private security. The lights you've seen in the past—were they all in the same vicinity?"

She stopped chewing. "Now that you mention it, yes."

"A few security cameras in that area would be helpful. I'll see if I can get her to spring for those. Has there been any pattern to your sightings?"

"Not that I can remember, except they've usually been later at night. After ten for sure, sometimes later."

"You're a night owl."

"Guilty as charged."

"What about days of the week?"

She shook her head. "I'm sorry. I can't remember what days I saw the others. I've only noticed the lights three or four times."

"No worries. There wasn't any reason you should have committed that information to memory." He brushed off his hands. "I'm going to walk down the path a ways and poke around before I talk to Steven and Natalie. But first—can we reschedule our dinner?"

The corners of her mouth rose. "I thought you'd never ask."

"Why don't we try for Wednesday next week?"

"I'll pencil it in."

"Write it in ink." He stood and held out the cookies. "You keep the rest."

She took the bag without argument. "Trust me, they won't go to waste. Or rather, they will. To *my* waist."

"An occasional indulgence never hurt anyone. And you look great to me." He gave her a slow, appreciative once-over that heightened her color.

A sudden urge to kiss her surged through him, too strong to resist. And since she'd initiated the last lip-lock, how risky could it be to take the lead today?

Without giving himself a chance to get cold feet or weigh pros and cons, he leaned down and pressed his lips to hers. Lingered. Pulled back at her sweet response before he overstepped.

"I'll call you this weekend." The promise came out hoarse, and he cleared his throat.

"Please do."

At her breathy encouragement, he almost succumbed to the temptation to claim another, more intense kiss. But somehow he managed to resist. Rushing this relationship would be a mistake, in light of their backgrounds.

He backed away, then turned and strode down the path toward the lake, glancing over his shoulder at the edge of the woods.

Cara was standing by the chairs, cookie bag clutched in her hand, fingers pressed to her lips. As if she was relishing the kiss as much as she had the other sweet treat he'd given her today.

The feeling was mutual.

But as Brad continued down the path, in the direction of Cara's mysterious sightings, he switched mental gears. His focus for the remainder of his visit had to be on the death of an innocent man.

Because all the troubling evidence that continued to accumulate was more and more suggesting that while the cause of Micah's death had been drowning, the manner may have been murder.

WHY COULDN'T HIS GRANDFATHER have been more clear about the location of the treasure?

Steven tossed back the dregs of his scotch, pulled out the bottle he'd tucked into his overnight bag for this weekend visit with Natalie, and refilled the glass.

A map would have been far more helpful than the reference to "tucked somewhere safe, down in the dark" that had led him on a fruitless, weeks-long search of Natalie's basement, poking into every nook and cranny and box and chest filled with decades of junk while his cousin slept at night.

Until the lightbulb had gone off in his head the day he'd shown Cara the hiking trail.

Of course his grandfather had meant the cave. Limestone caves were cool, dark, and dry. That's why the Nazis had stored much of their looted art treasures there during the war. Why the US government had warehoused vital federal records in caves for decades.

They were the perfect place to hide and preserve valuable objects.

Like the paintings and jewelry his grandfather had taken from an estate in Germany during World War II after the US Army moved into the area and the owners fled.

And since lore pegging the place as haunted would discourage unauthorized exploration, he was free to roam about in the cave without fear of discovery.

He paced over to the window in the guest bedroom of the

house where he'd been relegated after the professor took up residence in the cottage that had always been his private domain.

If she hadn't spotted his flashlight, no one would ever have suspected there was activity on the premises at night.

He took a gulp of the scotch and glared at the cottage.

At least Cara would be gone soon, back in Cape for the weekend, and he'd have free run of the place.

Unless the sheriff got Natalie to agree to install security cameras.

The man had made a valiant effort when he'd stopped in after sharing cookies and a kiss with Cara outside the cottage.

Steven scowled as he replayed the touching little scene he'd watched from his bedroom that had confirmed what he'd already concluded.

The two of them were smitten with each other—meaning Cara had the sheriff's ear. If she saw anything else suspicious, he'd be all over it.

Luckily, Natalie hadn't been convinced that installing cameras would produce results.

And he'd reinforce that conclusion over the next two days.

But at the moment, the cameras were less of a worry than the questions Brad Mitchell had asked him about his whereabouts the day Micah died.

Those had come out of left field, after Natalie retired to her room for her afternoon nap.

Steven finished his drink. Examined the empty glass.

Dare he have a third?

No.

He shouldn't be drinking at all. He had to keep his wits about him.

Fisting his free hand at his side, he drew a steadying breath.

Who knew why the sheriff was checking alibis? The man hadn't provided a rationale, other than to say he was talking to everyone who visited Natalie's place. It had all been very low key and friendly.

But his eyes had been sharp. Probing.

Conclusion?

Brad Mitchell wasn't wasting his time tracking people down to talk to unless he had serious cause to believe Micah's death hadn't been an accident.

Steven did his best to tamp down the sudden uptick in his pulse. There was no cause for worry. He was in the clear.

Thank goodness he'd had the foresight to leave Saturday evening and go to his gym on Sunday morning, where there had been plenty of witnesses to attest to his presence the day Micah had died.

What no one knew was that he'd hung out all night in his car on the vacant property he'd scouted out half a mile from Natalie's. Nor did anyone know he'd gone straight to the gym on Sunday morning after he'd done what he had to do, stopping en route only to dispose of the bloody ski cap in a quick-shop dumpster. All the witnesses knew was that he'd been on the elliptical by a few minutes after nine o'clock.

So whatever had the sheriff sniffing around would lead him nowhere.

Nevertheless, going forward it would be prudent to search only during Cara's absences. No need for any more Thursday arrivals. He'd just have to extend his Friday and Saturday hunts to compensate for the lost night. Since he could only disappear for so long on his daily "hikes," evening sessions would be in order again—just as they'd been after Micah had started giving him the evil eye. Shouldn't be a problem, though. Natalie had grown accustomed to him sleeping late.

And long nights would be worth it if his clandestine forays led somewhere.

He crossed to the bed and picked up the notebook where he'd been mapping the cave as he searched. Paged through it, frowning. The network of passageways was a literal maze, leading to a hunt that was long and frustrating.

Was it possible he'd missed some clue that would make it easier?

He zipped open the side pocket on his suitcase and pulled out the folder containing the letter he'd found among his father's papers last spring after his dad's sudden death, along with his grandfather's handwritten inventory. Sat on the edge of the bed to reread the letter.

Steven,

There is a less-than-honorable chapter in our family history that I must share with you. I didn't learn about it myself until shortly before my father died fifteen years ago.

As I sat with him during his final hours, he rambled quite a bit. One of the things he told me was that while he was overseas during the war, he took valuables from an estate in Germany after US forces captured the area. Once he returned home, he hid the valuables on Robert's property, unbeknownst to his brother. The most I could get from him was that the objects were tucked somewhere safe, down in the dark. He kept trying to throw the covers off his bed, saying he had to go back and get them, return them to their rightful owner.

I thought the story might be nothing more than a hallucination, which can happen near the end of life. But I found the enclosed list among his papers, along with the location of the estate in Germany, so I assume what he told me was true.

I always intended to follow through on his wish to return the items but had no idea where to look. And I've been occupied with other, more pressing issues. Perhaps you can take this up as time permits.

Steven closed the folder.

Yes, he'd definitely taken up the search.

But he had no intention of returning any treasures he found.

Maybe, if clients weren't fleeing and his business wasn't floundering after bad investment decisions, he'd have considered it. Likewise if his father had bequeathed him any money instead of losing his shirt in a bad business deal that had left liens on the property his son should have inherited—no doubt the pressing issues he'd referred to in his letter. Or if said son wasn't hanging by his fingernails financially, a hair's breadth away from losing everything.

That kind of jeopardy could lead a man to do desperate things.

Like commit murder.

The scotch gurgled in his stomach, and he swallowed.

That had been unfortunate.

But Micah had been unnerving, with his sudden propensity to materialize out of the woods and stare at him. Like he knew that the St. Louis cousin whose visits had mushroomed in recent months was up to something shady.

What choice had he had, except to eliminate that threat? It wasn't like anyone but Natalie had even noticed the passing of the man. He'd been a nobody, with nothing of value to his name. Not only warped but a loser through and through.

It might be possible to survive on a paltry salary living as a groundskeeper on a remote estate like this, but if you aspired to more, if you wanted to make your mark in the world, you needed solid financial footing.

The price the items on his grandfather's list would command on the black market would get him closer to that goal.

Access to Natalie's funds, which would be his someday anyway, would also help—if he could ever convince her to move to St. Louis and cede full control of her financial affairs to him. But that had been a losing battle up to this point.

Leaving him no other way to fix his money problems besides

exploiting the potential alternative source of income that had dropped into his lap.

If he could find the jewelry and the paintings.

Clearly there were many more trips to that abysmal cave in his future.

He suppressed a shudder as he slid the folder and notebook into his overnight bag.

That so-called haunted cave could freak a person out.

But he'd suck it up and get the job done. Just like he'd gotten the gory, stomach-churning job done with Micah. As long as the sheriff left him alone, Natalie remained convinced that security cameras were overkill, and Cara didn't stumble on any other helpful tips for law enforcement.

Because he was in too deep to back off. After all the hours he'd invested and all the unpleasantness he'd had to put up with, he wasn't giving up his quest. Spending his nights in a tomb-like cave was no fun. And Chloe was getting annoyed with his every-weekend visits to his cousin. Not that she wasn't busy on weekends too with her vet practice, but she wasn't going to play second fiddle forever.

And he needed to keep her around in case he had to restock his supply of sux on the sly.

Who knew when he'd started dating her that one day he'd have use for a drug designed to produce short-term paralysis?

He pulled his laptop from its case, moved to the overstuffed chair by the bed, and accessed the dark web.

Selling his bounty would be tricky, especially the paintings, but there were buyers for everything—including stolen goods—as long as you did your homework.

If the jewelry was as gem-studded as his grandfather's list suggested, however, it might be safer to take out the stones and sell them loose to remove the connection to their original setting.

Whichever option he chose, a source of serious money was

sitting in a cave almost within spitting distance, and he wasn't giving up until he had it in hand.

As for anyone else who got in his way?

Like his long-lost relative, Marie, they too would come to a bad and mysterious end.

TWENTY

"OH MY. THIS IS BECOMING QUITE . . . JUICY."

As Natalie paused in her translating on Tuesday morning, Cara looked up from her keyboard. "More about MSL?"

"Yes."

"He's taking up an increasing amount of space in her journal, isn't he?"

"Indeed he is. Let's see . . . this entry is how long past the first mention of him?"

Cara scrolled back until she found the original reference. "Three months."

"I think they've progressed beyond the conversation phase." Natalie adjusted her glasses and began translating again.

> *MSL is back! It feels as if he's been gone for years instead of weeks. Oh, how I live for the hours we can be together, limited though they are.*
>
> *We met in the usual spot tonight. He brought wine and I brought a picnic. From our perch up there, the moon was full and bright, the night so warm and clear. Somehow we forgot about the food.*
>
> *I know what happened next was wrong. All of our meetings have been wrong, of course, but this was very wrong. Still, I love him with all my heart, and I want him to know that. This seemed the best way to demonstrate the depth of my feelings.*

The stolen hours we shared have only made me want more, and God forgive me, I hope he feels the same. That someday he'll realize we were meant to be together. I know it's wicked of me to wish for that, and unfair to the others involved, but I can't help hoping my dreams will come true.

Cara stopped typing as Natalie finished. "I think your take is spot-on. They've moved past talking."

"And this entry does line up with the story Paul told me. But we may never know for sure if she doesn't reveal his name or offer any clues about his identity."

"She might, later on." Cara tapped a finger against the keyboard. "I wonder if her reference to a 'perch up there' could mean the clifftop here on the property?"

"I'd say that's a distinct possibility, since she also fell from there. Especially if this man was involved in that incident."

"You know . . . we could always skip ahead and read the final entries. They may answer our questions."

Natalie waved that suggestion aside. "I can wait. I like watching the story unfold in order. Besides, patience is a virtue."

"Not one of mine, sad to say."

"Nor the sheriff's. He called me yesterday to ask again if I'd be willing to put security cameras along the path to the lake. I'm as anxious as he is to catch whoever is trespassing in light of their possible connection to Micah's death, but unless we put in a dozen cameras, it seems like an exercise in futility. We're not even certain if the lights you've been seeing were on the path or in the woods."

It was hard to argue with that.

But if Brad was pushing for cameras, the suggestion had merit. He wasn't the type to waste time or money on efforts that hadn't much chance of producing results.

"I wonder if it would be worth putting in one or two as a test? See if any motion-detection alerts come through."

"That's a given, thanks to all the animals on the property. The deer alone would keep anyone monitoring the cameras busy. I did talk to Steven about this, and he's skeptical they would produce much beyond wildlife too. But I haven't taken the idea off the table. If you continue to see lights, I may revisit the decision. Shall we get back to the journal?"

And that was the end of that discussion for today.

Natalie continued translating for another forty minutes, ending their session promptly at eleven o'clock.

"Brad's housekeeper is coming by at noon today to talk with me about taking over for Lydia. Cross your fingers it works out." Natalie closed Marie's journal.

She already knew about that, thanks to Brad. But true to his word, when he'd passed on her name to Natalie, he'd simply said that he'd heard about Lydia's departure from someone in town. Which he had—*after* their discussion. Apparently, there was a server at the local diner who knew everything there was to know in town.

"If Brad likes her, I bet you will too." Cara shut down her laptop.

"He does appear to be an excellent judge of character." Winking, Natalie grasped her cane and stood.

Cara let that pass as Natalie walked the journal back to the desk. "You can tell me all about her tonight at dinner."

"I'll do that. I hope you have a productive afternoon."

After gathering up her tablet and pen, Cara headed back to the cottage.

The weather had turned a tad chilly, and she picked up her pace down the path. Fall was settling in, air crisp, sky deep blue, leaves brilliant shades of yellow and russet, light golden. Such a perfect autumn day.

It was hard to believe any dark currents could be rippling under the placid surface of such an idyllic setting.

Yet strange happenings had been occurring since the day

she arrived. Dizzy spells, a house fire, lights in the woods, the theft of a valuable stamp, a suspicious death. Not to mention the mystery of Marie, with its ominous overtones, which predated all of the current incidents.

Was it possible this place was jinxed?

She rolled her eyes.

No, of course not. That was ridiculous.

Nevertheless, all of the weird goings-on were more than a little perturbing.

So despite how much she enjoyed working with Natalie . . . despite her stimulating research and writing . . . she wouldn't mind if they wrapped up the translation sooner than scheduled. Then she could return to her safe, cozy condo back in Cape, where the scariest thing that ever happened was an occasional tornado warning that sent her scurrying to the basement to wait out storms far more predictable than the tempest churning below the surface here.

NOT AGAIN.

Biting back a word he never said, Brad punched the end button on his cell and dropped into his desk chair.

With the early flu wave sweeping through the department and decimating the ranks, he'd have to fill in and take on a patrol shift tomorrow night instead of enjoying his long-awaited dinner with Cara.

At this rate, she was going to think he didn't want to see her.

But he couldn't conjure up extra deputies out of thin air.

Heaving a sigh, he called her number.

She answered on the first ring. "Good morning. Or should I say afternoon, now that it's a few minutes past noon?" She sounded cheery and upbeat.

Not for long.

"It's afternoon—but either way, it's not good."

"Uh-oh." Her inflection deflated. "Why do I think I'm about to get bad news?"

"Because you're a smart, intuitive woman."

"Our date is off again, right?"

"Yes, and I'm totally bummed. But I've got three deputies out with the flu, and we're a small operation. There's only so much juggling I can do with the schedule unless I give people back-to-back shifts, and that's a last resort. I don't like having deputies on duty who are sleep-deprived. I'm going to have to run a patrol shift tonight."

"Dang."

"Ditto."

A sigh came over the line. "I can't tell you how disappointed I am—but I do understand. Do you want to reschedule?"

"Absolutely. Are you free tomorrow night? I can finagle the schedule to make that work." If he put in a double shift himself and made do with a quick nap before their date. But it would be worth a bout of exhaustion to have two or three uninterrupted off-duty hours with Cara.

"I wish I could, but I'm going back to Cape tomorrow afternoon. One of my doctoral students hit a glitch on his dissertation, and I offered to take a brief hiatus from my sabbatical and meet with him early Friday morning."

That figured.

But how could he complain, when his own job had messed with their plans twice?

"I get it. Duty calls."

"Can we pick a day next week?"

"Why don't I call you Sunday after I see how the department flu epidemic shakes out? I don't want to have to cancel a third time, or you might write me off."

"Not happening."

"Good to know." He leaned back in his chair. "Any more moving lights in the woods?"

"No. I check periodically at night now that I'm alerted to it, but everything's been quiet. Natalie told me you tried again to convince her to install cameras."

"I did. She wasn't ready to commit."

"That's what I heard. She seems convinced the only alerts you'd get would be from wandering deer."

"She could be right. All the same, I think it's worth a try. If Micah hadn't turned up dead, I wouldn't be as concerned, but I sense there's a connection between the two."

"She said if I saw any more lights, she'd rethink her decision."

"That's something, I guess." Rod appeared in his doorway, and he tipped his chair upright. "I have a visitor. Expect a call Sunday."

"I'll look forward to it."

As he ended the call, Brad motioned Rod in. "What's up?"

"I got the tox screen back on Micah Reeves."

"That was much quicker than usual."

"Must have been a slow week at the lab. Either that, or they got tired of me bugging them. This case has been on my mind."

"That makes two of us. What did you get?"

"Nothing. Screen was clean as a whistle."

Not unexpected, but it would have helped if the findings had offered even a tiny clue.

"I can't say I'm surprised in light of what I've learned about him."

Rod stuck his hands in his pockets. "I'm not coming up with grounds to rule this as anything but accidental, Brad—other than the unidentified vomit. Without a suspect to test for a match, though, that doesn't help us."

"I hear you. But there are a few other loose ends I'm trying to tie up that came to light during the investigation. Can you hold off on the final report for another couple of weeks?"

"Sure. You have any real leads, or are you going on instinct?"

May as well be honest.

"No leads in the sense you mean, but there are pieces of the puzzle that don't fit. My gut tells me that all it will take to connect the dots is one solid clue. However, if that doesn't surface soon, I'll have to let this go."

"No rush on my end to issue the final report. It's not like we have family clamoring for it."

"That's another incentive for me not to walk away from this too fast. If I don't push for answers, no one will. It's not like Micah has anyone else to speak for him. And if there was a violent element to his death, justice should be served."

Rod grinned and gave him a thumbs-up. "I knew there was a reason we elected you sheriff. Good luck with this one."

"Thanks."

But as Rod disappeared through the door, Brad wiped a hand down his face and sank back in his chair again.

Luck, good fortune, fate, providence—he'd take any of those he could get with this case.

Bottom line, he needed a lead. Soon. Otherwise, he'd have to drop this. There weren't enough hours in the day as it was, and beating his head against the wall with nothing to show for it would be foolish, even if his efforts were well intentioned.

All he could do was pray that if Micah's death wasn't as innocent as it had initially appeared, he'd get a break that would help him find the person who had killed a quiet, gentle man in cold blood.

CARA BLEW OUT A FRUSTRATED BREATH as she rounded a curve on the winding, two-lane road that led to Natalie's house.

How in the world could she have forgotten the laptop she needed for tomorrow's nine o'clock meeting with her doctoral candidate?

Except the constant thoughts about a handsome sheriff

that had taken up residence in her mind did have a tendency to short-circuit her usual concentration.

Which also meant the absence of her laptop hadn't registered until eight o'clock.

That's what romantic daydreams could do to you.

Cara slowed as she approached Natalie's driveway in the ten o'clock darkness, cut her headlights, and reduced her speed to a crawl. No sense announcing her arrival and waking up her hostess. If she heard someone driving up to the house at this hour, she could panic. Call the police.

And while seeing Brad would be lovely, a rendezvous under those circumstances would be less than ideal.

Tightening her grip on the wheel, she focused on the edges of the narrow gravel road. Difficult to discern, with the moon and stars hidden behind a heavy cloud cover. But it was a short drive, and she'd traveled it often in recent weeks. She ought to be able to navigate despite the limited visibility.

Nevertheless, when the house came into view over a small rise, she exhaled.

Almost there.

And no way was she retracing her steps to Cape tonight. She'd just have to get up at the crack of dawn and drive back super early for her meeting. Not how she'd planned to spend her Friday morning, but it was what it was.

As she drew close to the house, a BMW parked in front materialized out of the darkness.

Huh.

Steven must have come down for another long weekend.

Must be nice to have a job that was portable.

She pulled in behind his car on the circle drive, grabbed her purse, and closed the door gently after sliding from behind the wheel.

As she circled the dark house, she dug out her key to the cottage, angling sideways when a chilly wind buffeted her.

Fall had definitely arrived.

Key in hand, she started down the murky path, peering ahead toward the shadowy outline of the cottage to stay on track.

Maybe she should pull out her phone and turn on the—

She jolted to a stop as a light flashed in her peripheral vision to the left. In the woods.

Nerves tingling, she swiveled that direction.

All was dark.

Had she imagined the fleeting flare of light? Was her mind playing—

The light bobbed again, and her pulse surged.

No, she hadn't imagined it.

Putting her feet in gear, she hurried to the door, fitted her key in the lock, and let herself in. Then she slid the bolt into place and dug out her cell.

It was late, but this time she wasn't waiting to call Brad. If the person who'd been making nocturnal appearances on Natalie's property was back, this could be an opportunity to catch them. Assuming Brad or one of the deputies was available, and that whoever was here wasn't in a hurry to leave.

She tucked herself into a corner and peeked out the window as she placed the call. The light was still flickering through the trees, but it appeared farther away now.

"Cara? What's wrong?"

At Brad's terse question, she leaned back against the wall. "The person with the light is back."

A second ticked by.

"Where are you?"

"Natalie's. I'm in the cottage." She gave him a topline of her blunder, omitting the cause. It wasn't his fault her brain was shorting out, thanks to all the electricity sparking between them. "I know it's late, but—"

"No apology necessary. Your timing is impeccable. I'm on

patrol again, not far away. You didn't see any strange cars around when you pulled in, did you?"

"No."

"Lock the door and sit tight. I'm going to park out of sight, come in on foot, and scout around in the dark."

"Will you stop by after you're finished?"

"It could be late. If I don't find anything, I may hang around in the woods for a while. See if whoever is there starts moving again."

"I doubt I'll be asleep, and I'd like to know what you find."

"Okay. You may want to try and catch a few z's while you wait, though. You have your pepper gel?"

"Yes."

"Keep it handy, just in case."

"You think I'm in danger?" Her heart picked up speed again.

"No. I'm erring on the side of caution. This person hasn't bothered you in the past, and I doubt they'll change their pattern. Hang tight."

As Brad ended the call, Cara tucked her phone away and pulled out her pepper gel. Eyed the bed.

It could be a long night, and sitting in the dark as the minutes turtled by would be über stressful.

Why not at least lie down, even if the odds of falling asleep were tiny?

Wiping her palms one by one down her leggings, she crossed to the bed, pulled back the quilt, and slid under the comforting warmth, pepper gel in hand.

If fate was kind, Brad would find the person who'd been frequenting Natalie's property for weeks, at minimum. Perhaps much longer. Who knew how long they'd been around before she'd spotted them?

And if Brad confronted them, maybe they'd finally have answers that would help explain Micah's mysterious demise.

Except . . .

She frowned.

An encounter in the dark woods could also be dangerous. If someone was involved in criminal activity, they wouldn't want to get caught. And if whoever was out there was responsible for Micah's death, they could still have a murderous mindset.

Meaning Brad—or anyone—who got in their way could be in deadly peril.

TWENTY-ONE

NOTHING.
Nada.
Zip.
Reining in his frustration, Brad turned up the collar of his jacket. Gave the woods and path one more slow sweep from the concealed spot he'd staked out after he'd done a quiet, meticulous walk-through in the entire area visible from the guest cottage window.

No human movement then, no human movement now.

Whoever had been here must be long gone. Perhaps the person had passed through rather than lingered.

In any case, after more than two hours of silent, motionless surveillance in the bone-chilling wind, it was time to call it a night.

Brad pushed himself to his feet and shook out his stiff muscles.

He'd check in with Cara, let her know his reconnaissance had been a bust, and—

He froze.

Someone, or something, was on the move.

It could be a deer. A few had gone by earlier.

Except this didn't sound like a deer.

It sounded more like a pair of boots clumping along, breaking sticks and scattering stones along the way. Human footwear made far more noise than the small hooves of a buck or doe.

Brad cocked his ear toward the noise.

It was coming from the path, not the woods, in the direction of the lake. Otherwise, the dead leaves would rattle as branches were pushed aside.

Whoever or whatever it was would be within ten feet of him when they passed.

Pulse accelerating, he crouched down.

Waited.

A light flickered through the trees in the distance.

Definitely human.

Brad pulled out his cell and texted Larry for backup.

Sixty seconds later, a figure in black appeared on the trail, flashlight aimed at the ground. The tall, bulky build suggested the interloper was a man.

Best plan? Stay on the guy's tail until Larry arrived—and hope the man wasn't armed. A shooting match wasn't in his plans for this night, despite the pistol on his hip and all the hours he'd clocked at the range.

The intruder passed by, but his features would have been impossible to discern in the darkness even without the ski mask he wore.

Natalie's trespasser wasn't taking any chances on being recognized.

In light of his camouflage, the security cameras Natalie had rejected wouldn't have helped identify him.

As the masked man passed by, Brad edged out from his hiding spot. Fell in behind him.

Once they reached the clearing by the house and cottage at the edge of the woods, he'd have to stay farther back and—

He came to an abrupt halt as two does barreled through the brush a handful of yards in front of him and bounded out of the woods.

The man swung around. Froze when he realized he was being followed. Took off down the path, toward the cottage and house.

Brad sprinted after him, identifying himself and demanding that he stop.

He didn't.

Instead, he ran faster.

Brad surged forward too, but he didn't intend to get too close. Not without backup.

Now that the man was on the run, however, it would be tougher to keep tabs on him until Larry got here.

All at once, the intruder veered into the woods.

Wonderful.

Pursuit through a dense thicket would complicate this chase exponentially.

Nevertheless, Brad followed him in, pushing aside branches, keeping him in sight for the first twenty yards—until mother nature, in the form of a tree root, intervened.

His foot caught and he went down.

Hard.

Biting back a word he never used, he pushed himself to his feet. Gritted his teeth as pain exploded in his ankle the instant he tried to put weight on it.

The word spilled out.

Nothing felt broken, but at the very least he had a bad sprain. Worst case, he'd torn a tendon or ligament.

Didn't matter.

He was out of this race.

In the distance, the noise of someone hurtling headlong through the underbrush gradually receded.

The trespasser was history.

Expelling a breath, he gripped the tree beside him with one hand to prop himself up and called Larry.

"I'm ten minutes out." His chief deputy's tone was all business.

"Don't bother. I tripped while in pursuit and he got away."

A beat ticked by.

"You went after him without backup?"

Not the smartest choice in general, but he wanted this mystery solved. ASAP.

"Yeah. I intended to lay low and watch him until you got here, but two deer foiled that plan. I hoped he'd stop when I yelled at him."

"Do they ever?"

Good point.

"Only if they aren't guilty."

"Bingo. You sure you don't want me to come out there anyway?"

"There's nothing we can do tonight. It's dark as pitch in the woods. I'll come back tomorrow at first light and look the area over in case he dropped anything while he was running away. If he did, it will still be there."

"You're the boss. Ten-four."

As Brad stowed his phone, he listened again.

Nothing but the *hoo-h'HOO-hoo-hoo* of a great horned owl broke the stillness.

The trespasser was gone.

Holding on to trees for support, he limped back to the trail and continued toward the cottage, wincing with every step.

At the door, he took a steadying breath and gave a soft knock.

No response.

He tried again.

The curtain on the window beside the door fluttered, and he moved in front of it so Cara could see him.

Seconds later a bolt slid and the door opened. "Come in." She stepped back to give him access.

He moved inside. "Were you asleep?"

"Yes, believe it or not. I laid down to wait for you and drifted off."

"I'm not surprised. It's almost one."

"Did you see anything?"

"Oh yeah." He motioned to the café table and chairs against the wall. "Do you mind if I sit?" Maybe that would ease the throbbing in his ankle.

"Sure. Can I turn on a light?"

"No problem. The guy's long gone." He limped over to the chair and gingerly lowered himself to it, trying not to grimace.

A soft glow filled the room after Cara flicked a switch, and as she joined him, her eyebrows pinched together. "What happened to your leg?"

"Ankle." He gave her the short version. "It'll be fine." Even if his boot was getting uncomfortably tight. "The most important thing is that I did see a guy in the woods. I had him under surveillance and backup was on the way when two deer decided to wreak havoc with my plans. He took off, and while in pursuit I had my unfortunate encounter with the tree root. I'll come back in daylight to see if he may have dropped anything in his rush to get away."

"What happens if he didn't?"

"I wish I had the answer to that. It's possible I scared him and he'll never show again. If he does come back, though, you can bet he'll be extra cautious." He forked his fingers through his hair. "I'm going to talk to Natalie again tomorrow about cameras. With the guy concealing his face, we won't get a read on his identity, but at least we'll be alerted if he's on the premises and can try to get over here before he leaves. That shouldn't be hard, given the gap between your sighting and when he left."

"Which makes me wonder why he was on the property for so long and what he was doing while he was here."

"I had the same thought. What time are you leaving tomorrow?"

She wrinkled her nose. "I plan to be on the road by six. Is there any reason I should cancel my meeting?"

"No. The next steps with this are up to me and the deputies." He pushed himself to his feet, flinching as he tested his weight on the injured ankle. "I'll let you get back to sleep."

"Easier said than done after all this excitement."

"I hear you." He limped over to the door. "Lock up behind me."

"Trust me, that's my plan. Do you need a shoulder to lean on to get back to your car?"

A pair of crutches would be better, considering how far away he was parked, but he shook his head. "You'd have to walk back alone, and I'd rather know you're safe here. I'll call you with any news."

"You should get your ankle checked out."

"I'll think about it tomorrow." After a search of the woods. He leaned down and claimed a quick kiss. "Be careful driving."

"Always." She reached out and took his hand. Squeezed. "You be careful too. I don't have good feelings about whatever is going on here."

Neither did he.

"I always watch my back. Talk to you soon."

He exited, waited until he heard the bolt slide into place, then hobbled down the path toward the driveway.

The long walk back to his patrol car wasn't going to be fun.

Worse yet, he had little to show for his injury.

The ideal outcome tonight would have been to get the guy in custody, grill him to see if he knew anything about Micah's death, and find out what he was doing on the property for hours at a stretch.

But if nothing else, their suspicions about clandestine activity had been validated.

The challenge now was to figure out how to identify the nocturnal visitor who'd disrupted the peaceful ambiance of Natalie's place and determine whether his crimes were far more serious than mere trespassing.

STEVEN CLOSED HIS BATHROOM DOOR, yanked off his ski mask, and muttered a string of obscenities that would shock his dear cousin.

Tonight had been a disaster.

An utter, absolute, complete disaster.

And Cara was to blame, if the light that had come on in her cottage after the chase was any indication.

She must have seen his flashlight and alerted the sheriff to his presence. It couldn't have been Natalie. She'd gone to bed at nine thirty. And as she'd always told him, most nights she slept like a log as soon as her head hit the pillow—leaving her none the wiser about his late-night forays.

But what in blazes was Cara doing here, anyway? According to his cousin, she'd planned to leave early this week to go back to Cape. That's why he'd come for a long weekend again. It gave him an extra night to search in the cave. And her car hadn't been parked in front earlier.

So when had she come back? *Why* had she come back?

It didn't matter at this point, though.

He'd been seen.

Luckily he'd had the foresight to start covering his features, just in case he stumbled across anyone.

Nevertheless, the ski mask hadn't protected his face as he'd sprinted through the woods two hours ago, the sheriff in hot pursuit until he'd given up chase for unknown reasons.

Steven leaned closer to the mirror and examined the cut on

his forehead, courtesy of a branch that had grazed his temple as he ran through the dense thicket.

How was he going to explain that to Natalie tomorrow? Or the sheriff, if he showed up?

No, not if. When.

He *would* show up, no question about it.

Brad pulled a clean washcloth from the stash under the vanity, dampened it, and dabbed at the ragged edges of the cut. As blood soaked into the cloth, his stomach began to churn.

No.

He was *not* going to lose his dinner.

Swallowing past the bile that rose in this throat, he forced himself to clean the cut as best he could without upchucking. It wasn't deep, but it wasn't going to heal overnight, either.

Once he'd washed the abrasion, he threw the blood-stained cloth into the tub, slapped on a bandage he found in the medicine cabinet, and left the bathroom.

He ought to try and get some sleep. It was three in the morning, after all. Far later than he'd planned to be up. But returning to the house before the sheriff was gone would have been risky. Even when he'd finally snuck back, staying in the shadows, he'd been on full alert in case the man was hiding somewhere, like he'd been earlier.

He'd made it back undetected, though.

What he needed now was rest, to clear his head.

But before he slept, he had to come up with a credible explanation for the cut on his forehead.

He began to pace.

Planning his next moves was also critical. Like how to ramp up his efforts to get Natalie to leave and let him deal with the property. If she and the professor were gone, he'd have free rein of the place. He could stop worrying about someone finding out what he was up to, and he could search the cave during the day instead of into the wee hours of the night.

After the hellacious day he'd had dealing with creditors, a change like that couldn't come soon enough. Because the more hours he could devote to the search, the faster he'd find the treasure and put an end to his desperate financial straits.

But he could work on those plans tomorrow. Coming up with an explanation for the cut was more—

The hum of running water echoed in the house, and he froze.

Natalie must have gotten up to use the bathroom.

He strode over to the lamp on the nightstand and turned it off. She didn't tend to wander about at night, but if she did leave her room, she might notice the light shining under his door.

And he didn't want to have to come up with an excuse for that too.

As he waited in the darkness for silence to once again descend, an explanation for the cut began to form in his mind.

Yeah. That would work.

Doing what was necessary to give it credibility wouldn't help his queasy stomach, and he'd also have to time it well, but both were manageable.

The house grew quiet again, and Steven crossed to the bed. Shed his outerwear. Set his alarm.

It would be a short night, but he'd sleep in on Saturday.

Stretching out on the bed, he stared at the ceiling.

Of course the sheriff would tell Natalie what had happened tonight. First thing in the morning, if his take on the man was correct. And he'd no doubt try again to convince her to install security cameras. After listening to the man's story, it was possible she'd agree.

That shouldn't be a problem, however, as long as he knew where they were.

And he'd see that he did.

Filling his lungs, he forced his muscles to relax. To focus on the positive side of tonight's events.

Now that the sheriff had proof there was danger lurking here, it might be easier to convince Natalie to move to St. Louis and let him sell the place for her.

He smiled.

Who knew? Maybe tonight would end up working in his favor.

Because once she vacated the premises, and once the sheriff gave up his efforts to pin Micah's death on anything other than an accident, he should be home free.

He'd find the treasure, lock in the upscale lifestyle and image he'd created, and live the rest of his life on easy street—far away from the hand-to-mouth existence he'd endured growing up, thanks to his father's ineptitude with money.

And he'd never again have to visit this godforsaken piece of land, devote his weekends to an old lady, or spend his Friday and Saturday nights prowling through the dark bowels of a cursed, haunted hill from which a long-ago relative had plunged to her death.

TWENTY-TWO

BRAD PLANTED HIS FISTS ON HIS HIPS and surveyed the woods behind Natalie's house in the early morning light.

If last night's intruder had dropped anything in his haste to escape, it was well concealed. A thorough search had turned up nothing.

Nor had the hour-long hunt helped his ankle, even though he'd stopped at home to wrap it in an elastic bandage during the waning hours of his patrol last night. While compression had kept the swelling in check, tramping through dense wood on uneven terrain had only ratcheted up the pain again.

"You find anything?" Alan pushed through the brush and joined him in the small clearing.

"No. You?"

"Nothing a human would have dropped. But I did manage to find a pile of deer scat." He grimaced and lifted a boot.

Brad averted his head from the stench. "Get rid of it before you leave or you'll stink up the cruiser."

"That's my plan. You want to search anywhere else?"

"No. We covered a wide area in the vicinity the guy ran. I have no idea what direction he went from here." He rubbed the back of his neck. "This was a long shot anyway." But one he'd hoped would produce something. Anything.

"You going home to crash?"

"After I stop in to talk with Ms. Boyer."

Alan scanned his watch. "Isn't it kind of early?"

"A light came on in the kitchen about ten minutes ago. I'd say she's up. Thanks for lending your eagle eyes this morning."

"My eagle eyes didn't notice the deer scat."

Brad called up a weary grin. "You weren't looking for evidence of animals."

"True. If we're done here, I'll get back to my patrol duties." He struck off for the path that would take him past the cottage and around the house.

Brad followed at a slower pace, favoring his foot. It might not hurt to pay a quick visit to urgent care, on the off chance he'd done more serious damage than he thought.

Near as he could tell, though, it was a sprain. And he knew the treatment for that—rest, ice, compression, and elevation.

Like three of those four would happen anytime soon.

The light was still on in the kitchen, so rather than trek around to the front of the house on his sore foot, he climbed the stairs to the back galérie, grunting with each step.

Maybe he'd try the ice after he got home and take an aspirin . . . or two . . . or three.

He stopped at the back door and knocked.

Fifteen seconds later, a curtain was pushed aside on the window beside the door and Natalie's startled face appeared.

The fabric dropped back into place, the lock rattled, and the door opened.

"Brad! What on earth are you doing at my back door at this hour? And where's your car? I didn't see it out front."

"If I can come in, I'll be happy to answer all your questions."

"By all means." She pulled the door wide. "Have a seat. May I offer you coffee?"

He limped inside. "I'd be forever in your debt if you did. It's been a long night."

"You were on duty?"

"Yes." He gave her the short version of the rampaging flu bug and the department scheduling issues as he winced his way over to the table.

"What's wrong with your leg?"

"That's part of the story I have to tell you."

"Let me get your coffee and I'll give you my full attention." She crossed to a coffeemaker on the counter. "I like to have a pot at the ready for Steven. That boy is hooked on the stuff—the higher the octane, the better. I'm a tea woman, myself." She filled a mug and set it in front of him. "Black, as I recall from the dinner we shared the night of Micah's service."

"You have an excellent memory."

"Thank you." She sat beside him, lifted her tea, and waited.

"You didn't see my car because I parked it out of sight, farther down the drive. I didn't want to alarm you if you got up at the crack of dawn and saw it in front of the house."

"If you were on duty last night, why are you working again at this hour?"

He took a long, fortifying swig of coffee and gave her a full report on all that had happened during the night.

She listened as her tea grew cold, features taut, forehead furrowed. Only after he finished did she speak.

"This is most upsetting. The idea that someone is skulking about the property doing who knows what is—"

At a sudden, muted crash, she jerked.

Brad sprang to his feet. "Any idea what that was?"

"No, but I believe it came from the basement. Perhaps a box fell over. I've been down there rooting around lately."

"I'll check it out."

"Do be careful. We don't need any more excitement around here."

No kidding.

"Where's the basement access?"

"In the hall. First door on the right." She waved a hand that direction.

"Wait here." He left her at the table and moved quietly to the door. Eased it open just as Steven reached for the handle from the other side.

His pulse ratcheted down.

False alarm.

Or was it?

He frowned as the gash on the other man's temple registered.

"What happened? Are you hurt?"

"My pride more than anything else." Steven touched his forehead. Examined his bloody fingers. Paled. "But I did have a nasty encounter with a falling box."

"Come on up. Let me take a look."

He edged aside to allow the other man to emerge from the basement as Natalie appeared in the doorway.

"I heard voices and I—" She gaped at her cousin. "Steven! Was that you in the basement? And what happened to your head?"

"I woke up early and thought I'd make another attempt to find that box of your mother's personal items we were searching for last week. I lost my grip on one of the cartons on a top shelf. I was hoping to locate the one you were after and surprise you."

"Well, you succeeded on the surprise part." She laid a hand on her chest. "Come into the kitchen and we'll attend to that cut."

"I'll be fine. I'm sure I can take care of it myself."

"Humor me. Besides, I'd like Brad to weigh in on whether it requires stitches. You didn't black out, did you?"

"No, and I don't want to bother the sheriff with this. I

imagine he has far more important things to do than deal with a scratch."

Brad inspected the cut. "It's more than a scratch, and I can spare a few minutes."

"Well . . ." Steven shrugged. "If you're willing."

He followed Natalie into the kitchen and sat at the table.

She continued to a pantry on the other side of the room, removed a box, and set it beside her cousin. "First aid supplies. What do you think, Brad?"

"I'd like to clean it up, take a closer look. That okay with you, Steven?"

"Sure."

"There are latex gloves in here too." Natalie took the lid off the box. "Leftovers from the Covid era."

Brad pulled out a pair and tugged them on. After spraying a sterile gauze pad with antiseptic, he swabbed the gash. "Good news. No stitches required. But it should be cleaned and bandaged."

"Will you handle that if I play nurse?" Natalie positioned herself beside the box.

"I'll be happy to."

As Natalie handed him supplies while he took care of the cut, she filled Steven in on the events of the night.

He stared at her as the story wound down. "I can't believe all this is happening in such a quiet, out-of-the-way place."

"Me neither." She pulled a large bandage from the box. "We were lucky Cara had to come back or we'd never have confirmed that we have a trespasser. Brad, I believe I'll reconsider those cameras. Why don't we try two initially?"

"Sounds like a plan. I know a reputable firm that can handle installation for you. I'll have someone stop by." He reached past Steven and held out his hand for the bandage.

She passed it over. "Thank you for everything—including your housekeeper recommendation. I met with Margie Tuesday, and she'll be starting next week. She was very pleasant and struck me as a hard worker."

"Accurate on both counts." He finished securing the bandage and addressed Steven. "I don't expect you'll have any repercussions from that, but blows to the head can be tricky. If you get a severe headache or experience any nausea or dizziness, you should go to urgent care."

"Thanks. But you seem more in need of medical attention than I do, with that limp."

"I may stop there on my way home. Natalie, I'll be in touch."

"I'll walk you out. Steven, there's coffee on if you want a cup." She took the lead to the front door. "How far away are you parked?"

"Just over the rise."

"Would you like Steven or me to give you a lift to your car?"

"I appreciate the offer, but I can manage."

"Thank you again for all your efforts to get this puzzle figured out. And take care of that ankle."

"I will. Enjoy the rest of your day."

He two-footed it down the steps, leading with his uninjured foot on each one.

Despite his cautious descent, however, the ache in his ankle was inching up to an eight on the pain scale.

So before he went home, he'd drop in at urgent care.

And hope he got better results there than he had chasing his elusive quarry through the murky woods last night.

IT HAD WORKED LIKE A CHARM.

Steven smiled and sipped his java.

Reopening his early-morning wound hadn't been pleasant, but the story he'd concocted had given him a credible explanation for the cut. One both Natalie and the sheriff had bought without question.

On to step two.

"I'm so sorry about your injury, Steven." Natalie reentered the kitchen, clumping along with her cane. "But it was sweet of you to continue to search for the box of my mother's items. I know it's in the basement somewhere."

"We'll keep rummaging around until we find it." He set his mug down and feigned concern. "Natalie, after what happened last night, I'm more worried than ever about you being in this isolated place alone."

Her brow wrinkled. "I'm beginning to get a little worried myself."

That was the best news he'd had in weeks.

"You really ought to think about relocating to St. Louis. Help of every kind would be close at hand, and I'd be nearby too."

The grooves on her forehead deepened. "I do like the idea of having you within easy driving distance. And in case I haven't expressed my gratitude sufficiently, I do appreciate how you've devoted your weekends to me over the past few months. That's not fair to you, though. A young man like you shouldn't have to sacrifice all his free time for a distant relative."

"I don't think of it as a sacrifice." The lie glided off his tongue. "But I do have to admit my lady friend is becoming a bit annoyed with me." Perhaps playing the guilt card would expedite her decision.

Her eyebrows rose. "I didn't know you were dating anyone."

"It's been casual up to this point, but I think there could be serious potential if I gave her more attention."

Natalie's face sagged, her dismay clear. "And I've been keeping you from that." She sighed and pinched the bridge of her nose. "I don't want to be selfish. I do love this place, but perhaps holding on to the past isn't realistic. I can't stay here forever, I suppose—even if I found a retired couple or newlyweds to rent my cottage, like Cara suggested."

What?

He clenched his teeth.

The professor was all kinds of helpful, wasn't she?

Keeping his demeanor as pleasant as possible, he wrapped his hands around his mug. "When did that come up?"

"A week or two ago. I meant to discuss it with you, but my mind has been occupied with other matters."

"Understandable, in light of everything that's been happening around here."

"I'd have to expand the cottage to make that plan work, of course. I was going to get your input on the feasibility of that, but now you've given me another reason to move." She leaned over and laid her hand on his arm. "I don't want to stand in the way of your happiness, Steven."

Then she needed to move and give him control of her assets.

At least they were getting closer to that, thanks to the guilt play he'd made.

Why hadn't he tried that ruse sooner?

"I'm more concerned about *your* well-being, Natalie." He patted her hand. "Your safety is my priority."

"The cameras may help the sheriff find our trespasser."

"You wouldn't have to worry about trespassers in St. Louis."

"I do see the advantages of such a move. And I promise to give it serious consideration."

"If you decide to relocate, I can handle all the logistics for you."

"You're such a dear boy." She patted his hand and stood. "I'm going to reheat my tea. Would you like more coffee?"

"I'm fine." He drained his mug. "Is the new housekeeper coming today?"

"No, not until Tuesday." She slid her mug into the microwave, then crossed to the refrigerator and surveyed the contents. "I may have to run into town and do some grocery shopping today."

A perfect excuse to get away from her cloying solicitude.

"Why don't you let me do that for you?" He stood. "I was going to go in anyway. My cell service has been spotty since I arrived, and I have to call a few clients."

"Do you feel up to driving?"

"Yes. I think the fresh air will help. Write me out a list while I get my keys and wallet."

The corners of her lips rose. "I can see the benefits of having you close by. Much as I like Cara's suggestion about the cottage, it wouldn't be like having family on hand."

"Hold that thought."

He left the kitchen, his mouth flattening as he strode down the hall.

Cara was proving to be a colossal pain in the butt, with her flashlight sightings and cottage rental suggestions.

She couldn't be gone soon enough to suit him.

So it was possible he'd have to expedite her departure if Natalie continued to balk at his suggestion to move.

For now, though, he'd ratchet up his search and hope he'd strike pay dirt soon.

Because if he did, getting control of Natalie's financial affairs wouldn't be as urgent. He could always continue that campaign going forward, come up with tactics to make her doubt her self-sufficiency.

And who knew? Maybe the dizzy spells would return, or she'd have another lapse, like with the potholder.

Undermining her confidence in her ability to sustain an independent life would be child's play compared to what he'd had to do with Micah—and far less taxing than rooting about in a bat-filled cave.

He entered his bedroom and picked up his keys and wallet from the dresser. Blew out an annoyed breath.

Grocery shopping stunk. But it was a small price to pay for an excuse to get out of the house.

And when he came back, he'd take a long nap. Natalie wouldn't question that, after his injury.

But in reality, he wanted to be fully rested by tonight so he could put in extra hours searching for the treasure that had to be within grasp. There were a finite number of passageways, and all of them eventually dead-ended. Only a handful were left to explore.

And now that he'd done his homework, knew how to go about selling ill-gotten jewels and artwork, he was ready to cash in.

Jingling his keys, he retraced his steps down the hall, collected the list from Natalie, and let himself out through the front door.

If the cache in the cave was as rich as it sounded based on his grandfather's list, he might not even have to worry about convincing his cousin to move.

Wouldn't that be nice?

He could leave her here to rot in her forest and go back to the occasional obligatory visits designed to convince her he cared in order to secure his inheritance down the road. There was no question that she'd continue to fall hook, line, and sinker for his devoted cousin act, as she always had.

He snickered as he approached his BMW.

Old people were so easy to fool.

And Natalie was old. Gullible. Malleable.

She wasn't the one who could potentially thwart him.

That honor belonged to the sheriff and Cara.

But he'd deal with them if necessary, just like he'd dealt with Micah.

No one was going to stop him from securing the upscale life he'd grown accustomed to—and deserved.

No one.

TWENTY-THREE

WAS THAT... BLOOD?

Natalie paused as she straightened the sheets on Steven's bed—the least she could do after the dear boy had volunteered to trek into town for her groceries—and squinted at his pillow.

She leaned closer. Adjusted her glasses.

The faint smear certainly looked like blood.

Perhaps it was from a shaving nick that hadn't yet healed. Or a slight nosebleed.

Whatever the source, she ought to give him a fresh pillowcase. He deserved a spotless room after all the long drives he'd made down here and all the weekends he'd devoted to her.

He was such a treasure.

She shook the pillow out of the case and onto the bed, then started for the linen closet in the hall.

Stopped.

As long as she was tidying up, may as well check the bathroom. If he'd showered this morning, he'd welcome a fresh towel.

Pillowcase over her arm, she switched direction and walked over to the bathroom. Flipped on the light.

The pristine bath towel hung at the end of the tub.

No need to change that out.

As she turned away, a sliver of red caught her eye, peeking out from beyond the shower curtain.

Odd.

She entered the room and crossed to the tub.

A limp washcloth stained with blood lay in one corner. A lot more blood than was on the pillowcase.

What in the world?

A shaving nick would never have bled that much, though a nosebleed could have.

That had to be the explanation.

What else could it be?

Yet he'd never mentioned being prone to those.

However, many people kept physical ailments to themselves so those who cared about them didn't worry.

Her mouth bowed. That would be like Steven. He was such a considerate man.

Should she leave the cloth in the tub? If she took it, he might be embarrassed.

But they were family, and family watched out for each other. Besides, he hadn't minded letting her and Brad help him with the cut on his forehead today.

So she'd replace this cloth with a clean one and see what he had to say about the cause of the bleeding after he realized she'd freshened up his room.

She bent down, picked up the damp square, and added it to the pillowcase on her arm. Both of these would have to soak in the laundry room before being washed.

After taking care of that chore, she stopped at the linen closet, pulled out a new pillowcase and washcloth, and finished tidying up the room.

At the doorway, she looked back at the spruced-up space. Smiled.

One good turn deserved another, after all.

And wouldn't Steven be surprised by her thoughtfulness?

"**NO WORRIES.** I was glad to help. You're making excellent progress with your research, aside from this glitch. But I think we've worked that out."

As Cara spoke, the graduate student seated at the table in her office packed up his laptop and papers. "I do too. My problem was I got too immersed in the trees and lost sight of the forest."

"That can happen. Call me if you run into another snag."

"I will. Thanks again, Professor Tucker. Enjoy your weekend."

"You too."

As the student left, Cara rose, pulled out her phone, and walked over to the window, scrolling through messages.

Ah.

A text from Brad.

Her lips curved up as she scanned his note.

> Sorry again about our date. Hope your meeting this morning goes well. Wanted to let you know Natalie agreed to have two cameras installed. I'll arrange for that next week.

She put her fingers to work.

> Great news on the cameras. How's your ankle?

> Sprained, according to urgent care. It's wrapped and elevated as I type this. I'm about to crash. It was a long night.

> Did you find any trace of the trespasser?

> No.

>> Drat. Get some rest.

> That's the plan. Happy dancing tomorrow. I'll call you this weekend.

>> I'll look forward to it.

She started to slide the phone back into her pocket, only to have it begin vibrating again.

Maybe Brad had decided he'd rather hear her voice than communicate via text.

But the delicious tingle that rippled through her subsided quickly.

Jack's number was front and center on the screen.

Huh.

His calls had been few and far between since he'd been in Quantico.

She pressed talk. "This is a surprise."

"Are you all right?"

At his taut question, she frowned. "Of course. Why wouldn't I be?"

"I sent you three texts last night. You didn't return any of them."

Oh.

She scrolled back.

Yep, there they were.

"Sorry about that. I was a little frazzled by the end of the day."

"You never get frazzled. What's up?"

She watched a hawk swoop low over the athletic field in the distance, probably in pursuit of a quarry it had homed in on from high above with its keen eyes.

Like Jack homed in on comments that didn't ring true to him, thanks to his keen intuition.

She turned her back to the window. "You'd be frazzled too if you'd just finished a two-hour drive back to Cape and realized you had to retrace your steps because you'd forgotten the laptop you needed for an important meeting this morning. I had to get up at the crack of dawn to drive back."

"Ouch."

"Tell me about it."

"That sort of mistake isn't like you. You never forget anything. Is something else going on?"

He *would* ask that.

Now what?

She couldn't tell him about the furtive, late-night activity at Natalie's, or he'd get all protective on her.

And she certainly couldn't tell him about her distracting romantic daydreams.

"Cara?" His inflection had transitioned to interrogation mode.

"Yes. I'm here. It was just a busy week."

"Busy never frazzled you in the past."

"There's a first for everything."

Silence.

"What aren't you telling me?"

Oh, brother.

Only a close, homicide-detective sibling would tune into subtle cues and suspect she was holding back information.

But she ought to be able to divert him easier on the phone than in person.

"Would you like a progress report on my sabbatical?" She kept her tone chatty and conversational. "The translation is picking up speed, and I'm beginning to synthesize all the primary source material with my massive amounts of research. It's a huge job that's using all my brainpower. If you want more details, I'd be happy to share them. The historical data is fascinating."

"Um . . . that's okay. You don't have to rehash everything for me. I'm glad your time there has been productive."

"Very."

"So all's well in the hinterland?"

It appeared she wasn't finished playing dodgeball.

"Jack, I'm living a dream here. I get to spend my days in a historic house and work with amazing anthropological resources."

"Better you than me."

"I know history isn't your thing. How's Quantico?"

For the next five minutes he regaled her with tales of his training, then abruptly stopped as someone spoke in the background.

"Sorry. Gotta run to an exercise. Answer your texts from now on, okay?"

"I promise I'll be more diligent. Take care."

Jack ended the call, thank goodness.

Otherwise he could have circled back to whatever hint of trouble he'd picked up in her inflection.

She stowed her phone and returned to the table. Gathered up her papers and shut down her laptop.

Strange to have the rest of Friday stretching empty ahead of her.

Could she work in an extra ballet class today? That would be a treat. Even going to the studio for an hour to stretch instead of doing her routine at the condo today would be a nice change of—

Her phone began to ring again.

She pulled it out. Rolled her eyes as she skimmed the screen.

What were the odds Bri would be calling so soon after Jack unless their brother had planted a bug in their sister's ear?

But letting the call roll to voicemail wasn't an option. Bri was as persistent as Jack. If she'd decided not to wait until their usual Saturday call tomorrow morning to get in touch, she was on a mission. One no doubt instigated by Jack.

Shaking her head at the all-too-familiar sibling tag-team drill, Cara pressed the talk button. "Hi, Bri. Jack put you up to this, didn't he?"

Her sister didn't try to evade the question. "Yep. He said you told him you were frazzled. What's up with that?"

"Couldn't this wait until our call tomorrow?"

"No. I was going to ring you later today anyway. I got pulled into doing a presentation tomorrow morning for a civic group. Jack didn't buy your frazzled explanation, and he has solid instincts."

"He also has a tendency to overreact in matters concerning his siblings, as you know from personal experience." She repeated the story she'd told their brother, almost verbatim. "Wouldn't you be frazzled if you had to make a two-hour trek back thanks to an oversight?"

"Yeah. I'd also be annoyed. But I'm more interested in *why* you forgot the laptop. That doesn't sound like the buttoned-up, make-a-list-and-check-it-twice professor I know and love."

"Like I told Jack, I've been busy. The project is heating up."

A beat ticked by.

"Is that all that's heating up?"

Cara gaped at the phone.

She knew her sister—and based on Bri's playful inflection, the eldest Tucker sibling suspected that romance had entered the picture.

Seriously?

How on earth had she jumped to that conclusion right out of the gate?

"What are you talking about?" She maintained a calm, cool, collected tone.

"The only time my usual methodical, dot-all-the-i's MO got

out of whack was after I met Marc. Sparks can be a powerful distraction."

Dang.

This could be tricky.

Bri was even more adept than Jack at sniffing out romance. But it was too soon to mention Brad. If she did, Bri would want details—and a first date had yet to happen. Yes, Brad's interest appeared to be sincere, but he could end up backing off like all the other guys she dated.

So why create expectations in her family until there was a solid foundation under the relationship?

"Your silence is telling. Come on, Cara. Spill it."

"You're jumping to conclusions."

"Am I wrong?"

Short of telling an outright lie, she was stuck.

But maybe Bri would be satisfied with a few crumbs.

"More like premature. I did—"

"Sorry. Hold a sec." Background noise that came across as static filled the line for several seconds until Bri spoke again. "I have to go. I'm at a fire scene and I think a clue has emerged from the rubble. We'll pick this up later. I'll call you sometime over the weekend. Whoever this guy is, I hope he's a good one."

"No worries on that score."

"Happy to hear it. And I'm glad for you. We'll talk soon."

Once again, the line went dead.

Lips tipping up, Cara stowed her cell. Although her siblings' overprotective leanings could be stifling, it was also comforting to know they had her back.

Like Brad did.

She wandered over to the table and picked up her things.

While their fledgling romance could peter out after a few dates and she'd be back on the social sidelines, somehow she didn't think that was going to happen. Deep inside, this felt right . . . and meant to be.

Of course, that could be nothing more than wishful thinking. With Bri and Jack both meeting The One, romance had been swirling through the air around the Tucker clan for a solid year. No surprise it would be on her mind.

And in her heart.

But that wasn't all that was in her heart this time.

There was also hope.

So she'd savor the sense of possibility that had begun to brighten her days despite the disconcerting undercurrent of danger at Natalie's place.

Yet in spite of all the unsettling events that had occurred during her stay, if none of those had happened, she would never have met Brad.

How heartrending, though, that one of them had resulted in tragedy.

But Brad was on Micah's case, and if there was malice to be found, he'd uncover it.

Hopefully before Natalie's tucked-away acres hosted any more dangerous and disturbing incidents.

SOMETHING WAS OFF.

As daylight waned on Friday, Brad hobbled to the kitchen to refill his makeshift Ziplock-bag ice pack, frustration mounting.

He was missing an important piece of intel. One that had been niggling at his subconscious all day. Close, yet just beyond his grasp.

What was it?

He dumped the melted ice in the sink and refilled the bag from the icemaker in the fridge. Secured the top. Weighed it in his hand.

Had he failed last night to notice a key descriptive feature of the trespasser? Overlooked an item the man dropped as he and Alan were searching this morning, perhaps the corner of an object that may have registered only at a subliminal level in his peripheral vision? Forgotten to ask Natalie a critical question as he'd sat in her kitchen gulping down caffeine after his long, exasperating night?

He set the bag on the counter and massaged his forehead.

Any of those were possible—yet none of them were setting off any alerts in his mind.

Leaning back against the counter, he shifted his weight to his uninjured foot.

That helped.

At least while he was on patrol tomorrow, he shouldn't have to do much walking. Nothing like the effort he'd expended traipsing around in the woods this morning.

And if he kept his leg elevated while he slept tonight, that should help reduce the swelling.

He ought to nuke a frozen dinner and call it a night, considering how little sleep he'd gotten today after he'd come home from urgent care. Not that he hadn't tried to rest, but shuteye had been elusive as his mind kept chasing after whatever puzzle piece he was missing.

Problem was, he wasn't hungry.

Maybe he'd do a load of laundry first, see if his appetite perked up. The basket by the washer was overflowing.

Holding on to chair backs and countertops for support, he limped to the adjacent laundry room. Transferred the clothes from the basket to the washer, then leaned over and grabbed the uniform shirt draped over the adjoining dryer.

Why hadn't that been in the basket?

He started to throw it into the washer. Paused as a stain on the cuff registered.

Oh yeah.

He must have brushed the fabric across Steven's cut as he tended to the gash on the man's forehead. That's why he'd kept his shirt separate from the rest of the laundry. To remind himself to treat it with stain remover.

He opened the cabinet door above him and reached for the spray bottle.

Froze.

Steven.

His encounter with Natalie's cousin held the key to whatever had been bugging him all day. He knew that at a deep, intuitive level.

But what had raised a red flag in his sleep-deprived, pain-fogged state this morning?

Hard as he concentrated, nothing surfaced.

It wasn't as if the man had talked much. Natalie had carried the bulk of the conversation after her cousin emerged from the basement. So it couldn't have been anything the man said. There hadn't been—

Wait.

Brad stiffened.

That was it.

It was what Steven *hadn't* said that was peculiar.

He should have been surprised to find the sheriff on the other side of the basement door. His first logical question should have been, "What are you doing here?"

Instead, he'd acted as if the appearance of a law enforcement officer in the house at that early hour wasn't anything out of the ordinary. It was almost as if he'd expected him to be there.

But why would he have anticipated that unless he knew what had gone down last night?

Brad took a long, slow breath. Stared again at the blood on his shirt as a shocking theory began to take shape in his mind.

Steven's cut had been real, no question about it—but what if he hadn't gotten it in the basement? What if he'd been injured in the woods hours earlier and reopened the wound in the basement to create a plausible and innocent explanation for it?

What if Steven was the late-night trespasser?

Brad exhaled and leaned against the washer.

That theory seemed outrageous.

Yet it made sense.

Who would have better access to Natalie's property at night than someone staying on the premises? Someone who could come and go in the wee hours without anyone noticing—except a night-owl professor?

But if Steven *was* the trespasser, what was he doing in the woods?

Why did it have to be done covertly, under the cover of darkness?

And what connection, if any, did he have to Micah's death?

As questions tumbled through his mind, Brad fingered the cuff of the shirt.

Preposterous as it was to think that Natalie's beloved cousin could have any connection to all the strange happenings on the grounds or to Micah's death, the pieces fit.

And there was one simple way to find out if Steven knew more about Micah's death than he'd admitted.

A DNA test.

All they had to do was analyze this blood sample and see if there was a match to the vomit Rod had found on Micah's shirt.

Pulse picking up, Brad returned to the kitchen, shirt in hand, and pulled an evidence envelope from the stash he kept on hand. Slid the shirt in.

If he could get the test expedited, it wouldn't take long to see if there was a match.

But if a match *did* come back, his work would only be beginning. One piece of circumstantial evidence linking the two men wouldn't lead to a conviction. They'd have to have more.

Like a motive.

Whatever Steven was doing in the woods might provide that, however.

So if the lab confirmed they had a match, he'd have to figure out how best to play this to get the answers they needed.

In the meantime, it could be instructive to dig into his background. Delve into his history, run his credit, see how much information was available that didn't require a court order to access.

And hope that if Steven was their man, whatever he was up to in the dark of night didn't escalate before answers could be found that would provide an explanation for the tragic death of an innocent man.

TWENTY-FOUR

NATALIE WAS ACTING STRANGE.

As Steven finished the apple cobbler she'd baked for their Saturday night dessert, he gave her a surreptitious inspection across the silent table.

She was playing with her spoon, poking at her dessert but not eating it, twin grooves etched on her forehead.

Could she be feeling ill? Had she suffered another dizzy spell? Was she mulling over his suggestion that she sell this place and move to St. Louis?

Whatever the cause, her quietness was out of character. In general she kept the conversation flowing at a brisk pace while they ate their meals.

Not tonight.

It might behoove him to find out what was on her mind.

He finished chewing the tender crust on the cobbler, swallowed, and picked up his coffee mug. "Another excellent dinner, Natalie. You've spoiled me with these weekend feasts."

The smile she gave him was subdued. "I like having someone to cook for. That's another reason Cara's presence has been such a joy this fall. She appreciates my food too, and

I'm grateful for the companionship. Meals weren't meant to be eaten alone."

"I suppose that's true."

Instead of responding, she went back to playing with her dessert.

He quashed a sigh.

Apparently he'd have to be more direct if he wanted to get a read on her mood.

"You seem preoccupied tonight."

"Do I?" She broke off a bite of cobbler with the edge of her spoon. "I'm sorry if I've put a damper on our dinner. I have a lot on my mind."

"Understandable, with all the odd happenings around here in recent weeks."

"That's part of it, of course, but I'm also worried about you. You slept quite a bit yesterday, and again today."

Because he wasn't getting much shut-eye at night, thanks to his forays into the cave.

Not an excuse he could offer, but the cut on his forehead gave him a perfect out.

"This left me with a nagging headache." He touched the bandage the sheriff had put on yesterday. "Sleeping helps. But there's no need for you to fret. The cut will heal. I'm sorry if I haven't been good company."

"No apology necessary. I'm used to you working in your room or hiking around the property while you're here. Knowing you're close by has always been a comfort in itself." She picked up a crumb from the tablecloth and set it on the edge of her plate. "I know your injury will mend, but I've been wondering if you . . . if there might be anything else wrong."

His pulse took an uptick.

Had she found out about his dire financial situation? Was it possible she'd heard about the drastic erosion in his client base? Did she know he was behind on multiple bills, had maxed out his credit cards, and that a collection agency was on his tail for his late BMW payments?

Impossible.

He'd kept all of his problems close to his vest.

Nevertheless, it was possible she'd gotten wind of a woe or two. Stranger things had happened.

But before jumping to any conclusions, it would be prudent to feel her out. See if she knew about any of his distressing secrets.

"Like what?" He kept his manner nonchalant.

She caught her lower lip between her teeth for a moment. "I don't mean to pry, Steven, but when I straightened up your room yesterday, I found a bloody washcloth in the tub and a streak of blood on your pillow. I was concerned."

What?

She'd been in his room?

His stomach bottomed out.

Truth be told, he hadn't even noticed the bed was made when he got back. After everything that had happened since Thursday night, housekeeping had been the least of his concerns.

And he'd totally forgotten about the washcloth he'd pitched into the tub.

Somehow he held on to his placid expression as he kicked his brain into high gear and scrambled to come up with a credible response. "It was from this, Natalie." He tapped his temple again. "When I laid down, the bandage came loose and the cut started to bleed again. It must have seeped around the edges of the bandage and onto the pillow. I'm sorry you had to deal with the mess."

The creases on her forehead reappeared. "But you didn't lie down until you got back from the grocery store. I made the bed while you were gone."

His heart stumbled.

Mistake, mistake, mistake!

Except . . . his blunder could be an ideal opportunity to plant another seed of doubt about her mental capacity.

"I think you may have the sequence wrong, Natalie." He used his most placating tone, underscored with a hint of concern. "I laid down for a few minutes before I left. Not long, but enough to put a dent in my headache."

Confusion clouded her eyes. "That's not how I remember it. I thought you left right away. As soon as I wrote out the list."

"Not quite that fast. I laid down for about fifteen minutes. I imagine yesterday is a muddle for you, what with the early morning visit from the sheriff and the story he told, then your clumsy cousin almost knocking himself out in the basement." He called up a solicitous smile.

The grooves on her brow deepened. "I've never gotten muddled."

"You've never had to deal with masked intruders and kitchen fires and dizzy spells, either. Not to mention poor Micah." He reached over and patted her hand. "Cut yourself some slack, Natalie. You're not forty anymore."

"No, but my mind has always been sharp."

"I know. But I do think it's important to face facts. Age takes a toll. I noticed an occasional mental lapse in Dad during his last few years too, and he was younger than you are."

Natalie set her spoon down. "This is most disturbing."

"I think you're worrying too much. You had a stressful day yesterday. We both did. I'm sure it rattled you. I wouldn't be concerned unless the lapses begin to happen more often."

"I suppose not." The curve of her mouth seemed strained. "Would you like more cobbler?"

"No, thank you." He patted his stomach. "As it is, I'll have to do an extra lap around the lake tomorrow to burn off all the calories from dinner. Why don't I help you with the dishes tonight?"

She waved off his offer and stood. "Putting them in the dishwasher takes no effort. If you'll help me carry them to the kitchen as usual, though, I'd appreciate it."

"Always happy to assist."

They went about the task in silence, and once all the dishes were piled by the sink, he faked a yawn.

Natalie took the cue. "Why don't you lie down? You should take it easy until your head begins to heal."

"If you don't mind, I think I will. My temple is beginning to throb."

"Go rest." She shooed him away. "I don't have any pressing duties to attend to this evening. The dishes will keep me occupied, and then I'll crochet for a while. I may make it an early night too."

"Thank you, Natalie. You're the best." He crossed to her and leaned close to press his lips to her forehead, holding his breath against the faint hint of gardenia that had been her distinctive, nauseating scent for as long as he could remember.

She squeezed his arm. "No, *you're* the best. I've been blessed by your faithfulness and devotion. Sleep well."

Not likely. Very little slumber was on his agenda for this night.

But hopefully he could clock a few hours before he left for the cave.

"I hope you sleep well too. Are you going to church in the morning?"

"Yes. The eight o'clock Mass. You're welcome to join me. You'd like Father Johnson."

It was the same ritual they went through every Saturday night.

"Not this week, Natalie. But say a prayer for me."

"Always. Good night."

He left the kitchen and strolled down the hall to his room. Entered and shut the door. Stretched out on the bed.

Near as he could tell, Natalie had bought his story about the blood on the cloth and the pillow. Rather than doubt him, she'd begun to doubt herself.

It appeared all the glitches that had occurred in the past forty-eight hours were working in his favor.

But pushing his luck wouldn't be wise. He needed to double down and find the treasure.

So he'd put in an extra hour or two tonight. And he'd come down early again next week, even if Cara would be on the premises and cameras would be in place. If he was careful, he could avoid both.

It wouldn't be hard to fabricate an excuse for an extended visit. All he had to do was say the blow to his head had taken more out of him than he'd thought and that a few quiet days would help him recuperate. If pressed, he could claim he'd gone to urgent care and discovered he had a mild concussion.

Natalie would believe anything he told her.

And Cara shouldn't be a problem. He could find his way to the cave without lights at night. She'd never spot him.

But the search was getting old, and the longer it went on, the higher the risk of someone discovering his activity.

So while he put zero stock in praying and far less in a God who'd never once bailed him out of any of the scrapes he'd gotten in, perhaps the cosmos would smile on him, lead him to the treasure, and bring this unhappy chapter in his life to an end.

COULD SHE BE LOSING IT?

As the clock inched toward three o'clock, Natalie tugged the covers up to her chin and wadded them in her fists.

The question that had been strobing through her mind ever since she went to bed, through all the hours she'd tossed and turned and stared at the dark ceiling, continued to plague her.

Was it possible her recollection of the sequence of events around Steven's departure for the grocery store was off?

Yet she'd gone over and over it in her mind and kept coming up with the same scenario.

Steven had offered to do her grocery shopping for her.

While he'd gone to his room to collect his keys and wallet, she'd taken a quick inventory of the fridge and cabinets and written out a list. A mere eight items, the minimum she needed, so as not to burden him too much.

She'd finished writing the last item as he returned.

The whole process couldn't have taken more than five minutes, max.

Yet he said it had been at least fifteen. Long enough for him to lie down and take a brief rest.

That wasn't how she remembered it.

Moonlight leaked through the canted shutters of her room, creating a ghostly pattern on the ceiling, and she tucked the blanket higher as a shiver snaked through her.

The sequence of events wasn't the only piece of the picture that didn't fit.

There was also the bandage.

Steven still wore the same one Brad had applied, securely affixed. Yet he claimed it had come loose, that blood had leaked around the edge onto the pillow.

But the edge of the bandage remained pristine. No seepage was apparent.

Why would he fabricate such a story?

More troubling yet, if he wasn't being truthful about the blood, could his claim about her faulty memory also be disingenuous?

Again . . . why would he be deceitful?

She bunched the blanket tighter in her fingers, the soft

velour a sharp contrast to the hard, thorny questions shredding her peace of mind.

Could his aberrant behavior have anything to do with his head injury? Was he more hurt than he'd let on, to the extent that the blow had interfered with his thinking?

What other explanation could there be for his apparent confusion?

Because the more she thought about it, the more certain she was that if anyone was mistaken about the order of events on Friday morning, it was her cousin.

But how could she suggest that without upsetting him?

Maybe he should go to the ER and—

She stiffened.

What was that noise?

Staying as still as possible, she listened.

Five seconds ticked by.

Ten.

Nothing.

Had she imagined the slight thud that had sounded as if someone had dropped an object somewhere inside the—

A floorboard creaked.

Her pulse picked up speed.

She had *not* imagined that.

Had someone broken into the house?

Should she call the police?

Perhaps, if her phone wasn't charging in the kitchen.

But she could alert Steven. If there was an intruder, her strapping cousin was far better equipped to deal with the situation than she was.

Natalie threw back the covers, grasped her cane, and stood. After shoving her arms into the sleeves of the robe draped over the foot of her bed, she took a fortifying breath and crept toward the door as quietly as she could. Cracked it and peeked into the dark hall.

No one was there. Nor were there any more noises.

If someone *was* in the house, they were in the living room or study, not the bedroom wing.

Staying close to the wall, she crept down the hall toward Steven's room.

As she approached, it was apparent he was up. Light leaked from under his door.

Had he heard the noises too and risen to investigate?

She continued forward. Sounds of movement came from inside the room, and she gave a soft knock.

The room went silent.

She knocked again, a quiet rap hopefully only he would hear.

The thin band of light by the floor disappeared, and a few seconds later the door on the now-dark room cracked open.

"Natalie? What are you doing up at this hour?"

"I heard a noise in the house." As she whispered the words, she scanned the hall over her shoulder. "I thought maybe you did too. I saw the light under your door."

"No. I got up to get an aspirin for my headache. I didn't hear anything." He sounded a tad agitated. And annoyed.

"I'm sorry to bother you in the middle of the night, but would you mind taking a walk-through?"

"Sure. I can do that. Let me throw on my clothes. Go back to your room and lock the door. I'll knock after I finish."

"Thank you."

She retreated to her room, slipped inside, slid the bolt—and waited on the edge of her bed, in the dark.

Ten minutes later, a knock on her door announced his return.

"Natalie? All clear."

She rose and crossed to the door. Unlocked it and twisted the knob. The light in the hall was on now. "Did you see anything?"

"No. I checked all the rooms, the windows, and the doors. No signs of forced entry or any disruption."

"I wonder what I could have heard?"

He shrugged. "Old houses make noises."

That was true.

But she was accustomed to all the noises in this house, and the ones she'd heard hadn't been in the usual mix.

"I'm sorry to have bothered you."

"No worries. Go back to bed." He turned and walked down the hall toward his room.

As he retreated, she homed in on a streak of dried dirt that ran down the back of his jeans, above his left knee.

The hall went dark after he flicked the switch as he passed, and a moment later he entered his room. Shut the door.

Natalie remained where she was, a shiver racing through her.

The dirt on Steven's jeans hadn't been there at dinner.

Where could it have come from?

Unless . . .

Her lungs locked, and she pressed a hand to her chest.

No.

She quashed the sudden, ridiculous suspicion that skittered through her mind.

Steven wasn't wandering about the premises at night. Why would he do that when he had full run of the place during daylight hours?

Only someone involved in an underhanded activity would prowl around in the dead of night.

Like the man the sheriff had chased.

And that man wasn't Steven, despite the niggle of doubt polluting her mind. Why would a fine, successful young man skulk around in the dark or be involved in anything dishonest or deceitful?

That was crazy.

Nevertheless, a shroud-like sense of foreboding settled over her as she slowly closed her door. Locked it again. Returned to her bed.

And as she slipped under the covers and pulled them up to her chin, only one thing was clear in these predawn hours.

There would be no more sleep for her this night.

TWENTY-FIVE

"NATALIE, IS EVERYTHING OKAY?" As Cara broached the question, she studied the older woman. This was the second pause the woman had taken to rest her eyes a mere hour into their Monday session, and she looked weary and pale. As if she was feeling sick.

"Yes." The corners of Natalie's mouth tipped up, an attempt at reassurance that seemed to require far too much effort. "I'm just a little tired. I haven't slept well the past two nights."

Cara smoothed out a wrinkle in the top sheet of her tablet. Maybe she was overstepping, but Natalie was such a dear person, and her wan appearance was troubling. "From what you've told me, that's not like you. I remember you said once, back when I first arrived, that you were grateful you always slept like a baby. I don't mean to be nosy, but do you have any idea what's going on?"

"Yes and no." Her brow pinched, and she hesitated. As if she was thinking about explaining that ambiguous response. But in the end, she didn't. "It's a problem I have to work through. Nothing you need to be concerned about." She ran a finger across the text on the journal page in front of her. "You know, I've been thinking we should skip ahead and see what we can learn about Marie's death. Passively waiting for a story to unfold may not always be wise. And I know Paul would appreciate having answers sooner rather than later."

"I'm game if you are."

"Let's do it." She pushed her chair back, rose, and walked over to the desk, leaning more heavily on her cane than usual. After she pulled out the last journal, she returned to their worktable. "I'll translate the final entry, and if that doesn't provide answers, I'll work backward and see if any of the previous entries do."

"Ready whenever you are." Cara leaned forward, fingers poised over the keyboard.

Natalie slipped her glasses back on and flipped through to the last pages of writing, about midway through. "This entry is dated May 12, 1935. The day Marie died." After taking a sip of tea, she began to read.

> *I have thought about my situation day and night, tried to find a solution, but there is none. Not as long as he refuses to acknowledge that the—*

Natalie frowned at the text. "Oh my."

"What is it?" Cara stopped typing.

The other woman held up a finger and continued reading.

> *. . . that the baby is his. I know now all my fondest hopes have been nothing but dreams that will never come true. He isn't going to leave his wife or his family. He was very clear about that when we met two weeks ago. It would ruin him, he said, and his work in Washington is too important to give up. More important than me and his baby. So he's going to ruin me instead. I'll be a disgraced woman. An embarrassment to my family. No one in town will want to have anything to do with me.*
>
> *There is only one way I can remove the source of humiliation from*

my family and myself. This isn't how I wanted it to end, but what is the point of going on with a broken heart? I have no future anyway.

I'll do it tonight, where he and I spent such happy hours together. I know I should destroy my journals too, but somehow I can't. That would be like erasing the part of my life that gave me the most joy—and sadly, in the end, the most heartache. Instead, I'll hide them. Perhaps someone in the future will find them and learn a lesson from my mistakes.

And before I take the leap, I will put myself in God's hands, pray he understands my despair, and trust in his mercy and forgiveness for what I am going to do.

The room fell silent, and Natalie let out a slow breath. "So Papa was right, after all. His sister's death wasn't accidental. What a heartrending end for such a young woman."

Cara swallowed past the tightness in her throat. "At least we know why she did it."

"Yes. Despair can drive a person to take desperate measures. And finding oneself in a difficult situation can certainly trigger despair."

Cara scrutinized her.

She wasn't talking about Marie anymore. That was as obvious as the identity of Marie's suitor.

What was going on?

"Natalie." She leaned forward. "You seem beyond tired today. More like disturbed. Did something upsetting happen over the weekend?"

She sighed. "It's a long story, my dear. Would you mind if we canceled the rest of this morning's session? After reading Marie's last entry, my heart isn't in the work today. I should also call Paul. Tell him what we found."

"I'm assuming he'll conclude his grandfather was the man involved. Even though Marie never identified him by name, the reference to Washington is a solid clue."

"Yes, it is. I expect Paul will agree. And while his grandfather doesn't have direct culpability in her death, he did play a role." She tapped a finger against the journal. "The only identifying comment about him is the mention of Washington, as you noted. We may want to strike that reference from the translation. It's an irrelevant detail for our purposes, important only to the two affected families. I can scratch it out with indelible ink in the journal too before I turn the set over to the historical society."

Cara backed up to that section on her screen, highlighted the words "in Washington," and hit delete. "Done. We can do the same if there are any other specific references in the previous entries too, as we come to them."

"I believe that's a sound decision. Now I think I'll take a quick nap before lunch." Natalie rose again and carried the journals back to the desk. Secured them in the drawer. "We'll pick up where we left off tomorrow. I'm sorry to cancel the rest of the session for today. We can extend one of our sessions later in the week to compensate, if you like."

"That may not be necessary, with the excellent progress we're making. To be honest, I could use an extra hour today to go through all the research material I've amassed. That will keep me busy until dinner." And since her hostess didn't appear to be up to cooking, a visit to Chuck's Place might be in order. "Why don't you let me treat you to the diner in town tonight? We haven't gone out in a while."

Natalie's lips stretched into a joyless smile. "That's a very kind thought, but let's decide later in the afternoon. Chuck serves hearty food, and I'll have to see if my appetite is up to that challenge."

"All right. I'll check with you around four."

With a nod, Natalie left the room.

As she disappeared, Cara set her elbow on the table and propped her chin in her palm.

What was going on with her benefactor?

While she'd claimed her odd mood was due to fatigue, the anxiety radiating from her had nothing to do with tiredness.

Had she had another dizzy spell over the weekend? Could a new health issue have cropped up? Was she worried about being here alone after their project ended? Was it possible she'd had some sort of altercation with Steven?

Who knew?

And unless Natalie decided to share her concerns, Cara would have to resign herself to remaining in the dark.

All she could do was pray that the woman who'd gone from patron to friend during the weeks they'd worked together wouldn't have to cope with yet more upheaval in her life.

STEVEN BOYER WAS UP TO HIS EYEBALLS IN DEBT.

As Brad skimmed the man's credit report, he leaned forward in his desk chair and let out a soft whistle.

Apparently his gig as a financial consultant wasn't as successful or lucrative as he'd led Natalie to believe.

That didn't explain why he'd be prowling around the woods at night, however.

Nor did it explain why he might have wanted to kill a man whose material assets were meager. How would he have profited from that?

Unless Micah had witnessed clandestine activity on Natalie's property that the still-unidentified trespasser hadn't wanted seen . . . and that masked man wasn't a trespasser at all, but Steven.

But if it *was* Steven, what could Natalie's cousin have been doing at such a late hour night after—

His cell began to vibrate, and he pulled it out. Smiled as he put it to his ear. "Good morning to my favorite historical anthropologist."

"I'd be flattered, except I assume I'm the only historical anthropologist you know. We're a rare breed."

"True. But you'd be my favorite no matter how many I knew." He glanced at his watch. "I was going to call you this morning, but I assumed you'd be deep into a translating session with Natalie."

"I should be, but she bailed early."

"Isn't that out of pattern?"

"Yes."

"What's going on?"

"I have no idea. All I know is she seemed disturbed. I decided to call and see if you noticed anything odd in her behavior while you were talking to her Friday morning about the trespasser and trying to convince her again about security cameras."

"No. I wonder if she's worried about Steven."

"Why would she worry about him?"

Oh, right. Cara probably didn't know about the man's injury. Their phone conversation yesterday had been cut short after he'd had to take a call about a four-car pileup that had sent him double-timing it to the scene to lend a hand.

He briefed her on the basement incident, leaving out his suspicions about the man. At this stage they were in the purely speculative category. And it wasn't like Steven was hanging around the premises during the week presenting any danger to anyone—if he was, indeed, guilty of any crimes on Natalie's property.

"Maybe she's still worried about him." As he wrapped up the story, Rod appeared in the doorway. He waved the man in.

"I suppose that's possible. But why wouldn't she have admitted that when I asked her what was wrong?"

"I don't have an answer for that—but I do have a visitor who just walked into my office."

"I'll let you go."

"Not until we finalize our plans for this week. Does Thursday work?"

"Fine by me. Let's hope third time's the charm."

"Nothing short of a natural disaster is going to divert me from my mission this go-round. I'll call you back to discuss details."

"I'll put you on my calendar—and hope no tornadoes crop up. Talk to you soon."

As they ended the call, he looked over at Rod, who'd propped a shoulder against the doorframe. "What's up?"

"I talked to our private lab a few minutes ago. They said you dropped a blood sample off first thing this morning for DNA testing, along with a box of Danish. They were impressed by the personal delivery as well as the Danish. It got their attention."

"Good." That had been his goal.

"The lab's not exactly in our backyard. What time did you have to get up to be at their doorstep?"

"Early." But it had been worth the predawn rising. The private lab they used to handle backlog would process the sample fast. Who knew how long they'd have to wait if they sent it to the state facility?

"Must have been a hot sample if you were willing to ding the department budget for a private facility."

"Yeah. It may be a match for your vomit."

Rod arched his eyebrows. "No kidding? You have a suspect?"

"I'd put him in the semi long-shot category, but there are enough markers pointing to him to justify giving this a try."

"Let's hope it pans out. I'd like to wrap up the paperwork for that autopsy."

"We're getting there. I'm working the case on a couple of fronts."

In fact, his next call was to the firm he'd recommended to Natalie, to line up camera installation.

"Keep me in the loop." Rod pushed off from the doorframe.

"You got it."

As the coroner disappeared into the hall, Brad picked up his phone and scrolled through to the number for the security company.

In light of the decent scare he'd given the trespasser Thursday night, it was possible the guy was spooked and would stay away long enough to give them a chance to get cameras up and running before he came back. Best case, someone from the firm could go out there and get the cameras in place by midweek.

The only glitch?

If Steven happened to be their target, he'd have an inside track to any security measures Natalie implemented.

Meaning he'd know how to circumvent them.

That's why getting a read on the potential DNA match was urgent.

Because if it came back positive, the cameras might not be necessary.

And Natalie's nephew would have a whole lot of explaining to do.

HE WAS OUT OF TIME.

Shoving his cell back into his pocket, Steven stormed over to the bar in his condo, poured a scotch, and tossed it back. After refilling his glass, he continued to the window of the upscale high-rise unit that offered a panoramic view of the parkland-dotted cityscape.

These cushy digs were his home and giving them up was unthinkable.

But if he didn't come up with his back mortgage payments

pronto, he was going to be out on his ear. They were done with his stall tactics.

He gulped down the second drink and squeezed the glass.

Natalie would give him a short-term loan if he asked, but he'd have to explain why he was in such deep debt. Reveal how desperate he was. Acknowledge his bad judgment.

Not an option. He needed to maintain his image with her as a responsible money handler or she'd never trust him with her financial affairs.

It would be much better to find the jewels, which would provide instant cash.

Well, almost instant. He'd have to exchange his bitcoin profits for cash, since virtual currency was the monetary standard for the under-the-radar transactions he'd be doing. That would only take a few days, though. He could hold off his creditors until then.

Maybe.

But he was down to the dregs in the hourglass.

That's why he'd have to go back to Natalie's by Wednesday afternoon. Having two extra nights to search would expedite the process.

He'd just have to be extra careful not to drop one of his dirty boots again when he returned from his hunt, as he had Saturday night. If Natalie had come out of her room moments earlier, she would have seen him sneaking down the hall in his stockinged feet, shoes in hand.

That would have been difficult to explain on the fly.

After returning to the bar, he set his glass in the sink and scrolled through the messages from the two clients who'd fled his firm early on this Monday morning.

He had to respond to them soon.

But what could he say?

Certainly not the truth, that dabbling in options and futures had been a colossal mistake. The risk had been too high, and he hadn't had sufficient experience with those markets. He should have left speculative deals of that nature to institutional investors, which by virtue of size could absorb dramatic losses in one or two investments. By contrast, the bottom-line impact of such losses was far more profound on private-investor portfolios.

As he'd learned to his regret, attracting clients with promises of high returns was much easier than keeping them once dicey investments went south.

From here on out, he was sticking with sure bets.

Assuming he could rebuild his client base.

But perhaps the jewels and paintings would bring in sufficient money to not only pay off his debts but give him a sizable cushion going forward.

There were always Natalie's assets to tap too. Family lore said her father had inherited a fortune from his wife, and how much of it could Natalie have spent living in the middle of nowhere her whole life?

It was a shame she'd never let him invest her funds for her instead of keeping them in CDs. Then he'd know exactly how much she had.

On the other hand, if she *had* let him handle her money, she could be as broke as he was.

Going forward, though, he'd try to get a clearer read on her resources. For future lifestyle planning.

His lifestyle, not hers.

For now, however, his focus had to be on the jewels.

He strode into his office, pulled out the folder containing his drawing of the cave passages, and concentrated on planning his schedule for the coming trip. It was important to cover as much ground as possible with each visit to the subterranean corridors.

And hope he hit pay dirt before the life he'd built imploded and left his precarious world in ruins.

TWENTY-SIX

SWEET HEAVEN.

Steven *was* sneaking out of the house at night.

As Natalie peeked through the canted shutters in her room, her stomach clenched. There, in the moonlight, a dark figure hugged the shadowed edge of the galérie, then hurried toward the woods around the perimeter of the backyard and disappeared into the ten o'clock gloom.

The subtle noise she'd heard in the house, like the soft opening and closing of a door, had to have been her cousin. If she hadn't been wide awake and listening for it after his unexpected arrival on this Wednesday night, she would never have known he'd slipped out.

Unless . . . was it possible the person prowling about wasn't him? That the noise she'd heard hadn't been a door opening but simply the creak of old boards in the house?

Best to check his room and confirm it was empty before jumping to conclusions.

Clutching her cane, she crossed to the door. Peeked into the dark hall.

All was quiet.

She made her way down to his door as fast as she could

with her bad leg. Carefully twisted the knob and peeked in, sending a silent prayer heavenward that she'd find him asleep.

Her prayer went unanswered.

His bed was empty.

Breath hitching, she closed her eyes.

Oh, Lord, what am I supposed to do now?

Seconds ticked by, but when no answer came, she trudged back to her room. Closed the door. Sat on the edge of the bed and replayed the counsel Father Johnson had offered her after he'd slipped into the pew beside her at the back of the empty church after early Mass on Sunday.

The pastor had an uncanny ability to sense a troubled soul.

While she hadn't provided specifics, she'd given him enough information to capture the gist of her moral dilemma.

Namely, what do you do if you suspect someone you've always trusted and loved may be involved in a questionable activity?

The priest's advice had been sound for most such situations—verify your suspicions if possible, then bring your concerns forward and have a candid and compassionate conversation with that person.

If the person was engaged in anything criminal, however, the advice might not work as well. In such a case, a conversation like that could even be unsafe.

Except Steven would never do anything illegal. Nor was he dangerous. The two of them were family. He'd never hurt her. Her concern about danger was unfounded.

She set her cane aside and laid back on the bed. Pulled her grandmother's quilt over her.

There was no need to stay awake and listen for his return. She had the answer to her question about whether he was leaving the house at night.

What she didn't have was the answer to the more important question.

Why?

So come tomorrow, after she and Cara finished their morning session, she'd confront him.

It wouldn't be easy. Nor would it be comfortable. It was obvious Steven didn't want her to know what he was up to.

But this *was* her property, and his skulking about was nerve-racking.

If he hadn't mentioned a lady friend in St. Louis, she'd almost wonder if the situation with Marie and Paul's grandfather was being reenacted a century later.

That would be a stretch, though. Those sorts of illicit trysts were much more common these days, sad to say, and there were far more inviting places for a rendezvous than the top of a cliff on a chilly night.

No, romance had no role in Steven's nocturnal forays.

Perhaps, though, she was getting worked up over nothing. It was possible he'd have a simple explanation for all his clandestine activity.

Yet as the minutes ticked into hours while she lay awake in her dark room, she couldn't for the life of her think what that might be.

YES!

Despite the inky confines of the cave, lit only with his headlamp, the gloomy interior suddenly got brighter.

Because he felt something.

Something Mother Nature hadn't put there.

Pulse surging, Steven withdrew his hand from the crevice in the wall of the small passageway, leaned down, and peered in.

His light illuminated the top of a dirty canvas bag tucked far back, behind a few rocks. So well camouflaged he'd almost missed it.

But lady luck had smiled on him.

This had to be the treasure he'd been seeking for months.

Fingers tingling, he pulled out the rocks and set them on the floor of the passage beside him. Then he carefully grasped the bag and eased it from its hiding place.

It wasn't heavy—but jewels didn't have to weigh a lot to be valuable.

He set the bag on a rock ledge beside him and squinted into the crevice again.

Wedged farther back was a parcel wrapped in cloth.

That had to be the two paintings, though the package was much smaller than he'd anticipated.

Didn't matter. Stolen art was too identifiable and therefore worth far less on the black market. The jewels were his primary cash cow.

He pulled out the parcel, set it on the floor of the passageway, and removed his work gloves. After wiping his palms down his jeans, he picked up the soiled, sturdy bag again.

Fingers trembling, he untied the cord around the top . . . held his breath . . . and pulled the fabric apart to look inside.

The tension that had been his constant companion for months evaporated instantly, replaced by an elation verging on giddiness.

Yes, yes, yes, yes, yes!

He was holding a fortune in his hands.

Diamonds, emeralds, rubies, sapphires. They glinted in the light from his headlamp as he shifted the bag of bracelets, necklaces, earrings, broaches.

His money worries were over.

Grinning, he spread the contents onto the rock ledge beside him.

As he fingered the fortune displayed before him, the stones glittered in the light from his headlamp like the crown jewels.

Wow.

His grandfather's list hadn't begun to capture the breadth of his bounty.

Diamond necklace didn't come close to describing the jewel-encrusted choker studded with a fortune in sparkling precious stones.

He picked up a diamond-rimmed ruby broach. Examined it under the light from his headlamp.

Gorgeous.

It was a shame he'd have to ruin all these antique pieces by pulling out the stones, but it would be safer to sell loose gems. Intact jewelry could be identified if the owner had listed it on any of the international databases for stolen collectibles.

And considering all the valuables soldiers on both sides had plundered during World War II, it was very possible the owner had contacted one of those databases and—

At a sudden graze on his cheek, Steven jerked. Ducked. Uttered an oath.

The bats were on the move.

Thank goodness he wouldn't have to dodge the little devils again after tonight, or worry about getting bitten by a rabid winged mammal. He was done with caves for the rest of his life.

Another night marauder zipped by, and he ducked again.

He was out of here.

After hastily gathering up the jewels, he threw them back in the bag.

It hadn't been fun, but all the hours he'd spent in this crypt-like subterranean cavity had ended up paying off. Big time.

And he'd never have to come down here again. Going forward, he'd be able to sleep through the night. The disposal of his treasure could be done during normal waking hours.

He closed the bag again and secured it in his backpack with his bottle of water, extra jacket, and the crowbar he kept on hand in case he had to wedge any rocks loose. Tucked the bulky, twenty-by-twenty parcel of paintings under his arm. Took off for the entrance at a fast trot.

It might be wise to stash the paintings in his car tomorrow while Natalie was taking her midday nap—in case she decided to venture into his room again. He could bury the jewels deep in his overnight bag.

And now that his work here was done, maybe he'd leave Friday morning instead of staying through the weekend. Claim a work issue required his presence back in St. Louis. Which was true.

He had a ton of work to do to turn his treasure into cash.

Energy pulsing through him, he picked up his pace as he wove through the maze of passageways toward the entrance.

Once outside, he removed his headlamp and shoved it into his backpack. Touched the concealed carry holster he always wore on his treks into the woods. With mountain lion and black bear sightings becoming more common in Missouri, it would be foolish to wander about without any protection. The last thing he needed was an encounter with a wild animal.

He struck off down the path, keeping close tabs on his surroundings as the eerie hoot of an owl echoed through the treetops. Nighttime tramps in the forest were one more activity he wouldn't miss going forward.

Why anyone would choose to live in this rustic, godforsaken place was beyond him.

On the plus side, he didn't have to visit as often anymore. Once every few weeks should suffice. He could tell Natalie his romance was heating up. She'd understand. She always did.

He was her golden boy.

And maybe, if he stopped coming around as much, she'd get lonely and move to St. Louis. It would be far less bothersome to swing by to see her there, and if she was closer, he'd have more opportunities to convince her to let him handle her affairs.

As he approached the clearing behind the house, he paused.

A light was still on in the guest cottage, meaning Cara hadn't gone to bed yet. Not surprising. He'd finished much earlier tonight than usual. Less than an hour into his search.

No worries, though. He'd stay in the shadows until he got to the house. And since the sheriff hadn't managed to get his security cameras installed yet, he didn't have to dodge that potential trap either.

Nor would he ever have to.

He continued toward the back door, hugging the edge of the woods as he fished his key out, relief washing over him.

His search was over. The treasure was in hand, and no one would ever be the wiser.

He was safe.

And he'd never have to use the second vial of suxamethonium chloride he'd pilfered at the vet hospital—just in case—while Chloe attended to the canine emergency that had interrupted their date last week.

NATALIE LOOKED WORSE TODAY than she had on Monday—which was saying a lot.

As Cara set her laptop on the worktable in the study Thursday morning, she eyed the deep, parallel channels on the woman's forehead, her slight pallor, and the tremble in her fingers as she reached for her glasses.

Whatever was bothering her was getting worse.

And her distress was impossible to ignore.

"Good morning, Cara." Natalie put on her glasses and picked up the journal. Opened it to the bookmarked page. "Ready to dive in?"

"Not quite."

Natalie looked up. "What's wrong?"

"I think I should ask *you* that question. You seem upset. Is Steven all right?"

A pained expression tightened the older woman's features, suggesting the query had been on target.

Steven was the source of her concern.

After a brief hesitation, Natalie removed her glasses. "Did you know he came back last night?"

It wasn't an answer to her question, but it *was* news.

"No. He must have arrived late."

"About eight. He called thirty minutes out."

"Was the unexpected visit an issue?"

"Of course not. He knows he's always welcome here. And he can use the rest. He still gets headaches from his injury."

"If you're worried about his health, why don't you see if you can convince him to go to the urgent care center in town? It's possible he was hurt worse than everyone thought."

"That's not why I'm worried."

At least Natalie had admitted she was concerned.

"So what's going on?"

"I wish I knew. But I'm going to find out." Her lips settled into a firm line, and she lifted her chin. "However, that can wait until we finish our work for the day. I cut our session short once this week and I don't intend to do that again."

"I understand if a personal issue has come up that has to be dealt with."

"No. It's not that urgent. And it may be much ado about nothing anyway. Now, where did we leave off?"

Since it was obvious Natalie wasn't going to offer any more information about her problem with Steven, Cara transferred her attention to the screen and read the last sentence in the translation.

For the rest of their two-hour session, Natalie worked without a break, faltering only once when noise sounded from the hall around ten, indicating that Steven was up.

But she kept going until eleven o'clock sharp. Then she closed the journal, removed her glasses, and massaged the bridge of her nose.

"Another productive session." Cara shut down her laptop. "At this rate, we'll finish by Thanksgiving."

"I'd say that's a reasonable estimate. Not that I'm in a hurry to see you go, you know. I've enjoyed our collaboration."

"I have too, although the term collaboration may be generous. I've been more like a scribe."

"No, your knowledge of the culture has been very beneficial in helping me interpret fuzzy passages. I'll stick with collaboration." She rose and picked up the journal. Crossed the room toward the desk to deposit it. "I'll see you at dinner, my dear. Enjoy the rest of your day."

Cara stood, gathered up her laptop and tablet, and headed for the hall—but with worry about Natalie front and center in her mind, enjoying the rest of her day would be difficult.

Whatever was troubling the woman was serious.

But what could be wrong between her and Steven? As far as she'd been able to discern, the two of them had an excellent relationship. And they couldn't have had a falling-out. He wouldn't have come down here to recuperate from his injury if any rancor had developed between them.

She continued down the hall and into the kitchen, stopping as she passed the table to glance at the note on top, addressed to Natalie.

Hmm.

Steven must be feeling better if he'd been up to a walk to the lake.

As she stepped onto the galérie, she scanned the cloudless blue sky. Inhaled the crisp fall air.

What a glorious day for a hike around the property. The perfect way to clear her head after two hours of intense work with Natalie as they'd struggled to decipher several difficult passages.

And it should be safe to wander around with an able-bodied man in the vicinity.

In fact, perhaps she ought to seek Steven out. Alert him to Natalie's distress and see if he offered any clues about its source.

At the very least, she could help set the stage for whatever discussion Natalie wanted to have with him. Encourage him to put her mind at ease. It would be such a shame if anything interfered with their relationship. Family was everything, after all, and they only had each other.

She picked up her pace toward the cottage.

Butting into other people's business wasn't her usual style, but surely Natalie and Steven wouldn't mind if she was able to help them smooth out whatever turbulence had disrupted their placid relationship.

Besides, given all the stressful incidents she'd endured over the past few weeks, Natalie didn't deserve any more turmoil.

TWENTY-SEVEN

THE DNA MATCHED.

His crazy hunch hadn't been so crazy after all.

Pulse picking up, Brad used his thumbs to type in a return thank-you email to the lab for their expedited turnaround and saved the attached report. It would contain details that could be necessary in court, but for now he had all he needed.

Namely, confirmation that Steven Boyer had thrown up in very close proximity to Micah's body.

That didn't make the man a killer, but it did leave him with a boatload of explaining to do. Face-to-face explaining. Body language and visual cues would be critical as the man told his story.

Their conversation might even merit a trip to St. Louis—unless Steven was coming down tomorrow for the weekend, as seemed to be his pattern.

From his position beside the cruiser, Brad surveyed the crime scene where he and Larry had spent the past fifteen minutes. His chief deputy was taking a statement from the farmer whose equipment had been stolen, but that didn't require two people.

Nevertheless, his agenda for today was full thanks to the

flu wave that continued to decimate the department. While deferring the discussion with Steven for twenty-four hours wasn't ideal, a drive to St. Louis would take a chunk out of his packed schedule.

Besides, it wasn't as if the man was hanging around Natalie's house today and in a position to cause any further disruption. He rarely came down until Friday afternoon.

May as well wait. Deferring their conversation until tomorrow would give him an opportunity to practice his patience.

Brad huffed out a breath.

As if.

The odds of him ever mastering that when it came to solving a case were nil.

At least he could call Natalie and confirm Steven was planning to visit this weekend, using an update on the camera installation delay as an excuse for getting in touch. No sense raising any alarms with the woman until he talked to her cousin.

He also needed to work through the inconsistencies with his theory about the man's involvement in the incidents on the property.

Like the alibi Steven had provided for the Sunday morning Micah had been killed, complete with the names of patrons and staff who'd been on hand at the gym he frequented. Given how easy it would be to verify those facts, it was doubtful he'd lied about his presence. Plus, Natalie had said he'd left Saturday night.

But he hadn't. Otherwise his vomit wouldn't have been on Micah's shirt.

Meaning he must have connected with the groundskeeper at the beginning of the time-of-death window Rod had identified, then driven straight to St. Louis to be at the gym early.

If Micah's cause of death ended up being homicide, and Steven was responsible, he'd planned the crime in meticulous detail.

How Steven's financial straits fit into the picture was a mystery, but they *did* fit. Brad could feel it in his gut. He just had to connect the dots.

He pulled up Natalie's number on his cell and tapped it in.

After three rings, she picked up.

"Natalie, it's Brad. I hope I'm not interrupting anything."

"No. Cara and I finished our morning translation session about five minutes ago. How can I help you?"

"I wanted to apologize for the delay in getting the cameras in place. The company I recommended is working through an unusual backlog. They promised to be there bright and early Monday morning."

Silence.

"Natalie?"

"Yes, I'm here. I was going to call you today about that. I'm going to hold off on the cameras."

He frowned as he watched a combine harvest soybeans in a field across the road.

What was that odd inflection in her voice all about?

He kept his tone conversational even as his antennas went up. "Why wait? My encounter with the man may have put a temporary stop to his trespassing, but since Cara's seen lights in the woods on multiple occasions, I think we can assume he'll be back. The cameras may be our best hope of spotting him and getting someone over there to intercept."

More silence.

This time he waited her out.

At last a sigh came over the line. "That won't be necessary, Brad. I know who the man is. It's Steven. I wanted to talk with him before I said anything to anyone. I'm sure there's a simple explanation for his nighttime trips. I intend to ask him about those as soon as he gets back from his walk to the lake."

An alert began pinging in Brad's mind.

"He's there now?"

"Yes. He came down last night for a few days of rest after the blow to his head. I heard him go out last night about ten, and I spotted him through the window, in the yard."

So he was still roaming around.

Why?

"Can you think of any reason he'd be leaving the house at that hour?"

"No, and I've racked my brain trying to come up with a plausible explanation. But cameras won't be necessary now that I know who's roaming around the property. I'll straighten this out with him when he gets back."

Not the safest plan if homicide was in the picture. The sort of questioning Natalie had in mind should be handled by law enforcement.

Brad pulled out his keys. "May I ask a favor? I have some questions I want to ask him on another subject. If he comes back before I get there, I'd appreciate it if you didn't say anything about your concerns. I can bring up his nighttime activity during our conversation."

"I don't know, Brad." Worry scored her voice. "He may be upset with me if *you* broach it. He could think I've been telling tales out of school. He's such a good boy, and he's been very kind to me. I don't want him to think I've been going behind his back, or that I don't trust him."

If Boyer was as guilty as Brad was beginning to believe, he wasn't worthy of trust—or all the kindness Natalie had shown him.

And if he'd killed Micah, he was also dangerous. Anyone who got in his way or threatened to expose him would be at grave risk.

Including the cousin who doted on him.

Cornered people, like trapped animals, could lash out with little regard for consequences.

He signaled to Larry, tension bunching in his shoulders as

he spoke into the phone again. "Natalie, I understand your concern. Protecting those we care about is admirable. But I have information indicating Steven may also know more about Micah's death than he's told us. I'd like to talk to him about that before you ask him about his evening activities. I know you want justice served on behalf of Micah as much as I do."

"Of course. But what could Steven know about that?" She sounded baffled.

"I'll explain when I get there." After he talked to her cousin. "Why don't you wait for me in your room? That way, if Steven comes back, you won't have to engage with him until after he and I connect."

A few beats passed.

"Very well. I'll trust your judgment on this."

"Thank you. Expect me in less than twenty minutes. Where's Cara?"

"She went back to the cottage."

Good. She should be safe there.

"Sit tight until I arrive." He ended the call and spoke to Larry, who'd walked over to join him. "How much longer do you think you'll be here?"

"Half an hour, tops. I want to poke around behind the barn, see if the guilty parties left us anything to work with. There had to be two of them, minimum. Stealing a five-hundred-pound generator worth thousands of dollars isn't a one-person job."

"I hear you. I'm going over to Natalie Boyer's place. I have a lead on the Micah Reeves case and her trespasser. After you're done here, check in with me. I may want to bring in backup, depending on what I find."

"Will do."

Brad pulled out his keys, slid behind the wheel of his cruiser, and pressed hard on the accelerator once he cleared the end of the dirt drive at the farm.

It was possible Natalie was right. There could be a simple explanation for Steven's actions.

But every instinct he'd honed through thirteen years of police work wasn't buying that.

In fact, as he barreled down the rural roads that wound among the wooded hillsides, one word kept strobing through his mind.

Guilty.

IT HAD TO BE HERE.

Every other piece of jewelry in his grandfather's inventory was accounted for except a diamond-and-emerald bracelet, as he'd discovered when he'd cross-checked his bounty against the list this morning.

Cursing the stupid bats, Steven ducked into the passageway where he'd found the man's stash, flashlight aimed at the floor as he approached the crevice that had held the treasure.

If the flying creatures hadn't unnerved him last night, he would never have been in such a rush to shove all the jewelry back into the bag, beat a hasty retreat—and apparently drop one precious item as he fled.

Waiting until tonight to come back and search for it may have been more prudent, but the thought of another trip out here in the dark turned his stomach. Besides, a daylight excursion wasn't risky. He wasn't likely to run into anyone, and he had a right to walk around his cousin's property.

His beam picked up a sparkle, and he dropped to one knee. Yes!

The bracelet was wedged under an overhang of jagged rock, where he must have kicked it as he fled.

He worked his fingers under the ledge and gently extracted the bracelet. Examined it.

It appeared to be fine, but he'd give it a more thorough inspection in the light.

After securing it in his shirt pocket, he retraced his route to the entrance of the cave. Stepped outside and filled his lungs with the fresh air.

Claustrophobia had never been one of his liabilities, but in the future he planned to walk a wide circle around small, enclosed spaces.

He started to reach for the bracelet to give it a once-over. Hesitated.

Maybe it would be smarter to go back down to the main path, find a brighter spot that would better highlight the gems. The dense trees by the cave entrance created deep shadows, and the angry clouds swirling overhead had snuffed out the weak light trying to filter through the branches.

Leaving the bracelet in his pocket, he descended the rocky, sloping trail.

Smiled.

At last his quest to recover the spoils of war his grandfather had claimed long ago in Germany had been completed.

And he didn't share one iota of the guilt his long-dead relative must have nursed after the theft. Why else would the man have hidden his plunder from the world and decided not to profit from it?

What a fool.

His grandfather had taken these items from the enemy. All soldiers did that, even if it was against the rules of war.

Heck, look at all the artwork the Nazis had stolen. This was small potatoes compared to their pillaging.

Not that he cared about what had happened eighty-plus years ago.

All that mattered was that the stuff was his now.

He emerged from the narrow trail that led up to the cave, onto the main path to the lake.

It was definitely brighter here. A perfect place to examine the merchandise.

And gloat over a job well done.

THERE HE WAS.

As Cara rounded the curve in the path, she spotted Steven just up ahead, angled away from her as he examined an object in his hand.

Could be a buckeye. There were lots of them on the ground. Beautiful, with their egg-like shape, glossy-wood finish, and distinctive white eye on one end. She'd collected a few herself, near the perimeter of the yard at the edge of the woods, and put them in a small glass bowl to admire after sun drying them for several days.

Or perhaps he'd stumbled upon a piece of lace agate, like the one she'd found on her wanderings that rested on the windowsill in the cottage, sparkling in the sun.

He appeared to be engrossed in whatever he'd discovered and apparently didn't hear her approach.

"Hi, Steven." She called out from several yards away to alert him to her presence so he wouldn't be startled.

Didn't help.

He jerked toward her, and the object in his hand flew her direction.

She jolted to a stop as it came to rest a few feet in front of her on top of the bright yellow leaves shed by a tall poplar tree beside the path.

Her jaw dropped as she stared at it.

Was that a diamond-and-emerald bracelet?

Before she could process what she was seeing, Steven swept in, snatched it up, and shoved it into his shirt pocket.

Several silent seconds crawled by as she tried to make sense of the scenario.

"You should see your face." He smiled, but unless she was misreading him, he was seriously rattled. "Then again, I suppose it's not every day you see a piece of fine jewelry lying in the woods."

"So my eyes weren't deceiving me."

"Nope. It's real." He shifted his weight, his expression growing sheepish as he propped his hands on his hips. "This is a mite awkward. I guess I should have mentioned that I'm seeing a woman in St. Louis. The bracelet is for her. She has a birthday coming up. I hope I didn't mislead you about my interest."

"No. Not at all." Truth be told, it was possible she'd misinterpreted the glint of attraction in his eyes early on. And once Brad had taken center stage, she hadn't cared what, if any, romantic signals Steven had been sending. She certainly hadn't sent *him* any, that much she knew. "She's a lucky woman. That's quite a gift."

"I hope she agrees."

She glanced down at his other hand.

Why was he carrying a flashlight in broad daylight?

He lifted it and spoke as if he'd read her mind. "I was thinking about exploring the cave. Spelunking has never been high on my radar, but since I know every inch of this property above ground, I thought I should take a peek into the cave."

While carrying around an expensive piece of jewelry?

Why would he do that?

And what was the bracelet doing in his pocket, anyway? Shouldn't it be in the elegant, protective case the jeweler must have provided?

Maybe Steven's head injury was muddling his thinking.

Whatever was going on, however, it wasn't giving her a warm and fuzzy feeling. Strange vibes were swirling through the air, and an alert began to beep in her mind.

"Well . . ." She took a step back. Forced up the corners

of her lips. "I'll let you get to it. I was going to take a walk by the lake, but I think the weather is about to get nasty. I'd rather be inside if a storm is brewing." She turned and began to walk away.

Fast.

"Cara."

As he called out to her, she stopped. Looked back.

Sucked in a breath.

What in the world?

Steven was Natalie's kind, caring cousin. The man who gave up his weekends to keep her company and watch over her. Who'd accompanied the visiting professor on hikes around the property and entertained her with witty banter as they'd laughed and chatted.

So who was this gun-toting stranger putting her heart in his crosshairs?

TWENTY-EIGHT

THIS MUST BE THE MONTH for missing children.

And finding a child who had vanished was more urgent than a conversation with Steven, eager as he was to talk to the man.

Brad ended his exchange with the dispatcher on the radio, put his phone on hands-free, and called Natalie again.

She answered on the first ring.

After he identified himself, he got straight to business. "Any sign of Steven?"

"No. I'm in my room, and I have a clear view of the yard behind the house. He hasn't come back yet."

"Slight change in plans. I just had a call about a missing child. That has to take precedence. I may not get to your place until later in the afternoon. I'd still like you to wait and let me talk to Steven first about his nighttime excursions on the property. It ties into the other questions I have for him."

"About Micah's death?"

"Yes."

"I've been thinking about that since your first call. You must be mistaken, Brad. If he knew anything about what happened to Micah, he would have told us."

Not if he'd killed the man.

But he couldn't drop that bombshell on Natalie over the phone.

"You know him better than I do." He kept his tone conversational. "But I'm obligated to investigate any evidence that turns up."

"I understand. That's your job. I'm sure he'll have an explanation for whatever you found, though."

Yes, he would—especially if he had time to conjure one up.

That was why it was important to catch him by surprise.

"Let's hope we can clear it up later this afternoon. Would you hold off talking to him about your concerns until after he and I chat?"

"It will be a bit awkward. But I suppose I could go to the study and work. He never interrupts if I shut the door, and it would be far less suspicious than me hiding in my room all afternoon."

"Sounds like a plan. I'll get there as soon as I can."

The instant they said their goodbyes, he hit the siren and picked up speed.

Hopefully the missing six-year-old would be found safe and unharmed fast so he could move on to Natalie's.

And as long as she didn't alert her cousin to the fact that he was on the sheriff's radar, there shouldn't be any imminent danger on the Boyer property.

PULLING HIS GUN HAD BEEN A MISTAKE.

And now he'd have to deal with it.

Stifling a curse as Cara gaped at him from ten feet away, Steven tried to work through the muddle in his brain.

Failed.

There was no simple fix for this problem.

With Micah, he'd had time to plan. Working on the fly had never been his strong suit.

"W-what's going on?"

At Cara's question, he closed the distance between them. "Shut up and let me think. Don't get any ideas about screaming, either. Natalie won't hear you inside the house, and I won't hesitate to pull the trigger. With all the hunting that goes on around here, one more shot won't even be noticed."

Her gaze dropped to his pistol, and sweat beaded on her forehead despite the chill in the air.

She was scared.

Good.

That should keep her in line while he figured out what to do next.

If he'd let her walk away a minute ago, he wouldn't be in this mess—except that would have been a mistake too. Her expression had telegraphed her suspicions loud and clear, making it obvious she hadn't bought his explanation about the bracelet. And who could blame her? No one took an expensive piece of jewelry on a spelunking expedition.

If she wasn't best buds with the sheriff, their encounter might not have been as much of an issue. Natalie wouldn't have questioned his explanation if Cara brought the incident up to her.

But Brad Mitchell would.

And he didn't want the man asking any more questions. Mitchell had grilled him about his whereabouts the day Micah died, and while his alibi was sound, anything that cast further suspicion on him could be damaging. The sheriff might dig deeper. What if he somehow found out the identity of the late-night trespasser?

That would open a whole new can of worms.

No, Cara couldn't talk to him about this.

And there was only one way to stop her from doing that—just as there'd been only one way to stop Micah from potentially thwarting his plans.

Cara had to die.

There was no choice.

His stomach gurgled, and he swallowed past the sour taste in his mouth.

Another killing hadn't been in his plans. *No* killings had ever been in his plans.

But he was in too deep to back out.

What he needed to do was put other concerns aside and focus on how to accomplish the task.

It had to look like an accident, as Micah's had. That was a given.

With the lake close at hand, that was the easiest solution. But drowning wouldn't work a second time.

So what could happen to a healthy young woman that would appear accidental and raise no red flags?

"Steven, whatever is wrong can be fixed." A tremor ran through Cara's voice. "You don't have to—"

"I said, shut up!"

Hands clenched at her sides, she pressed her lips together and watched him.

Keeping the pistol pointed at her, he considered scenarios.

A car crash could work. The narrow, winding roads in this area were accident alley.

That would be hard to stage without advance planning, though.

She could trip on the path while hiking, hit her head. That kind of injury could be fatal.

But it was possible she'd survive that—and survival wasn't an option.

What could he do that would—

He froze.

Of course!

Why hadn't he thought of that immediately?

The perfect weapon was close at hand.

It would be easy to pull off too. And unlike the situation with Micah, there would be no blood on his hands.

This go-round, he could accomplish the distasteful deed without having to worry about losing his breakfast.

CRISIS AVERTED.

Brad finished the call with dispatch, swung into a gravel driveway on his right, backed out onto the road, and reversed course.

With the six-year-old found safely asleep beside the family dog in the woods abutting the field beside his house, the situation with Steven once more took top billing.

Natalie answered his call on the first ring, as she had before. "I didn't expect to hear from you so soon."

"The situation I had to deal with resolved itself. I should be at your place within fifteen minutes. Any sign of Steven?"

"No. All's quiet here. I haven't heard him come back yet."

"Stay put if you do. I'll be there shortly."

As soon as he ended that conversation, Brad called Cara's cell and pressed on the accelerator. She was probably heads-down in the cottage with her research, but it wouldn't hurt to advise her to lock her doors until he'd had an opportunity to talk to Steven.

Besides, it was a legitimate excuse to hear her voice, even if he'd be swinging back by the property in a mere six hours to pick her up for their much-delayed dinner date.

Brad's lips bowed as he took a curve at a fast clip, keeping a firm grip on the wheel.

The gourmet restaurant where he'd reserved an intimate table for two would surprise her. The eatery was a hidden gem, out in the middle of nowhere, but it attracted patrons from a huge radius. The tab would set him back a hefty amount, but it would be well worth it to—

Cara's cell rolled to voicemail.

Huh.

Why wasn't she answering?

He ended the call without leaving a message.

Five minutes later, he tried her again.

Same result.

A tingle of unease slithered up his spine.

She always kept her phone close at hand. Unless she was taking a shower, she should have noticed the call. But how many people took showers in the middle of the day?

In all likelihood there was a logical explanation for her lack of response. Absent his concerns over Steven, the lapse would only cause the tiniest blip on his worry meter.

But Steven was a big worry—and he was on the premises.

Still, he'd have no reason to bother Cara.

Then again, he'd had no apparent reason to bother Micah, either. And he'd done more than bother the groundskeeper, if the red alerts the DNA results had set off were accurate.

So as soon as he checked in with Natalie at the house, he'd circle around to the cottage and make sure Cara was okay before he shared a cup of tea with the older woman and waited for her cousin to finish his trek around the lake.

THIS WAS SURREAL.

As Cara faced off with Steven on the path to the lake, mind processing at warp speed, the pieces began to fall into place.

Steven had never found caves appealing. He'd told her that on their first hike.

Either he'd been lying, or there was another explanation for his sudden interest in visiting the subterranean space.

Did it have anything to do with the bracelet in his pocket?

And could all of this be connected to the late-night lights she'd seen on the property?

Was Steven the trespasser?

"Stop thinking so hard, Cara."

At Steven's comment, she studied him.

He wasn't quite as agitated as he'd been moments ago.

Why not?

He didn't wait long to give her an answer.

"Let's take a walk." He motioned to the trail behind her. The one that led back to the cottage and the house.

What?

He was going to take her at gunpoint to a place where Natalie could see them?

That didn't make sense.

Because Cara would bet her life the older woman didn't have a clue her cousin had a dark side. Why would Steven want to risk changing that?

"Move." Steven extended his hand, aiming the gun at her center mass.

Her breath hitched, and she turned around. Started up the path.

She had to do something.

But what?

This scenario was more the bailiwick of her siblings. Jack would already have the situation in hand, and Bri wouldn't be far behind. Either of them would be capable of kicking the gun out of Steven's—

Wait.

She could kick.

While she didn't have the self-defense moves her siblings had mastered, her ballet experience ought to give her the tools to deliver a kick that would dislodge the gun from Steven's hand if the opportunity presented itself.

Of course, after that, her only defense would be to run.

Unless . . . was it possible she could talk her way out of this?

Even as that thought crossed her mind, she dismissed it.

What Steven was doing was a criminal offense. He wasn't going to want to pay the price for that.

And who knew what else he'd done, this man with jewels in his pocket, who was likely the person who'd been skulking around in the dark that she'd assumed was Micah.

Micah.

Cara's stomach began to churn.

All along, Natalie had been skeptical about the circumstances around her trusted groundskeeper's death. The same man who'd left her a warning to be careful, which she'd attributed to the kitchen fire.

But maybe Micah had discovered there was underhanded activity on the premises.

Maybe he'd known Steven was involved.

Maybe Steven had found out he'd known.

And maybe Steven had eliminated that threat because he didn't want his project, whatever it was, to be exposed.

Cara's pulse spiked, and she stumbled on a rock.

Could Steven be a . . . a murderer?

The notion seemed absurd.

But if he was . . . if he'd killed Micah . . . then there was little chance he'd hesitate to kill again.

And right now, she was literally in his sights.

Bile rose in her throat as she struggled to get her fear under control. To engage the left side of her brain and think this through. To try to anticipate his next steps.

Shooting her would be a mistake. He had to know that. It would obviously be murder. And if he'd killed Micah, he'd gone to great lengths to make it seem like an accident. No matter how he framed it, a gunshot wound wouldn't be an accident.

So how was he going to—

"Turn right."

She paused. Stared at the narrow trail that had become overgrown since Micah's death.

And with sudden, sickening certainty, she realized what he had in store for her.

Steven was taking her up to the cliff where Marie and Paul's grandfather had held their trysts.

To the cliff from which that despondent young woman had jumped to her death.

The cliff where Steven no doubt intended to stage a fall by the visiting professor who'd wandered up there to see the view and gotten a tad too close to the edge.

"Go up the trail, Cara." He bent down and tucked his flashlight among the foliage, perhaps to keep his hands free so he could deal with her on the hike if she decided to object to his plan.

A hard object nudged her in the kidney, and she lurched forward as her respiration went haywire and fear clogged her throat.

She could scream, but Steven was right. Natalie would never hear her inside the house, and the closest neighbors were too far away to pick up a cry for help.

"Keep walking—and remember, I'll use this gun if I have to. The shot won't be noticed, and a few minutes after that, the gun will be at the bottom of the lake. The shooter will never be identified."

"They'll . . . they'll suspect you. You're on site." Somehow she choked out the reply.

"Suspicions are useless without proof."

True. But there would be proof. Trace evidence on her body, if nothing else. Like his skin under her fingernails.

Because she wasn't going over the edge without a fight.

In the critical minutes ahead, however, she intended to do everything in her power to ensure that history didn't repeat itself.

Marie had chosen to die.

But *she* intended to live.

TWENTY-NINE

BRAD TOOK THE DRIVE UP to Natalie's house far faster than was prudent, gravel pinging against the underside of the cruiser.

But cars were replaceable.

People weren't.

He skidded to a stop on the circle drive behind Cara's Accord, set the brake, and vaulted from the car.

As he strode up the walk and ascended the steps to the galérie, he scanned the property. All appeared quiet.

Didn't mean a thing.

Sometimes the quietest moments held the deepest danger.

He rang the bell, trying to curb his impatience as he waited for Natalie to answer.

At last the muffled sound of a sliding bolt broke the silence. Seconds later she opened the door. "Sorry to keep you waiting. It seems I move slower every day."

"Is Steven back?"

"No. Would you like to come in and wait?"

"Yes, but I want to swing by the cottage first. Give me a few minutes."

"Don't rush on my account. Would you like a cup of coffee?"

"If it's not too much trouble." Wired as he was, he didn't need the caffeine. But juggling a mug would keep his hands occupied.

"It's no trouble. Do you want to cut through the house?"

"No. I'll circle around from the outside."

"I'll unlock the back door for you. Come in through there after you finish."

He acknowledged her comment with a dip of his head, then descended the steps and took off at a jog around the house, scrutinizing the cottage at the back of the yard after it came into view.

Nothing appeared to be amiss.

Hopefully, his worry was for naught. Cara would be hard at work on her laptop or engrossed in one of the books she'd borrowed from the study in the main house.

At her door, he gave a soft knock.

No response.

He tried again, rapping harder. With her hearing issues, it was possible she hadn't heard his first attempt.

Still nothing.

He frowned.

Could she have turned off her implants?

He crossed to the window, cupped his hands around his face, and peered in.

The cottage was empty.

A tingle of alarm raced through him.

Since she wasn't at the main house and her car was in front, she had to be on the property.

But where?

Had she decided to take a hike around the lake on this beautiful day?

She'd said she'd given those up after he'd expressed concern about her wandering around alone, but what if she'd changed her mind?

What if she'd run into Steven?

He tamped down a surge of panic.

It shouldn't matter if they'd met up. The man would have no reason to hurt her.

Yet he'd had no apparent reason to hurt Micah, either.

And Micah was dead.

Pulse kicking into high gear, he texted Larry with a request for backup before jogging back toward the main house. It wouldn't hurt to have his chief deputy on hand in case this went south.

As he drew close, Natalie came out onto the galérie. "Is everything all right?"

"Cara's not in the cottage. I'm going to see if I can find her. Do me a favor and bolt all the doors while I'm gone."

Her eyebrows rose. "What if Steven comes back?"

"Talk to him through a window. Ask him to wait outside."

Natalie blinked. "Why?"

"It would be safer."

"I'm not afraid of Steven."

"Trust me on this, Natalie." He began backing up. "If I'm wrong, I'll apologize to both of you later. But if I'm not, at least you'll be secure until I get back." He swiveled around and took off at a fast trot.

He couldn't make Natalie follow his instructions. All he could do was hope she listened to him.

Because if Steven had somehow realized that the risk of exposure for whatever he was up to had escalated, no one would be safe.

Including the cousin who'd never shown him anything but kindness and love.

"STEVEN . . . I DON'T UNDERSTAND what's going on." Cara pushed aside a branch as they ascended the trail to the cliff.

Maybe if she could get him to talk, she could buy herself a few more minutes.

"You don't have to understand."

His reply was a bit garbled, but she got the gist.

He didn't want to talk.

She surveyed the path ahead.

They were halfway to the top of the cliff, and the clock was ticking down fast.

It couldn't hurt to try again to engage him. What did she have to lose?

"Look . . . you don't have to do whatever you're planning to do." She stopped and pivoted toward him. "I don't know anything about whatever you've got going on."

"You know about the bracelet. And I pulled a gun on you. Your sheriff friend wouldn't be happy about that."

"I don't have to tell him about it."

Steven barked out a laugh. "Like that's gonna happen."

"Even if I did tell him, pulling a gun is far less of a crime than using it."

"I'm hoping I don't have to do that. Get moving." He waved the gun toward the trail. "And pick up the pace. You're going too slow."

"The path is overgrown."

"Yeah." He surveyed the trail ahead. "I suppose Micah was good for something. But he ended up being as much of a problem as you did."

Cara's lungs stalled. "Are you saying you . . . that he didn't drown?"

"No. He did drown—with a little help."

As the man's comment sank in, two facts registered.

Steven had killed Micah.

And if he was willing to admit his culpability, he couldn't let her live to tell that tale.

Cara began to shake.

She had to come up with a strategy to foil his plan. Now.

"Keep going." Steven pointed the gun at her again.

Doing her best to rein in her snowballing panic, she stumbled forward, moving as slow as possible. They were approaching the top too quickly, and her brain felt mired in muck.

A bramble snagged her sleeve, halting her forward momentum.

"Now what?" Steven sounded annoyed.

"I'm stuck on a thorny vine."

"Pull it off."

She pretended to focus on freeing her sleeve, but in reality she was concentrating on getting her brain in gear.

Could she enlist Steven's help with the barbed stem? Draw him close enough to perhaps kick the gun out of his hand?

Problem was, the path was narrow, the brush on either side was too thick to plunge through, and he was a lot stronger than she was. It would be better to find an open spot for her kick, where she had room to maneuver and could attempt to outrun him.

At a sudden prick on her finger, she jerked her hand back. "Ouch!"

Muttering a word that burned her ears, Steven moved closer, jabbed the gun into her kidney again, and yanked the bramble free of her sweater. "You're more trouble than Micah was."

The coldness in his eyes sent a shiver through her.

"Why did you kill him, Steven?" She searched his face. "He never did anything to you."

A muscle in his jaw clenched. "He saw too much. Like you did. But I had time to plan with him."

Keep him talking while you think, Cara.

"You did an impressive job." She tried to inject a note of admiration into her voice without gagging. "It looked like an accident." Even if Natalie had her doubts and Brad was still investigating the death.

"That was the plan."

"You must have mapped it out to the last detail, minute by minute."

It was possible he'd tell her to shut up again—but if he wanted to brag about his plotting skills, she'd listen. That would eke out a few more minutes for her.

He took the bait.

"Yeah. I did."

"I thought you left the night before Micah died."

A smirk twisted his lips. "So did everyone else. But I hung out down the road."

"And you came back Sunday?"

"Yes. Early. I went down to Micah's cabin before dawn, hid outside, and played a YouTube video of a whimpering raccoon. He could never resist an injured animal. When he came out to investigate, I hit him with a pipe. Once I got him into the boat, all I had to do was inject him with the sux I'd brought and dump him over the side."

At his matter-of-fact recounting of the ruthless murder, Cara groped for the tree next to her. Held on.

How could she have been fooled by the pleasant façade he'd displayed to the world?

But Natalie had been duped too, and she'd known Steven far longer.

Despite the nausea threatening to choke her, she forced out another question. "What's sux?"

"A drug that causes short-term paralysis. Vets use a ton of it. I knew it would keep Micah immobilized if he woke up while I was trying to get him into the water."

"Also while he was drowning." This man was heartless.

"That too."

"Weren't you worried it would show up in the drug screening the coroner did?"

"No. He'd have to test for it specifically, and why would

he? The cause of death was obvious. Drowning." Steven's eyes narrowed. "You're only delaying the inevitable, you know. And I don't want to be gone too long from the house. Natalie will wonder what I'm doing. Start walking."

She turned back to the path and began to climb again, her heart picking up speed as her palms grew clammy.

They were getting very close to the top.

And unless there was room up there to maneuver . . . unless she got an opportunity to deliver a well-placed kick . . . unless the clifftop offered an escape route . . . her life could be over in a handful of minutes.

HE COULD CALL OUT TO CARA. See if she answered.

But as Brad took the path from the cottage toward the lake, his gut told him to stay quiet.

And he always listened to his gut.

In fact, he took extra pains to keep his footfalls as silent as possible.

Of course, there was a chance he'd come across Steven and Cara either individually or together, both out for an innocent walk.

That was the best-case outcome.

Worst case, he'd be plunged into danger.

That's why Larry was en route, with instructions to come in quietly and text once he arrived.

It was also why his hand wasn't straying far from his pistol.

As Brad approached the offshoot trail that led to the clifftop, he paused. Leaned close to examine the broken branches along the edge of the overgrown trail that indicated someone had ventured that way in the recent past.

Deer were a distinct possibility.

He hesitated.

The most prudent course seemed to be to continue on,

toward the lake. It was doubtful Cara would tackle the overgrown track, and Natalie had said Steven intended to go to the lake.

He started to turn away from the cliff route.

Stopped as a glint registered in his peripheral vision.

Using his toe, he pushed the foliage aside. Bent down to inspect the black cylindrical item with a metal clip on the side.

Huh.

What was a flashlight doing here?

And it hadn't been in that spot long, either. The barrel wasn't dirty or stained or weather-beaten.

Brad looked up the trail to the cliff. Back down the path to the lake.

A wrong decision could cost him precious time.

If danger was lurking on these premises today, minutes or even seconds could mark the difference between—

He froze.

What was that?

Cocking his ear toward the cliff trail, he tuned in to the skittering noise.

It sounded like rocks slipping and sliding. As if someone was ascending the steep slope.

Decision made.

After texting Larry his location, he veered onto the path and began to climb, doing his best to remain as silent as possible. Announcing his presence to whoever was up there would be a mistake.

But he had to move fast.

Because every instinct in his body was screaming that whatever was happening on the cliff path had nothing to do with a casual afternoon stroll to admire the view.

He picked up his pace, cringing at the rustle of every leaf he stepped on, but the noise coming from above him ought to be sufficient to cover his missteps.

When he rounded a curve near the top and caught sight of who was ahead of him, his pulse stuttered.

Cara was in front of Steven as the two of them emerged onto the clifftop, and when she swung toward the man, he extended his arm.

There was a gun in his hand.

And it was aimed at her heart.

Brad's heart lurched as icy fingers squeezed his windpipe. What the . . . ?

This didn't make any sense.

Why would Steven be holding her at gunpoint?

Unless she'd stumbled into something he didn't want anyone to see—as Micah perhaps had.

Brad pulled out his pistol, but there were too many trees between him and Steven to give him a clean line of sight.

And he was only going to get one shot.

He charged ahead.

If Boyer was planning to kill Cara anyway, there was no longer any point in trying to mask his presence.

When his approach registered with the man, Steven glanced over his shoulder.

The instant he did, Cara executed a high kick that connected with the man's hand. The one holding the pistol.

A shot rang through the quiet air, and Brad's lungs shut down.

But Cara was still on her feet.

As Steven lunged for the gun lying on the ground a few feet away, Cara dived at his legs.

He twisted toward her. Tried to shake her off as they both fell to the ground.

She held tight.

And as they grappled, they inched closer and closer to the edge of the cliff.

Too close.

One wrong move, and they'd both plunge over the precipice.

Brad surged forward. "Steven—stop! This is over."

No response.

Brad reached the crest of the trail and dashed for the gun lying near the duo.

"No!" The bellow came from Steven as he kicked free of Cara's grasp, vaulted to his feet, and yanked her up in front of him. Clamping his arm under her chin, he pulled her back against him. "Stay away from my gun and put yours down or she goes over."

Cara clutched at Steven's arm, trying to pull free, but he held on tight, his eyes crazed. Desperate.

And desperate people didn't think straight.

Brad stopped fifteen feet away, lowered his weapon, and tried to keep his voice calm. An almost impossible task when the woman who he was more and more certain represented his future was literally on the brink of death. "Let her go, Steven."

"No."

Stalemate.

Would negotiation work?

"Tell me what you want."

"Nothing you can give me. Not now." He eyed his gun again, resting on the ground halfway between them.

That pistol was not getting back into his hands.

Maybe he could coax him away from the edge of the cliff, remove the imminent danger, and then—

All at once, Cara lifted her arm and started banging the side of her fist against Steven's face.

The blows were enough to cause him to loosen his grip, and she twisted again in his arms. Wrenched free and stumbled back, away from the cliff top.

Steven didn't recover as well.

Thrown off balance, he lost his footing. Tottered on the edge, arms flailing.

But he couldn't defy gravity.

A second later he pitched over the edge, his scream echoing . . . fading . . . as he disappeared from view.

Shock reverberated through the silent air.

Until Cara's sudden, quiet sob propelled Brad into action.

He erased the distance between them in several long strides and wrapped her in his arms as tremors racked her body.

Or were the tremors his?

Didn't matter.

She was safe. That was all that counted.

Murmuring comforting words, he held her until she at last eased back within the circle of his arms, the distress in her eyes almost palpable.

"How will we ever tell Natalie about this? Steven was all the family she had."

Brad stared at her.

After all she'd been through, her first thought was about Natalie rather than her own near-death experience?

If he wasn't already half in love with her, her incredible unselfishness and compassion would have given him a major push along that road.

"I'll handle that. But first, I need to check on Steven." Not that there was much urgency. The odds of surviving a fall from such a height were infinitesimal. "Are you up to walking down the trail with me?"

"Yes. I want off this cliff as fast as possible."

"I hear you. Let's go."

He took the lead on the steep track, calling Larry during the descent with an update and a request that he have an ambulance dispatched. Just in case.

By the time they arrived at the bottom, his chief deputy was striding down the path.

"Ambulance is on the way." Larry glanced at Cara. Back at him. "You want to stay with the professor while I get a read on the situation?"

"Yes. Thanks. We'll go back to the house. Text me with whatever you find. The next trail you come to will take you to the cliff base."

"Got it."

Larry continued down the path, and Brad folded Cara's icy hand in his. If anything, her trembling was worse.

Not surprising.

Reaction was setting in.

"Let's stop at your cottage for a minute. You can get a drink and tell me what happened before I talk to Natalie."

"He killed Micah, Brad." Her irises began to shimmer.

Theory confirmed.

"Did he admit that?"

"Yes. After I found him with the bracelet."

Bracelet?

Apparently there were more pieces to this story than he'd anticipated.

"Let's go back to the cottage, and you can fill me in."

She didn't protest.

They paused only once in their trek, for him to read the text from Larry.

"Is Steven . . . did he survive?" Cara gripped his hand tighter.

"No."

"So he died just like Marie." A shiver rippled through her. "I think that cliff is cursed."

He didn't argue with her.

But there were still answers to find and bad news to share—and telling a caring woman that her beloved cousin was not only dead but a killer would be one of the hardest tasks he'd ever performed during his law enforcement career.

THIRTY

BY THE TIME THEY EMERGED from the woods, Brad's brain was on overload trying to integrate the new information Cara had relayed during the walk back with the facts he already knew. Steven's dire financial situation. Micah's death. The expensive jewelry Cara had seen. The flashlight he'd found, and Steven's reference to the cave. The man's late-night excursions.

All of those disparate pieces were somehow related, and it was up to him to figure out how.

On the plus side, he had far more to work with now than he'd had an hour ago.

The faint wail of a siren sounded in the distance as they walked across the lawn toward the cottage, and the back door of the main house opened.

He paused as Natalie stepped onto the galérie. The place would soon be swarming with emergency crews, and keeping her in the dark any longer than necessary would be cruel.

"Why don't you go on to the cottage and chill while I talk to Natalie?"

Cara's brow puckered as she looked toward the house. "No. I'll go with you."

"This isn't going to be easy, and you've been through enough today."

"I have to be there when you tell her, Brad. We've grown close during my stay, and she's about to get the shock of her life. I want her to know she's not alone."

Throat constricting, he squeezed the hand of the remarkable woman beside him who never seemed to put herself first. "Okay. We'll do this together."

She held on tight to his fingers as they headed for the galérie.

The older woman remained in the shadows under the overhang as they approached, cane gripped in one hand, fingers of the other wrapped around the railing.

She watched them as they ascended the steps, eyes sad, complexion pale.

"Natalie, why don't we go inside for a few minutes and talk?" Brad motioned toward the back door.

"Steven's dead, isn't he?" Her tone was flat. Resigned.

Brad sucked in a breath as Cara stiffened beside him.

How could she know that?

But sometimes people sensed when someone they loved was gone.

And since she'd intuited the truth, there was no point in sugarcoating it.

"Yes. I'm sorry."

Her features crumpled.

Cara tugged her hand free of his and crossed to the older woman. Pulled her into a hug.

Natalie clung to her, lashes spiky with moisture. "I knew there was something wrong once I realized it was Steven sneaking around at night. I had a feeling it would all come to a bad end." A quiver ran through her words.

"Let's go inside. I'll make us some tea." Cara stroked the woman's back, her own voice tear-laced.

After a few moments, Natalie eased away and turned toward the house.

Brad moved forward and took her arm in a steadying grip.

"Thank you." She sent him a grateful look.

He guided her to the living room while Cara brewed tea for Natalie and poured a cup of coffee for herself and him, but he waited until she joined them before launching into his story.

Both women listened without speaking as he told them about his suspicions and the evidence he'd compiled linking Steven to Micah's death, along with the information he'd gathered about the man's finances.

When he got to the part about today's cliffside drama, Natalie's complexion lost what little color remained.

"You mean Steven was going to push you over the edge?" Shock rose off her in waves as she turned to Cara and clasped her hand.

"But he didn't. Once Brad showed up, I knew I'd be fine."

"Oh, my dear, I'm so sorry." Natalie touched Cara's cheek, distress etching deep brackets beside her mouth.

"There's nothing to be sorry about. Steven fooled everyone."

"And poor Micah . . ." She pulled a tissue from her pocket. Dabbed at her lashes. "This is an even more tragic story than Marie's."

"And we don't know all of it yet." Brad rejoined the conversation. "Natalie, do you have any idea why Steven would have such a valuable piece of jewelry in his possession?"

"No. And if his financial problems were as severe as your research suggests, where would he have gotten the money for such a purchase?"

Excellent question.

Perhaps the guestroom would hold some clues.

"Would you mind if I go through his room?"

"Not at all. It's down the hall, first door on the left."

He glanced at Cara. "I'll be back in a few minutes."

"Natalie and I will finish our tea."

He left the two women in the living room and strode down the hall to Steven's bedroom, pausing to place a quick but important call en route.

His subsequent thorough search yielded pay dirt.

A headlamp like miners used. Hand-drawn maps of what appeared to be cave passages. An inventory of items, and a letter from Steven's father. A soiled bag full of stunning antique jewelry. And a dirty, wrapped parcel that must contain the paintings referenced on the inventory.

It didn't take a genius to do the math.

Steven had intended to sell his grandfather's World War II contraband on the black market to fix his financial problems.

It was possible, of course, that he'd never intended to kill anyone.

But somewhere along the way, when his plan had been put in jeopardy, he'd taken the huge leap from black market dealer of stolen goods to murderer.

A leap only someone without the merest shred of a conscience could have made.

Meaning it was impossible to dredge up the tiniest scrap of empathy for the man.

Brad took the bag of jewels, the inventory, and the letter back to the living room.

"Did you find any answers?" Natalie wadded the tissue tighter in her hand as he entered.

"Yes." He gave them a recap of his search, then handed Natalie the letter and inventory.

As she scanned it, he opened the bag of jewels and spread them on the coffee table.

Cara gaped at the glittering array. "Those must be worth a fortune."

"Indeed—and they must be returned to the rightful owner. The paintings too, just as my uncle directed." Natalie passed the letter and inventory back. "Can you make that happen, Brad?"

"Yes. I'll contact the FBI Art Crime Team. They'll know the correct procedure to follow." The doorbell rang, and he rose. "I'll get that."

Thirty seconds later, he opened the door to find Father Johnson on the other side.

The priest from the historic church where locals had worshipped for almost two centuries must have dropped everything and driven faster than was prudent after their phone chat.

"Thank you for coming so fast, Father." He stepped back and ushered the man in. "Like I told you on the phone, I thought it would comfort Natalie to speak with you."

"I'm always happy to tend the flock, and Natalie's been a faithful parishioner for decades. Thank *you* for thinking of calling me."

Brad led him into the living room.

"Natalie, you have a visitor."

The older woman shifted sideways on the couch. "Father Johnson!" She started to stand.

"Don't get up." He waved her back.

Cara rose from beside Natalie. "Why don't you take my seat? I'd like to go freshen up."

"I'll walk back to the cottage with you." Brad waited for her in the doorway. "Natalie, I'll stop by again before I leave. And I'll be back later with dinner for you and Cara and me. Father, you're welcome to join us."

"Thank you, but I have a sick call later this afternoon." He sat beside Natalie.

Cara slipped into the hall and Brad fell in beside her, the murmur of conversation following them until they exited through the back door.

"Did you call the priest?" Cara looked up at him as they crossed the galérie and descended the steps.

"Yes."

"That was kind of you. As was the offer to provide dinner."

He took her hand. "I hope you don't mind one more deferral of our date, but I didn't think Natalie should be alone this evening. I know it won't be much of a date, and certainly nothing like the one I had planned. I'm sorry if—"

"Brad." She stopped. Tightened her grip on his fingers. "Don't apologize. Our dinner for two can wait. There's a more pressing need here tonight. If you hadn't suggested this, I would have." She smiled up at him, the warmth in her gaze seeping deep into his heart. "No fancy restaurant date would have impressed me half as much as your thoughtfulness and compassion."

"And here I was afraid you might be upset."

"Then you have a lot to learn about me."

"And I'll enjoy every minute of it." They continued to the cottage, stopping by her front door. "I promise I'll make up for tonight. We *will* have a real dinner date. One to remember."

"I'll hold you to that."

"Until then, why don't we go inside where it's more private and I'll give you a preview of dessert?"

Without a word, she dug out her key, inserted it into the lock, and opened the door.

He followed her in, closed it behind him, and held out his hand.

When she placed hers inside his, he drew her toward him.

She came without protest, the soft curve of her mouth an invitation that was impossible to resist.

Never breaking eye contact, he lifted his other hand. Traced the arch of her eyebrow. Brushed his knuckles over her cheek. Trailed his fingers across her lips.

At the catch in her breath, his pulse picked up and he slowly, very slowly, leaned down and pressed his lips to hers.

This long-awaited moment was to be savored.

Her hands crept around his neck, and he wrapped her in his arms, pulling her close until no more than a whisper separated them and the world faded away.

How long the kiss went on, Brad had no idea. But at last, with a triumph of will over desire, he broke contact. Rested his forehead against hers as he came up for air.

"You know . . ." She cleared her throat when her voice rasped. "I never overindulge on d-dessert, but I could go for second helpings of that one anytime."

At her husky comment, a chuckle rumbled deep in his chest. "I think that could be arranged. Write me in ink on your calendar for Sunday night—if you're willing to come back from Cape in time for dinner."

"I'll camp out here all weekend if necessary. I am *not* missing our next date."

"I like your enthusiasm."

"I have plenty of enthusiasm—but to tell you the truth, I planned to come back early Sunday anyway. I'd rather not leave Natalie on her own for too long. I'm also going to contact Paul and see if he'll stop by Saturday."

"Good idea. And now I need to get back to work." He pulled slightly away and studied her. "You'll be okay here by yourself?"

She nodded. "With Steven gone, there's no danger anymore. I'll be fine. I'm more worried about Natalie."

"You may be surprised at how well she weathers this. She lived through polio and the challenges that brought, not to mention all the years she's managed out here on her own. I expect she has deep reserves of strength and fortitude."

"I hope you're right."

"She also has you for the next few weeks."

"I'm glad for that."

"So am I. May I suggest you take a nap this afternoon? You have to be exhausted."

"I don't typically sleep while the sun's up, but I think I'll make an exception today."

After stealing one more quick kiss, he slipped through the door and struck off toward the path to the cave, where the emergency crew was waiting for Rod to arrive. They wouldn't move the body until the coroner weighed in, though there were two witnesses who could testify to manner of death.

What a tragic end for such a young man, thanks to a host of bad choices.

Yet sorry as he was for Natalie, who would not only be grieving the death of her beloved cousin but also dealing with her disillusionment about the man she'd held in such high esteem, he couldn't help but be relieved that at long last the mysterious happenings on this isolated property were over.

And at least there would be a happy ending for a family in Germany, soon destined to be reunited with a long-lost treasure that had been hidden for decades in a cave thousands of miles from where it belonged.

"**I STILL CAN'T BELIEVE** a place like this exists in the hinterland, as Jack would call it." Cara took another bite of the luscious chocolate mousse she'd ordered on their first visit to this hidden gem too, during their first date two weeks ago.

"There are signs of civilization here and there." Brad smiled at her over the rim of his coffee cup, as distractingly hot in his sport jacket and open-necked dress shirt as he was in his uniform.

Cara took a sip of her ice water.

Didn't help her cool down.

Maybe discussing a serious topic would do the trick.

"So what's the news you said you'd share about the case after dinner?"

"Do you really want to talk business in this romantic spot?"

He waggled his eyebrows, the flickering votive candle in the center of the table casting a golden glow over his handsome face.

No, she did *not* want to talk business.

What she wanted to do was claim another one of the incredible kisses he'd been offering on a regular basis for the past two weeks.

But this wasn't the place for that.

"To tell you the truth, I can think of another activity I'd enjoy more—but in the interest of decorum, a business discussion would be more prudent."

"We'll move on to the other activity later." At his intimate wink, a delicious tingle of anticipation zipped through her. "I heard from the FBI this morning."

She forced herself to refocus. "They located the owners of the jewels and the paintings?"

"Yes. The family was ecstatic to get the paintings back. Turns out the two small canvases are a Vermeer and a Rembrandt. Worth a fortune—though not on the black market. They were listed on two international databases for stolen collectibles. No reputable dealer would touch them, and buyers of less stellar character would have paid only a fraction of their value. Steven wouldn't have profited much from them. Certainly not enough to cover all his debts."

"So I guess he was going to rely on the jewels, probably broken down into loose stones. I doubt he could sell them intact if they were listed in the databases too."

"They weren't."

Cara stopped eating her mousse, spoon poised halfway to her mouth. "Why not?"

"Here's where the story gets interesting—and ironic. After the war started, the owners knew the family jewels would be a target if their land was ever occupied by enemy soldiers. They were afraid that hiding them wouldn't be sufficient, because anyone looting the premises would expect to find jewels in such a magnificent setting. If they didn't, they'd tear the place apart searching for them, causing major damage to the ancestral home. So the family had paste copies made, which they kept in a very visible cabinet in the master suite. That's what Natalie's uncle stole."

Cara stared at him. Set her spoon down. "You mean Steven spent all those nights searching—and killed a man—for jewelry that was worth nothing?"

"Yes."

"Wow."

"I had the same reaction."

"Have you told Natalie?"

"No. She's had enough trauma planning Steven's funeral and sorting out his affairs. I decided to wait a couple of weeks to pass on this news."

"I concur with that decision." Cara nodded her thanks at the waiter who topped off her coffee. Stirred in a dash of cream to cut the blackness. "On a happier note, she's decided to proceed with plans to expand the guest cottage. Paul's been helping her get that rolling. With the election over and his son bound for Washington, he's had more time to spend with her. I'm glad she has such a staunch friend."

"Speaking of friends . . ." Brad reached across the table and captured her hand, his fingers warm and strong, his touch ratcheting up her pulse. "I don't want to rush you, but I'm hoping the two of us are on the road to a much more serious relationship."

"I'm hoping the same thing. And you're not rushing me."

One side of his mouth rose. "I'm glad to hear that. Because I talked with a realtor today about putting my house on the market."

Cara blinked.

That had come out of nowhere—and it was a bit nerve-racking this early in their relationship. Hoping for a happy ending was fine, but not all such hopes came to fruition.

"Um . . . do you think that's premature? I mean, what if we fizzle?"

He hiked up the other side of his mouth, giving her a full-fledged smile. "I don't think that's going to happen." Then he grew more serious. "But in all honesty, I've been toying for a while with the idea of selling the house. There are too many memories there, and if I keep clinging to the past, I won't ever have a future. What I thought I'd do is rent an apartment as close to Cape as I can without leaving the county. The commute will still be a challenge after you go back, but it will be much more manageable than from my house. And fair warning—I plan to do a *lot* of commuting."

Joy bubbled up in her heart. Spilled over.

But before she got carried away, there was another issue they had to address.

"I like the sound of that. But what happens if we get more serious? That commute wouldn't be tenable for either of us long term."

He stroked his thumb over the back of her hand, causing a major disruption in her concentration. "Like I told you once, there are other jobs in law enforcement."

"It doesn't seem fair to ask you to give up your position as sheriff."

"Law enforcement is law enforcement, and my career is more portable than yours. I'd rather be married to a beautiful, intelligent, articulate, kind, generous, and loving woman than to a job any day—no pressure intended." He tapped the edge of her mousse goblet as his eyes began to smolder. "Are you going to finish that?"

She picked up her spoon and dug into the sweet confection, the electricity in the air setting off a tingle in her fingertips. "Yes, but I'm a fast eater."

"I'll get the check." He signaled to the waiter. "I don't know about you, but I'm ready to proceed to the second dessert course."

Cara made short work of her remaining mousse, and minutes later they were walking hand-in-hand out of the restaurant and into the chilly November night.

"The temperature's dropped." She angled sideways as a gust of wind whipped by.

"I have a fix for that." He positioned himself to block the breeze, pulled her close, and wrapped her in his arms. "Warmer?"

"Much. Now only my lips are cold." She lifted her head and rose on her tiptoes.

"I think I can fix that too."

And so he did.

In a way that was far sweeter and much more delicious than her delectable chocolate mousse.

EPILOGUE

AMAZING.

As Cara wrapped up her presentation about the paper she'd written on the Missouri settlement time forgot and its fast-disappearing language, Brad surveyed the audience in the university auditorium.

Everyone's attention was riveted on the woman he loved—rightly so—as she spoke from behind a microphone in the center of the stage. Cara had taken a specialized subject that could have been dry and tedious and injected it with life and vitality by masterfully weaving in snippets from Marie's journal and the woman's history to put a face on the subject matter.

She'd done the same with her more scholarly-style paper, which may have been why it had garnered national attention in academic circles and prompted an invitation for her to present it during a prestigious spring conference at a prominent East Coast university.

Now, two weeks later, she was repeating the presentation at her own university in a session that had been widely publicized. And both the media and the public had come out in force.

He glanced around again at the rapt audience.

Impressive.

Even more impressive, though?

Her hard-won self-confidence, on full display as she spoke with poise and authority to the large crowd.

Incredible, after all she'd had to overcome.

He couldn't be prouder of her if she'd won the Nobel Prize.

Nor could he love her more.

Brad's lips curved up as he shifted his attention back to the woman who'd staked a claim on his heart over the past seven months with her kindness and grace and generous, loving nature.

God had blessed him beyond measure the day she'd walked into his life, and he'd give thanks for that gift as long as he lived.

"Before I close, I want to recognize a very special person in the audience." Cara gave the crowd a sweep. "Without her gracious assistance, my project wouldn't have been possible. Please join me in thanking Natalie Boyer, whose translation of Marie's journal has made an incalculable contribution to our understanding of a unique era in history and a vanishing language. Natalie, would you please stand?"

Beside him, the older woman's hand fluttered to her chest as a wave of applause swept through the auditorium.

"Oh my. I didn't expect this."

"The recognition is well deserved. Take a bow." He gave her an assist up with a hand under her elbow.

Once the applause died down and Natalie retook her seat, Cara closed her folder of notes. "Thank you all for coming, and please stay to enjoy the reception in the foyer."

Another extended round of applause, this one for Cara, rang through the room.

"She's quite remarkable, isn't she? A brilliant young woman." Natalie watched Cara leave the stage, then turned to him. "I hope the university recognizes what a treasure she is."

"Treasure is an apt description."

She gave an approving nod and reached for her cane. "I thought you'd agree. And now I want to speak to her before we head home."

"So do I." Paul chimed in from the seat on her other side as he rose and crooked an elbow to her.

Natalie slipped her hand through his arm and stood.

A reporter from a local station swooped in to commandeer Natalie as they all exited the row, and Brad spoke to the older woman as he eased away to give the journalist access. "I'll stop in to see you soon."

"I'll look forward to that."

Natalie began fielding the man's questions with aplomb, and Brad left her to enjoy her moment in the spotlight. Up front, Cara was likewise occupied.

Fine by him. He was in no hurry. His afternoon and evening were hers—though he'd have to share her for a while with her siblings and their significant others, who'd driven down from St. Louis for the event.

No worries.

He had plans for later that, if all went as he hoped, would end this already happy day on a very high note.

"GOOD JOB, KIDDO. You managed to keep me awake through the whole thing." Jack grinned as Cara walked over to join her family in the foyer.

"Jack!" His fiancée elbowed him.

"Don't worry, Lindsey." Cara waved aside her concern. "I'm used to his eyes glazing over whenever I mention anything related to my work. I consider it a major compliment that he didn't doze off."

"The talk was excellent." Bri gave her a hug and nudged her husband. "Don't you think so, Marc?"

"Yes. I have to admit I was afraid this would be like one of the insomnia-curing lectures my western civ teacher in college used to give." One side of his mouth quirked up. "Not even close. Your presentation was not only educational but entertaining."

"Thank you." In the background, Natalie motioned her over, and Cara acknowledged the summons with a lift of her hand. "Would you all excuse me for a minute? I think Natalie may be leaving, and I want to say goodbye."

"Take your time. We'll check out the eats." Jack took Lindsey's arm and steered her toward the buffet table.

Bri rolled her eyes. "Leave it to our chef brother to make a beeline for the food."

"Hey, don't knock that idea." Marc twined his fingers with hers. "I'm hungry too."

"I'll catch up with you." Cara waved them off as he towed her sister toward the buffet.

She wound through the crowd to where Natalie waited in a quiet corner with Paul.

"My dear, that was magnificent." The older woman grasped her hand.

"Thank you. And Paul, thank you for coming and bringing Natalie."

"I wouldn't have missed it for the world. If you ever want a job at our historical society, the door is open. Although the pay is much higher at the university."

"But the volunteers at the historical society do an admirable job." Natalie patted his arm.

"I'll second that." Cara motioned toward the food table. "Can you stay for a few minutes to enjoy the reception?"

"I wish we could, but Becky and I have the grandkids this weekend and I promised her I wouldn't linger." Paul pulled out his keys. "Natalie, I'll get the car and pick you up in front. Cara, wonderful job."

As he walked away, Natalie turned back to her. "I did want to share two pieces of news with you today. Margie and her husband have agreed to move into the cottage as soon as the remodeling wraps up in a couple of weeks."

"That's wonderful, Natalie. I've had my fingers crossed ever since you told me you'd broached that idea to them."

"Trust me, I have too. I'm grateful they're willing to take me up on my offer. It's truly an ideal arrangement all around. I get a housekeeper and handyman on site, they get a private place to live with far more reasonable rent than what they've been paying. It's a win-win, as you young folks like to say. I couldn't be happier."

"I'm glad you'll have other people living on the property."

"I am too. I so enjoyed having you close by in the fall, and I've missed our daily interactions." She patted her hand. "But Paul and Becky come by often, as does Father Johnson. And I've started spending half a day each week at the pregnancy resource center. Crocheting baby afghans is a fine contribution, but I've discovered that many of the women welcome a sympathetic ear too."

What a dynamo this woman was.

And Brad had been right about her fortitude. She was strong and resilient. Despite the shock over Steven's death and the revelations about his character, she'd carried on with grace and grit.

"Good for you, Natalie."

"My other piece of news is about Lydia. I received a letter from her last week. She sent back the stamp she took."

Cara hiked up her eyebrows. "I never expected that."

"Me neither. But I've been praying for her. She seemed like such a troubled soul. She said that because I was always kind to her, her conscience wouldn't let her sell the stamp. She also apologized for her mistake. It sounds like she's had a change of heart and is building a new life in Kansas."

"What a wonderful example of someone turning their life around."

"Yes, it is. I wish Steven had done the same." Her countenance clouded for a fleeting instant, then brightened again. "You'll come visit soon, I hope?"

"It will be my pleasure. You aren't going to get rid of me just because our project is finished."

"As if I would ever want to do that." Natalie motioned to the large window in the front of the foyer. "I see Paul has arrived, and I don't want to keep him waiting after he was kind enough to be my chauffeur today." She took her hand again and gave it a squeeze. "You've been a great blessing to me, my dear. May all the happiness you've brought me return tenfold."

Pressure built in Cara's throat as she watched the woman walk away.

The blessing had worked both ways. Despite all the distressing incidents that had tainted her tenure at Natalie's, she'd always be grateful for the weeks she'd spent there and the opportunity to get to know such an inspiring woman.

As Natalie disappeared through the door, Cara searched the crowd.

Where was Brad? He'd been sitting next to her former hostess in the audience, but after the presentation ended, she'd lost—

"Looking for me?"

At a touch on her shoulder, she swiveled around to find him standing behind her, admiration, appreciation . . . and something more . . . deepening the green of his eyes.

Oh, how she loved this man who'd brought such joy and light and warmth into her life. Who'd filled her heart with hope and her days with the tantalizing promise of even sweeter tomorrows.

"Yes, I was."

"I have only one word. Your paper was extraordinary, but your presentation? Phenomenal."

At his praise, happiness bubbled up inside her. "Thank you."

"I would have approached you sooner, but I was waiting for your fans to disperse."

She took his hand. "I'm all yours now."

"Hey, Cara, you have to try this spanakopita." Jack joined them and thrust a phyllo triangle perched on a cocktail napkin at her. "They have a first-class spread here. You must really rate."

Cara sent Brad a silent apology. "A slight delay in my promise."

"No worries. It will be worth the wait." His slow, intimate smile sent a rush of warmth radiating through her.

Thank heaven the man she'd given her heart to was a good sport. One who liked her siblings and their significant others, and who'd blended seamlessly into the family group. He'd handled Jack's third degree at their first meeting with consummate skill, winning kudos from Bri and respect from her brother.

As her family chatted and chowed down, a newspaper reporter approached, demanding her attention. After that, several members of the audience cornered her to ask questions about her research and offer tidbits about relatives who'd lived in the Old Mines area.

Through it all, Brad stayed by her side, offering support but never trying to step into the spotlight or inject himself into the conversation. Thanks to the quiet self-confidence he radiated that instilled trust and respect in everyone he met, he didn't have to seek the limelight to shore up his own sense of worth.

Heaven had smiled on her the day he'd walked into her life.

An hour later, after the last guests departed and she waved

goodbye to her siblings with a promise to arrive early next week to help Bri set up for Lindsey's bridal shower, Cara expelled a long breath. "I am so ready to ditch these heels and chill."

"Then let's go." Brad took her hand and led her out the door, toward the parking lot. "You and I have some celebrating to do."

"I thought we just did that. The university put on a lovely reception."

"How much did you eat?"

"Hmm. A spanakopita?"

"That's what I figured. I have a dinner reservation for us."

Of course he did.

Brad was thoughtfulness personified.

"Thank you for that. Where are we going?"

At the high-end spot he named, she did a double take. "After all the dinners you've treated me to at our favorite hideaway in the hinterland, you don't have to break the bank tonight."

"Special days merit special attention. I'm glad the paper you wrote, and all the research you did, got the acclaim they deserved, but I want to do my small part to mark the occasion."

"Well . . . since you put it that way." She rose on tiptoe and stole a kiss before she slid into the passenger seat of his car.

But when he pulled out of the parking lot, she frowned. "Wait. The restaurant is the other direction."

"I know. It's a little early for dinner, though. I thought we could take a short drive through the countryside on this beautiful April afternoon. That work for you?"

Unexpected—but why not?

"Sure."

She toed off her heels, settled back in her seat . . . and gave him a surreptitious scan as he accelerated down the road.

Nothing obvious was amiss, but there was an odd undercurrent buzzing through the car.

Something was up.

Strange.

It wasn't like him to keep her in the dark. In general, he shared whatever was on his mind.

Apparently she'd have to prompt him this time.

"Do you want to tell me what's going on?"

He gave her a quick glance. Grinned. "It's hard to keep secrets from you. You know me too well."

"You have a secret?"

"I do. One I'm not going to reveal quite yet. Why don't you tell me what Natalie had to say? She was thrilled with the accolade you gave her, by the way."

Cara hesitated.

She could press him—but she *did* know him well. And from the set of his jaw, he wasn't going to budge.

So she played along, sharing the news about Margie.

He kept the conversation flowing after that until he pulled over to the side of a street in one of the towns a short drive away from Cape.

"Why are you stopping?" She sent him a puzzled look.

He set the brake and motioned to a modern building up ahead.

She squinted at the sign.

The police department?

"Do you have official business here?"

"No. Personal business." He angled toward her. "I have it on credible authority that the chief here is going to retire in the fall. My term's up in November. Instead of running for sheriff again, I'm thinking a new job closer to Cape may be in order—and based on a few discreet inquiries, I think I'd have an excellent shot at this one. But before I make such a huge change, I'd need a guarantee."

"What sort of guarantee?"

"That I won't be starting over in a new place alone." He reached into the inner pocket of his sport coat.

Cara's heart missed a beat . . . or two . . . or three as he withdrew a small square box. When he lifted the lid to reveal a sparkling round diamond, the platinum band inset with several smaller diamonds on each side of the main stone, her voice deserted her.

As silent seconds ticked by, Brad shifted in his seat. "If you don't like the style, the jeweler said you could—"

"No." Cara somehow convinced her vocal cords to kick back in. "It just . . . it took my breath away. Is there . . . is there a proposal to go with it?"

"Yes." His lips flexed, yet this man who was always in control and confident seemed endearingly nervous. "Would you like to hear it now, or should I save it for the romantic candlelit restaurant?"

"Anywhere I'm with you is romantic." She twisted sideways and focused on his face.

Because she didn't intend to miss a word of what he had to say.

"I guess I'm on." His Adam's apple bobbed, and he took her hand, cradling it in his strong fingers. "I never expected to find love again, Cara. I didn't think I *deserved* to find it again. But after you walked into my world and filled my days with happiness and warmth and hope, I realized that maybe God was offering me a second chance. A new beginning with a woman whose sweetness and grace and empathy and kindness illuminated all the dark, lonely places in my heart."

He set the box on the console between them and cupped her face with his hands, the tremble in his fingers clear evidence of the magnitude of this moment, when both their futures were poised to change forever with one simple word from her.

"Professor Cara Tucker, I love you with every ounce of my being. Would you please do me the honor of becoming my wife?"

Pressure built behind her eyes as she gazed at the man who'd made her believe that maybe . . . just maybe . . . the youngest Tucker sibling had at last met the partner of her dreams. A man who hadn't viewed the inconveniences of her deafness as an obstacle and who was willing to make a dramatic change in his life so she could continue to do the work she loved. A man of integrity and commitment and deep compassion.

"You won't have to start over in a new place alone. Guaranteed." Cara lifted her left hand. "Yes."

He exhaled, as if he'd been holding his breath. Fumbled with the box while he removed the ring. Slipped the band on with unsteady fingers.

It was a perfect fit.

Just as they were a perfect fit.

"It suits you." He lifted her hand to examine the ring.

She blinked to clear her vision. "You know, until I met you, I was beginning to think this would never happen. That the romance in my life would be confined to novels and chick flicks." She leaned closer, across the console. "But you, Brad Mitchell, made all my romantic dreams come true. You're better than any heartthrob in a book or a movie. And I feel like the luckiest woman in the world."

"The luck was all mine." He closed the distance between them, until they were a whisper apart. "I think we should make this engagement official."

"I'm in." She put her arms around his neck.

Without wasting another moment, he pressed his lips to hers in an achingly tender kiss that expressed with wordless eloquence the depth of his love and devotion. A kiss that told her she was cherished beyond measure. A kiss filled with a promise of the passion to come for all their tomorrows as man and wife.

The world around them vanished as Cara gave herself to the embrace on this street in a small Missouri town that no one else might think was anything special.

But for her, it was magic.

Because this was the official beginning of their happily ever after.

Guaranteed.

AUTHOR'S NOTE

With this book, my Undaunted Courage series comes to an end. It's been an amazing journey, and I've loved every minute of it.

As I say goodbye to the Tucker siblings, there are some real-life people I need to thank.

On the professional front, I'm grateful to FBI veteran and retired police chief Tom Becker, who answered my questions during the writing of this book with patience and precision, as always. A shout-out as well to former Monroe County, Missouri, sheriff David Hoffman, who provided invaluable insights into law enforcement in a rural setting. I also owe a debt of gratitude to fellow author Lynette Eason, who read the manuscript and offered much-appreciated input on the sections related to deafness and hearing challenges. And finally, a huge thank-you to the team at Revell that works so hard to ensure my books are the best they can be and to make certain they get noticed in the marketplace.

On the personal side, my deepest thanks to my husband Tom for his delight in my successes (which makes them all the sweeter), his unwavering support, and his boundless love and encouragement. He makes the sun shine for me, even on rainy days. And though my parents are gone now, their inspiring influence lives on in my life . . . as their infinite love lives on in my heart. I will never stop missing them.

Looking ahead, book 12 in my Hope Harbor series will release in April 2026 (you can read a preview at the end of this book). In *Harbor Pointe* you'll meet ballet dancer Devyn Lee, who returns to her hometown to deal with a family emergency. But her quick visit turns into an extended stay after complications arise—including a romance that is *not* in her plans. Charley and his tacos will be back too, of course, along with the bantering clerics and the resident seagull couple, Floyd and Gladys. Mark your calendars for another trip to the Oregon coast! ☺

Until next time, stay well and stay happy!

Can't get enough of Irene Hannon?

Turn the page and journey with her to Hope Harbor!

COMING SOON

HER SISTER WAS IN A COMA.

Sucking in a lungful of Oregon seaside air, Devyn Lee swung into a parking space, set the brake on her rental car, and unclamped her white-knuckled fingers from the wheel.

How could so much change so fast?

Last night, she'd been dancing the title role in *Giselle* at Lincoln Center.

Now, she was sitting outside the Coos Bay hospital where her sister lay unresponsive after tripping on broken pavement.

There was only one word to describe all that had happened in the past eighteen hours.

Surreal.

As the sequence of events scrolled through her mind, she closed her eyes and massaged her forehead.

A late-night call from a neurologist at this hospital.

A frantic online search for the next available flight from New York City to Oregon.

A midnight phone conversation with the ballet master to alert him that an understudy would have to dance her role for today's final performance of the spring season.

A futile attempt to catch three hours of sleep before her dawn flight on this last Sunday in May.

Nine-plus travel hours from boarding to arrival, followed by a short drive from the North Bend airport to the hospital.

Hectic as her typical days were as a principal dancer with one of the most prestigious ballet companies in the world, none of them had ever been this chaotic or frenzied.

Calling up every ounce of her waning stamina, Devyn

reached for her purse. It might only be two in the afternoon in Oregon, but it was five o'clock New York time. And whatever energy boost she'd gleaned from the turkey wrap she'd gulped down in San Francisco between flights had evaporated hours ago.

Yet as she slid from behind the wheel and walked toward the hospital entrance, a tingle of anxiety-laced adrenaline vibrated through her nerve endings.

Because in mere minutes, she'd be face-to-face with the sister she hadn't seen since their father's funeral thirteen years ago.

Stomach knotting, she walked through the doors that slid open as she approached. Stopped at the reception desk to get directions. Strode toward the elevator as the questions that had plagued her since last night's summons looped through her mind yet again.

Why had she been listed as Lauren's emergency contact instead of her sister's husband?

And why had she gotten a "no longer in service" message when she'd called the number she'd long ago tucked away for Dennis?

Frowning, she pressed the up button.

What was going on with her sister's marriage?

A call to Mom at the crack of dawn Paris-time to share the news about the accident hadn't provided any clues. According to her, Lauren hadn't been in touch for months and had snubbed her during their last exchange.

No surprise there. Mom and her oldest offspring had never been close.

Nor had her two daughters.

Regrettable . . . but understandable.

The elevator doors slid open, and Devyn stepped inside. Pushed the button for the second floor.

It was hard to fault Lauren for resenting the younger sister who'd usurped their mother's attention and whose ballet aspirations had made any semblance of normal family life impossible.

But after she woke up, maybe they could initiate a few repairs in their relationship—a task long relegated to the back burner that had suddenly taken on new urgency.

And her sister *would* wake up. Any other outcome was unthinkable.

The elevator doors parted, and Devyn stepped out. Clenching her fingers around the strap of her purse, she approached the ICU. Stopped beside the intercom. Took a steadying breath and depressed the button.

When the doors swooshed open, she forced herself to walk through.

A scrubs-clad woman at a central station looked over. "Can I help you?"

"Yes. I'm here to see Lauren Collier. I'm her sister."

"Oh yes. I spoke with you when you called from San Francisco." She circled around the counter. "I'll take you back."

"How is she doing?" Devyn followed the woman, lungs balking as she waited for the answer. Hopefully no complications had arisen since she'd checked in during her layover.

"No changes. All her vitals remain strong." The woman paused by a room with glass doors. "I'll let her neurologist know you're here. She wanted to speak with you as soon as you arrived."

A tingle of unease zipped through her. "Why?"

"To discuss treatment options, I expect." The woman motioned toward the room. "Feel free to talk to your sister. Often people who are otherwise unresponsive can hear what's being said. Would you like a soft drink or water? We also have coffee and tea."

After declining that offer, Devyn took a slow breath and entered the room.

The woman in the bed was Lauren, no question about it. Same pert nose. Same naturally long, curving lashes. Same high cheekbones.

But her big sister had aged.

A lot, for someone who was only thirty-five.

Though her features were slack in repose, the embedded twin creases above her nose were new. So was the fan of fine lines at the corner of each eye. Her once-long dark hair was gone, replaced by short-cropped locks containing a few strands of silver.

The past thirteen years must have held some serious challenges for her, even if she'd never indicated there were any problems during their infrequent phone calls and texts.

Yet though the changes wrought by time and stress were apparent, there was little visible evidence of the injuries she'd suffered in the fall, other than an elastic bandage on her left wrist.

Except for all the medical devices she was hooked up to.

Devyn took a quick inventory.

Heart and blood pressure monitor. IV drip. Nasal cannula. Oxygen monitor on Lauren's finger.

The rest of the equipment was unfamiliar.

And what other stuff was attached to her beneath the sheet?

Devyn groped for the bottom of the bed. Held on tight.

Hard as she'd tried to prepare for this moment, seeing her sister comatose was like a punch in the gut.

Maybe she and Lauren weren't as close as they could have been for sisters separated in age by a mere two years, but with Dad gone, Mom remarried and living a new life in Paris, and Dennis apparently out of the picture, the only real family the two of them had was each other.

Lauren had to recover so they could make a new start.

Blinking back the sudden mist in her vision, Devyn moved beside the bed and laid her hand over Lauren's. Tried to call up a cheery tone. "Hey, sis. It's me, Devyn. I heard you were off in la-la land and decided to come out here to keep an eye on you. And I'm sticking close until you decide to rejoin the human race. We have a ton of catching up to do. I'm between seasons now, and I plan to stay awhile."

"That's good news."

The voice of the neurologist who'd called last night spoke from the doorway.

Devyn twisted sideways. "Dr. Sherman?"

"Yes." The white-coated woman, who looked to be in her fifties, remained on the threshold. "Having family on hand is always helpful during a health crisis, especially with head injuries. Why don't we talk for a few minutes? There's a small lounge near the ICU."

"Okay." Devyn leaned close to her sister and brushed a stray wisp of hair back from her face. "I'll be back in a few minutes, sis."

The doctor led the way down the hall, out of the ICU and to a small, deserted lounge. "Have a seat." She motioned to one of the chairs and took the adjacent one. "Thank you for coming so fast. I'm sure you're exhausted after our late call and your cross-country flight."

Devyn waved that aside. "This is what family does in an emergency." Not counting Mom, who'd said she'd wait for an update before embarking on the long trip from Paris—no doubt hoping Lauren would wake up, rendering such a trek unnecessary.

"Not always." The doctor's lips contorted into a rueful twist, leveling out as she continued. "I was just leaving the hospital when I got the call you'd arrived, and I decided to come back up to talk with you in person. I'll try to use layman's language, but don't hesitate to stop me if I start to throw in too many medical terms."

"I already did some research on comas during my flights,

but the information I found online was kind of mind boggling. And scary." To say the least.

"Brain injuries are complicated. On the plus side, your sister didn't suffer any other trauma beyond a few minor bruises and a sprained wrist. That lets us concentrate on the brain. As I told you last night, the original CT scan showed minor swelling, but there was no indication of major structural injuries or bleeding. Your sister's pupils are responsive, her reflexes are functioning, she reacts to pain, and she's breathing on her own. Those are all hopeful signs. Our goal now is to create conditions conducive to recovery, including letting the brain rest. We also want to reduce the swelling to prevent any potential damage from intracranial pressure."

"Have you tried diuretics and steroids?" Based on her in-air research, those were the first line of attack for brain swelling.

"Yes. They haven't had any effect. And the newest CT scan indicates that the swelling has increased. We're concerned about a reduction in oxygen supply and blood flow to the brain, as well as brain stem issues."

Devyn fisted her hands until her nails bit into her palms. Every site she'd found said brain stem issues were a recipe for disaster. "So what do we do?"

"My recommendation is to lower her body temperature and put her into a medically induced coma for a couple of days, then reevaluate. Allowing her brain to focus most of its energy on regeneration could reduce the swelling."

"What if it doesn't?"

"A portion of her skull can be removed to give the brain more room to expand. I briefed a neurosurgeon in Eugene on the case earlier today, but I'm hoping the swelling will go down and that step won't be necessary."

Because it was a last resort, according to online sources.

"I guess we'll go with your plan." What other choice was there?

"It's the logical next step. We'll also put your sister on a ventilator while she's in the induced coma to maintain normal respiration. It's standard procedure for this type of intervention. Don't be alarmed by it."

Devyn's heart stumbled.

She was supposed to remain calm while they put her sister on a ventilator?

In what universe?

IRENE HANNON is the bestselling, award-winning author of more than sixty-five contemporary romance and romantic suspense novels. She is also a three-time winner of the RITA award—the "Oscar" of romance fiction—from Romance Writers of America and is a member of that organization's elite Hall of Fame.

Her many other awards include National Readers' Choice, Daphne du Maurier, Retailers' Choice, Booksellers' Best, Carol, and Reviewers' Choice from RT *Book Reviews* magazine, which also honored her with a Career Achievement award for her entire body of work. In addition, she is a HOLT Medallion winner and a two-time Christy award finalist.

Millions of her books have been sold worldwide, and her novels have been translated into multiple languages.

Irene, who holds a BA in psychology and an MA in journalism, juggled two careers for many years until she gave up her executive corporate communications position with a Fortune 500 company to write full-time. She is happy to say she has no regrets.

A trained vocalist, Irene has sung the leading role in numerous community musical theater productions and is also a soloist at her church. She and her husband enjoy traveling, long hikes, gardening, impromptu dates, and spending time with family. They make their home in Missouri.

To learn more about Irene and her books, visit IreneHannon.com. She occasionally posts on Instagram but is most active on Facebook, where she loves to chat with readers.

Meet
IRENE HANNON
at IreneHannon.com

Learn news, sign up for her mailing list,
and more!

Find her on

Be the first to hear about new books from Revell!

Stay up to date with our authors and books by signing up for our newsletters at

RevellBooks.com/SignUp

FOLLOW US ON SOCIAL MEDIA

@RevellFiction

A Note from the Publisher

Dear Reader,

Thank you for selecting a Revell novel! We're so happy to be part of your reading life through this work. Our mission here at Revell is to publish stories that reach the heart. Through friendship, romance, suspense, or a travel back in time, we bring stories that will entertain, inspire, and encourage you. We believe in the power of stories to change our lives and are grateful for the privilege of sharing these stories with you.

We believe in building lasting relationships with readers, and we'd love to get to know you better. If you have any feedback, questions, or just want to chat about your experience reading this book, please email us directly at publisher@revellbooks.com. Your insights are incredibly important to us, and it would be our pleasure to hear how we can better serve you.

We look forward to hearing from you and having the chance to enhance your experience with Revell Books.

The Publishing Team at Revell Books
A Division of Baker Publishing Group
publisher@revellbooks.com

Revell